SKELMERSDALE

FICTION RESERVE STOCK LL50

John Buchan

THE COMPLETE SHORT STORIES

◆

Volume One

John Buchan

THE COMPLETE SHORT STORIES

◆

Volume One

Edited by
ANDREW LOWNIE

Foreword by
WILLIAM BUCHAN

THISTLE PUBLISHING

First published in Great Britain in 1996 by
Thistle Publishing
122 Bedford Court Mansions
London WC1B 3AH

Copyright © 1996 by The Right Honourable Lord Tweedsmuir
Introduction and selection © 1996 by Andrew Lownie
Foreword © 1996 by The Honourable William Buchan

A CIP catalogue record for this book is available from the British Library

ISBN 0-9526756-0-9

Designed by Wendy Bann

Typeset by DP Photosetting, Aylesbury, Bucks

Printed and bound in England by Short Run Press, Exeter

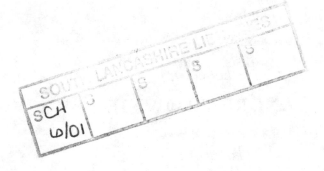

Contents

Foreword by William Buchan

John Buchan's father, a Presbyterian minister, served parishes in Perth, Pathhead and Glasgow, and so his eldest son had much of his upbringing in towns. For the long summer holidays, however, he was set free to visit his mother's family, farmers at Broughton in Peebleshire, close by the upper reaches of the River Tweed. He came to know every one of the numerous glens in the Tweed valley between Peebles and the river's source beyond Tweedsmuir, fishing every tributary down to the very smallest burns and climbing the hills in every kind of weather.

The weather in that part of Scotland is highly capricious, liable to produce a blanketing hill-fog on a fine summer day, as well as furious thunderstorms, great blizzards of snow, or deluges of rain on the hill-tops which cause the floods so notably described in this book. The upper Tweed valley is beautiful, but its atmosphere can be harsh in the extreme. Not surprisingly some of Buchan's best writing has to do with landscape and weather as they affect his characters and their affairs.

Extremes of weather were one aspect of Tweedside. Others were old stories of battles, of skirmishes with English troops, of cattle-stealing, of witchcraft and many bloody deeds. Running like a bright thread through these is the humour, sometimes grim, usually sardonic, often compassionate with human idiocy, of the Border people. Religion and politics played important parts. The Scottish Church and the Liberal Party were powerful in John Buchan's day, and they make themselves felt in these stories.

Wandering far and near, John Buchan made many friends among the shepherds and farmers of the valley, and often helped with his uncles' sheep. In his memoirs he wrote: 'These Border shepherds, the men of the long stride and the clear eye, were a great race – I have never known a greater ... I acquired a reverence and affection for the "plain people" who, to Walter Scott and Abraham Lincoln were what mattered most in the world'.

Beyond doubt the 'plain people' in these stories have a clear-cut and powerful life, and their creator manages their 'Lallans' speech superbly. For the non-Scot the latter must, at first, make difficult reading but perseverance will bring its reward, for the pith and acuity, the wealth of arresting words and phrases which it displays.

Introduction by Andrew Lownie

John Buchan is now principally remembered for his thrillers, and in particular *The Thirty-Nine Steps*, but in a writing career that spanned almost fifty years and over a hundred books he also wrote biographies, children's stories, poetry, history books, historical novels, essays and hundreds of newspaper and magazine articles. What is hardly known is that he was a prolific and highly successful short-story writer, especially as a young man. Writing to his school and university friend, Charles Dick, in January 1900 he claimed 'that to a person of my habits the short story is the real form'. A third of his sixty short stories were written or published in the five years between his second year at Glasgow University and his leaving Oxford at the end of 1899. It is these twenty-one stories that I have selected for this first volume of a projected three-volume collection of Buchan's complete short stories. The stories appear in chronological order of first publication or, where known, the date of their composition. Some, like 'A Captain of Salvation' and 'Gideon Scott', are appearing for the first time in book form, while four others from his short-story collection *Grey Weather* have not been in print for almost a century.

Buchan is often accused of being a snob and careerist, only interested in the activities of fictional characters such as the aristocrats Archie Roylance and Sandy Arbuthnot and successful men like Sir Richard Hannay and Sir Edward Leithen. This collection shows just how false a picture that represents of his writing. Almost all the stories here are about the people and places of the Scottish Borders, and especially the shepherds, poachers, gamekeepers and drovers of the Upper Tweed Valley, home to the families of both his parents. This is a book not about clubland but moorland heroes. The stories are about the power of religion, drink or the weather; many revolve around death, temptation and retribution, centre around a single, not necessarily dramatic, event and rely heavily on the use of local dialects. They are a far cry from the adventures of Richard Hannay and Edward Leithen.

Buchan's first published short story, 'On Cademuir Hill', appeared in the *Glasgow University Magazine* in December 1894 when he was still a teenager, but it was not until he went up to Oxford in the autumn of 1895 and took on a literary agent, Alexander Watt, that he began to publish stories on a regular basis. Watt was able to sell Buchan's stories not just to British outlets, such as *Macmillan's Magazine, Chamber's Journal* and *Black & White*, but also to American papers, such as *The Living Age.* This meant that relatively quickly Buchan found he could support himself from his writing and he soon learnt the importance of a transatlantic appeal.

Three of the stories were originally published in *The Yellow Book.* It is often forgotten that Buchan was a contributor to Aubrey Beardsley's famous magazine of the Aesthetic Movement. John Betjeman's lines in 'The Arrest of Oscar Wilde at the Cadogan Hotel' give some indication of the surprise with which this news is sometimes received, even if Betjeman takes some artistic licence since Wilde was arrested before Buchan actually began to contribute to the magazine:

> So you've brought me the latest *Yellow Book*
> And Buchan has got in it now;
> Approval of what is approved of
> Is as false as a well-kept vow.

The Yellow Book only existed for thirteen issues, between April 1894 and April 1897, but it published many of the most interesting writers of the period, including George Gissing, Kenneth Grahame and W.B. Yeats – not writers one normally associates with the author of *The Thirty-Nine Steps*. Buchan's link with the magazine came through a Glasgow friend, the illustrator D.Y. Cameron, and its publisher John Lane, for whom Buchan acted as reader and who published several of his early books.

Buchan's first novel, an historical romance called *Sir Quixote of the Moors*, was published in the autumn of 1895, just after he went up to Brasenose College, Oxford and this was followed the next year with a collection of essays and stories, *Scholar Gipsies*, which Buchan described as 'a few pictures of character and nature, pieces of sentiment torn from their setting, a fragment of criticism, some moralisings of little worth – the baggage of a vagrant in letters and life'. Over the next three years he produced a short life of Sir Walter Raleigh (his Stanhope essay prize at Oxford), two further historical romances – *John Burnet of*

Barns (1898) and *A Lost Lady of Old Years* (1899), a history of his Oxford college and another short-story collection, *Grey Weather* (1899), which he subtitled 'moorland tales of my own people'. The stories in *Grey Weather* constitute the bulk of the stories in this volume.

What is interesting is that though the countryside of Upper Tweeddale, which he knew well from long holidays staying with his maternal relations at Broughton and father's family in Peebles, would provide the inspiration for most of the stories of this period, few of his subsequent stories are set in the area. Upper Tweeddale was a crucial literary influence, but only for a limited period. Amazingly, there are no stories in this volume set in Fife or Glasgow, where he had grown up, nor – apart from a brief mention in 'No-Man's Land' – in Oxford, which was to be such a formative influence on his life.

One of the strong undercurrents, particularly evident in these early short stories, is Buchan's fascination with the supernatural. Many of them involve some encounter with the forces of the unknown and the way in which the 'other' world impinges on the 'ordinary' world, a theme he would later develop in stories such as 'The Kings of Orion' and *'Tendebant Manus'*. This susceptibility was heightened at Oxford by attending lectures on pre-Christian cults and living in rooms at Brasenose, where reputedly a former President of the Brasenose Hellfire Club had been literally snatched by the Devil. The stories were also much influenced by his wide reading of Celtic myths, fairy tales, Border ballads, the Bible and Shakespeare, as well as the work of more contemporary writers such as R.L. Stevenson, Conan Doyle, Ibsen, Maupassant and Edgar Allan Poe, whose *Tales of Mystery and Imagination* he edited for Thomas Nelson in 1911.

By education and temperament Buchan was a classicist and his grounding in the classics is evident in these stories, marked as they are by a clear and economical prose style and use of classical imagery. He was also a Son of the Manse, brought up to accept an omnipotent and benevolent God and a Devil that was half-humorous and half-earthy, aware of the teachings of John Knox, Erasmus, Galileo and Hume. Another influence was Andrew Lang, a neighbour in the Borders, and especially Lang's *Custom and Myth*, which dealt with the survival of ancient customs in a modern society. Buchan's angling anthology, *Musa Piscatrix* (1896), is dedicated to Lang. Indeed, a feature of these stories are the many references to fishing, a particular love of Buchan's. His first published piece of work was an essay about a day's fishing on the Tweed, published in *Gentleman's Magazine* just before his eighteenth birthday in August 1893, and during the five years covered by this volume he was editing for publication both *Musa Piscatrix* and Izaak Walton's *The Compleat Angler* (1901). Yet another interest was politics – he was elected President of the Oxford Union in 1899 – and many of the stories, not just those written in the 1890s, have a political theme. 'Politics and the May-Fly' and 'The Herd of Standlan' allow him to poke fun at politics, as he would subsequently do in stories such as 'A Lucid Interval'.

Graham Greene, a great admirer of Buchan's writing, wrote in 1940 that 'John Buchan was the first to realize the enormous dramatic value of adventure in familiar surroundings happening to unadventurous men'. He was referring to the thrillers, but his comment could as easily apply to these early stories. Here, too, the menace comes from the familiar and trusted – streams that flood their banks, hosts who are not what they initially appear, sons who make unusual demonstrations of filial love – but where later in the thrillers the threat is to the political and moral *status quo*, here it is more often seen simply in terms of good and evil.

Greene also noticed 'the completeness of the world they describe'. In his novels Buchan continually included the same places and people to create a recognisable world. The same is true of these early stories, in which his fictional map is already beginning to take shape. The town of Gledsmuir appears in six stories and there are numerous references to Clachlands, Callowa, Aller, the Gled, the Forest of Rhynns and St. Chad's College at Oxford. Castle Gay, the title of a novel published in 1933, is mentioned in 'The Rime of True Thomas' ('The Moor Song'), a story written in 1897. Names, often taken from local Border landmarks, recur. Lord Manorwater, a character in 'Politics and the May-Fly' and the title Buchan considered for himself when he was raised to the peerage in 1935, is presumably related to the Lady Manorwater in Buchan's novel *The Half-Hearted* (1900) and the Manorwaters in the stories 'The Far Islands' and 'The Company of the Marjolaine' and the novel *The Dancing Floor* (1926). Lady Clanroyden in 'A Reputation' is no doubt a relative of the Clanroydens in the stories 'The Watcher By The Threshold' and 'Fountainblue' and of one of Buchan's central figures, Sandy Arbuthnot, later Lord Clanroyden. The Raden family, which figures so prominently in the novel *John Macnab* (1925), is introduced in 'The Far Islands'. Lady Afflint appears in both 'A Reputation' and 'The Far Islands', Gideon Scott is the eponymous hero of one story and appears as Gidden Scott in 'The Herd of Standlan', while Jock Rorison features in both 'Streams of Water in the South' and 'Comedy in the Full Moon'.

The stories in this collection can be enjoyed at different levels – as simply moorland tales about his own people, as delicate expositions of human character which demonstrate that Buchan's gift for strong descriptive writing was apparent from his early twenties, or as explorations of themes to be developed more fully later in his novels. For many of the recurrent Buchan themes are present – the power of place, the use of the sacred place *temenos*, the importance of landscape to plot, the strong descriptive writing, the emptiness of success, the call of the wild, the contrast between the city and the countryside and between England and Scotland, the narrow thread between the primitive and civilised. It is true that these early stories are not among his best; the stories selected for the two successive volumes cover a wider range of subjects, with a greater sense of depth and more narrative tension. They are apprentice work, but, given they were all written while Buchan was at school or university, they are an extraordinary achievement. I have deliberately used less well-known versions of the stories and have added a glossary covering some of the less familiar Scots words.

John Buchan may now largely be remembered for his 'shockers', but these early and quite different stories deserve to be more widely known. They show how Buchan first drew literary inspiration from the countryside he knew so well from school and university holidays and how he might have developed as an archetypally Scottish writer, more interested in social observation than a gripping yarn. The second volume will demonstrate his continuing preoccupation with the supernatural, but his canvas will move from the Upper Tweed Valley to Galloway, Switzerland, Africa and the Aegean. Instead of setting his stories in the present, as he has hitherto done, many of them will be set in the past, have a twist at the end and a more recognisable Buchan style will be apparent. The stories of volume two and three are more obviously the work of the author of *The Thirty-Nine Steps* and as a result are likely to be more popular than these early tales. Yet it is their very unexpectedness that is part of the appeal of these highly personal and moving stories. They are also a reminder that John Buchan was a far more accomplished and complex writer than his reputation has allowed.

On Cademuir Hill

'On Cademuir Hill', Buchan's first published short story, appeared in the *Glasgow University Magazine* for 19 December 1894 and was one of only three stories in his essay collection, *Scholar Gipsies* (1896).

I

THE GAMEKEEPER OF Cademuir strode in leisurely fashion over the green side of the hill. The bright chilly morning was past, and the heat had all but begun, but he had lain long a-bed, deeming that life was too short at the best, and there was little need to hurry it over. He was a man of a bold carriage, with the indescribable air of one whose life is connected with sport and rough moors. A steady grey eye and a clean chin were his best features; otherwise, he was of the ordinary make of a man, looking like one born for neither good nor evil in any high degree. The sunlight danced around him, and flickered among the brackens; and though it was an everyday sight with him, he was pleased, and felt cheerful, just like any wild animal on a bright day. If he had had his dog with him, he would have sworn at it to show his pleasure; as it was, he contented himself with whistling 'The Linton Ploughman', and setting his heels deep into the soft green moss.

The day was early and his way was long, for he purposed to go up Manor Water to the shepherd's house about a matter of some foxes. It might be ten miles, it might be more; and the keeper was in no great haste, for there was abundant time to get his dinner and a smoke with the herd, and then come back in the cool of the evening; for it was summer-time, when men of his class have their holiday. Two miles more, and he would strike the highway; he could see it even now coiling beneath the straight sides of the glen. There it was easy walking, and he would get on quickly; but now he might take his time. So he lit his pipe, and looked complacently around him.

[7]

At the turn of the hill, where a strip of wood runs up the slope, he stopped, and a dark shadow came over his face. This was the place where, not two weeks ago, he had chased a poacher, and but for the fellow's skill in doubling, would have caught him. He cursed the whole tribe in his heart. They were the bane of his easy life. They came at night, and took him out on the bleak hillside when he should have been in his bed. They might have a trap there even now. He would go and see, for it was not two hundred yards from his path.

So he climbed up the little howe in the hill beside the firwood, where the long thickets of rushes, and the rabbit-warrens made a happy hunting-ground for the enemies of the law. A snipe or two flew up as he approached, and a legion of rabbits scurried into their holes. He had all but given up the quest, when the gleam of something among the long grass caught his attention, and in a trice he had pulled back the herbage, and disclosed a neatly set and well-constructed trap.

It was a very admirable trap. He had never seen one like it; so in a sort of angry exultation, as he thought of how he would spoil this fine game, he knelt down to examine it. It was no mere running noose, but of strong steel, and firmly fixed to the trunk of an old tree. No unhappy pheasant would ever move it, were its feet once caught in its strong teeth. He felt the iron with his hand, feeling down the sides for the spring; when suddenly with a horrid snap the thing closed on him, pinning his hand below the mid-finger, and he was powerless.

The pain was terrible, agonising. His hand burned like white fire, and every nerve of his body tingled. With his left hand he attempted to loosen it, but the spring was so well concealed, that he could not find it. Perhaps, too, he may have lost his wits, for in any great suffering the brain is seldom clear. After a few minutes of feeble searching and tugging, every motion of which gave agony to his imprisoned hand, he gave it up, and, in something very like panic, sought for his knife to try to cut the trap loose from the trunk. And now a fresh terror awaited him, for he found that he had no knife; he had left it in another coat, which was in his room at home. With a sigh of infinite pain, he stopped the search, and stared drearily before him.

He confusedly considered his position. He was fixed with no possibility of escape, some two miles from the track of any chance passer-by. They would not look for him at home until the evening, and the shepherd at Manor did not know of his coming. Some one might be on the hill, but then this howe was on a remote side where few ever came, unless their duty brought them. Below him in the valley was the road with some white cottages beside it. There were women in those houses, living and moving not far from him; they might see him if he were to wave something as a signal. But then, he reflected with a groan, that though he could see their dwellings, they could not see him, for he was hidden by the shoulder of the hill.

Once more he made one frantic effort to escape, but it was unsuccessful. Then he leant back upon the heather, gnawing his lips to help him to endure the agony of the wound. He was a strong man, broad and sinewy, and where a weaker might have swooned, he was left to endure the burden of a painful consciousness. Again he thought of escape. The man who had set the trap must come to see it, but it might not be that day, nor the next. He pictured his friends hunting up and down Manor Water, every pool and wood; passing and re-passing not two hundred yards from where he was lying dead, or worse than dead. His mind grew sick at the thought, and he had almost fainted in spite of his strength.

Then he fell into a panic, the terror of rough 'hard-handed men, which never laboured in their mind.' His brain whirled, his eyes were stelled, and a shiver shook him like a reed. He puzzled over his past life, feeling, in a dim way, that it had not been as it should be. He had been drunk often; he had not been over-careful of the name of the Almighty; was not this some sort of retribution? He strove to pray, but he could think of no words. He had been at church last Sunday, and he tried to think of what he had heard; but try as he would, nothing came to his mind, but the chorus of a drinking-song he had often heard sung in the public-house at Peebles:

> When the hoose is rinnin' round about,
>   It's time eneuch to flit;
> For we've lippened aye to Providence,
>   And sae will we yet.

The irony of the words did not strike him; but fervently, feverishly, he repeated them, as if for the price of his soul.

The fit passed, and a wild frenzy of rage took him. He cursed like a fiend, and yelled horrible menaces upon the still air. If he had the man who set this trap, he would strangle the life out of him here on this spot. No, that was too merciful. He would force his arm into the trap,

[9]

and take him to some lonely place where never a human being came from one year's end to the other. Then he would let him die, and come to gloat over his suffering. With every turn of his body he wrenched his hand, and with every wrench, he yelled more madly, till he lay back exhausted, and the green hills were left again in peace.

Then he slept a sleep which was half a swoon, for maybe an hour, though to him it seemed like ages. He seemed to be dead, and in torment; and the place of his torment was this same hillside. On the brae face, a thousand evil spirits were mocking his anguish, and not only his hand, but his whole body was imprisoned in a remorseless trap. He felt the keen steel crush through his bones, like a spade through a frosted turnip. He woke screaming with nameless dread, looking on every side for the infernal faces of his dreams, but seeing nothing but a little chaffinch hopping across the turf.

Then came for him a long period of slow, despairing agony. The hot air glowed, and the fierce sun beat upon his face. A thousand insects hummed about him, bees and butterflies and little hill-moths. The wholesome smell of thyme and bent was all about him, and every now and then a little breeze broke the stillness, and sent a ripple over the grass. The genial warmth seemed stifling; his head ached, and his breath came in sudden gasps. An overpowering thirst came upon him, and his tongue was like a burnt stick in his mouth. Not ten feet off, a little burn danced over a minute cascade. He could see the dust of spray, which wet the cool green rushes. The pleasant tinkle sang in his ears, and mocked his fever. He tried to think of snow and ice and cold water, but his brain refused to do its part, and he could get nothing but an intolerable void.

Far across the valley, the great forehead of Dollar Law raised itself, austere and lofty. To his unquiet sight, it seemed as if it rolled over on Scrape, and the two played pranks among the lower hills beyond. The idea came to him, how singularly unpleasant it would be for the people there – among them a shepherd to whom he owed two pounds. He would be crushed to powder, and there would be no more of the debt at any rate. Then a text from the Scriptures came to haunt him, something, he could scarce tell exactly, about the hills and mountains leaping like rams. Here it was realised before his very eyes. Below him, in the peaceful valley, Manor Water seemed to be wrinkled across it, like a scrawl from the pen of a bad writer. When a bird flew past, or a hare started from its form, he screamed with terror, and all the wholesome sights of a summer day were wrought by his frenzied brain into terrible phantoms. So true is it that Natura Benigna and Natura Maligna may walk hand in hand upon the same hill-side.

Then came the time when the strings of the reason are all but snapped, and a man becomes maudlin. He thought of his young wife, not six weeks married, and grieved over her approaching sorrow. He wept unnatural tears, which, if any one had been there to see him, would have been far more terrible than his frantic ravings. He pictured to himself in gruesome detail, the finding of his body, how his wife would sob, and his friends would shake their heads, and swear that he had been an honest fellow, and that it was a pity that he was away. The place would soon forget him; his wife would marry again; his dogs would get a new master, and he – ay, that was the question, where would he be? and a new dread took him, as he thought of the fate which might await him. The unlettered man, in his times of dire necessity, has nothing to go back upon but a mind full of vivid traditions, which are the most merciless of things.

It might be about three or four o'clock, but by the clock in his brain it was weeks later, that he suffered that last and awful pain, which any one who has met it once, would walk to the end of the earth to avoid. The world shrank away from him; his wits forsook him; and he cried out, till the lonely rocks rang, and the whaups mingled their startled cries with his. With a last effort, he crushed down his head with his unwounded hand upon the tree-trunk, till blessed unconsciousness took him into her merciful embrace.

II

At nine o'clock that evening, a ragged, unshorn man, with the look of one not well at ease with the world, crept up the little plantation. He had a sack on his back for his ill-gotten plunder, and a mighty stick in case of a chance encounter. He visited his traps, hidden away in little nooks, where no man might find them, and it would have seemed as if trade were brisk, for his sack was heavy, and his air was cheerful. He looked out from behind the dyke at his last snare carefully, as behoved one in danger; and then with a start he crouched, for he saw the figure of a man.

There was no doubt about it; it was his bitterest enemy, the keeper of Cademuir. He made as if to crawl away, when by chance he looked again. The man lay very still. A minute later he had rushed forward with a white face, and was working as if for his life.

In half an hour two men might have been seen in that little glen. One, with a grey, sickened face, was gazing vacantly around him, with the look of some one awakened from a long sleep. By dint of much toil, and half a bottle of brandy, he had been brought back from what was like to have been the longest sleep he had ever taken. Beside him on the grass, with wild eyes, sat the poacher, shedding hysterical tears. 'Dae onything ye like wi' me,' he was saying, 'kick me or kill me, an' am ready. I'll gang to jail wi' ye, to Peebles or the Calton, an' no say a word. But oh –! ma God, I thocht ye were bye wi't.'

Afternoon

The second of the stories in *Scholar Gipsies* (1896), 'Afternoon' is a highly self-conscious and literary story by a precocious undergraduate, inspired in part by two of his favourite books, *Lorna Doone* and Kenneth Grahame's *The Golden Age*. It is perhaps too full of references to Scottish history and classical literature but gives an early indication of Buchan's ability to evoke the sounds, smells and sights of nature.

THE JACOBITE RUSHED from the house into the garden, swung himself wildly across a paling, and landed on all fours in the road. It was just past the noon; the cloudless summer day had left its zenith behind it; and the first minute degree of decadence had joined with the sun. July was not yet merged in August; the festival of nature was at its height, and the whole earth throbbed with joy. The hum of bees and the tirra of the lark, the cooing of wood-doves, the far-away calls of haymakers, and the plash of the mill-burn filled the air. It was one great world of flowers, green leaves, and the sunlit heaven above, cool waters, solemn hills, and a blue distance.

The Jacobite was of noble appearance and gallant attire, as became his name. His age might have been twelve, but he was somewhat taller than the common. He was clothed in corduroys, formerly green, now many-coloured as Joseph's coat, and worn at the elbows to the likeness of chamois. Black, short-cut hair, thin shanks though stout as steel, a head held straight above the shoulders, a most cavalier carriage, and there you have him. A sprig of heath and a feather from a crow's wing were stuck in his hat, and in his hand was a well-used stick with a bar nailed thwart-wise, which did duty as a sword. In his belt was a knife with a broken blade, and an old news-sheet, for he made pretence that he carried state papers of high import. He stood there in the road, well-pleased with himself and content with the world. The hurried exit had been but the exuberance of his spirits. He was on no fixed journey bound. With much searching he produced from a deep pocket a George III penny, and spun it in the air. It fell face foremost in the dust, whence he picked it. Now was his course decided, and he turned resolutely to the highway.

In a little he came to a shop, a window in a flower-surrounded cottage, which proclaimed the residence of a wayside trafficker. The Jacobite considered his financial position. He possessed, he reflected, moneys to the extent of one penny and one halfpenny; this found on the road, that given by a benevolent grandfather. So he marched through the honeysuckled entrance, and stood delighted, inhaling the quaint, pleasing odours of bread and ancient brandy-balls, bacon and paraffin. He thought how proud the owner of such a place must be, and wondered mildly how such a man condescended to treat with so small a customer, from which it will be seen that he had no contempt for trade. He bought a pen'orth of treacle toffy, and stowed it about him. Fain would he have expended the other coin, but that it would have left him without supplies – a position he held hateful to the spirit of a cavalier.

Once more he stood in the sunshine, with the world before him and a thousand voices calling him hither and thither. He raced tumul-tuously over a field of close turf, scattering sheep before him like chaff. Then over a fence and into a byway, where he loitered for a second to fling a stone at a casual rat; and then with a whoop and a skirl of delight he was at the river.

Down its banks he strolled in all the glory of undoubted possession. There was no boy in the place who dared lift hand against him. For had he not fought his way to renown, till in a battle the week before, attended by half the village, he had defeated William Laidlaw, the shepherd's son, who was earning his own living, and so no more in the field of fair encounter, and severely battered the said William's face? From this combat he had been dragged by an irate grandparent, and even now he was dreeing his weird in the loss of his dog, his most faithful ally, who in a lonely kennel sadly bemoaned its master. For grown-up persons he cared naught, for he knew by long experience that they were a weak-kneed folk and feeble in the race. So amid the nodding grasses he swung along, whisking the heads off the meadow-sweet with his sword, in most unmilitary fashion, telling himself that he was setting out on a journey as great as erst Sir Galahad or Sir John

Mandeville, that sweetest and most truthful of knights. He had his store of provisions in his pocket; he was armed with sword and dagger and a stout heart; with another bellow of defiance he drew his blade and stalked on like Goliath of Gath, or Ajax defying the celestial lightning.

A sound in the bushes, a rustle, a movement, and the Jacobite was on his face, breathing hard and peering warily forth. It was only a thrush, so once more he got upon his feet and advanced. Just where the woods began he had a sharp conflict with a rabbit, which escaped amid a volley of stones. Once inside the cover, among the long, ghostlike firs and tremulous beeches, he felt he was on classic ground. There was every probability that an enchanter lurked among the shadows or a wild-boar in the rocks. To be sure, he had never seen such things, but they must be somewhere about. He clasped his sword a little timorously, but still with strong purpose. The river looked black and unfriendly, a fitting haunt for kelpies and mermaidens.

Soon he came to where another stream entered, a bright, prattling, sunshiny burn, such as his soul loved. Thither he felt his course lay. Now was the time to emulate the heroic John Ridd, when he tracked the Bagworthy stream and met the girl Lorna.

Without doubt some Lorna awaited his coming among the meadows by the water-side. He felt the surer when he reflected that this expedition, too, was not without danger. The land was the ground of a manor-house, watched by zealous gardeners and keepers, full of choice flowers and pleasant fruits as the garden of the Hesperides. He had once essayed the venture before and met with a sad discomfiture. While he kept the stream he had fared well enough, but it so fell out that in the meadow he espied a horse, and there his troubles began; for, approaching it in the Indian manner, he crawled under its belly in the most orthodox way, and proceeded delicately to mount it. The horse clearly was of no Indian breed, for it made off after sadly barking his shins. To add to it all, he had to flee homewards, limping across ploughed lands and through marshy woods, pursued by two irate grooms and a vociferous coachman. No. There was no lack of danger in that direction. So for form's sake he pulled his belt tighter, looked to the edge of his dagger and the point of his sword, and made a pretence of seeking the aid of Heaven in pious, knightly fashion.

It was a gracious and comely land he entered upon. The clear water crooned among irises and white ranunculus or rippled across broad, shining shallows, or fell in a valorous plunge over a little cauld. There was no lack of fish, and had the Jacobite not been on high mission intent he would have thrown off his jacket and groped for trout beneath the banks. But not for him now were such sports. The yellow sunlight clothed the fields as in a cloth of gold, and from the midst great beech trees raised their masses of rich browns and cool greens. There were sheep there and horses, but he did not turn aside, for, like Ulysses, he had learned from misfortune. The place had an enchanting effect upon his spirits. It was like some domain in faëry, the slumbrous forest which girt the sleeping princess, or the wood beyond the world. John Ridd was forgotten, and the Jacobite, forgetful of his special calling, had fled to regions beyond history. He was recalled of a sudden by an unlooked-for barrier to his progress. The stream issued from below a high weir, and unfriendly-looking walls barred its sides.

Without an effort he rose to the occasion. Now was the opportunity for a master-mind, which had never yet met its match among the boys of his restricted acquaintance. He set himself tooth and nail to the wall. Projecting stone and mossy interstices gave him foothold. In a trice he had gained the top and was looking into a sort of refined Elysium, a paradise within a paradise. A broad pond had been formed by the stream, whereon sailed a swan and some brave-liveried ducks, and near whose margin floated water-lilies, yellow and white. Clean-shaven turf fell away from the edge, barred by the shadows of trees and bright in many places with half-opened heather. Beyond the water were little glades of the greenest grass, through which came a glimpse of stone and turret. The Jacobite's breath went quick and fast. Things were becoming, he felt, altogether too true to nature. He had come straight upon a castle without so much as a mishap. The burden of his good fortune bore heavily on him; and he was strongly tempted to retreat. But in the end romance prevailed; with wavering footsteps he crept along the edge, ready at a glance to flop among the reeds.

But these violent tactics were not needed. Sleep seemed to have fallen upon the race of grooms and gardeners. Nothing stirred save a linnet, which came down to drink, and a moorhen which scuttled across the pool. Grasshoppers were chirping in the silence, and the faraway sound of a bell came clear and thin through the air. In a little he came to where the pond ceased and the stream began once more, not like the stream in the meadows below, but a slow, dark current among trees and steep mossy banks. Once more the adventurer's heart beat irresolutely; once more his courage prevailed. He scrambled below trailing branches, slipped oftentimes into the shallows, and rolled among red earth till the last vestige of green was gone from his corduroys. But harsh is the decree of fate. Again he came to a barrier – this time a waterfall of great sound and volume.

Joy filled the heart of the Jacobite. This was the water-slide in the Bagworthy wood, and at the top must be the Doone's valley. So with boldness and skill he addressed himself to the ascent. I have no inkling what the real cascade in Devon is like, but I will take my oath it was not more perilous than this. The black rocks were slippery with ooze, few helping boughs of trees were at hand, and the pool at the bottom yawned horrific and deep. But the Jacobite was skilled in such break-neck ventures. With the ease of a practised climber he swung himself from one foothold to another till he gripped the great rock which stood midway in the stream just at the summit, and, dripping and triumphant, raised himself to the dry land.

And there before him on a fallen trunk, in the most lovely dell that nature ever conceived, sat the Lady.

For a moment the Jacobite, notwithstanding his expectations, was staggered. Then his training asserted itself. He pulled a torn cap from his head, and 'I thought you would be here,' said he.

'Who are you?' said the Lady, with the curiosity of her sex, 'and where do you come from?'

The Jacobite reflected. It was only consistent with tradition, he felt, to give some account of himself. So he proceeded compendiously to explain his birth, his antecedents, his calling, and his adventures of the day. He was delighted with the princess now he had found her. She was tall and lithe, with hair like gold, and the most charming eyes. She wore a dress of white, like a true princess, and a great hat, made according to the most correct canons of romance. She had been reading in a little book, which lay face downward at her feet. He thought of all his special heroines, Helen of Troy and Ariadne, Joan of Arc, the Queen of Scots, Rosalind, and Amy Robsart, and that most hapless and beautiful of dames, the wife of the Secretary Murray. He inwardly decided that the Lady was most like the last, which indeed was only fitting, seeing that tradition said that this place was once her home.

'O, you delightful boy,' said the Lady. 'I never met any one like you before. Tell me what you think of me.'

[17]

'You're all right,' said the wanderer, 'only where do you come from? I hope you're not going to disappear.'

'No, indeed,' said she. 'I come from a place to which you will go some day, a big, stupid town, where the finest and the worst things in the world are to be found. I'm here to escape from it for a little.'

The Jacobite was keenly interested in this account of his prospective dwelling-place.

'What are the fine things?' he asked. 'Ships and palaces and dogs and guns and – oh, you know what I mean?'

'Yes,' she said, 'these things are there. And the people take very little interest in them. What they chiefly like is money.'

The Jacobite pulled out his halfpenny, and regarded it with critical interest.

'Yes,' she went on, 'and lots of people don't go to bed much at night, but they put on fine clothes and go to other people's houses and have dinner and talk, even when they would rather be at home.'

The Jacobite looked philosophically at his clothes. They could not be called fine. He wasn't given to talking to people whom he didn't like, and he told the Lady so.

'And there are others, who rule the country and don't know anything about it, and are only good for making long speeches.'

'But,' said the Jacobite, incredulously, 'don't they know how to fight, or how do they rule if they don't?'

'They don't know how to fight,' said the Lady sadly; 'and more, they say fighting is wrong, and want to settle everything by talking.'

The Jacobite looked mournfully skyward. If this was true, his future was dismal indeed. He had much skill in fighting, but talk he held in deep contempt.

'But there must be heaps of knights and cavaliers left; or are they all gone to heaven?' said he.

The Lady sighed. 'There are some, but very few, I am afraid. And these mostly go away to foreign lands, where there is still fighting, or they hunt lions and tigers, or they stay at home very sad. And people say there is no such place as heaven, but that all that is left for us when we die is a "period of sensationless, objective existence". Do you know what that means?'

'No,' said the Jacobite, stoutly, 'and I don't care. What awful rot!'

'And they say that there never were such things as fairies, and that all the stories about Hector and Ulysses and William Tell and Arthur are nonsense. But we know better.'

'Yes,' said he, 'we know better. They're true to us, and it is only to stupids that they're not true.'

'Good,' said the Lady. 'There was once a man called Horace, who lived long ago, who said the same thing. You will read his book some day.' And she repeated softly to herself,

> Prætulerim scriptor delirus inersque videri,
> Dum mea delectent mala me vel denique fallant,
> Quam sapere et ringi.

But the Jacobite saw the slanting sun over the treetops, and he knew it was time to go home.

'I am afraid I must go,' he said mournfully. 'When I grow up I will stop all that nonsense. I will hang a lot of them and banish others, and then you will like it, won't you? Will you have some treacle toffy? It is very good.'

'Thank you,' said the Lady, 'it *is* good.'

'Good-bye,' said he, 'I will come and see you when I grow up and go to the place you spoke of.'

'Yes, I am sure you will,' said she, and gave him her hand.

He bent low and kissed it in true cavalier fashion.

'There is the road up there,' she said, 'it's your quickest way.' And she looked after him as he disappeared through the trees.

The road ran east and west, and as the sun bent aslant it, it was one great belt of golden light. The Jacobite was wonderfully elated. What an afternoon he had had, just like a bit out of a book! Now there remained for him the three miles of a walk home; then tea with fresh butter and cakes such as his heart rejoiced in; and then the delights of taking the horses to drink, and riding his pony to the smithy. The prospect was soothing and serene. A mellow gaiety diffused through his being.

And yet he could not get rid of the Lady's news. Ah! There was a true princess for you, one who agreed with him in everything; but how sad was the tale she told! Would he ever have to meet such misfortune? He felt that some day he would, and the notion pained him. But he turned back for a moment to look to the westward. The crimson heart of evening was glowing like a furnace; the long shafts of orange light were lengthening, and the apple-green was growing over the blue. Somehow or other the sight gave him heart. The valiant West, that home of El Dorados and golden cities, whither all the romance of life seems to flee, raised his sinking courage. He would, alone, like Douglas among the Saracens, lift the standard and rout all foolish and feeble folks. Some day, when he was great and tall, he would ride into the city where the Lady dwelt, and, after he had scattered her enemies, would marry her and live happy for evermore.

That for the future. For the present home and tea and a summer evening.

An Individualist

Another story from *Scholar Gipsies* (1896), 'An Individualist' touches on a consistent theme in Buchan's writing: 'the place of ambition in the scale of the virtues'.

THE AFTERNOON WAS fast waning to twilight, and the man who for the last few hours had been alternately sleeping in the heather and dabbling in the rocky pools of the burn awoke to the consciousness of time. He rose and looked around him. Hills crowded upon hills, blue, purple, and black; distant spaces of green meadow; barren pines waving desolately on a scarp; many streams falling in a chain of cascades to the glens; and over all a June sky, clear, deep, and tender. The place was goodly, and the idleness which is inseparable from the true enjoyment of afternoon weather dragged heavily upon him to keep him where he was.

He had come out that morn with his mind a chaos of many cares. Projects, fragments of wise and foolish thoughts, a thousand half-conceptions, had crowded upon him thick and fast, for the habit of unceasing mental toil is not shaken off in an hour. But June and the near presence of great hills are wondrous correctives; they are like an inverted spy-glass, which makes large things seem of the smallest; and ere long he found himself aimless and thoughtless. The drift of clouds, the twitter of mountain linnets, seemed all in the world of moment, and he would have gladly bartered his many plans for some share in this wild lore. And so for that day there was one pervert from the gospel of success in life, till lengthening shadows came and he gathered together his wits and laughed at his folly.

With lingering regrets he set off homewards, and the vista before him was one of work awaiting and a whole host of anxieties. Yet for once in a while he had been at peace, and to don the harness again was not so repellent, now that he had found how it could be shaken off at will. So he went along the grassy hill-path whistling an old air, till he

[21]

had gained the edge of the decline, and lo! before him went another wayfarer.

It was the figure of a man about the middle height, with a forward stoop, and a walk which was neither shuffle nor stride, but the elegant lounge of the idler. His general aspect was one of breeding and ease; it was not till a nearer approach that one perceived the contradiction of the details. For all things about him were in rags, from the torn cap to the fragmentary shoes, and the pristine excellence of the cloth only served to accentuate its present state of defection. He also whistled as he walked, and his roving eyes devoured the manifold landscape. Then some other mood seemed to take him, and he flung himself on the short hill grass, lying back with his head on his hands.

At the sound of the other's footsteps he sat up and greeted him.

'Good-day,' said the tramp, civilly. 'Do you go far?' Then, as if he had forgotten himself, he went back to his Scots. 'I was wonderin' if ye could tell me the time o' day, sir,' he said, hastily.

The other stopped short and looked at the stranger before him. Something in his frank eye and strange appearance attracted him, for he did not go on, but glanced at his watch and sat down beside him. Darkness was not yet, and the air was as soft as mid-day.

For a few minutes there was silence, and the one broke it with a laugh. 'I seem to have come into a new land to-day,' he said. 'All things have seemed enchanted, and I scarcely know whether I am sleeping or waking. I suppose it is the weather and those great hills.' And even as he spoke he found himself wondering at himself for speaking thus in such company.

But the other reassured him. 'Good,' said he, and again he dropped the dialect. 'At last I have found some one like-minded. You are a—?'

'Oh, I am a man of affairs, busy from year's end to year's end. For eleven months I am chained, but for once in a while I am free. And you—?'

'Oh I,' and the tramp laughed. 'Ulysses, you know. A wanderer is man from his birth. I see we have not so much in common.'

'No,' said the other, 'I am afraid we have not. You see I believe really at the bottom of my heart in getting on in life, and doing one's duty, and that sort of thing. I see that you have no such pre-judices.'

'Not a bit of it,' and the tramp whistled lackadaisically. 'It's all a question of nature. Some men – well, some, you know, are born to be good citizens. Others lack the domestic virtues. How does the thing go?

> Non illum tectis ullæ, non mœnibus urbes
> Accepere, neque ipse manus feritate dedisset,
> Pastorum et solis exegit montibus ævum.

'Brunck emends the passage, but the words are good as they are. In them you have my character and watchword.'

'It is the character of many,' said the other. 'We can all hear the Piper if we listen, but some of us stop our ears against him. For myself, this hill air makes me daft, and the smell of heather and burning wood, and the sound of water and the wind. I can sympathise with you. And now I am going back to toil, and it will be very hard for days, till the routine lays its spell over me once more.'

'And for what good?' asked the wayfarer. 'I apologise for asking you the foolish question, but it is the inevitable one in my philosophy.'

'Oh,' said the other, 'I can scarcely tell. For the sake of feeling that one is fighting in the ranks of life and not skulking from the battle line; that one is doing the work for which God has given him talents; to know that one is mixing with men, and playing his part well in the human tragi-comedy. These reasons and many others.'

'Hum,' said the tramp. 'Again I must say, "temper of mind". You will excuse me if I say that they do not commend themselves to me. I cannot see the necessity for making the world a battle-field. It is a pilgrimage, if you like, where it is a man's duty and best wisdom to choose the easiest course. All the pleasure in life can be got apart from the turmoil of the market-place — love and kindness, the taste of bread to a hungry man and water to a thirsty, the delight of rest when tired, and the pleasure of motion when fresh and alert, and, above all, the thousand things of nature.'

'You chose the life? You were not born to it?'

'Born to it?' and the wayfarer laughed again. 'No, I was very little born to it. I shall not trouble you with my story, it is too old-fashioned to amuse you. I had good prospects, as people say, but, as I have said, I lacked the civil virtues. I was too restless to stay long anywhere and too rich to have any need, and the upshot of it all is — this!' And he fingered lovingly the multiform rents in his coat.

Below them, as they talked, ran the sandy hill-road, with its white gravel glistening in the westering sunlight. Far down lay a cottage, which was as clear as if it had been not a score of yards away. Thither a man was walking, a shepherd in his Sabbath clothes, who had been to the country town and was returning laden with many parcels. Distant as it was, the whole scene lay plain before the two. A child, a little girl, ran from the cottage at her father's approach, and clung lovingly to his knee. Then with childish strength she clutched a package, and in another second the pair had entered the house. By some simultaneous impulse both men had directed their eyes to the place and had seen the whole of the little comedy.

And lo! to the other's amazement the tramp's eyes glistened as he looked.

'You do not believe in the domestic virtues?' said the one very slowly.

'Not I,' said the tramp. 'I have told you that I don't. The essence of social life, civil and domestic, is bearing one another's burdens and sharing one another's pleasures. I am an individualist with all my heart. I grant you things would come to a pretty pass if all were of my way of thinking; but there – it is a matter of temperament, and such temperaments are scarce.'

'Is it not,' said his interrogator, 'the old question whether man or nature is the more productive study? You cannot maintain that these hills afford the same view-ground of character as the city and the bustle of life. I speak solely as a spectator. I do not even ask you to go down and mix with the crowd and taste its life.' And there seemed no incongruity in talking thus to the man of the wayside and many tatters.

'No, no,' said the other. 'God forbid that I should talk so callously of the sorrows and toils of my fellows. I do not seek to scrutinise the character of others. All my concern is with myself. It is not a man's duty to seek out his kind and strive with them and live among them. All that he must do is to play his part well as he may chance upon them. It is not richness and fulness of life that I want. I am not ambitious. Ease, *ataraxia*, you know, is enough for me.'

'But the rewards?' said the one, questioningly.

'Ah, the rewards! You cannot know them.' And the man's voice took a new tone. His eyes lit up, and, looking over the darkening valley, he spoke to his comrade many things, and sang in his ear ever so sweetly the 'Song of the Open Road'. He told of the changes of the season – the rigours of winter, the early flush of spring, the mellow joys of summer, and autumn with her pomp and decay. He told of clear starlit nights, when the hill breezes blow over the moors and the birds wake the sleeper; of windy mornings, when the mist trails from the hills and dun clouds scud across the sky; of long hot days in the heather among the odours of thyme and bog-myrtle and the lark's clear song. Then he changed his tune, and spoke of the old romance of the wayside, that romance which gipsies and wanderers feel, of motion amid rest, of ease in the hurry of the seasons, of progress over the hills and far away, into that land unknown which dawns upon the sight with each new morrow. And he spoke, too, of the human element in it all which is so dear to the man versed in its mysteries, of heroism amid the sordid, the pathetic in the coarse, the kindly in the most repulsive. And as he spoke he grew eloquent with it all, and his hearer marvelled at such words, till he looked away from the rags to the keen, eager face, and then he marvelled no more.

But by this time the darkness had all but come, and the speaker cut himself short, laughing at his own rhetoric.

'Losh, it's comin' on for nicht,' he said, speaking broadly, as if to point a contrast, 'and time slips by when ye get on the crack. I'll hae to be movin' if I'm to win to Jock Rorison's the nicht. I aye bide wi' Jock, when I'm hereaways, if I dinna sleep ootbye. Will ye be gaun doun the road?'

'Yes, I go by that way too. I'll be glad to accompany you'; and the two went down the winding path together. Overhead the stars, faint with haze, winked and glittered, and below in the valley a light or two shone out from the blue darkness. The soft, fragrant night airs rustled over the heather, and borne on them came the faint twitter of sleepy birds. To one of the pair all seemed so new, so strange, that it was like an excerpt from the caliph's journal. The wondrous natural loveliness around seemed to be a fitting environment for the strange being at his side; and he reflected somewhat ruefully as he walked that what folk call the romance of life springs in the main from people of hot heads and ill-balanced judgments, who seek to put their imperfect, immature little philosophies into action.

They stopped at the first wayside cottage, and the tramp knocked. The door was opened by a grave-faced woman, for in these uplands the sharp air seems to form the human countenance into a passive mould. But at the sight of the man her eyes brightened and she half-offered admittance.

'I'm no comin' in the now,' he explained. 'I juist ca'ed as I passed to tell ye that as I cam' bye the schule at Callowa', the maister gave me a wheen buiks to tak' to your laddie.'

'Thank ye, and it's rale guid o' ye to bring them. He's awfu' keen o' the readin', and gettin' on uncommon weel. It's a wunnerfu' thing eddication; how it mak's a thing different to some folk. But of course you, that never kenned what it was, canna understand it in the same way.'

'No,' said the tramp humbly, 'we canna, but it's a wunnerfu' thing. Na, I'll no come in. Gude nicht,' and again they took the road.

By the time they crossed the water the darkness had fairly come, and a bright horn rose behind the pines. Somewhere in thicket a bird sang – no nightingale – and the two men stopped to listen. Beyond lay the little hamlet of a dozen houses, a rambling, tangled clachan, looking grey and ghostlike in the night.

At one door he knocked and a man came, an old man bent with age and toil, who greeted them kindly.

'I juist cam' frae your son,' the visitor explained. 'I gave him a ca' in as I was passin'. He's verra weel, and he bade me tell ye that he's comin' ower the morn's week to see ye. I was to tell ye, tae, that he's sold his hoggs at twenty-seven, and that he's bocht Crichope yins this 'ear.'

Again he halted, and this time it was at a very little dwelling somewhat beyond the others, standing alone in its garden of gooseberry and marigold. This time the man who waited at the gate saw a pretty, slim lass stand in the doorway, who blushed at the message which was brought her. For her lover lived many a mile over the hills and saw her but every second Sabbath, so their primitive love-letters were sent by word of mouth. And sometimes there came a present from the market town, and there went back something knitted by the girl's own fair fingers; and so the harmless comedy was played, as it is played and will be played all the world over.

Once more the two went on their way, the one silent, the other humming a light country catch. The mind of the one was occupied with many problems, among them that hard one of the adjustment of a man to his neighbours, and the place of ambition in the scale of the virtues. Somehow or other his pride of intellect, of strength, seemed to be deserting him, and in its place there came a better feeling, humble and kindly, a sense that the world is full of more things than any man has ever writ in black and white.

But now it was the cross-road where their paths were severed. They had known each other a bare hour, and now they were the fastest friends. At parting the one shook the other's hand. 'You are a very pretty kind of individualist,' he said.

A Captain of Salvation

'A Captain of Salvation' was the first of three Buchan stories to be published in *The Yellow Book* and has not been reprinted since its first appearance in January 1896, alongside contributions from George Gissing, A.C. Benson, Kenneth Grahame and H.G. Wells.

As with many of Buchan's early stories it revolves around a man brought low by drink, but it is an unusual story for the period in not being set in Scotland. Buchan's actual knowledge of London's East End was probably nonexistent when he wrote the tale – his hitherto brief visits had been confined to the West End and his relatives in Clapham – but he skilfully brings alive the poverty and suffering of the area. This ability to evoke places which he had never visited was later notably demonstrated in his depictions of Virginia in *Salute to Adventurers* (1915) and Olifa in *The Courts of the Morning* (1929).

'A Captain of Salvation' not only draws on Buchan's Calvinistic upbringing, with its concern about the temptation between good and evil, but is also about the differences between the town and the country, the civilised and the primitive.

Nor is it any matter of sorrow to us that the gods of the Pagans are no more. For whatsoever virtue was theirs is embodied in our most blessed faith. For whereas Apollo was the most noble of men in appearance and seemed to his devotees the incarnation (if I may use so sacred a word in a profane sense) of the beauty of the male, we have learned to apprehend a higher beauty of the Spirit, as in our blessed Saints. And whereas Jupiter was the king of the world, we have another and more excellent King, even God the Father, the holy Trinity. And whereas Mars was the god of war, the strongest and most warlike of beings, we have the great soldier of our cause, even the Captain of our Salvation. And whereas the most lovely of women was Venus, beautiful alike in spirit and body, to wit our Blessed Lady. So it is seen that whatever delights are carnal and of the flesh, such are met by greater delights of Christ and His Church.

An Extract from the writings of Donisarius, a Monk of Padua

THE SALVATION CAPTAIN sat in his room at the close of a windy March day. It had been a time of storm and sun, blustering showers and flying scuds of wind. The spring was at the threshold with its unrest and promise; it was the season of turmoil and disquietude in Nature, and turmoil and disquietude in those whose ears are open to her piping. Even there, in a three-pair back, in the odoriferous lands of Limehouse, the spring penetrated with scarcely diminished vigour. Dust had been whistling in the narrow streets; the leaden sky, filled with vanishing spaces of blue, had made the dull brick seem doubly sordid; and the sudden fresh gusts had caused the heavy sickening smells of stale food and unwholesome lodging to seem by contrast more hateful than words.

The Captain was a man of some forty years, tall, with a face deeply marked with weather and evil living. An air of super-induced gravity served only to accentuate the original. His countenance was a sort of epitome of life, full of traces of passion and nobler impulse, with now and then a shadow of refinement and a passing glimpse of breeding. His history had been of that kind which we would call striking, were it not so common. A gentleman born, a scholar after a fashion, with a full experience of the better side of civilisation, he had begun life as well as one can nowadays. For some time things had gone well; then came the utter and irretrievable ruin. A temptation which meets many men in their career met him, and he was overthrown. His name disappeared from the books of his clubs, people spoke of him in a whisper, his friends were crushed with shame. As for the man himself, he took it otherwise. He simply *went under*, disappeared from the ranks of life into the seething, struggling, disordered crowd below. He, if anything, rather enjoyed the change, for there was in him something of that brutality which is a necessary part of the natures of great leaders of men and great scoundrels. The accidents of his environment had made him the latter; he had almost the power of proving the former, for in his masterful brow and firm mouth there were hints of extraordinary strength. His history after his downfall was as picturesque a record as needs be. Years of wandering and fighting, sin and cruelty, generosity and meanness followed. There were few trades and few parts of the earth in which he had not tried his luck. Then there had come a violent change. Somewhere on the face of the globe he had met a man and heard words; and the direction of his life veered round of a sudden to the opposite. Culture, family ties, social bonds had been of no avail to wean him from his headstrong impulses. An ignorant man, speaking plainly some strong sentences which are unintelligible to three-fourths of the world, had worked the change; and spring found him already two years a servant in that body of men and women who had first sought to teach him the way of life.

These two years had been years of struggle, which only a man who has lived such a life can hope to enter upon. A nature which has run riot for two decades is not cabined and confined at a moment's notice. He had been a wanderer like Cain, and the very dwelling in houses had its hardships for him. But in this matter even his former vice came to aid him. He had been proud and self-willed before in his conflict with virtue. He would be proud and self-willed now in his fight with evil. To his comrades and to himself he said that only the grace of God kept him from wrong; in his inmost heart he felt that the grace of God was only an elegant name for his own pride of will.

As he sat now in that unlovely place, he felt sick of his surroundings and unnaturally restive. The day had been a trying one for him. In the morning he had gone West on some money-collecting errand, one which his soul loathed, performed only as an exercise in resignation. It was a bitter experience for him to pass along Piccadilly in his shabby uniform, the badge in the eyes of most people of half-crazy weakness. He had passed restaurants and eating-houses, and his hunger had pained him, for at home he lived on the barest. He had seen crowds of well-dressed men and women, some of whom he dimly recognised, who had no time even to glance at the insignificant wayfarer. Old ungodly longings after luxury had come to disturb him. He had striven to banish them from his mind, and had muttered to himself many texts of Scripture and spoken many catchword prayers, for the fiend was hard to exorcise.

The afternoon had been something worse, for he had been deputed to go to a little meeting in Poplar, a gathering of factory-girls and mechanics who met there to talk of the furtherance of Christ's kingdom. On his way the spirit of spring had been at work in him. The whistling of the wind among the crazy chimneys, the occasional sharp gust from the river, the strong smell of a tanyard, even the rough working-dress of the men he passed, recalled to him the roughness and vigour of his old life. In the forenoon his memories had been of the fashion and luxury of his youth; in the afternoon they were of his world-wide wanderings, their hardships and delights. When he came to the stuffy upper-room where the meeting was held, his state of mind was far from the meek resignation which he sought to cultivate. A sort of angry unrest held him, which he struggled with till his whole nature was in a ferment. The meeting did not tend to soothe him. Brother followed sister in aimless remarks, seething with false sentiment and sickly enthusiasm, till the strong man was near to disgust. The things which he thought he loved most dearly, of a sudden became loathsome. The hysterical fervours of the girls, which only yesterday he would have been ready to call 'love for the Lord', seemed now perilously near absurdity. The loud 'Amens' and 'Hallelujahs' of the men jarred, not on his good taste (that had long gone under), but on his sense of the ludicrous. He found himself more than once admitting the unregenerate thought, 'What wretched nonsense is this? When men are living and dying, fighting and making love all around, when the glorious earth is calling with a hundred voices, what fools and children they are to babble in this way!' But this ordeal went by. He was able to make some conventional remarks at the end, which his hearers treasured as 'precious and true', and he left the place with the shamefaced feeling that for the first time in his new life he had acted a part.

It was about five in the evening ere he reached his room and sat down to his meal. There was half a stale loaf, a pot of cheap tea, and some of that extraordinary compound which the humorous grocers of the East call butter. He was hungry and ate without difficulty, but such fragments of æsthetic liking as he still possessed rose against it. He looked around his room. The table was common deal, supported by three legs and a bit of an old clothes-prop. On the horsehair sofa among the dusty tidies was his Bible, one or two publications of the Army, two bundles of the *War Cry*, some hymn-books, and – strange relic of the past – a battered Gaboriau. On the mantelpiece was a little Burmese idol, which acted as a watch-stand, some hideous photographs framed in black, and a china Duke of Wellington. Near it was his bed, ill-made and dingy, and at the bottom an old sea-trunk. On the top lay one relic of gentility, which had escaped the wreck of his fortunes, a silver-backed hair-brush.

The place filled him with violent repugnance. A smell of rich, greasy fish came upstairs to his nostrils; outside a woman was crying; and two children sprawled and giggled beside his door. This certainly was a wretched hole, and his life was hard almost beyond words. He solemnly reviewed his recent existence. On the one side he set down the evils – bad pay, severe and painful work, poor lodgings, poor food and dismal company. Something stopped him just as he was about to set down the other. 'Oh,' he cried, 'is the love of Jesus nothing that I think like that?' And he began to pray rapidly, 'Lord, I believe, forgive my unbelief.'

For a little he sat in his chair looking straight before him. It would be impossible to put down in words the peculiar hardness of his struggle. For he had to fight with his memory and his inclinations, both of which are to a certain extent independent of the will; and he did this not by sheer strength of resolution, but by fixing his thought upon an abstraction and attempting to clothe it in warm, lovable attributes. He thought upon the countless mercies of God towards him, as his creed showed them; and so strong was the man that in a little he had gotten the victory.

By-and-by he got up and put on his overcoat, thin and patched, and called so only by courtesy. He suddenly remembered his work, how he was engaged that night to lead a crusade through some of the worst streets by the river. Such a crusade was the romantic description by certain imaginative Salvationists of a procession of some dozen men and women with tambourines and concertinas, singing hymns, and sowing the good seed broadcast in the shape of vociferous invitations to mercy and pardon. He hailed it as a sort of anodyne to his pain. There was small time for morbid recollection and introspection if one were engaged in leading a crew of excited followers in places where they were by no means sure of a favourable reception.

There was a noise without on the stairs, then a rap at the door, and Brother Leather entered, whom Whitechapel and the Mile-End Road knew for the most vigilant of soldiers and violent of exhorters.

'Are you strong in the Lord, Captain?' he asked. 'For to-night we're goin' to the stronghold of Satan. It haint no use a invitin' and invitin'. It haint no good 'nless you compel them to come in. And by the 'elp of

God we 'opes to do it. Sister Stokes, she has her tamb'rine, and there's five concertinies from Gray Street, and Brother Clover's been prayin' all day for a great outpourin' of blessin'. "The fields are wite unto th' 'arvest," ' he quoted.

The Captain rose hastily. 'Then hadn't we better be going?' he said. 'We're to start at seven, and it's half-past six already.'

'Let's have a word of prayer fust,' said the other; and straightway, in defiance of all supposed rules of precedence, this strange private soldier flopped on his knees beside the sofa and poured forth entreaties to his Master. This done he arose, and along with the Captain went down the dingy stairway to the door, and out into the narrow darkening street. The newly-lit gas lamps sent a flicker on the men's faces – the one flabby, soft and weak, but with eyes like coals of fire; the other as strong as steel, but listless and uneager. As they passed, a few ragged street-boys cried the old phrase of derision, 'I love Jesus,' at the sight of the caps and the red-banded coats. Here again the one smiled as if he had heard the highest praise, while the other glanced angrily through the gloom as if he would fain rend the urchins, as the bears did the children who mocked Elisha.

At last they turned down a stone-paved passage and came into a little room lined with texts which represented the headquarters of the Army in the district. Sitting on the benches or leaning against the wall were a dozen or so of men and women, all wearing the familiar badge, save one man who had come in his working corduroys, and one girl in a black waterproof. The faces of the men were thin and eager, telling of many sacrifices cheerfully made for their cause, of spare dinners, and nights spent out o' bed, of heart-searchings and painful self-communings, of fervent praying and violent speaking. Thin were the women too, thin and weary, with eyes in which utter lassitude strove against enthusiasm, and backs which ached as they rested. They had come from their labours, as seamstresses and milliners, as shop-girls and laundry-maids, and, instead of enjoying a well-won rest, were devoting their few hours of freedom to the furtherance of an ideal which many clever men have derided. Verily it is well for the world that abstract truth is not the measure of right and wrong, of joy and sorrow.

The Captain gave a few directions to the band and then proceeded to business. They were silent men and women in private life. The world was far too grave a matter for them to talk idly. It was only in the streets that speech came thick and fast; here they were as silent as sphinxes – sphinxes a little tired, not with sitting but with going to and fro on the earth.

'Where are we going?' asked one woman.

The Captain considered for a minute ere he replied. 'Down by the Mordon Wharves,' he said, 'then up Blind Street and Gray Alley to Juke's Buildings, where we can stop and speak. You know the place, friend Leather?'

'Do I know my own dwellin'?' asked the man thus addressed in a surprised tone. 'Wy, I've lived there off an' on for twenty year, and I could tell some tyles o' the plyce as would make yer that keen you couldn't wait a minute but must be off doin' Christ's work.'

'We'll be off now,' said the Captain, who had no desire for his assistant's reminiscences. 'I'll go first with the flag and the rest of you can come in rank. See that you sing out well, for the Lord has much need of singing in these barren lands.' The desultory band clattered down the wooden stair into the street.

Once here the Captain raised the hymn. It was 'Oh, haven't I been happy since I met the Lord?', some rhapsodical words set to a popular music-hall air. To the chance hearer who hailed from more civilised places the thing must have seemed little better than a blasphemous parody. But all element of farce was absent from the hearts of the grim-faced men and women; and the scene as it lay, the squalid street with its filth stirred by the March wind, the high shifting sky overhead, the flicker and glare of the street lamps as each gust jostled them, the irregular singing, the marching amid the laughs or silent scorn of the bystanders – all this formed a picture which had in it more of the elements of the tragic or the noble than the ludicrous.

And the heart of the man at the head of the little procession was the stage of a drama which had little of the comic about it. The street, the open air, had inflamed again the old longings. Something of the enthusiasm of his following had entered into his blood; but it was a perverted feeling, and instead of desiring earnestly the success of his mission, he longed madly, fiercely for forbidden things. In the short encounter in his room he had come off the victor; but it had only been a forced peace, and now the adversary was at him tooth and nail once more. The meeting with the others had roused in him a deep disgust. Heaven above, was it possible that he, the cock of his troop, the man

[34]

whom all had respected after a fashion, as men will respect a strong man, should be a bear-leader to fools! The shame of it took him of a sudden, and as he shouted the more loudly he felt his heart growing hot within him at the thought. But, strangely enough, his very pride came once more to help him. At the thought, 'Have I really come to care what men say and think about me?' the strong pride within him rose in revolt and restored him to himself.

But the quiet was to be of short duration. A hateful, bitter thought, began to rise in him – 'What am I in the world but a man of no importance? And I might have been – oh, I might have been anything I chose! I made a mess of it at the beginning, but is it not possible for a man to right himself again with the world? Have I ever tried it? Instead of setting manfully to the task, I let myself drift, and this is what I have become. And I might have been so different. I might have been back at my old clubs with my old friends, married, maybe, to a pretty wife, with a house near the Park, and a place in the country with shooting and riding to hounds, and a devilish fine time of it. And here I must go on slaving and gabbling, doing a fool's work at a drainer's pay.' Then came a burst of sharp mental anguish, remorse, hate, evil craving. But it passed, and a flood of counter-thoughts came to oppose it. The Captain was still unregenerate in nature, as the phrase goes, but the leaven was working in him. The thought of all that he had gained – God's mercy, pardon for his sins, a sure hope of happiness hereafter, and a glorified ideal to live by – made him stop short in his regrets.

The hymn had just dragged itself out to its quavering close. Wheeling round, he turned a burning eye on his followers. 'Let us raise another, friends,' he cried; and began, 'The Devil and me we can't agree' – which the rest heartily joined in.

And now the little procession reached a new stage in its journey. The narrow street had grown still more restricted. Gin palaces poured broad splashes of garish light across the pavement. Slatternly women and brutal men lined the footpath, and in the kennels filthy little urchins grinned and quarrelled. Every now and then some well-dressed, rakish artiste, or lady of the half-world, pushed her way through the crowds, or a policeman, tall and silent, stalked among the disorderly. Vanity Fair and its denizens were everywhere, from the chattering hucksters to the leering blackguards and sleek traffickers in iniquity. If anything on earth can bring a ray of decency into such a place, then in God's name let it come, whether it be called sense or rant by stay-at-home philosophers.

The hymn-singing added one more element to the discordant noise. But there was in it a suggestion of better things, which was absent from the song of the streets. The obvious chords of the music in that place acquired an adventitious beauty, just as the song of a humble hedge-linnet is lovely amid the croaking of ravens and hooting of owls. The people on the pavement looked on with varying interest. To most it was an everyday exhibition of the unaccountable. Women laughed, and shrieked coarse railleries; some of the men threatened, others looked on in amused scorn; but there was no impulse to active violence. The thing was tolerated as yonder seller of cheap watchguards was borne; for it is an unwritten law in the slums, that folk may do their own pleasure, as long as they cease from interfering offensively with the enjoyment of others.

' 'Oo's the cove wi' the flag, Bill?' asked one woman. ' 'E haint so bad as the rest. Most loikely 'e's taken up the job to dodge the nick.'

'Dodge the nick yersel', Lizer,' said the man addressed. 'Wy, it's the chap's wye o' making his livin', a roarin' and a preachin' like that. S'help me, I'd rather cry "Welks" any dye than go about wi' sich a crew.'

A woman, garishly adorned, with a handsome flushed face, looked up at the Captain.

'Why, it's Jack,' she cried. 'Bless me if it ain't Jack. Jack, Jack, what are you after now, not coming to speak to me. Don't you mind Sal, your little Sal. I'm coming to yer, I ain't forgotten yer.' And she began to push her way into mid-street.

The Captain looked to the side, and his glance rested upon her face. It was as if the Devil and all his angels were upon him that night. Evil memories of his past life thronged thick and fast upon him. He had already met and resisted the world, and now the flesh had come to torment him. But here his armour was true and fast. This was a temptation which he had choked at the very outset of his reformation. He looked for one moment at her, and in the utter loathing and repugnance of that look, she fell back; and the next instant was left behind.

The little streets, which radiate from the wharf known as Mordon's, are so interlaced and crooked that to find one's way in them is more a matter of chance than good guiding even to the initiated. The houses are small and close, the residence of the very sweepings of the population; the shops are ship-chandlers and low eating-houses, pawnshops, emporia of cheap jewellery, and remnant drapers. At this hour of the night there is a blaze of dull gas-light on either side, and the proprietors of the places of custom stand at their doors inviting the bystanders to inspect their goods. This is the hotbed of legalised crime, the rendezvous of half the wickedness of the earth. Lascars, Spaniards, Frenchmen jostle Irishmen, and Scotsmen, and the true-born Englishmen in these narrow purlieus. If a man disappears utterly from view you may be sure to find him somewhere in the network of alleys, for there it would be hard for the law to penetrate *incolis invitis*. It is a sort of Cave of Adullam on the one hand, to which the morally halt and maimed of all nations resort; and, on the other, a nursery of young vice and unformed devilry. Sailors straddled about the pavement, or stood in knots telling their tales in loud voices and plentiful oaths; every beershop was continually discharging its stream of filthy occupants, filthy and prosperous. The element of squalor and misery was here far less in evidence. All the inhabitants seemed gorged and well clad, but their faces were stained with vice so horrible that poverty and tatters would have been a welcome relief.

The Salvation band penetrated into this Sodom with fear in the heart of each member. It was hard for the Gospel to strive with such seared and branded consciences. The repulsive, self-satisfied faces of the men, the smug countenances of the women, made that little band seem hopeless and Quixotic in the extreme. The Captain felt it, too; but in him there was mingled another feeling. He thought of himself as a combatant entering the arena. He felt dimly that some great struggle was impending, some monstrous temptation, some subtle wile of the Evil One. The thought made him the more earnest. 'Sing up, men,' he cried, 'the Devil is strong in this place.'

It was the truth, and the proof awaited him. A man stepped out from among the bystanders and slapped his shoulder. The Captain started and looked. It was the Devil in person.

'Hullo, Jack!' said the new-comer. 'Good God, who'd have thought of seeing you here? Have you gone off your head now?'

The Captain shivered. He knew the speaker for one of his comrades of the old days, the most daring and jovial of them all. The two had been hand and glove in all manner of evil. They had loved each other like brothers, till the great change came over the one, which fixed a gulf between them for ever.

'You don't mean to tell me you've taken up with this infernal nonsense, Jack? No, I won't believe it. It's just another of your larks. You were always the one for originality.'

'Go away, Hilton,' said the Captain hoarsely, 'go away. I've done with you. I can't see you any more.'

'What the deuce has come over you, Jack? Not speak to me any more! Why, what foolery is this? You've gone and turned a regular old wife, bless me if you haven't. Oh, man, give it up. It's not worth it. Don't you remember the fun we've had in our time? Gad, Jack, when you and I stood behind yon big tree in Kaffraria with twenty yelling devils wanting our blood; don't you remember how I fell and you got over me, and, though you were bleeding like a pig, you kept them off till the Cape troopers came up? And when we were lost, doing picketing up in the Drakenberg, you mind how we chummed together for our last meal? And heavens! it was near our last. I feel that infernal giddiness still. And yet you tell me to go away.'

'Oh, Hilton,' said the Captain, 'come and be one of us. The Lord's willing to receive you, if you'll only come. I've got the blessing, and there's one waiting for you if you'll only take it.'

'Blessing be damned!' said the other with a laugh. 'What do I want with your blessing when there's life and the world to see? What's the good of poking round here, and crying about the love of Jesus and singing twaddle, and seeing nobody but old wives and white-faced shopmen, when you might be out on the open road, with the wind and the stars and the sun, and meet with men, and have your fling like a man. Don't you remember the days at Port Said, when the old Frenchman twanged his banjo and the girls danced and – hang it, don't you feel the smell of the sand and the heat in your nostrils, you old fool?'

'Oh, my God!' said the Captain, 'I do. Go away, Hilton. For God's sake, go away and leave me!'

'Can't you think,' went on the other, 'of the long nights when we dropped down the Irrawaddy, of the whistle of the wind in the white sails, and the singing of the boatmen, and the sick-suck of the alligators among the reeds; and how we went ashore at the little village and got arrack from the natives, and made a holy sight of the place in the morning? It was worth it, though we got the sack for it, old man.'

The Captain made no answer. He was muttering something to himself. It might have been a prayer.

'And then there was that time when we were up country in Queensland, sugar farming in the bush, thinking a billy of tea the best thing on earth, and like to faint with the work and the heat. But, Jove, wasn't it fine to head off the cattle when you knew you might have a big bull's horn in your side every minute? And then at night to sit outside the huts and smoke pig-tail and tell stories that would make your hair rise! We were a queer lot, Jack, but we were men, *men*, do you hear?'

A flood of recollection came over the Captain, vehement, all-powerful. He felt the magic of the East, the wonder of the South, the glory of the North burning in his heart. The old wild voices were calling him, voices of land and sea, the tongues of the moon and the stars and the beasts of the field, the halcyon voices of paganism and nature which are still strong in the earth. Behind him rose the irregular notes of the hymn; at his side was the tempter, and in his own heart was the prince of the world, the master of pleasure, the great juggler of pain. In that man there was being fought the old fight, which began in the Garden, and will never end, the struggle between the hateful right and the delicious wrong.

'Oh man, come with me,' cried Hilton, 'I've got a berth down there in a ship which sails to-morrow, and we'll go out to our old place, where they'll be glad to get us, and we'll have a devilish good time. I can't be staying here, with muggy stinks, and white-faced people, and preaching and praying, and sloppy weather. Come on, and in a month we'll be seeing the old Coal-sack above us, and smelling the palms and the sea-water; and then, after that, there'll be the Bush, the pines and the gum-trees and the blue sky, and the hot, clear air, and rough-riding and adventure; and by God we'll live like gentlemen and fine fellows, and never come back to this cursed hole any more. Come on, and leave the psalm-singing.'

A spasm of convulsive pain, of exquisite agony, of heart-breaking struggle came over the Captain's face, stayed a moment, and passed. He turned round to his followers. 'Sing louder, lads,' he cried, 'we're fighting a good fight.' And then his voice broke down, and he stumbled blindly on, still clutching the flag.

A Journey of Little Profit

This second *Yellow Book* story appeared in April 1896 and was chosen for a subsequent collection of stories from the magazine *The Yellow Book: A Selection*. It was one of the stories included in *Grey Weather* (1899).

> The Devil he sang, the Devil he played
>   High and fast and free.
> And this was ever the song he made,
>   As it was told to me.
> Oh, I am the king of the air and the ground,
>   And lord of the seasons' roll,
> And I will give you a hundred pound,
>   If you will give me your soul!
>
> from The Ballad of Grey Weather

THE CATTLE MARKET of Inverforth is, as all men know north of the Tweed, the greatest market of the kind in the land. For days in the late Autumn there is the lowing of oxen and the bleating of sheep among its high wooden pens, and in the rickety sale-rings the loud clamour of auctioneers and the talk of farmers. In the open yard where are the drovers and the butchers, a race always ungodly and law-despising, there is such a Babel of cries and curses as might wake the Seven Sleepers. From twenty different adjacent eating-houses comes the clatter of knives, where the country folk eat their dinner of beef and potatoes, with beer for sauce, and the collies grovel on the ground for stray morsels. Hither come a hundred types of men from the Highland cateran with scarce a word of English, and the shentleman-farmer of Inverness and Ross, to lowland graziers and city tradesmen, not to speak of blackguards of many nationalities and more professions.

It was there I first met Duncan Stewart of Clachamharstan, in the

Moor of Rannoch, and there I heard this story. He was an old man when I knew him, grizzled and wind-beaten; a prosperous man, too, with many herds like Jacob and much pasture. He had come down from the North with kyloes, and as he waited on the Englishmen with whom he had trysted, he sat with me through the long day and beguiled the time with many stories. He had been a drover in his youth, and had travelled on foot the length and breadth of Scotland; and his memory went back hale and vigorous to times which are now all but historical. This tale I heard among many others as we sat on a pen amid the smell of beasts and the jabber of Gaelic:

'When I was just turned of twenty-five I was a wild young lad as ever was heard of. I had taken to the droving for the love of a wild life, and a wild life I led. My father's heart would be broken long syne with my doings, and well for my mother that she was in her grave since I was six years old. I paid no heed to the ministrations of godly Mr. Mac-dougall of the Isles, who bade me turn from the error of my ways, but went on my own evil course, making siller, for I was a braw lad at the work and a trusted, and knowing the inside of every public from the pier of Cromarty to the streets of York. I was a wild drinker, caring in my cups for neither God nor man, a great hand with the cards, and fond of the lasses past all telling. It makes me shameful to this day to think on my evil life when I was twenty-five.

'Well, it chanced that in the back of the month of September I found myself in the city of Edinburgh with a flock of fifty sheep which I had bought as a venture from a drunken bonnet-laird and was thinking of selling somewhere wast the country. They were braw beasts, Leicester every one of them, well-fed and dirt-cheap at the price I gave. So it was with a light heart that I drove them out of the town by the Merchiston Road along by the face of the Pentlands. Two or three friends came with me, all like myself for folly, but maybe a little bit poorer. Indeed, I cared little for them, and they valued me only for the whisky which I gave them to drink my health in at the parting. They left me on the near side of Colinton, and I went on my way alone.

'Now, if you'll be remembering the road, you will mind that at the place called Kirk Newton, just afore the road begins to twine over the Big Muir and almost at the head of the Water o' Leith, there is a verra fine public. Indeed, it would be no lee to call it the best public between

[41]

Embro' and Glesca. The good wife, Lucky Craik by name, was an old friend of mine, for many a good gill of her prandy have I bought; so what would I be doing but just turning aside for refreshment? She met me at the door, verra pleased-like to see me, and soon I had my legs aneath her table and a basin of toddy on the board before me. And whom did I find in the same place but my old comrade Toshie Maclean from the backside of Glen-Lyon. Toshie and I were acquaintances so old that it did not behoove us to be parting quick. Forbye the day was chill without; and within the fire was grand and the crack of the best.

'Then Toshie and I got on quarrelling about the price of Lachlan Farawa's beasts that he sold at Falkirk; and, the drink having aye a bad effect on my temper, I was for giving him the lie and coming off in a great rage. It was about six o'clock in the evening and an hour to nightfall, so Mistress Craik comes in to try and keep me. "Losh, Duncan," says she, "ye'll never try and win ower the muir the nicht. It's mae than ten mile to Carnwath, and there's nocht atween it and this but whaups and heathery braes." But when I am roused I will be more obstinate than ten mules, so I would be going, though I knew not under Heaven where I was going till. I was too full of good liquor and good meat to be much worth at thinking, so I got my sheep on the road an a big bottle in my pouch and set off into the heather. I knew not what my purpose was, whether I thought to reach the shieling of Carnwath, or whether I expected some house of enter- tainment to spring up by the wayside. But my fool's mind was set on my purpose of getting some miles further in my journey ere the coming of darkness.

'For some time I jogged happily on, with my sheep running well before me and my dogs trotting at my heels. We left the trees behind and struck out on the proad grassy path which bands the moor like the waist-strap of a sword. It was most dreary and lonesome with never a house in view, only bogs and grey hillsides and ill-looking waters. It was stony, too, and this more than aught else caused my Dutch courage to fail me, for I soon fell wearied, since much whisky is bad travelling fare, and began to curse my folly. Had my pride no kept me back, I would have returned to Lucky Craik's; but I was like the devil, for stiff-neckedness and thought of nothing but to push on.

'I own that I was verra well tired and quite spiritless when I first saw the House. I had scarce been an hour on the way, and the light was not

quite gone; but still it was geyan dark, and the place sprang somewhat
suddenly on my sight. For, looking a little to the left, I saw over a little
strip of grass a big square dwelling with many outhouses, half farm
and half pleasure-house. This, I thought, is the verra place I have been
seeking and made sure of finding; so whistling a gay tune, I drove my
flock toward it.

'When I came to the gate of the court, I saw better of what sort was
the building I had arrived at. There was a square yard with monstrous
high walls, at the left of which was the main block of the house, and
on the right what I took to be the byres and stables. The place looked
ancient, and the stone in many places was crumbling away; but the
style was of yesterday and in no way differing from that of a hundred
steadings in the land. There were some kind of arms above the
gateway, and a bit of an iron stanchion; and when I had my sheep
inside of it, I saw that the court was all grown up with green grass.
And what seemed queer in that dusky half-light was the want of
sound. There was no neichering of horses, nor routing of kye, nor clack
of hens, but all as still as the top of Ben Cruachan. It was warm and
pleasant too, though the night was chill without.

'I had no sooner entered the place than a row of sheep-pens caught
my eye, fixed against the wall in front. This I thought mighty convenient, so I made all haste to put my beasts into them; and finding
that there was a good supply of hay within, I left them easy in my
mind, and turned about to look for the door of the house.

'To my wonder, when I found it, it was open wide to the wall;
so, being confident with much whisky, I never took thought to
knock, but walked boldly in. There's some careless folk here, thinks
I to myself, and I much misdoubt if the man knows aught about
farming. He'll maybe just be a town's body taking the air on the
muirs.

'The place I entered upon was a hall, not like a muirland farmhouse,
but more fine than I had ever seen. It was laid with a verra fine carpet,
all red and blue and gay colours, and in the corner in a fireplace a great
fire crackled. There were chairs, too, and a walth of old rusty arms on
the walls, and all manner of whigmaleeries that folk think ornamental.
But nobody was there, so I made for the staircase which was at the
further side, and went up it stoutly. I made scarce any noise so thickly
was it carpeted, and I will own it kind of terrified me to be walking in
such a place. But when a man has drunk well he is troubled not

overmuckle with modesty or fear, so I e'en stepped out and soon came to a landing where was a door.

'Now, thinks I, at last I have won to the habitable parts of the house; so laying my finger on the sneck I lifted it and entered. And there before me was the finest room in all the world; indeed I abate not a jot of the phrase, for I cannot think of anything finer. It was hung with braw pictures and lined with big bookcases of oak well-filled with books in fine bindings. The furnishing seemed carved by a skilled hand, and the cushions and curtains were soft velvet. But the best thing was the table, which was covered with a clean white cloth and set with all kind of good meat and drink. The dishes were of silver and as bright as Loch Awe water in an April sun. Eh, but it was a braw braw sight for a drover! And there at the far end, with a great pottle of wine before him, sat the master.

'He rose as I entered, and I saw him to be dressed in the pink of town fashion, a man of maybe fifty years, but hale and well-looking, with a peaked beard and trimmed moustache and thick eyebrows. His eyes were slanted a thought, which is a thing I hate in any man, but his whole appearance was pleasing.

' "Mr. Stewart?" says he courteously, looking at me. "Is it Mr. Duncan Stewart that I will be indebted to for the honour of this visit?"

'I stared at him blankly, for how did he ken my name?

' "That is my name," I said, "but who the tevil tell't you about it?"

' "Oh, my name is Stewart myself," says he, "and all Stewarts should be well acquaint."

' "True," said I, "though I don't mind your face before. But now I am here, I think you have a most gallant place, Mr. Stewart."

' "Well enough. But how have you come to't? We've few visitors."

'So I told him where I had come from, and where I was going, and why I was forwandered at this time of night among the muirs. He listened keenly, and when I had finished, he says verra friendly-like, "Then you'll bide all night and take supper with me. It would never be doing to let one of the clan go away without breaking bread. Sit ye down, Mr. Duncan."

'I sat down gladly enough, though I own that at first I did not half-like the whole business. There was something unchristian about the place, and for certain it was not seemly that the man's name should be the same as my own, and that he should be so well posted in my doings. But he seemed so well-disposed that my misgivings soon vanished.

'So I seated myself at the table opposite my entertainer. There was a place laid ready for me, and beside the knife and fork a long horn-handled spoon. I had never seen a spoon so long and queer, and I asked the man what it meant. "Oh," says he, "the broth in this house is very often hot, so we need a long spoon to sup it. It is a common enough thing, is it not?"

'I could answer nothing to this, though it did not seem to me sense, and I had an inkling of something I had heard about long spoons which I thought was not good; but my wits were not clear, as I have told you already. A serving man brought me a great bowl of soup and set it before me. I had hardly plunged spoon intil it, when Mr. Stewart cries out from the other end: "Now, Mr. Duncan, I call you to witness that you sit down to supper of your own accord. I've an ill name in these parts for compelling folk to take meat with me when they dinna want it. But you'll bear me witness that you're willing."

' "Yes, by God, I am that," I said, for the savoury smell of the broth was rising to my nostrils. The other smiled at this as if well-pleased.

'I have tasted many soups, but I swear there never was one like that. It was as if all the good things in the world were mixed thegether – whisky and kale and shortbread and cocky-leeky and honey and salmon. The taste of it was enough to make a body's heart loup with fair gratitude. The smell of it was like the spicy winds of Arabia, that you read about in the Bible, and when you had taken a spoonful you felt as happy as if you had sellt a hundred yowes at twice their reasonable worth. Oh, it was grand soup!

' "What Stewarts did you say you comed from?" I asked my entertainer.

' "Oh," he says, "I'm connected with them all, Athole Stewarts, Appin Stewarts, Rannoch Stewarts; and a' I've a heap o' land there-aways."

' "Whereabouts?" says I, wondering. "Is't at the Blair o' Athole, or along by Tummel side, or wast the Loch o'Rannoch, or on the Muir, or in Mamore?"

' "In all the places you name," says he.

' "Got damn," says I, "then what for do you not bide there instead of in these stinking lawlands?"

'At this he laughed softly to himself. "Why, for maybe the same reason as yoursel, Mr. Duncan. You know the proverb, 'A' Stewarts are sib to the Deil.' "

[45]

'I laughed loudly; "Oh, you've been a wild one, too, have you? Then you're not worse than mysel. I ken the inside of every public in the Cowgate and Cannongate, and there's no another drover on the road my match at fechting and drinking and dicing." And I started on a long shameless catalogue of my misdeeds. Mr. Stewart meantime listened with a satisfied smirk on his face.

'"Yes, I've heard tell of you, Mr. Duncan," he says. "But here's something more, and you'll doubtless be hungry."

'And now there was set on the table a round of beef garnished with pot-herbs, all most delicately fine to the taste. From a great cupboard were brought many bottles of wine, and in a massive silver bowl at the table's head were put whisky and lemons and sugar. I do not know well what I drank, but whatever it might be it was the best ever brewed. It made you scarce feel the earth round about you, and you were so happy you could scarce keep from singing. I wad give much siller to this day for the receipt.

'Now, the wine made me talk, and I began to boast of my own great qualities, the things I had done and the things I was going to do. I was a drover just now, but it was not long that I would be being a drover. I had bought a flock of my own, and would sell it for a hundred pounds, no less; with that I would buy a bigger one till I had made money enough to stock a farm; and then I would leave the road and spend my days in peace, seeing to my land and living in good company. Was not my father, I cried, own cousin, thrice removed, to the Macleans o' Duart, and my mother's uncle's wife a Rory of Balnacroy? And I am a scholar too, said I, for I was a matter of two years at Embro' College, and might have been roaring in the pulpit, if I hadna liked the drink and the lassies too well.

'"See," said I, "I will prove it to you"; and I rose from the table and went to one of the bookcases. There were all manner of books, Latin and Greek, poets and philosophers, but in the main, divinity. For there I saw Richard Baxter's "Call to the Unconverted", and Thomas Boston of Ettrick's "Fourfold State", not to speak of the *Sermons* of half a hundred auld ministers, and the "Hind let Loose", and many books of the covenanting folk.

'"Faith," I says, "you've a fine collection, Mr. What's-your-name," for the wine had made me free in my talk. "There is many a minister and professor in the Kirk, I'll warrant, who has a less godly library. I begin to suspect you of piety, sir."

' "Does it not behoove us," he answered in an unctuous voice, "to mind the words of Holy Writ that evil communications corrupt good manners, and have an eye to our company? These are all the company I have, except when some stranger such as you honours me – with a visit."

'I had meantime been opening a book of plays, I think by the famous William Shakespeare, and I here proke into a loud laugh. "Ha, ha, Mr. Stewart," I says, "here's a sentence I've lighted on which is hard on you. Listen! 'The Devil can quote Scripture to advantage.' "

'The other laughed long. "He who wrote that was a shrewd man," he said, "but I'll warrant if you'll open another volume, you'll find some quip on yourself."

'I did as I was bidden, and picked up a white-backed book, and opening it at random, read: "There be many who spend their days in evil and wine-bibbing, in lusting and cheating, who think to mend while yet there is time; but the opportunity is to them for ever awanting, and they go down open-mouthed to the great fire."

' "Psa," I cried, "some wretched preaching book, I will have none of them. Good wine will be better than bad theology." So I sat down once more at the table.

' "You're a clever man, Mr. Duncan," he says, "and a well-read one. I commend your spirit in breaking away from the bands of the kirk and the college, though your father was so thrawn against you."

' "Enough of that," I said, "though I don't know who telled you;" I was angry to hear my father spoken of, as though the grieving him was a thing to be proud of.

' "Oh, as you please," he says; "I was just going to say that I commended your spirit in sticking the knife into the man in the Pleasaunce, the time you had to hide for a month about the backs o' Leith."

' "How do you ken that," I asked hotly, "you've heard more about me than ought to be repeated, let me tell you."

' "Don't be angry," he said sweetly; "I like you well for these things, and you mind the lassie in Athole that was so fond of you. You treated her well, did you not?"

'I made no answer, being too much surprised at his knowledge of things which I thought none knew but myself.

' "Oh yes, Mr. Duncan. I could tell you what you were doing to-day, how you cheated Jock Gallowa out of six pounds, and sold a horse to the farmer of Haypath that was scarce fit to carry him home. And I know what you are meaning to do the morn at Glesca, and I wish you well of it."

' "I think you must be the Devil," I said blankly.

' "The same, at your service," said he, still smiling.

'I looked at him in terror, and even as I looked I kenned by something in his eyes and the twitch of his lips that he was speaking the truth.

' "And what place is this, you . . ." I stammered.

' "Call me Mr. S.," he says gently, "and enjoy your stay while you are here and don't concern yourself about the lawing."

' "The lawing!" I cried in astonishment, "and is this a house of public entertainment?"

' "To be sure, else how is a poor man to live?"

' "Name it," said I, "and I will pay and be gone."

' "Well," said he, "I make it a habit to give a man his choice. In your case it will be your wealth or your chances hereafter, in plain English your flock or your—"

' "My immortal soul," I gasped.

' "Your soul," said Mr. S., bowing, "though I think you call it by too flattering an adjective."

' "You damned thief," I roared, "you would entice a man into your accursed house and then strip him bare."

' "Hold hard," said he, "don't let us spoil our good fellowship by incivilities. And, mind you, I took you to witness to begin with that you sat down of your own accord."

' "So you did," said I, and could say no more.

' "Come, come," he says, "don't take it so bad. You may keep all your gear and yet part from here in safety. You've but to sign your name, which is no hard task to a college-bred man, and go on living as you live just now to the end. And let me tell you, Mr. Duncan Stewart, that you should take it as a great obligement that I am willing to take your bit soul instead of fifty sheep. There's no many would value it so high."

' "Maybe no, maybe no," I said sadly, "but it's all I have. D'ye no see that if I gave it up, there would be no chance left of mending? And I'm sure I do not want your company to all eternity."

' "Faith, that's uncivil," he says; "I was just about to say that we had had a very pleasant evening."

'I sat back in my chair very down-hearted. I must leave this place as poor as a kirk-mouse, and begin again with little but the clothes on my back. I was strongly tempted to sign the bit paper thing and have done with it all, but somehow I could not bring myself to do it. So at last I says to him: "Well, I've made up my mind. I'll give you my sheep, sorry though I be to lose them, and I hope I may never come near this place again as long as I live."

' "On the contrary," he said, "I hope often to have the pleasure of your company. And seeing that you've paid well for your lodging, I hope you'll make the best of it. Don't be sparing on the drink."

'I looked hard at him for a second. "You've an ill name, and an ill trade, but you're no a bad sort yoursel, and, do you ken, I like you."

' "I'm much obliged to you for the character," says he, "and I'll take your hand on't."

'So I filled up my glass and we set to, and such an evening I never mind of. We never got fou, but just in a fine good temper and very entertaining. The stories we told and the jokes we cracked are still a kind of memory with me, though I could not come over one of them. And then, when I got sleepy, I was shown to the brawest bedroom, all hung with pictures and looking-glasses, and with bed-clothes of the finest linen and a coverlet of silk. I bade Mr. S. good-night, and my head was scarce on the pillow ere I was sound asleep.

'When I awoke the sun was just newly risen, and the frost of a September morning was on my clothes. I was lying among green braes with nothing near me but crying whaups and heathery hills, and my two dogs running round about and howling as they were mad.'

Politics and the May-Fly

'Politics and the May-Fly' was published in *Chamber's Journal* on 9 May 1896, a month later in the Boston magazine *The Living Age* and was subsequently included in *Grey Weather* (1899).

It introduces the town of Gledsmuir – called Marchthorn in the original magazine version – and is the first of several stories that revolve around angling and an examination of social change in the Scottish countryside, a subject at the centre of his novel *John Macnab* (1925), and on which he often spoke after he was elected as a Scottish Member of Parliament in 1927.

THE FARMER OF Clachlands was a Tory, stern and unbending. It was the tradition of his family, from his grandfather, who had been land-steward to Lord Manorwater, down to his father, who had once seconded a vote of confidence in the sitting member. Such traditions, he felt, were not to be lightly despised; things might change, empires might wax and wane, but his obligation continued; a sort of perverted *noblesse oblige* was the farmer's watchword in life; and by dint of much energy and bad language, he lived up to it.

As fate would have it, the Clachlands ploughman was a Radical of Radicals. He had imbibed his opinions early in life from a speaker on the green of Gledsmuir, and ever since, by the help of a weekly penny paper and an odd volume of Gladstone's speeches, had continued his education. Such opinions in a conservative countryside carry with them a reputation for either abnormal cleverness or abnormal folly. The fact that he was a keen fisher, a famed singer of songs, and the best judge of horses in the place, caused the verdict of his neighbours to incline to the former, and he passed for something of an oracle among his fellows. The blacksmith, who was the critic of the neigh-bourhood, summed up his character in a few words. 'Him,' said he, in a tone of mingled dislike and admiration, 'him! He would sweer white was black the morn, and dod! he would prove it tae.'

It so happened in the early summer, when the land was green and the trout plashed in the river, that Her Majesty's Government saw fit to appeal to an intelligent country. Among a people whose politics fight hard with their religion for a monopoly of their interests, feeling ran high and brotherly kindness departed. Houses were divided against themselves. Men formerly of no consideration found themselves suddenly important, and discovered that their intellects and conscience, which they had hitherto valued at little, were things of serious interest to their betters. The lurid light of publicity was shed upon the lives of the rival candidates; men formerly accounted worthy and respectable were proved no better than white sepulchres; and each man was filled with a morbid concern for his fellow's character and beliefs.

The farmer of Clachlands called a meeting of his labourers in the great dusty barn, which had been the scene of many similar gatherings. His speech on the occasion was rigorous and to the point. 'Ye are a' my men,' he said, 'an' I'll see that ye vote richt. Y're uneddicated folk, and ken naething aboot the matter, sae ye just tak' my word for't, that the Tories are in the richt and vote accordingly. I've been a guid maister to ye, and it's shurely better to pleesure me, than a wheen leein' scoondrels whae tramp the country with leather bags and printit trash.'

Then arose from the back the ploughman, strong in his convictions, 'Listen to me, you men,' says he; 'just vote as ye think best. The maister's a guid maister, as he says, but he's nocht to dae wi' your votin'. It's what they ca' inteemedation to interfere wi' onybody in this matter. So mind that, an' vote for the workin'-man an' his richts.'

Then ensued a war of violent words.

'Is this a meetin' in my barn, or a pennywaddin?'

'Ca 't what ye please. I canna let ye mislead the men.'

'Whae talks about misleadin'? Is 't misleadin' to lead them richt?'

'The question,' said the ploughman solemnly, 'is what you ca' richt.'

'William Laverhope, if ye werena a guid plooman, ye wad gang post-haste oot o' here the morn.'

'I carena what ye say. I'll stand up for the richts o' thae men.'

'Men!' – this with deep scorn. 'I could mak' better men than thae wi' a stick oot o' the plantin'.'

'Ay, ye say that noo, an' the morn ye'll be ca'in' ilka yin o' them *Mister*, a' for their votes.'

The farmer left in dignified disgust, vanquished but still dangerous; the ploughman in triumph mingled with despair. For he knew that his fellow-labourers cared not a whit for politics, but would follow to the letter their master's bidding.

The next morning rose clear and fine. There had been a great rain for the past few days, and the burns were coming down broad and surly. The Clachlands Water was chafing by bank and bridge and threatening to enter the hay-field, and every little ditch and sheep-drain was carrying its tribute of peaty water to the greater flood. The farmer of Clachlands, as he looked over the landscape from the doorstep of his dwelling, marked the state of the weather and pondered over it.

He was not in a pleasant frame of mind that morning. He had been crossed by a ploughman, his servant. He liked the man, and so the obvious way of dealing with him – by making things uncomfortable or turning him off – was shut against him. But he burned to get the upper hand of him, and discomfit once for all one who had dared to question his wisdom and good sense. If only he could get him to vote on the other side – but that was out of the question. If only he could keep him from voting – that was possible but unlikely. He might forcibly detain him, in which case he would lay himself open to the penalties of the law, and be nothing the gainer. For the victory which he desired was a moral one, not a triumph of force. He would like to circumvent him by cleverness, to score against him fairly and honourably on his own ground. But the thing was hard, and, as it seemed to him at the moment, impossible.

Suddenly, as he looked over the morning landscape, a thought struck him and made him slap his legs and chuckle hugely. He walked quickly up and down the gravelled walk. 'Losh, it's guid. I'll dae't. I'll dae't, if the weather juist hauds.'

His unseemly mirth was checked by the approach of someone who found the farmer engaged in the minute examination of gooseberry leaves. 'I'm concerned aboot thae busses,' he was saying; 'they've been ill lookit to, an' we'll no hae half a crop.' And he went off, still smiling, and spent a restless forenoon in the Gledsmuir market.

In the evening he met the ploughman, as he returned from the turnip-singling, with his hoe on his shoulder. The two men looked at one another with the air of those who know that all is not well between them. Then the farmer spoke with much humility.

'I maybe spoke rayther severe yestreen,' he said. 'I hope I didna hurt your feelings.'

'Na, na! No me!' said the ploughman airily.

'Because I've been thinking ower the matter, an' I admit that a man has a richt to his ain thochts. A'body should hae principles an' stick to them,' said the farmer, with the manner of one making a recondite quotation.

'Ay,' he went on, 'I respect ye, William, for your consistency. Ye're an example to us a'.'

The other shuffled and looked unhappy. He and his master were on the best of terms, but these unnecessary compliments were not usual in their intercourse. He began to suspect, and the farmer, who saw his mistake, hastened to change the subject.

'Graund weather for the fishin',' said he.

'Oh, is it no?' said the other, roused to excited interest by this home topic. 'I tell ye by the morn they'll be takin' as they've never ta'en this 'ear. Doon in the big pool in the Clachlands Water, at the turn o' the turnip-field, there are twae or three pounders, and aiblins yin o' twae pund, I saw them mysel' when the water was low. It's ower big the noo, but when it gangs doon the morn, and gets the colour o' porter, I'se warrant I could whup them oot o' there wi' the flee.'

'D' ye say sae?' said the farmer, sweetly. 'Weel, it's a lang time since I tried the fishin', but I yince was keen on 't. Come in bye, William; I've something ye micht like to see.'

From a corner he produced a rod, and handed it to the other. It was a very fine rod indeed, one which the owner had gained in a fishing competition many years before, and treasured accordingly. The ploughman examined it long and critically. Then he gave his verdict. 'It's the brawest rod I ever saw, wi' a fine hickory butt, an' guid greenhert tap and middle. It wad cast the sma'est flee, and haud the biggest troot.'

'Weel,' said the farmer, genially smiling, 'ye have a half-holiday the morn when ye gang to the poll. There'll be plenty o' time in the evening to try a cast wi' 't. I'll lend it ye for the day.'

The man's face brightened. 'I wad tak' it verra kindly,' he said, 'if ye wad. My ain yin is no muckle worth, and, as ye say, I'll hae time for a cast the morn's nicht.'

'Dinna mention it. Did I ever let ye see my flee-book? Here it is,' and he produced a thick flannel book from a drawer. 'There's a maist miscellaneous collection, for a' waters an' a' weathers. I got a heap o' them frae auld Lord Manorwater, when I was a laddie, and used to cairry his basket.'

But the ploughman heeded him not, being deep in the examination of its mysteries. Very gingerly he handled the tiny spiders and hackles, surveying them with the eye of a connoisseur.

'If there's anything there ye think at a' like the water, I'll be verra pleased if ye'll try 't.'

The other was somewhat put out by this extreme friendliness. At another time he would have refused shamefacedly, but now the love of sport was too strong in him. 'Ye're far ower guid,' he said; 'thae twae paitrick wings are the verra things I want, an' I dinna think I've ony at hame. I'm awfu' gratefu' to ye, an' I'll bring them back the morn's nicht.'

'Guid-e'en,' said the farmer, as he opened the door, 'an' I wish ye may hae a guid catch.' And he turned in again, smiling sardonically.

The next morning was like the last, save that a little wind had risen, which blew freshly from the west. White cloudlets drifted across the blue, and the air was as clear as spring-water. Down in the hollow the roaring torrent had sunk to a full, lipping stream, and the colour had changed from a turbid yellow to a clear, delicate brown. In the town of Gledsmuir, it was a day of wild excitement, and the quiet Clachlands road bustled with horses and men. The labourers in the field scarce stopped to look at the passers, for in the afternoon they too would have their chance, when they might journey to the town in all importance, and record their opinions of the late Government.

The ploughman of Clachlands spent a troubled fore-noon. His nightly dreams had been of landing great fish, and now his waking thoughts were of the same. Politics for the time were forgotten. This was the day which he had looked forward to for so long, when he was to have been busied in deciding doubtful voters, and breathing activity into the ranks of his cause. And lo! the day had come and found his thoughts elsewhere. For all such things are, at the best, of fleeting interest, and do not stir men otherwise than sentimentally; but the old kindly love of field-sports, the joy in the smell of the earth and the living air, lie very close to a man's heart. So this apostate, as he cleaned his turnip rows, was filled with the excitement of the sport, and had no thoughts above the memory of past exploits and the anticipation of greater to come.

Mid-day came, and with it his release. He roughly calculated that he could go to the town, vote, and be back in two hours, and so have the evening clear for his fishing. There had never been such a day for the trout in his memory, so cool and breezy and soft, nor had he ever seen so glorious a water. 'If ye dinna get a fou basket the nicht, an' a feed the morn, William Laverhope, your richt hand has forgot its cunning,' said he to himself.

He took the rod carefully out, put it together, and made trial casts on the green. He tied the flies on a cast and put it ready for use in his own primitive fly-book, and then bestowed the whole in the breast-pocket of his coat. He had arrayed himself in his best, with a white rose in his button-hole, for it behoved a man to be well dressed on such an occasion as voting. But yet he did not start. Some fascination in the rod made him linger and try it again and again.

Then he resolutely laid it down and made to go. But something caught his eye – the swirl of the stream as it left the great pool at the hay-field, or the glimpse of still, gleaming water. The impulse was too strong to be resisted. There was time enough and to spare. The pool was on his way to the town, he would try one cast ere he started, just to see if the water was good. So, with rod on his shoulder, he set off.

Somewhere in the background a man, who had been watching his movements, turned away, laughing silently, and filling his pipe.

A great trout rose to the fly in the hay-field pool, and ran the line up-stream till he broke it. The ploughman swore deeply, and stamped on the ground with irritation. His blood was up, and he prepared for battle. Carefully, skilfully he fished, with every nerve on tension and ever-watchful eyes. Meanwhile, miles off in the town the bustle went on, but the eager fisherman by the river heeded it not.

Late in the evening, just at the darkening, a figure arrayed in Sunday clothes, but all wet and mud-stained, came up the road to the farm. Over his shoulder he carried a rod, and in one hand a long string of noble trout. But the expression on his face was not triumphant; a settled melancholy overspread his countenance, and he groaned as he walked.

Mephistopheles stood by the garden-gate, smoking and surveying his fields. A well-satisfied smile hovered about his mouth, and his air was the air of one well at ease with the world.

'Weel, I see ye've had guid sport,' said he to the melancholy Faust. 'By-the-bye, I didna notice ye in the toun. And losh! man, what in the warld have ye dune to your guid claes?'

The other made no answer. Slowly he took the rod to pieces and strapped it up; he took the fly-book from his pocket; he selected two fish from the heap; and laid the whole before the farmer.

'There ye are,' said he, 'and I'm verra much obleeged to ye for your kindness.' But his tone was of desperation and not of gratitude; and his face, as he went onward, was a study in eloquence repressed.

The Herd of Standlan

First published in the magazine *Black and White* on 13 June 1896, 'The Herd of Standlan' was reprinted in *Grey Weather* (1899).

It is another satirical story about politics and religion, but with a supernatural element and traces of scenes from two future novels, *The Half-Hearted* (1900) and *Witch Wood* (1927).

When the wind is nigh and the moon is high
    And the mist on the riverside,
Let such as fare have a very good care
    Of the Folk who come to ride.
For they may meet with the riders fleet
    Who fare from the place of dread;
And hard it is for a mortal man
    To sort at ease with the Dead.
        from *The Ballad of Grey Weather*

WHEN STANDLAN BURN leaves the mosses and hags which gave it birth, it tumbles over a succession of falls into a deep, precipitous glen, whence in time it issues into a land of level green meadows, and finally finds its rest in the Gled. Just at the opening of the ravine there is a pool shut in by high, dark cliffs, and black even on the most sunshiny day. The rocks are never dry but always black with damp and shadow. There is scarce any vegetation save stunted birks, juniper bushes, and draggled fern; and the hoot of owls and the croak of hooded crows is seldom absent from the spot. It is the famous Black Linn where in winter sheep stray and are never more heard of, and where more than once an unwary shepherd has gone to his account. It is an Inferno on the brink of a Paradise, for not a stone's throw off is the green, lawn-like turf, the hazel thicket, and the broad, clear pools, by the edge of which on that July day the Herd of Standlan and I sat drowsily smoking and talking of fishing and the hills. There he told me this story, which I here set down as I remember it, and as it bears repetition.

'D'ye mind Airthur Morrant?' said the shepherd, suddenly.

I did remember Arthur Mordaunt. Ten years past he and I had been inseparables, despite some half-dozen summers difference in age. We had fished and shot together, and together we had tramped every hill within thirty miles. He had come up from the South to try sheep-farming, and as he came of a great family and had no need to earn his bread, he found the profession pleasing. Then irresistible fate had swept me southward to college, and when after two years I came back to the place, his father was dead and he had come into his own. The next I heard of him was that in politics he was regarded as the most promising of the younger men, one of the staunchest and ablest upstays of the Constitution. His name was rapidly rising into pro-minence, for he seemed to exhibit that rare phenomenon of a man of birth and culture in direct sympathy with the wants of the people.

'You mean Lord Brodakers?' said I.

'Dinna call him by that name,' said the shepherd, darkly. 'I hae nae thocht o' him now. He's a disgrace to his country, servin' the Deil wi' baith hands. But nine year syne he was a bit innocent callant wi' nae Tory deevilry in his heid. Well, as I was sayin', Airthur Morrant has cause to mind that place till his dying day'; and he pointed his finger to the Black Linn.

I looked up the chasm. The treacherous water, so bright and joyful at our feet, was like ink in the great gorge. The swish and plunge of the cataract came like the regular beating of a clock, and though the weather was dry, streams of moisture seamed the perpendicular walls. It was a place eerie even on that bright summer's day.

'I don't think I ever heard the story,' I said casually.

'Maybe no,' said the shepherd. 'It's no yin I like to tell'; and he puffed sternly at his pipe, while I awaited the continuation.

'Ye see it was like this,' he said, after a while. 'It was just the beginning o' the back-end, and that year we had an awfu' spate o' rain. For near a week it poured hale water, and a' doon by Drumeller and the Mossfennan haughs was yae muckle loch. Then it stopped, and an awfu' heat came on. It dried the grund in nae time, but it hardly touched the burns; and it was rale queer to be pourin' wi' sweat and the grund aneath ye as dry as a potato-sack, and a' the time the water neither to haud nor bind. A' the waterside fields were clean stripped o' stooks, and a guid wheen hay-ricks gaed doon tae Berwick, no to speak o' sheep and nowt beast. But that's anither thing.

'Weel, ye'll mind that Airthur was terrible keen on fishing. He wad gang oot in a' weather, and he wasna feared for ony mortal or naitural thing. Dod, I've seen him in Gled wi' the water rinnin' ower his shouthers yae cauld March day playin' a saumon. He kenned weel aboot the fishing, for he had traivelled in Norroway and siccan out-landish places, where there's a heap o' big fish. So that day – and it was a Setterday tae and far ower near the Sabbath – he maun gang awa' up Standlan Burn wi' his rod and creel to try his luck.

'I was bidin' at that time, as ye mind, in the wee cot-house at the back o' the faulds. I was alane, for it was three year afore I mairried Jess, and I wasna begun yet to the coortin'. I had been at Gledsmuir that day for some o' the new stuff for killing sheep-mawks, and I wasna very fresh on my legs when I gaed oot after my tea that night to hae a look at the hill-sheep. I had had a bad year on the hill. First the lambin'-time was snaw, snaw ilka day, and I lost mair than I wad like to tell. Syne the grass a' summer was so short wi' the drought that the puir beasts could scarcely get a bite and were as thin as pipe-stapples. And then, to crown a', auld Will Broun, the man that helpit me, turned ill wi' his back, and had to bide at hame. So I had twae man's work on yae man's shouthers, and was nane so weel pleased.

'As I was saying, I gaed oot that nicht, and after lookin' a' the Dun Rig and the Yellow Mire and the back o' Cramalt Craig, I cam down the burn by the road frae the auld faulds. It was geyan dark, being about seven o'clock o' a September nicht, and I keepit weel back frae that wanchancy hole o' a burn. Weel, I was comin' kind o' quick, thinkin' o' supper and a story book that I was readin' at the time, when just abune that place there, at the foot o' the Linn, I saw a man fishing. I wondered what ony body in his senses could be daein' at that time o' nicht in sic a dangerous place, so I gave him a roar and bade him come back. He turned his face round and I saw in a jiffey that it was Mr. Airthur.

' "O, sir," I cried, "What for are ye fishing there? The water's awfu' dangerous, and the rocks are far ower slid."

' "Never mind, Scott,' he roars back cheery-like. "I'll take care o' mysel'."

'I lookit at him for twa-three meenutes, and then I saw by his rod he had yin on, and a big yin tae. He ran it up and doon the pool, and he had uncommin wark wi' 't, for it was strong and there was little licht. But bye and bye he got it almost tae his feet, and was just about to lift it oot when a maist awfu' thing happened. The tackets o' his boots maun hae slithered on the stane, for the next thing I saw was Mr. Airthur in the muckle hungry water.

'I dinna exactly ken what happened after that, till I found myself on the very stone he had slipped off. I maun hae come doon the face o' the rocks, a thing I can scarcely believe when I look at them, and a thing no man ever did afore. At ony rate I ken I fell the last fifteen feet or sae, and lichted on my left airm, for I felt it crack like a rotten branch, and an awfu' sairness ran up it.

'Now, the pool is a whirlpool as ye ken, and if anything fa's in, the water first smashes it against the muckle rock at the foot, then it brings it round below the fall again, and syne at the second time it carries it doon the burn. Weel, that was what happened to Mr. Airthur. I heard his heid gang dunt on the stane wi' a sound that made me sick. This must hae dung him clean senseless, and indeed it was a wonder it didna knock his brains oot. At ony rate there was nae mair word o' swimming, and he was swirled round below the fa' just like a corp.

'I kenned fine that nae time was to be lost, for if he once gaed doun the burn he wad be in Gled or ever I could say a word, and nane wad ever see him mair in life. So doon I got on my hunkers on the stane, and waited for the turnin'. Round he came, whirling in the foam, wi' a lang line o' blood across his brow where the stane had cut him. It was a terrible meenute. My heart fair stood still. I put out my airm, and as he passed I grippit him and wi' an awfu' pu' got him out o' the current into the side.

'But now I found that a waur thing still was on me. My left airm was broken, and my richt sae numbed and weak wi' my fall that, try as I micht, I couldna raise him ony further. I thocht I wad burst a blood-vessel i' my face and my muscles fair cracked wi' the strain, but I would make nothing o' 't. There he stuck wi' his heid and shouthers abune the water, pu'd close until the edge of a rock.

'What was I to dae? If I once let him slip he wad be into the stream and lost forever. But I couldna hang on here a' nicht, and as far as I could see there wad be naebody near till the mornin', when Ebie

Blackstock passed frae the Head o' the Hope. I roared wi' a' my power; but I got nae answer, naething but the rummle o' the water and the whistling o' some whaups on the hill.

'Then I turned very sick wi' terror and pain and weakness and I kenna what. My broken airm seemed a great lump o' burnin' coal. I maun hae given it some extra wrench when I hauled him out, for it was sae sair now that I thocht I could scarcely thole it. Forbye, pain and a', I could hae gone off to sleep wi' fair weariness. I had heard o' men sleepin' on their feet, but I never felt it till then. Man, if I hadna warstled wi' mysel, I wad hae dropped off as deid's a peery.

'Then there was the awfu' strain o' keepin' Mr. Airthur up. He was a great big man, twelve stone I'll warrant, and weighing a terrible lot mair wi' his fishing togs and things. If I had had the use o' my ither airm I micht hae taen off his jacket and creel and lichtened the burden, but I could do naething. I scarcely like to tell ye how I was tempted in that hour. Again and again I says to mysel, "Gidden Scott," say I, "what do ye care for this man? He's no a drap's bluid to you, and forbye ye'll never be able to save him. Ye micht as weel let him gang. Ye've dune a' ye could. Ye're a brave man, Gidden Scott, and ye've nae cause to be ashamed o' givin' up the fecht." But I says to mysel again: "Gidden Scott, ye're a coward. Wad ye let a man die, when there's a breath in your body? Think shame o' yoursel, man." So I aye kept haudin' on, although I was very near bye wi' 't. Whenever I lookit at Mr. Airthur's face, as white's death and a' blood, and his een sae stelled-like, I got a kind o' groo and felt awfu' pitiful for the bit laddie. Then I thocht on his faither, the auld Lord, wha was sae built up in him, and I couldna bear to think o' his son droonin' in that awfu' hole. So I set mysel to the wark o' keepin' him up a' nicht, though I had nae hope in the matter. It wasna what ye ca' bravery that made me dae't, for I had nae ither choice. It was just a kind o' dourness that runs in my folk, and a kind o' vexedness for sae young a callant in sic an ill place.

'The nicht was hot and there was scarcely a sound o' wind. I felt the sweat standin' on my face like frost on tatties, and abune me the sky was a' misty and nae mune visible. I thocht very likely that it micht come a thunder-shower and I kind o' lookit forrit tae't. For I was aye feared at lichtning, and if it came that nicht I was bound to get clean dazed and likely tummle in. I was a lonely man wi' nae kin to speak o', so it wouldna maitter muckle.

'But now I come to tell ye about the queer side o' that nicht's wark, whilk I never telled to nane but yoursel, though a' the folk about here ken the rest. I maun hae been geyan weak, for I got into a kind o' doze, no sleepin', ye understand, but awfu' like it. And then a' sort o' daft things began to dance afore my een. Witches and bogles and brownies and things oot o' the Bible, and leviathans and brazen bulls — a' cam fleerin' and flauntin' on the tap o' the water straucht afore me. I didna pay muckle heed to them, for I half kenned it was a' nonsense, and syne they gaed awa'. Then an auld wife wi' a mutch and a hale procession o' auld wives passed, and just about the last I saw yin I thocht I kenned.

'"Is that you, grannie?" says I.

'"Aye, it's me, Gidden," says she; and as shure as I'm a leevin' man, it was my auld grannie, whae had been deid thae sax year. She had on the same mutch as she aye wore, and the same auld black stickie in her hand, and, Dod, she had the same snuff-box I made for her out o' a sheep's horn when I first took to the herdin'. I thocht she was lookin' rale weel.

'"Losh, Grannie," says I, "Where in the warld hae ye come frae? It's no canny to see ye danderin' about there."

'"Ye've been badly brocht up," she says, "and ye ken nocht about it. Is't no a decent and comely thing that I should get a breath o' air yince in the while?"

'"Deed," said I, "I had forgotten. Ye were sae like yoursel I never had a mind ye were deid. And how d' ye like the Guid Place?"

'"Wheesht, Gidden," says she, very solemn like, "I'm no there."

'Now at this I was fair flabbergasted. Grannie had aye been a guid contentit auld wumman, and to think that they hadna let her intil Heeven made me think ill o' my ain chances.

'"Help us, ye dinna mean to tell me ye're in Hell?" I cries.

'"No exactly," says she, "But I'll trouble ye, Gidden, to speak mair respectful about holy things. That's a name ye uttered the noo whilk we dinna daur to mention."

'"I'm sorry, Grannie," says I, "but ye maun allow it's an astonishin' thing for me to hear. We aye counted ye shure, and ye died wi' the Buik in your hands."

'"Weel," she says, "it was like this. When I gaed up till the gate o' Heeven a man wi' a lang white robe comes and says, 'Wha may ye be?' Says I, 'I'm Elspeth Scott.' He gangs awa' and consults a wee and then he says, 'I think, Elspeth my wumman, ye'll hae to gang doon the brae a bit. Ye're no quite guid eneuch for this place, but ye'll get a very comfortable doonsittin' whaur I tell ye.' So off I gaed and cam' to a place whaur the air was like the inside of the glass-houses at the Lodge. They took me in wi'oot a word and I've been rale comfortable. Ye see they keep the bad part o' the Ill Place for the reg'lar bad folk, but they've a very nice half-way house where the likes o' me stop."

' "And what kind o' company hae ye?"

' "No very select," says she. "There's maist o' the ministers o' the countryside and a pickle fairmers, tho' the maist o' them are further ben. But there's my son Jock, your ain faither, Gidden, and a heap o' folk from the village, and oh, I'm nane sae bad."

' "Is there naething mair ye wad like then, Grannie?"

' "Oh aye," says she, "we've each yae thing which we canna get. It's a' the punishment we hae. Mine's butter. I canna get fresh butter for my bread, for ye see it winna keep, it just melts. So I've to tak jeely to ilka slice, whilk is rale sair on the teeth. Ye'll no hae ony wi' ye?"

' "No," I says, "I've naething but some tobaccy. D' ye want it? Ye were aye fond o' 't."

' "Na, na," says she. "I get plenty o' tobaccy doon bye. The pipe's never out o' the folks' mouth there. But I'm no speakin' about yoursel, Gidden. Ye're in a geyan ticht place."

' "I'm a' that," I said. "Can ye no help me?"

' "I micht try." And she raxes out her hand to grip mine. I put out mine to tak it, never thinkin' that that wasna the richt side, and that if Grannie grippit it she wad pu' the broken airm and haul me into the water. Something touched my fingers like a hot poker; I gave a great yell; and ere ever I kenned I was awake, a' but off the rock, wi' my left airm aching like hell-fire. Mr. Airthur I had let slunge ower the heid and my ain legs were in the water.

'I gae an awfu' whammle and edged my way back though it was near bye my strength. And now anither thing happened. For the cauld water roused Mr. Airthur frae his dwam. His een opened and he gave a wild look around him. "Where am I?" he cries, "Oh, God!" and he gaed off intil anither faint.

'I can tell ye, sir, I never felt anything in this warld and I hope never to feel anything in anither sae bad as the next meenutes on that rock. I was fair sick wi' pain and weariness and a kind o' fever. The lip-lap o' the water, curling round Mr. Airthur, and the great *crush* o' the Black Linn itsel dang me fair silly. Then there was my airm, which was bad eneuch, and abune a' I was gotten into sic a state that I was fleyed at ilka shadow just like a bairn. I felt fine I was gaun daft, and if the thing had lasted another score o' meenutes I wad be in a madhouse this day. But soon I felt the sleepiness comin' back, and I was off again dozin' and dreamin'.

'This time it was nae auld wumman but a muckle black-avised man that was standin' in the water glowrin' at me. I kenned him fine by the bandy-legs o' him and the broken nose (whilk I did mysel), for Dan Kyle the poacher deid thae twae year. He was a man, as I remembered him weel, wi' a great black beard and een that were stuck sae far in his heid that they looked like twae wull-cats keekin' oot o' a hole. He stands and just stares at me, and never speaks a word.

' "What d'ye want?" I yells, for by this time I had lost a' grip o' mysel. "Speak, man, and dinna stand there like a dummy."

' "I want naething," he says in a mournfu' sing-song voice; "I'm just thinkin'."

' "Whaur d' ye come frae?" I asked, "and are ye keepin' weel?"

' "Weel," he says bitterly. "In this warld I was ill to my wife, and twa-three times I near killed a man, and I stole like a pyet, and I was never sober. How d' ye think I should be weel in the next?"

'I was sorry for the man. "D' ye ken I'm vexed for ye, Dan," says I; "I never likit ye when ye were here, but I'm wae to think ye're sae ill off yonder."

' "I'm no alane," he says. "There's Mistress Courhope of the Big House, she's waur. Ye mind she was awfu' fond o' gumflowers. Weel, she canna keep them Yonder, for they a' melt wi' the heat. She's in an ill way about it, puir body." Then he broke off. "Whae's that ye've got there? Is't Airthur Morrant?"

' "Ay, it's Airthur Morrant," I said.

' "His family's weel kent doon bye," says he. "We've maist o' his forbears, and we're expectin' the auld Lord every day. May be we'll sune get the lad himsel."

' "That's a damned lee," says I, for I was angry at the man's presumption.

'Dan lookit at me sorrowfu'-like. "We'll be gettin' you tae, if ye swear that gate," says he, "and then ye'll ken what it's like."

'Of a sudden I fell into a great fear. "Dinna say that, Dan," I cried;

"I'm better than ye think. I'm a deacon, and 'll maybe sune be an elder, and I never swear except at my dowg."

' "Tak care, Gidden," said the face afore me. "Where I am, a' things are taken into account."

' "Then they'll hae a gey big account for you," says I. "What-like do they treat you, may be?"

'The man groaned.

' "I'll tell ye what they dae to ye doon there," he said. "They put ye intil a place a' paved wi' stanes and wi' four square walls around. And there's naething in 't, nae grass, nae shadow. And abune you there's a sky like brass. And sune ye get terrible hot and thirsty, and your tongue sticks to your mouth, and your eyes get blind wi' lookin' on the white stane. Then ye gang clean fey, and dad your heid on the ground and the walls to try and kill yoursel. But though ye dae't till a' eternity ye couldna feel pain. A' that ye feel is just the awfu' devourin' thirst, and the heat and the weariness. And if ye lie doon the ground burns ye and ye're fain to get up. And ye canna lean on the walls for the heat, and bye and bye when ye're fair perished wi' the thing, they tak ye out to try some ither ploy."

' "Nae mair," I cried, "nae mair, Dan!"

'But he went on malicious-like, –

' "Na, na, Gidden, I'm no dune yet. Syne they tak you to a fine room but awfu' warm. And there's a big fire in the grate and thick woollen rugs on the floor. And in the corner there's a braw feather bed. And they lay ye down on 't, and then they pile on the tap o' ye mattresses and blankets and sacks and great rolls o' woollen stuff miles wide. And then ye see what they're after, tryin' to suffocate ye as they dae to folk that a mad dowg has bitten. And ye try to kick them off, but they're ower heavy, and ye canna move your feet nor your airms nor gee your heid. Then ye gang clean gyte and skirl to yoursel, but your voice is choked and naebody is near. And the warst o' 't is that ye canna die and get it ower. It's like death a hundred times and yet ye're aye leevin'. Bye and bye when they think ye've got eneuch they tak you out and put ye somewhere else."

' "Oh," I cries, "stop, man, or you'll ding me silly."

'But he says never a word, just glowrin' at me.

' "Aye, Gidden, and waur than that. For they put ye in a great loch wi' big waves just like the sea at the Pier o' Leith. And there's nae chance o' soomin', for as sune as ye put out your airms a billow gulfs ye

[65]

down. Then ye swallow water and your heid dozes round and ye're chokin'. But ye canna die, ye must just thole. And down ye gang, down, down, in the cruel deep, till your heid's like to burst and your een are fu' o' bluid. And there's a' kind o' fearfu' monsters about, muckle slimy things wi' blind een and white scales, that claw at ye wi' claws just like the paws o' a drooned dog. And ye canna get away though ye fecht and fleech, and bye and bye ye're fair mad wi' horror and choking and the feel o' thae awfu' things. Then—''

'But now I think something snapped in my heid, and I went daft in doonricht earnest. The man before me danced about like a lantern's shine on a windy nicht and then disappeared. And I woke yelling like a pig at a killing, fair wud wi' terror, and my skellochs made the rocks ring. I found mysel in the pool a' but yae airm – the broken yin – which had hankit in a crack o' rock. Nae wonder I had been dreaming o' deep waters among the torments o' the Ill Place, when I was in them mysel. The pain in my airm was sae fearsome and my heid was gaun round sae wi' horror that I just skirled on and on, shrieking and groaning wi'oot a thocht what I was daein'. I was as near death as ever I will be, and as for Mr. Airthur he was on the very nick o' 't, for by this time he was a' in the water, though I still kept a grip o' him.

'When I think ower it often I wonder how it was possible that I could be here the day. But the Lord's very gracious, and he works in a queer way. For it so happened that Ebie Blackstock, whae had left Gledsmuir an hour afore me and whom I thocht by this time to be snorin' in his bed at the Head o' the Hope, had gone intil the herd's house at the Waterfit, and had got sae muckle drink there that he was sweered to start for hame till aboot half-past twal i' the night. Weel, he was comin' up the burnside, gey happy and contentit, for he had nae wife at hame to speir about his ongaeings, when, as he's telled me himsel, he heard sic an uproar doon by the Black Linn that made him turn pale and think that the Deil, whom he had long served, had gotten him at last. But he was a brave man, was Ebie, and he thinks to himsel that some fellow-creature micht be perishin'. So he gangs forrit wi' a' his pith, trying to think on the Lord's Prayer and last Sabbath's sermon. And, lookin' ower the edge, he saw nae-thing for a while, naething but the black water wi' the awfu' yells coming out o' 't. Then he made out something like a heid near the side. So he rins doon by the road, no ower the rocks as I had come, but round by the burnside road, and soon he gets to the pool, where the crying was getting aye fainter and fainter. And then he saw me. And he grips me by the collar, for he was a sensible man, was Ebie, and hauls me oot. If he hadna been geyan strong he couldna hae dune it, for I was a deid wecht, forbye having a heavy man hanging on to me. When he got me up, what was his astonishment to find anither man at the end o' my airm, a man like a corp a' bloody about the heid. So he got us baith out, and we twae baith senseless; and he laid us in a safe bit back frae the water, and syne gaed off for help. So bye and bye we were baith got home, me to my house and Mr. Airthur up to the Lodge.'

'And was that the end of it?' I asked.

'Na,' said the shepherd. 'I lay for twae month there ravin' wi' brain fever, and when I cam to my senses I was as weak as a bairn. It was many months ere I was mysel again, and my left airm to this day is stiff and no muckle to lippin to. But Mr. Airthur was far waur, for the dad he had gotten on the rock was thocht to have broken his skull, and he lay long atween life and death. And the warst thing was that his faither was sae vexed about him that he never got ower the shock, but dee'd afore Airthur was out o' bed. And so when he cam out again he was My Lord, and a monstrously rich man.'

The shepherd puffed meditatively at his pipe for a few minutes.

'But that's no a' yet. For Mr. Airthur wad tak nae refusal but that I maun gang awa' doon wi' him to his braw house in England and be a land o' factor or steward or something like that. And I had a rale fine cottage a' to mysel, wi' a very bonny gairden and guid wages, so I stayed there maybe sax month and then I gaed up till him. "I canna bide nae longer," says I. "I canna stand this place. It's far ower laigh, and I'm fair sick to get hills to rest my een on. I'm awfu' gratefu' to ye for your kindness, but I maun gie up my job." He was very sorry to lose me, and was for giein' me a present o' money or stockin' a fairm for me, because he said that it was to me he owed his life. But I wad hae nane o' his gifts. "It wad be a terrible thing," I says, "to tak siller for daein' what ony body wad hae dune out o' pity." So I cam awa' back to Standlan, and I maun say I'm rale contentit here. Mr. Airthur used whiles to write to me and ca' in and see me when he cam North for the shooting; but since he's gane sae far wrang wi' the Tories, I've had naething mair to dae wi' him.'

I made no answer, being busy pondering in my mind on the depth of the shepherd's political principles, before which the ties of friendship were as nothing.

'Ay,' said he, standing up, 'I did what I thocht my duty at the time and I was rale glad I saved the callant's life. But now, when I think on a' the ill he's daein' to the country and the Guid Cause, I whiles think I wad hae been daein' better if I had just drappit him in.

'But whae kens? It's a queer warld.' And the shepherd knocked the ashes out of his pipe.

Streams of Water in the South

Buchan rarely included the same material in different books but 'Streams of Water in the South' is an exception. Written in 1896, it appeared in slightly different versions in both *Grey Weather* (1899) and *The Moon Endureth* (1912). It exhibits certain parallels with Walter Scott's 'Wandering Willie's Tale'.

As streams of water in the South,
Our bondage, Lord, recall.

Psalm CXXVI
Scots Metrical Version

I

IT WAS AT the ford of the Clachlands Water in a tempestuous August that I, an idle boy, first learned the hardships of the Lammas droving. The shepherd of the Redswirehead, my very good friend, and his three shaggy dogs, were working for their lives in an angry water. The path behind was thronged with scores of sheep bound for the Gledsmuir market, and beyond it was possible to discern through the mist the few dripping dozen which had made the passage. Between raged yards of brown foam coming down from murky hills, and the air echoed with the yelp of dogs and the perplexed cursing of men.

Before I knew I was helping in the task, with water lapping round my waist and my arms filled with a terrified sheep. It was no light task, for though the water was no more than three feet deep it was swift and strong, and a kicking hogg is a sore burden. But this was the only road; the stream might rise higher at any moment; and somehow or other those bleating flocks had to be transferred to their fellows beyond. There were six men at the labour, six men and myself, and all were cross and wearied and heavy with water.

I made my passages side by side with my friend the shepherd, and thereby felt much elated. This was a man who had dwelt all his days in the wilds, and was familiar with torrents as with his own doorstep. Now and then a swimming dog would bark feebly as he was washed against us, and flatter his fool's heart that he was aiding the work. And so we wrought on, till by midday I was dead-beat, and could scarce stagger through the surf, while all the men had the same gasping faces. I saw the shepherd look with longing eye up the long green valley, and mutter disconsolately in his beard.

'Is the water rising?' I asked.

'It's no rising,' said he, 'but I likena the look o' yon big black clud upon Cairncraw. I doubt there's been a shoor up the muirs, and a shoor there means twae mair feet o' water in the Clachlands. God help Sandy Jamieson's lambs, if there is.'

'How many are left?' I asked.

'Three, fower — no abune a score and a half,' said he, running his eye over the lessened flocks. 'I maun try to tak twae at a time.'

So for ten minutes he struggled with a double burden, and panted painfully at each return. Then with a sudden swift look up-stream he broke off and stood up. 'Get ower the water, every yin o' ye, and leave the sheep,' he said, and to my wonder every man of the five obeyed his word.

And then I saw the reason of his command, for with a sudden swift leap forward the Clachlands rose, and flooded up to where I had stood an instant before high and dry.

'It's come,' said the shepherd in a tone of fate, 'and there's fifteen no ower yet, and Lord kens how they'll dae't. They'll hae to gang roond by Gledsmuir Brig, and that's twenty mile o' a differ. 'Deed, it's no like that Sandy Jamieson will get a guid price the morn for sic sair forfochen beasts.'

Then with firmly gripped staff he marched stoutly into the tide till it ran hissing below his armpits. 'I could dae't alane,' he cried, 'but no wi' a burden. For, losh, if ye slippit, ye'd be in the Tod's Pool afore ye could draw breath.'

And so we waited with the great white droves and five angry men beyond, and the path blocked by a surging flood. For half an hour we waited, holding anxious consultation across the stream, when to us thus busied there entered a newcomer, a helper from the ends of the earth.

He was a man of something over middle size, but with a stoop forward that shortened him to something beneath it. His dress was ragged homespun, the cast-off clothes of some sportsman, and in his arms he bore a bundle of sticks and heather-roots which marked his calling. I knew him for a tramp who long had wandered in the place, but I could not account for the whole-voiced shout of greeting which met him as he stalked down the path. He lifted his eyes and looked solemnly and long at the scene. Then something of delight came into his eye, his face relaxed, and flinging down his burden he stripped his coat and came toward us.

'Come on, Yeddie, ye're sair needed,' said the shepherd, and I watched with amazement this grizzled, crooked man seize a sheep by the fleece and drag it to the water. Then he was in the midst, stepping warily, now up, now down the channel, but always nearing the farther bank. At last with a final struggle he landed his charge, and turned to journey back. Fifteen times did he cross that water, and at the end his mean figure had wholly changed. For now he was straighter and stronger, his eye flashed, and his voice, as he cried out to the drovers, had in it a tone of command. I marvelled at the transformation; and when at length he had donned once more his ragged coat and shouldered his bundle, I asked the shepherd his name.

'They ca' him Adam Logan,' said my friend, his face still bright with excitement, 'but maist folk ca' him "Streams o' Water".'

'Ay,' said I, 'and why "Streams of Water"?'

'Juist for the reason ye see,' said he.

Now I knew the shepherd's way, and I held my peace, for it was clear that his mind was revolving other matters, concerned most probably with the high subject of the morrow's prices. But in a little, as we crossed the moor toward his dwelling, his thoughts relaxed and he remembered my question. So he answered me thus, –

'Oh, ay; as ye were sayin', he's a queer man, Yeddie – aye been; guid kens whaur he cam frae first, for he's been trampin' the countryside since ever I mind, and that's no yesterday. He maun be sixty year, and yet he's as fresh as ever. If onything, he's a thocht dafter in his ongaein's and mair silent-like. But ye'll hae heard tell o' him afore?'

I owned ignorance.

'Tut,' said he, 'ye ken nocht. But Yeddie had aye a queer crakin' for waters. He never gangs on the road. Wi' him it's juist up yae glen and doon anither, and aye keepin' by the burnside. He kens every water i' the warld, every bit sheuch and burnie frae Gallowa' to Berwick. And he kens the way o' spates the best I ever seen, and I've heard tell o' him fordin' waters when nae ither thing could leeve i' them. He can weyse and wark his road sae cunnin'ly on the stanes that the roughest flood, if it's no juist fair ower his heid, canna upset him. Mony a sheep has he saved to me, and it's mony a guid drove wad never hae won to Gledsmuir market but for Yeddie.'

I listened with a boy's interest in any romantic narration. Somehow, the strange figure wrestling in the brown stream took fast hold on my mind, and I asked the shepherd for further tales.

'There's little mair to tell,' he said, 'for a gangrel life is nane o' the liveliest. But d'ye ken the langnebbit hill that cocks its tap abune the Clachlands heid? Weel, he's got a wee bit o' grund on the tap frae the Yerl, and there he's howkit a grave for himsel'. He's sworn me and twae-three ithers to bury him there, wherever he may dee. It's a queer fancy in the auld dotterel.'

So the shepherd talked, and as at evening we stood by his door we saw a figure moving into the gathering shadows. I knew it at once, and did not need my friend's 'There gangs "Streams o' Water"' to recognise it. Something wild and pathetic in the old man's face haunted me like a dream, and as the dusk swallowed him up, he seemed like some old Druid recalled of the gods to his ancient habitation of the moors.

II

Two years passed, and April came with her suns and rains, and again the waters brimmed full in the valleys. Under the clear, shining sky the lambing went on, and the faint bleat of sheep brooded on the hills. In a land of young heather and green upland meads, of faint odours of moor-burn, and hill-tops falling in clean ridges to the sky-line, the veriest St. Anthony would not abide indoors; so I flung all else to the winds and went a-fishing.

At the first pool on the Callowa, where the great flood sweeps nobly round a ragged shoulder of hill, and spreads into broad deeps beneath a tangle of birches, I began my labours. The turf was still wet with dew and the young leaves gleamed in the glow of morning. Far up the stream rose the grim hills which hem the mosses and tarns of the tableland, whence flow the greater waters of the countryside. An ineffable freshness, as of the morning alike of the day and the seasons, filled the clear hill air, and the remote peaks gave the needed touch of intangible romance.

But as I fished, I came on a man sitting in a green dell, busy at the making of brooms. I knew his face and dress, for who could forget such eclectic raggedness? – and I remembered that day two years before when he first hobbled into my ken. Now, as I saw him there, I was captivated by the nameless mystery of his appearance. There was something startling to one, accustomed to the lack-lustre gaze of town-bred folk, in the sight of an eye as keen and wild as a hawk's from sheer solitude and lonely travelling. He was so bent and scarred with weather that he seemed as much a part of that woodland place as the birks themselves, and the noise of his labours did not startle the birds that hopped on the branches.

Little by little I won his acquaintance – by a chance reminiscence, a single tale, the mention of a friend. Then he made me free of his knowledge, and my fishing fared well that day. He dragged me up little streams to sequestered pools, where I had astonishing success; and then back to some great swirl in the Callowa where he had seen monstrous takes. And all the while he delighted me with his talk, of men and things, of weather and place, pitched high in his thin, old voice, and garnished with many tones of lingering sentiment. He spoke in a broad, slow Scots, with so quaint a lilt in his speech that one seemed to be in an elder time among people of a quieter life and a quainter kindliness.

Then by chance I asked him of a burn of which I had heard, and how it might be reached. I shall never forget the tone of his answer as his face grew eager and he poured forth his knowledge.

'Ye'll gang up the Knowe Burn, which comes doun into the Cauldshaw. It's a wee tricklin' thing, trowin' in and out o' pools i' the rock, and comin' doun out o' the side o' Caerfraun. Yince a merry-maiden bided there, I've heard folks say, and used to win the sheep frae the Cauldshaw herd, and bile them i' the muckle pool below the fa'. They say that there's a road to the Ill Place there, and when the Deil likit he sent up the lowe and garred the water faem and fizzle like an auld kettle. But if ye're gaun to the Colm Burn ye maun haud atower the rig o' the hill frae the Knowe heid, and ye'll come to it wimplin' among green brae faces. It's a bonny bit, lonesome but awfu' bonny, and there's mony braw trout in its siller flow.'

Then I remembered all I had heard of the old man's craze, and I humoured him.

'It's a fine countryside for burns,' I said.

'Ye may say that,' said he gladly, 'a weel-watered land. But a' this braw south country is the same. I've traivelled frae the Yeavering Hill in the Cheviots to the Caldons in Galloway, and it's a' the same. When I was young, I've seen me gang north to the Hielands and doun to the English lawlands, but now that I'm gettin' auld I maun bide i' the yae place. There's no a burn in the South I dinna ken, and I never cam to the water I couldna ford.'

'No?' said I. 'I've seen you at the ford o' Clachlands in the Lammas floods.'

'Often I've been there,' he went on, speaking like one calling up vague memories. 'Yince, when Tam Rorison was drooned, honest man. Yince again, when the brigs were ta'en awa', and the Back House o' Clachlands had nae bread for a week. But oh, Clachlands is a bit easy water. But I've seen the muckle Aller come roarin' sae high that it washed awa' a sheepfauld that stood weel up on the hill. And I've seen this verra burn, this bonny clear Callowa, lyin' like a loch for miles i' the haugh. But I never heeds a spate, for if a man just kens the way o't it's a canny, hairmless thing. I couldna wish to dee better than just be happit i' the waters o' my ain countryside, when my legs fail and I'm ower auld for the trampin'.'

Something in that queer figure in the setting of the hills struck a note of curious pathos. And towards evening as we returned down the glen the note grew keener. A spring sunset of gold and crimson flamed in our backs and turned the pools to fire. Far off down the vale the plains and the sea gleamed half in shadow. Somehow in the fragrance and colour and the delectable crooning of the stream, the fantastic and the dim seemed tangible and present, and high sentiment revelled for once in my prosaic heart.

And still more in the breast of my companion. He stopped and sniffed the evening air, as he looked far over hill and dale and then back to the great hills above us. 'Yon's Crappel, and Caerdon, and the Laigh Law,' he said, lingering with relish over each name, 'and the Gled comes doun atween them. I haena been there for a twalmonth, and I maun hae another glisk o't, for it's a braw place.' Some bitter thought seemed to seize him, and his mouth twitched. 'I'm an auld man,' he cried, 'and I canna see ye a' again. There's burns and mair burns in the high hills that

I'll never win to.' Then he remembered my presence, and stopped. 'Ye maunna mind me,' he said huskily, 'but the sicht o' thae lang blue hills makes me daft, now that I've faun i' the vale o' years. Yince I was young and could get where I wantit, but now I am auld and maun bide i' the same bit. And I'm aye thinkin' o' the waters I've been to, and the green heichs and howes and the linns that I canna win to again. I maun e'en be content wi' the Callowa, which is as guid as the best.'

I left him wandering down by the streamside and telling his crazy meditations to himself.

III

A space of years elapsed ere I met him, for fate had carried me far from the upland valleys. But once again I was afoot on the white moor roads; and, as I swung along one autumn afternoon up the path which leads from the Glen of Callowa to the Gled, I saw a figure before me which I knew for my friend. When I overtook him, his appearance puzzled and troubled me. Age seemed to have come on him at a bound, and in the tottering figure and the stoop of weakness I had difficulty in recognising the hardy frame of the man as I had known him. Something, too, had come over his face. His brow was clouded, and the tan of weather stood out hard and cruel on a blanched cheek. His eye seemed both wilder and sicklier, and for the first time I saw him with none of the appurtenances of his trade.

He greeted me feebly and dully, and showed little wish to speak. He walked with slow, uncertain step, and his breath laboured with a new panting. Every now and then he would look at me sidewise, and in his feverish glance I could detect none of the free kindliness of old. The man was ill in body and mind.

I asked him how he had done since I saw him last.

'It's an ill world now,' he said in a slow, querulous voice. 'There's nae need for honest men, and nae leevin'. Folk dinna heed me ava now. They dinna buy my besoms, they winna let me bide a nicht in their byres, and they're no like the kind canty folk in the auld times. And a' the countryside is changin'. Doun by Goldieslaw they're makkin' a dam for takin' water to the toun, and they're thinkin' o' daein' the like wi' the Callowa. Guid help us, can they no let the works o' God alane? Is there nae room for them in the dirty lawlands that they maun file the hills wi' their biggins?'

I conceived dimly that the cause of his wrath was a scheme for waterworks at the border of the uplands, but I had less concern for this than his strangely feeble health.

'You are looking ill,' I said. 'What has come over you?'

'Oh, I canna last for aye,' he said mournfully. 'My auld body's about dune. I've warkit it ower sair when I had it, and it's gaun to fail on my hands. Sleepin' out o' wat nichts and gangin' lang wantin' meat are no the best ways for a long life'; and he smiled the ghost of a smile.

And then he fell to wild telling of the ruin of the place and the hardness of the people, and I saw that want and bare living had gone far to loosen his wits. I knew the countryside, and I recognised that change was only in his mind. A great pity seized me for this lonely figure toiling on in the bitterness of regret. I tried to comfort him, but my words were useless, for he took no heed of me; with bent head and faltering step he mumbled his sorrows to himself.

Then of a sudden we came to the crest of the ridge where the road dips from the hill-top to the sheltered valley. Sheer from the heather ran the white streak till it lost itself among the reddening rowans and the yellow birks of the wood. The land was rich in autumn colour, and the shining waters dipped and fell through a pageant of russet and gold. And all around hills huddled in silent spaces, long brown moors crowned with cairns, or steep fortresses of rock and shingle rising to foreheads of steel-like grey. The autumn blue faded in the far sky-line to white, and lent distance to the farther peaks. The hush of the wilderness, which is far different from the hush of death, brooded over the scene, and like faint music came the sound of a distant scythe-swing, and the tinkling whisper which is the flow of a hundred streams.

I am an old connoisseur in the beauties of the uplands, but I held my breath at the sight. And when I glanced at my companion, he too had raised his head, and stood with wide nostrils and gleaming eye revelling in this glimpse of Arcady. Then he found his voice, and the weakness and craziness seemed for one moment to leave him.

'It's my ain land,' he cried, 'and I'll never leave it. D'ye see yon lang broun hill wi' the cairn?' and he gripped my arm fiercely and directed my gaze. 'Yon's my bit. I howkit it richt on the verra tap, and ilka year I gang there to mak it neat and orderly. I've trystit wi' fower men in different pairishes, that whenever they hear o' my death, they'll cairry me up yonder and bury me there. And then I'll never leave it, but lie still and quiet to the warld's end. I'll aye hae the sound o' water in my ear, for there's five burns tak' their rise on that hillside, and on a' airts the glens gang doun to the Gled and the Aller.'

Then his spirit failed him, his voice sank, and he was almost the feeble gangrel once more. But not yet, for again his eye swept the ring of hills, and he muttered to himself names which I knew for streams, lingeringly, lovingly as of old affections. 'Aller and Gled and Callowa,' he crooned, 'braw names, and Clachlands and Cauld-shaw and the Lanely Water. And I maunna forget the Stark and the Lin and the bonny streams o' the Creran. And what mair? I canna mind a' the burns, the Howe and the Hollies and the Fawn and the links o' the Manor. What says the Psalmist about them?

> "As streams of water in the South,
> Our bondage, Lord, recall."

Ay, but yon's the name for them. "Streams o' water in the South."'

As we went down the slopes to the darkening vale I heard him crooning to himself in a high, quavering voice the single distich; then in a little his weariness took him again, and he plodded on with no thought save for his sorrows.

IV

The conclusion of this tale belongs not to me, but to the shepherd of the Redswirehead, and I heard it from him in his dwelling, as I stayed the night, belated on the darkening moors. He told me it after supper in a flood of misty Doric, and his voice grew rough at times, and he poked viciously at the dying peat.

'In the last back-end I was at Gledfoot wi' sheep, and a weary job I had and sma' credit. Ye ken the place, a lang dreich shore wi' the wind swirlin' and bitin' to the bane, and the broun Gled water choked wi' Solloway sand. There was nae room in ony inn in the town, so I bude to try a bit public on the Harbour Walk, where sailor-folk and fish-ermen feucht and drank, and nae dacent men frae the hills thocht o' gangin'. I was in a gey ill way, for I had sell't my beasts dooms cheap, and I thocht o' the lang miles hame in the wintry weather. So after a bite o' meat I gangs oot to get the air and clear my heid, which was a' rammled wi' the auction-ring.

'And whae did I find, sittin' on a bench at the door, but the auld man

Yeddie? He was waur changed than ever. His lang hair was hingin' ower his broo, and his face was thin and white as a ghaist's. His claes fell loose about him, and he sat wi' his hand on his auld stick and his chin on his hand, hearin' nocht and glowerin' afore him. He never saw nor kenned me till I shook him by the shouthers, and cried him by his name.

' "Whae are ye?" says he, in a thin voice that gaed to my hert.

' "Ye ken me fine, ye auld fule," says I. "I'm Jock Rorison o' the Redswirehead, whaur ye've stoppit often."

' "Redswirehead," he says, like a man in a dream. "Redswirehead! That's at the tap o' the Clachlands Burn as ye gang ower to the Dreichil."

' "And what are ye daein' here? It's no your countryside ava, and ye're no fit noo for lang trampin'."

' "No," says he, in the same weak voice and wi' nae fushion in him, "but they winna hae me up yonder noo. I'm ower auld and useless. Yince a'body was gled to see me, and wad keep me as lang's I wantit, and had aye a guid word at meeting and pairting. Noo it's a' changed, and my wark's dune."

'I saw fine that the man was daft, but what answer could I gie to his havers? Folk in the Callowa glens are as kind as afore, but ill weather and auld age had put queer notions intil his heid. Forbye, he was seeck, seeck unto death, and I saw mair in his ee than I likit to think.

' "Come in-by and get some meat, man," I said. "Ye're famishin' wi' cauld and hunger."

' "I canna eat," he says, and his voice never changed. "It's lang since I had a bite, for I'm no hungry. But I'm awfu' thirsty. I cam here yestreen, and I can get nae water to drink like the water in the hills. I maun be settin' out back the morn, if the Lord spares me."

'I mindit fine that the body wad tak nae drink like an honest man, but maun aye draibble wi' burn water, and noo he had got the thing on the brain. I never spak a word, for the maitter was bye ony mortal's aid.

'For lang he sat quiet. Then he lifts his heid and looks awa ower the grey sea. A licht for a moment cam intil his een.

' "Whatna big water's yon?" he said, wi' his puir mind aye rinnin' on waters.

' "That's the Solloway," says I.

' "The Solloway," says he; "it's a big water, and it wad be an ill job to ford it."

'"Nae man ever fordit it," I said.

'"But I never yet cam to the water I couldna ford," says he. "But what's that queer smell i' the air? Something snell and cauld and unfreendly."

'"That's the salt, for we're at the sea here, the mighty ocean."

'He keepit repeatin' the word ower in his mouth. "The salt, the salt! I've heard tell o' it afore, but I dinna like it. It's terrible cauld."

'By this time an on-ding o' rain was coming up frae the water, and I bade the man come indoors to the fire. He followed me, as biddable as a sheep, draggin' his legs like yin far gone in seeckness. I set him by the fire, and put whisky at his elbow, but he wadna touch it.

'"I've nae need o' it," said he. "I'm fine and warm"; and he sits staring at the fire, aye comin' ower again and again, "The Solloway, the Solloway. It's a guid name and a muckle water." But sune I gaed to my bed, being heavy wi' sleep, for I had traivelled for twae days.

'The next morn I was up at six and oot to see the weather. It was a' changed. The muckle tides lay lang and still as our ain Loch o' the Lee, and far ayont I saw the big blue hills o' England shine bricht and clear. I thankit Providence for the day, for it was better to tak the lang miles back in the sun than in a blast o' rain.

'But as I lookit I saw folk comin' up frae the beach cairryin' something atween them. My hert gied a loup, and "Some puir, drooned sailor body," says I to mysel', "whae has perished in yesterday's storm." But as they cam nearer I got a glisk which made me run like daft, and lang ere I was up on them I saw it was Yeddie.

'He lay drippin' and white, wi' his puir auld hair lyin' back frae his broo and the duds clingin' to his legs. But oot o' the face there had gane a' the seeckness and weariness. His een were stelled as if he had been lookin' forrit to something, and his lips were set like a man on a lang errand. And mair, his stick was grippit sae firm in his hand that nae man could lowse it, so they e'en let it be.

'Then they tell't me the tale o't, how at the earliest licht they had seen him wanderin' alang the sands, juist as they were putting out their boats to sea. They wondered and watched him, till of a sudden he turned to the water and wadit in, keeping straucht on till he was oot o' sicht. They rowed a' their pith to the place, but they were ower late. Yince they saw his heid appear abune water, still wi' his face to the other side; and then they got his body, for the tide was rinnin' low in the mornin'.

'We brocht him up to the house and laid him there till the folk i' the town had heard o' the business. Syne the procurator-fiscal came and certifeed the death, and the rest was left to me. I got a wooden coffin made and put him in it, juist as he was, wi' his staff in his hand and his auld duds about him. I mindit o' my sworn word, for I was yin o' the four that had promised, and I ettled to dae his bidding. It was saxteen miles to the hills, and yin and twenty to the lanely tap whaur he had howkit his grave. But I never heedit it. I'm a strong man, weel used to the walkin', and my hert was sair for the auld body. Now that he had gotten deliverance from his affliction, it was for me to leave him in the place he wantit. Forbye, he wasna muckle heavier than a bairn.

'It was a long road, a sair road, but I did it, and by seven o'clock I was at the edge o' the muirlands. There was a braw mune, and a' the glens and taps stood out as clear as midday. Bit by bit, for I was gey tired, I warstled ower the rigs and up the cleuchs to the Gled-head; syne up the stany Gled-cleuch to the lang grey hill which they ca' the Hurlybackit. By ten I had come to the cairn, and black i' the mune I saw the grave. So there I buried him, and though I'm no a releegious man, I couldna help sayin' ower him the guid words o' the Psalmist –

> "As streams of water in the South,
> Our bondage, Lord, recall." '

So if you go from the Gled to the Aller, and keep far over the north side of the Muckle Muneraw, you will come in time to a stony ridge which ends in a cairn. There you will see the whole hill country of the south, a hundred lochs, a myriad streams, and a forest of hill-tops. There on the very crest lies the old man, in the heart of his own land, at the fountain-head of his many waters. If you listen you will hear a noise as of a swaying of trees or a ripple on the sea. It is the sound of the rising of burns, which, innumerable and unnumbered, flow thence to the silent glens for evermore.

At the Article of Death

Buchan's third story in *The Yellow Book* appeared alongside
Henry James and Kenneth Grahame in the January 1897
issue. It was later included in *Grey Weather* (1899).

'At the Article of Death' is one of Buchan's bleakest short
stories and a good example of why it is quite wrong to suggest
he is part of the sentimental Kailyard School of Scottish
writing. Whereas in his other tales the characters overcome
their problems through force of character or religious superstition, here religion offers no comfort.

Nullum
Sacra caput Proserpina fugit.

A NOISELESS EVENING fell chill and dank on the moorlands. The
Dreichil was mist to the very rim of its precipitous face, and the long,
dun sides of the Little Muneraw faded into grey vapour. Underfoot
were plashy moss and dripping heather, and all the air was choked
with autumnal heaviness. The herd of the Lanely Bield stumbled
wearily homeward in this, the late afternoon, with the roof-tree of his
cottage to guide him over the waste.

For weeks, months, he had been ill, fighting the battle of a lonely
sickness. Two years agone his wife had died, and as there had been no
child, he was left to fend for himself. He had no need for any woman,
he declared, for his wants were few and his means of the scantiest, so
he had cooked his own meals and done his own household work since
the day he had stood by the grave in the Gledsmuir kirkyard. And for
a little he did well; and then, inch by inch, trouble crept upon him. He
would come home late in the winter nights, soaked to the skin, and sit
in the peat-reek till his clothes dried on his body. The countless little
ways in which a woman's hand makes a place healthy and habitable

were unknown to him, and soon he began to pay the price of his folly. For he was not a strong man, though a careless onlooker might have guessed the opposite from his mighty frame. His folk had all been short-lived, and already his was the age of his father at his death. Such a fact might have warned him to circumspection; but he took little heed till that night in the March before, when, coming up the Little Muneraw and breathing hard, a chill wind on the summit cut him to the bone. He rose the next morn, shaking like a leaf, and then for weeks he lay ill in bed, while a young shepherd from the next sheep-farm did his work on the hill. In the early summer he rose a broken man, without strength or nerve, and always oppressed with an ominous sinking in the chest; but he toiled through his duties, and told no man his sorrow. The summer was parchingly hot, and the hillsides grew brown and dry as ashes. Often as he laboured up the interminable ridges, he found himself sickening at heart with a poignant regret. These were the places where once he had strode so freely with the crisp air cool on his forehead. Now he had no eye for the pastoral loveliness, no ear for the witch-song of the desert. When he reached a summit, it was only to fall panting, and when he came home at nightfall he sank wearily on a seat.

And so through the lingering summer the year waned to an autumn of storm. Now his malady seemed nearing its end. He had seen no man's face for a week, for long miles of moor severed him from a homestead. He could scarce struggle from his bed by mid-day, and his daily round of the hill was gone through with tottering feet. The time would soon come for drawing the ewes and driving them to the Gledsmuir market. If he could but hold on till the word came, he might yet have speech of a fellow man and bequeath his duties to another. But if he died first, the charge would wander uncared for, while he himself would lie in that lonely cot till such time as the lowland farmer sent the messenger. With anxious care he tended his flickering spark of life — he had long ceased to hope — and with something like heroism looked blankly towards his end.

But on this afternoon all things had changed. At the edge of the water-meadow he had found blood dripping from his lips, and half-swooned under an agonizing pain at his heart. With burning eyes he turned his face to home, and fought his way inch by inch through the desert. He counted the steps crazily, and with pitiful sobs looked upon mist and moorland. A faint bleat of a sheep came to his ear; he heard it clearly, and the hearing wrung his soul. Not for him any more the hills of sheep and a shepherd's free and wholesome life. He was creeping, stricken, to his homestead to die, like a wounded fox crawling to its earth. And the loneliness of it all, the pity, choked him more than the fell grip of his sickness.

Inside the house a great banked fire of peats was smouldering. Unwashed dishes stood on the table, and the bed in the corner was unmade, for such things were of little moment in the extremity of his days. As he dragged his leaden foot over the threshold, the autumn dusk thickened through the white fog, and shadows awaited him, lurking in every corner. He dropped carelessly on the bed's edge, and lay back in deadly weakness. No sound broke the stillness, for the clock had long ago stopped for lack of winding. Only the shaggy collie which had lain down by the fire looked to the bed and whined mournfully.

In a little he raised his eyes and saw that the place was filled with darkness, save where the red eye of the fire glowed hot and silent. His strength was too far gone to light the lamp, but he could make a crackling fire. Some power other than himself made him heap bog-sticks on the peat and poke it feebly, for he shuddered at the ominous long shades which peopled floor and ceiling. If he had but a leaping blaze he might yet die in a less gross mockery of comfort.

Long he lay in the firelight, sunk in the lethargy of illimitable feebleness. Then the strong spirit of the man began to flicker within him and rise to sight ere it sank in death. He had always been a godly liver, one who had no youth of folly to look back upon, but a well-spent life of toil lit by the lamp of a half-understood devotion. He it was who at his wife's death-bed had administered words of comfort and hope; and had passed all his days with the thought of his own end fixed like a bull's eye in the target of his meditations. In his lonely hill-watches, in the weariful lambing days, and on droving journeys to faraway towns, he had whiled the hours with self-communing, and self-examination, by the help of a rigid Word. Nay, there had been far more than the mere punctilios of obedience to the letter; there had been the living fire of love, the heroical attitude of self-denial, to be the halo of his solitary life. And now God had sent him the last fiery trial, and he was left alone to put off the garments of mortality.

He dragged himself to a cupboard where all the appurtenances of the religious life lay to his hands. There were Spurgeon's sermons in torn covers, and a dozen musty 'Christian Treasuries'. Some anti-quated theology, which he had got from his father, lay lowest, and on the top was the gaudy Bible, which he had once received from a grateful Sabbath class while he yet sojourned in the lowlands. It was lined and re-lined, and there he had often found consolation. Now in the last faltering of mind he had braced himself to the thought that he must die as became his possession, with the Word of God in his hand, and his thoughts fixed on that better country, which is an heavenly.

The thin leaves mocked his hands, and he could not turn to any well-remembered text. In vain he struggled to reach the gospels; the obstinate leaves blew ever back to a dismal psalm or a prophet's lamentation. A word caught his eye and he read vaguely: 'The shepherds slumber, O King, ... the people is scattered upon the mountains ... and no man gathereth them ... there is no healing of the hurt, for the wound is grievous.' Something in the poignant sorrow of the phrase caught his attention for one second, and then he was back in a fantasy of pain and impotence. He could not fix his mind, and even as he strove he remembered the warning he had so often given to others against death-bed repentance. Then, he had often said, a man has no time to make his peace with his Maker, when he is wrestling with death. Now the adage came back to him; and gleams of comfort shot for one moment through his soul. He at any rate had long since chosen for God, and the good Lord would see and pity His servant's weakness.

A sheep bleated near the window, and then another. The flocks were huddling down, and wind and wet must be coming. Then a long dreary wind sighed round the dwelling, and at the same moment a bright tongue of flame shot up from the fire, and queer crooked shadows flickered over the ceiling. The sight caught his eyes, and he shuddered in nameless terror. He had never been a coward, but like all religious folk he had imagination and emotion. Now his fancy was perturbed, and he shrank from these uncanny shapes. In the failure of all else he had fallen to the repetition of bare phrases, telling of the fragrance and glory of the city of God. 'River of the water of Life,' he said to himself, ... 'the glory and honour of the nations ... and the street of the city was pure gold ... and the saved shall walk in the light of it ... and God shall wipe away all tears from their eyes.'

Again a sound without, the cry of sheep and the sough of a lone wind. He was sinking fast, but the noise gave him a spasm of strength.

The dog rose and sniffed uneasily at the door, a trickle of rain dripped from the roofing, and all the while the silent heart of the fire glowed and hissed at his side. It seemed an uncanny thing that now in the moment of his anguish the sheep should bleat as they had done in the old strong days of herding.

Again the sound, and again the morris-dance of shadows among the rafters. The thing was too much for his failing mind. Some words of hope – 'streams in the desert, and' – died on his lips, and he crawled from the bed to a cupboard. He had not tasted strong drink for a score of years, for to the true saint in the uplands abstinence is a primary virtue; but he kept brandy in the house for illness or wintry weather. Now it would give him strength, and it was no sin to cherish the spark of life.

He found the spirits and gulped down a mouthful – one, two, till the little flask was drained, and the raw fluid spilled over beard and coat. In his days of health it would have made him drunk, but now all the fibres of his being were relaxed, and it merely stung him to a fantasmal vigour. More, it maddened his brain, already tottering under the assaults of death. Before he had thought feebly and greyly, now his mind surged in an ecstasy.

The pain that lay heavy on his chest, that clutched his throat, that tugged at his heart, was as fierce as ever, but for one short second the utter weariness of spirit was gone. The old fair words of Scripture came back to him, and he murmured promises and hopes till his strength failed him for all but thought, and with closed eyes he fell back to dream.

But only for one moment; the next he was staring blankly in a mysterious terror. Again the voices of the wind, again the shapes on floor and wall and the relentless eye of the fire. He was too helpless to move and too crazy to pray; he could only lie and stare, numb with expectancy. The liquor seemed to have driven all memory from him, and left him with a child's heritage of dreams and stories.

Crazily he pattered to himself a child's charm against evil fairies, which the little folk of the moors still speak at their play, –

> Wearie, Ovie, gang awa',
> Dinna show your face at a',
> Ower the muir and down the burn,
> Wearie, Ovie, ne'er return.

The black crook of the chimney was the object of his spells, for the kindly ingle was no less than a malignant twisted devil, with an awful red eye glowering through smoke.

His breath was winnowing through his worn chest like an autumn blast in bare rafters. The horror of the black night without, all filled with the wail of sheep, and the deeper fear of the red light within, stirred his brain, not with the far-reaching fanciful terror of men, but with the crude homely fright of a little child. He would have sought, had his strength suffered him, to cower one moment in the light as a refuge from the other, and the next to hide in the darkest corner to shun the maddening glow. And with it all he was acutely conscious of the last pangs of mortality. He felt the grating of cheekbones on skin, and the sighing, which did duty for breath, rocked him with agony.

Then a great shadow rose out of the gloom and stood shaggy in the firelight. The man's mind was tottering, and once more he was back at his Scripture memories and vague repetitions. Aforetime his fancy had toyed with green fields, now it held to the darker places. 'It was the day when Evil Merodach was king in Babylon,' came the quaint recollection, and some lingering ray of thought made him link the odd name with the amorphous presence before him. The thing moved and came nearer, touched him, and brooded by his side. He made to shriek, but no sound came, only a dry rasp in the throat and a convulsive twitch of the limbs.

For a second he lay in the agony of a terror worse than the extremes of death. It was only his dog, returned from his watch by the door, and seeking his master. He, poor beast, knew of some sorrow vaguely and afar, and nuzzled into his side with dumb affection.

Then from the chaos of faculties a shred of will survived. For an instant his brain cleared, for to most there comes a lull at the very article of death. He saw the bare moorland room, he felt the dissolution of his members, the palpable ebb of life. His religion had been swept from him like a rotten garment. His mind was vacant of memories, for all were driven forth by purging terror. Only some relic of manliness, the heritage of cleanly and honest days, was with him to the uttermost. With blank thoughts, without hope or vision, with naught save an aimless resolution and a causeless bravery, he passed into the short anguish which is death.

At the Rising of the Waters

By his second year at Oxford Buchan was a regular contributor to *Chamber's Journal*. This story appeared there on 13 March 1897 and was later one of the moorland tales in *Grey Weather* (1899).

'At the Rising of the Waters' is another story about the effects of flooding and the casualness with which human life is regarded.

———————

IN MID-SEPTEMBER the moors are changing from red to a dusky brown, as the fire of the heather wanes, and the long grass yellows with advancing autumn. Then, too, the rain falls heavily on the hills, and vexes the shallow upland streams, till every glen is ribbed with its churning torrent. This for the uplands; but below, at the rim of the plains, where the glens expand to vales, and trim fields edge the wastes, there is wreck and lamentation. The cabined waters lip over cornland and meadow, and bear destruction to crop and cattle.

This is the tale of Robert Linklater, farmer in Clachlands, and the events which befell him on the night of September 20th, in the year of grace 1880. I am aware that there are characters in the countryside which stand higher in repute than his, for imagination and love of point and completeness in a story are qualities which little commend themselves to the prosaic. I have heard him called 'Leein' Rob', and answer to the same with cheerfulness; but he was wont in private to brag of minutest truthfulness, and attribute his ill name to the universal dullness of man.

On this evening he came home, by his own account, from market about the hour of six. He had had a week of festivity. On the Monday he had gone to a distant cattle-show, and on Tuesday to a marriage. On the Wednesday he had attended upon a cousin's funeral, and, being flown with whisky, brought everlasting disgrace upon himself by rising to propose the health of the bride and bridegroom. On

Thursday he had been at the market of Gledsmuir, and, getting two shillings more for his ewes than he had reckoned, returned in a fine fervour of spirit and ripe hilarity.

The weather had been shower and blast for days. The grey skies dissolved in dreary rain, and on that very morn there had come a downpour so fierce that the highways ran like a hillside torrent. Now, as he sat at supper and looked down at the green vale and red waters leaping by bank and brae, a sudden fear came to his heart. Hitherto he had had no concern – for was not his harvest safely inned? But now he minds of the laigh parks and the nowt beasts there, which he had bought the week before at the sale of Iverforth. They were Kyloe and Galloway mixed, and on them, when fattened through winter and spring, lay great hopes of profit. He gulped his meal down hurriedly, and went forthwith to the garden-foot. There he saw something that did not allay his fears. Gled had split itself in two, at the place where Clachlands water came to swell its flow, and a long, gleaming line of black current stole round by the side of the laigh meadow, where stood the huddled cattle. Let but the waters rise a little, and the valley would be one uniform, turgid sea.

This was pleasing news for an honest man after a hard day's work, and the farmer went grumbling back. He took a mighty plaid and flung it over his shoulders, chose the largest and toughest of his many sticks, and set off to see wherein he could better the peril.

Now, some hundreds of yards above the laigh meadow, a crazy wooden bridge spanned the stream. By this way he might bring his beasts to safety, for no nowt could hope to swim the red flood. So he splashed through the dripping stubble to the river's brink, where, with tawny swirl, it licked the edge of banks which in summer weather stood high and flower-decked. Ruefully he reflected that many good palings would by this time be whirling to a distant sea.

When he came to the wooden bridge he set his teeth manfully and crossed. It creaked and swayed with his weight, and dipped till it all but touched the flow. It could not stand even as the water was, for already its mid prop had lurched forward, like a drunken man, and was groaning at each wave. But if a rise came, it would be torn from its foundations like a reed, and then heigh-ho! for cattle and man.

With painful haste he laboured through the shallows which rimmed the haughlands, and came to the snake-like current which had even now spread itself beyond the laigh meadow. He measured its depth with his eyes and ventured. It did not reach beyond his middle, but its force gave him much ado to keep his feet. At length it was passed, and he stood triumphant on the spongy land, where the cattle huddled in mute discomfort and terror.

Darkness was falling, and he could scarcely see the homestead on the affronting hillside. So with all speed he set about collecting the shivering beasts, and forcing them through the ring of water to the bridge. Up to their flanks they went, and then stood lowing helplessly. He saw that something was wrong, and made to ford the current himself. But now it was beyond him. He looked down at the yellow water running round his middle, and saw that it had risen, and was rising inch by inch with every minute. Then he glanced to where aforetime stood the crazy planking of the bridge. Suddenly hope and complacency fled, and the gravest fear settled in his heart; for he saw no bridge, only a ragged, saw-like end of timber where once he had crossed.

Here was a plight for a solitary man to be in at nightfall. There would be no wooden bridge on all the water, and the nearest one of stone was at distant Gledsmuir, over some score of miles of weary moorland. It was clear that his cattle must bide on this farther bank, and he himself, when once he had seen them in safety, would set off for the nearest farm and pass the night. It seemed the craziest of matters, that he should be thus in peril and discomfort, with the lights of his house blinking not a quarter mile away.

Once more he tried to break the water-ring and once more he failed. The flood was still rising, and the space of green which showed grey and black beneath a fitful moon was quickly lessening. Before, irritation had been his upper feeling, now terror succeeded. He could not swim a stroke, and if the field were covered he would drown like a cat in a bag. He lifted up his voice and roared with all the strength of his mighty lungs, 'Sammle', 'Andra', 'Jock', 'come and help 's', till the place rang with echoes. Meantime, with strained eyes he watched the rise of the cruel water, which crept, black and pitiless, over the shadowy grey.

He drove the beasts to a little knoll, which stood somewhat above the meadow, and there they stood, cattle and man, in the fellowship of misfortune. They had been as wild as peat-reek, and had suffered none to approach them, but now with some instinct of peril they stood quietly by his side, turning great billowy foreheads to the surging waste. Upward and nearer came the torrent, rising with steady gurgling which told of great storms in his hills and roaring torrents in every gorge. Now the sound grew louder and seemed almost at his feet, now it ceased and nought was heard save the dull hum of the main stream pouring its choking floods to the sea. Suddenly his eyes wandered to the lights of his house and the wide slope beyond, and for a second he mused on some alien trifle. Then he was brought to himself with a pull as he looked and saw a line of black water not three feet from the farthest beast. His heart stood still, and with awe he reflected that in half-an-hour by this rate of rising he would be with his Maker.

For five minutes he waited, scarce daring to look around him, but dreading each instant to feel a cold wave lick his boot. Then he glanced timorously, and to his joy it was scarce an inch higher. It was stopping, and he might yet be safe. With renewed energy he cried out for aid, till the very cattle started at the sound and moved uneasily among themselves.

In a little there came an answering voice across the dark. 'Whae's in the laigh meedy?' and it was the voice of the herd of Clachlands, sounding hoarse through the driving of the stream.

'It's me,' went back the mournful response.

'And whae are *ye*?' came the sepulchral voice.

'Your ain maister, William Smail, forewandered among water and nowt beast.'

For some time there was no reply, since the shepherd was engaged in a severe mental struggle; with the readiness of his class he went straight to the heart of the peril, and mentally reviewed the ways and waters of the land. Then he calmly accepted the hopelessness of it all, and cried loudly through the void, –

'There's nae way for't but juist to bide where ye are. The water's stoppit, and gin mornin' we'll get ye aff. I'll send a laddie down to the Dow Pule to bring up a boat in a cairt. But that's a lang gait, and it'll be a sair job gettin' it up, and I misdoot it'll be daylicht or he comes. But haud up hour hert, and we'll get ye oot. Are the beasts a' richt?'

'A' richt, William; but, 'od man! their maister is cauld. Could ye no fling something ower?'

'No, when there's twae hunner yairds o' deep water atween.'

'Then, William, ye maun licht a fire, a great muckle roarin' fire, juist fornenst me. It'll cheer me to see the licht o' 't.'

The shepherd did as he was bid, and for many minutes the farmer could hear the noise of men heaping wood, in the pauses of wind and through the thicker murmur of the water. Then a glare shot up, and revealed the dusky forms of the four serving-men straining their eyes across the channel. The gleam lit up a yard of water by the other bank, but all mid-way was inky shadow. It was about eight o'clock, and the moon was just arisen. The air had coldened and a light chill wind rose from the river.

The farmer of Clachlands, standing among shivering and dripping oxen, himself wet to the skin and cold as a stone, with no wrapping save his plaid, and no outlook save a black moving water and a gleam of fire — in such a position, the farmer of Clachlands collected his thoughts and mustered his resolution. His first consideration was the safety of his stock. The effort gave him comfort. His crops were in, and he could lose nothing there; his sheep were far removed from scaith, and his cattle would survive the night with ease, if the water kept its level. With some satisfaction he reflected that the only care he need have in the matter was for his own bodily comfort in an autumn night. This was serious, yet not deadly, for the farmer was a man of many toils and cared little for the rigours of weather. But he would gladly have given the price of a beast for a bottle of whisky to comfort himself in his emergency.

He stood on a knuckle of green land some twenty feet long, with a crowd of cattle pressing around him and a little forest of horns showing faintly. There was warmth in these great shaggy hides if they had not been drenched and icy from long standing. His fingers were soon as numb as his feet, and it was in vain that he stamped on the plashy grass or wrapped his hands in a fold of plaid. There was no doubt in the matter. He was keenly uncomfortable, and the growing chill of night would not mend his condition.

Some ray of comfort was to be got from the sight of the crackling fire. There at least was homely warmth, and light, and ease. With gusto he conjured up all the delights of the past week, the roaring evenings in market ale-house, and the fragrance of good drink and piping food. Necessity sharpened his fancy, and he could almost feel the flavour of tobacco. A sudden hope took him. He clapped hand to pocket and pulled forth pipe and shag. Curse it! He had left his match-box on the chimney-top in his kitchen, and there was an end to his only chance of comfort.

So in all cold and damp he set himself to pass the night in the midst of that ceaseless swirl of black moss water. Even as he looked at the dancing glimmer of fire, the moon broke forth silent and full, and lit the vale with misty glamour. The great hills, whence came the Gled, shone blue and high with fleecy trails of vapour drifting athwart them. He saw clearly the walls of his dwelling, the light shining from the window, the struggling fire on the bank, and the dark forms of men. Its transient flashes on the waves were scarce seen in the broad belt of moonshine which girdled the valley. And around him, before and behind, rolled the unending desert waters with that heavy, resolute flow, which one who knows the floods fears a thousandfold more than the boisterous stir of a torrent.

And so he stood till maybe one o'clock of the morning, cold to the bone, and awed by the eternal silence, which choked him, despite the myriad noises of the night. For there are few things more awful than the calm of nature in her madness – the stillness which follows a snow-slip or the monotony of a great flood. By this hour he was falling from his first high confidence. His knees stooped under him, and he was fain to lean upon the beasts at his side. His shoulders ached with the wet, and his eyes grew sore with the sight of yellow glare and remote distance.

From this point I shall tell his tale in his own words, as he has told it me, but stripped of its garnishing and detail. For it were vain to translate Lallan into orthodox speech, when the very salt of the night air clings to the Scots as it did to that queer tale.

'The mune had been lang out,' he said, 'and I had grown weary o' her blinkin'. I was as cauld as death, and as wat as the sea, no to speak o' haein' the rheumatics in my back. The nowt were glowrin' and glunchin', rubbin' heid to heid, and whiles stampin' on my taes wi' their cloven hooves. But I was mortal glad o' the beasts' company, for I think I wad hae gane daft mysel in that muckle dowie water. Whiles I thocht it was risin', and then my hert stood still; an' whiles fa'in', and then it loupit wi' joy. But it keepit geyan near the bit, and aye as I heard it lip-lappin' I prayed the Lord to keep it whaur it was.

'About half-past yin in the mornin', as I saw by my watch, I got sleepy, and but for the nowt steerin', I micht hae drappit aff. Syne I begood to watch the water, and it was rale interestin', for a' sort o' queer things were comin' doun. I could see bits o' brigs and palin's wi'oot end dippin' in the tide, and whiles swirlin' in sae near that I could hae grippit them. Then beasts began to come by, whiles upside doun, whiles soomin' brawly, sheep and stirks frae the farms up the water. I got graund amusement for a wee while watchin' them, and notin' the marks on their necks.

' "That's Clachlands Mains," says I, "and that's Nether Fallo, and the Back o' the Muneraw. Gudesake, sic a spate it maun hae been up the muirs to work siccan a destruction!" I keepit coont o' the stock, and feegured to mysel what the farmer-bodies wad lose. The thocht that I wad keep a' my ain was some kind o' comfort.

'But about the hour o' twae the mune cloudit ower, and I saw nae mair than twenty feet afore me. I got awesome cauld, and a sort o' stound o' fricht took me, as I lookit into that black, unholy water. The nowt shivered sair and drappit their heids, and the fire on the ither side seemed to gang out a' of a sudden, and leave the hale glen thick wi' nicht. I shivered mysel wi' something mair than the snell air, and there and then I wad hae gien the price o' fower stirks for my ain bed at hame.

'It was as quiet as a kirkyaird, for suddenly the roar o' the water stoppit, and the stream lay still as a loch. Then I heard a queer lappin' as o' something floatin' doun, and it soundcd miles aff in that dreidfu' silence. I listened wi' een stertin', and aye it cam' nearer and nearer, wi' a sound like a dowg soomin' a burn. It was sae black, I could see nocht, but somewhere frae the edge o' a cloud, a thin ray o' licht drappit on the water, and there, soomin' doun by me, I saw something that lookit like a man.

'My hert was burstin' wi' terror, but, thinks I, here's a droonin' body, and I maun try and save it. So I waded in as far as I daured, though my feet were sae cauld that they bowed aneath me.

'Ahint me I heard a splashin' and fechtin', and then I saw the nowt, fair wild wi' fricht, standin' in the water on the ither side o' the green bit, and lookin' wi' muckle feared een at something in the water afore me.

'Doun the thing came, and aye I got caulder as I looked. Then it was by my side, and I claught at it and pu'd it after me on to the land.

'I heard anither splash. The nowt gaed farther into the water, and stood shakin' like young birks in a storm.

'I got the thing upon the green bank and turned it ower. It was a drooned man wi' his hair hingin' back on his broo, and his mouth wide open. But first I saw his een, which glowered like scrapit lead out o' his clay-cauld face, and had in them a' the fear o' death and hell which follows after.

'The next moment I was up to my waist among the nowt, fechtin' in the water aside them, and snowkin' into their wet backs to hide mysel like a feared bairn.

'Maybe half an 'oor I stood, and then my mind returned to me. I misca'ed mysel for a fule and a coward. And my legs were sae numb, and my strength sae far gane, that I kenned fine that I couldna lang thole to stand this way like a heron in the water.

'I lookit round, and then turned again wi' a stert, for there were thae leaden een o' that awfu' deid thing staring at me still.

'For anither quarter-hour I stood and shivered, and then my guid sense returned, and I tried again. I walkit backward, never lookin' round, through the water to the shore, whaur I thocht the corp was lyin'. And a' the time I could hear my hert chokin' in my breist.

'My God, I fell ower it, and for one moment lay aside it, wi' my heid touchin' its deathly skin. Then wi' a skelloch like a daft man, I took the thing in my airms and flung it wi' a' my strength into the water. The swirl took it, and it dipped and swam like a fish till it gaed out o'sicht.

'I sat doun on the grass and grat like a bairn wi' fair horror and weakness. Yin by yin the nowt came back, and shouthered anither around me, and the puir beasts brocht me yince mair to myself. But I keepit my een on the grund, and thocht o' hame and a' thing decent and kindly, for I daurna for my life look out to the black water in dreid o' what it micht bring.

'At the first licht, the herd and twae ither men cam' ower in a boat to tak me aff and bring fodder for the beasts. They fand me still sittin' wi' my heid atween my knees, and my face like a peeled wand. They lifted me intil the boat and rowed me ower, driftin' far doun wi' the angry current. At the ither side the shepherd says to me in an awed voice, –

' "There's a fearfu' thing happened. The young laird o' Manor-water's drooned in the spate. He was ridin' back late and tried the ford o' the Cauldshaw foot. Ye ken his wild cantrips, but there's an end o' them noo. The horse cam' hame in the nicht wi' an empty saddle, and the Gled Water rinnin' frae him in streams. The corp'll be far on to the sea by this time, and they'll never see 't mair." '

' "I ken," I cried wi' a dry throat, "I ken; I saw him floatin' by."

And then I broke yince mair into a silly greetin', while the men watched me as if they thocht I was out o' my mind.'

So much the farmer of Clachlands told me, but to the countryside he repeated merely the bare facts of weariness and discomfort. I have heard that he was accosted a week later by the minister of the place, a well-intentioned, phrasing man, who had strayed from his native city with its familiar air of tea and temperance to those stony uplands.

'And what thoughts had you, Mr. Linklater, in that awful position? Had you no serious reflection upon your life?'

'Me,' said the farmer; 'no me. I juist was thinkin' that it was dooms cauld, and that I wad hae gien a guid deal for a pipe o' tobaccy.' This in the racy, careless tone of one to whom such incidents were the merest child's play.

Prester John

The legend of Prester John, the African Christian king, was one that fascinated Buchan. He refers to it in his short story 'The Kings of Orion' and it is the title of his famous novel about Black Nationalism. Here, setting it around Gledsmuir, he links it to the tale of an old man who claims he is completely self-sufficient and needs neither wife nor religion. The story is most remarkable for Buchan's ability to convey a sense of weather and terrain, as much as its insights into character.

It was first published in *Chamber's Journal* for 5 June 1897 and has not subsequently appeared since its inclusion in *Grey Weather* (1899).

Or he, who in the wilderness, where no man travels and few may live, dwelled in all good reason and kindness.

Chronicle of S. Jean de Remy

THE EXACT TALE of my misadventure on that September day I can scarcely now remember. One thing I have clear in my mind – the weather. For it was in that curious time of year when autumn's caprices reach their height either in the loveliest of skies or a resolute storm. Now it was the latter, and for two days the clear tints of the season had been drowned in monotonous grey. The mighty hill-streams came down like fields in breadth, and when the wind ceased for a time, the roar of many waters was heard in the land. Ragged leaves blocked the path, heather and bracken were sodden as the meadow turf, and the mountain backs were now shrouded to their bases in mist, and now looming ominous and near in a pause of the shifting wrack.

In the third day of the weather I was tempted by the Evil One and went a-fishing. The attempt was futile, and I knew it, for the streams were boiling like a caldron, and no man may take fish in such a water. Nevertheless, the blustering air and the infinite distance of shadowy hill-top took hold on me so that I could not choose but face the storm. And, once outside, the north wind slashed and buffeted me till my breath was almost gone; and when I came to the river's edge, I looked down on an acre of churning foam and mountainous wave.

Now, the way of the place is this. The Gled comes down from flat desolate moorlands to the narrower glen, which in turn opens upon the great river of the countryside. On the left it is bounded by gentle slopes of brown heather, which sink after some score of miles into the fields of a plain; but to the right there lies a tract of fierce country, rugged and scarred with torrents; while at the back of all rise the pathless hills which cradle the Callowa and the Aller. It is a land wild on the fairest summer noon, but in the autumn storms it is black as a pit and impregnable as a fortress.

As ill-fortune would have it, I raised a good fish in my first pool, ran it, and lost it in a tangle of driftwood. What with the excitement and the stinging air my blood grew high, I laughed in the face of the heavens, and wrestled in the gale's teeth for four miles up-stream. It was the purest madness, for my casting-line was blown out of the water at almost every gust, and never another fish looked near me. But the keenness abode with me, and so it happened that about mid-day I stood at the foot of the glen whence the Cauldshaw Burn pours its troubled waters to the Gled.

Something in the quiet strength of the great brown flood attracted me against my better judgment. I persuaded myself that in this narrower vale there must be some measure of shelter, and that in its silent pools there were chances of fish. So, with a fine sense of the adventurous, I turned to the right and struck up by the green meadow-lands and the lipping water. Before me was a bank of mist; but even as I looked it opened, and a line of monstrous blue shoulders, ribbed and serrated with a thousand gullies, frowned on my path. The sight put new energy into my limbs. These were the hills which loomed far to the distant lowlands, which few ever climbed, and at whose back lay a land almost unknown to man. I named them to myself with the names which had always been like music to my ear — Craigcreich, the Yirnie, the two Muneraws, and the awful precipice of the Dreichil. With zest I fell to my fishing, and came in a little to the place where the vale ceased and the gorge began.

Here for the first time my efforts prospered, and I had one, two, and three out of the inky pots, which the spate had ringed and dappled with foam. Then, from some unknown cause, the wind fell, and there succeeded the silence which comes from a soaked and dripping world. I fished on and on, but the stillness oppressed me, and the straight craigs, tipped with heather and black with ooze, struck me with something like awe.

Then, ere I knew, I had come to the edge of the gorge, and was out on the peat-moss which gives the Cauldshaw its birth. Once more there came a clearing in the mist, and hill-faces looked out a little nearer, a little more awful. Just beyond that moss lay their foot, and over that barrier of heath and crag lay a new land which I had not yet seen, and scarcely heard of. Suddenly my whole purpose changed. Storm or no storm, I would climb the ridge and look down on the other side. At the top of the Little Muneraw there rose two streams – one, the Callowa, which flowed to the haughlands and meadows of the low country; the other, the Aller, which fought its way to the very centre of the black deserts, and issued some fifty miles distant on another seaboard. I would reach the top, haply see the sight I had often longed for, and then take my weary way down the Callowa home.

So, putting up my rod and strapping tight my creel, I set my face to the knuckle of these mountains which loomed beyond the bog. How I crossed that treacherous land I can scarcely tell, for the rain had left great lagoons which covered shifting sand and clinging mud. Twice I was bogged to my knees, but by dint of many flying leaps from heather to heather, and many lowly scrambles over loose peat, I came to the hard ground whence the slope began. Here I rested, panting, marvelling greatly at my foolhardiness and folly. When honest men were dwelling in comfort at home, I in my fool's heart chose to be playing cantrips among mosses and scaurs and pathless rocks. I was already soaked and half tired, so in no great bodily ease I set myself to the ascent.

In two hours I had toiled to the front shoulder of the Muneraw, and sat looking down on a pit of mist whence three black lochs gleamed faint and shadowy. The place was hushed save for the croak of ravens and the rare scream of a hawk. Curlews and plovers were left far below; the place was too wild for rushes or bracken; and nothing met the eye but stunted heather, grey lichen-clad boulders, and dark craigs streaked with the fall of streams. I loosened a stone and sent it hurling to the loch below, and in a trice the air was thick with echoes of splash and rush and splinter.

Then once more I set my face to the steep and scrambled upward. And now there came to trouble me that very accident which I most feared; for the wind brought the accursed mist down on me like a plaid, and I struggled through utter blindness. The thickness of mirk is bad enough, but the thickness of white, illimitable ether is worse a thousandfold, for it closes the eye and mazes the wits. I kept as straight as might be for what I knew was the head of the hill, and now upon great banks of rotten granite, now upon almost sheer craigs, I made my track. In maybe an hour the steeps ceased, and I lay and panted on a flat bed of shingle, while the clammy mist drenched me to the bone.

Now for the first time I began to repent of my journey, and took grace to regret my madcap ploy. For the full perils of the place began to dawn upon me. I was here, in this dismal weather, a score of miles from any village, and nigh half as many from the nearest human habitation. A sprain or a broken limb would mean death, and at any moment I might step over a cliff-face into eternity. My one course of safety lay in finding the Callowa springs, and following the trickle to the glens. The way was long, but it was safe, and sooner or later I must come to a dwelling-house.

I knew well that the Callowa rose on the south side of the Muneraw, and the Aller somewhere on the north. But I had lost all sense of direction, I had no compass, and had it not been for the wind, I should have been without guidance. But I remembered that it had blown clear from the north on all my way up the Gled, and now, as I felt its sting on my cheek, I turned with it to what I guessed to be the south. With some satisfaction I began to descend, now sliding for yards, now falling suddenly in a rocky pool, whence a trickle issued among a chaos of stones. Once I came to a high fall, which must have been wonderful indeed had the water been of any size, but was now no more than a silver thread on a great grey face. Sometimes I found myself in ravines where the huge sides seemed to mock the tiny brawling water. A lurking fear began to grow upon me. Hitherto I had found no loch, though I had gone for miles. Now, though I had never been at Callowa head, I had seen it afar off, and knew that the Back Loch o' the Muneraw lay near the source. But now the glen was opening, peat and heather were taking the place of stone, and yet I had seen no gleam of water.

I sat down to consider, and even as I looked the mist drew back again. And this was what I saw. Brown bog lay flat down a valley, with a stream in its midst making leaden pools. Now there are bogs and bogs, and some are harmless enough; but there was that in the look of this which I could not like. Some two miles down the stream turned, and a ridge of dark and craggy hills fronted the eye. Their edges were jagged, and their inky face was seamed and crossed with a thousand little cataracts. And beneath their shadow lay the cruel moss, with flows and lochs scattered over it like a map on a child's slate.

To my wonder, in the very lee of the hill I saw what seemed to be a cottage. There was a stunted tree, a piece of stone wall, and a plain glimpse of a grey gable-end. Then I knew whither I had come. The wind had changed. I had followed north for south, and struck the Aller instead of the Callowa. I could not return over that fierce hill and those interminable moorland miles. There was naught to be done save to make for the stones, which might be a dwelling. If the place was ruined, I would even sleep the night in its shelter, and strive to return in the morning. If it was still dwelled in, there was hope of supper and bed. I had always heard of the Aller as the wildest of all waters, flowing, for most of its course, in a mossland untenanted of man. Something of curiosity took me, in spite of my weariness, to meet with a dweller in this desert. And always as I looked at the black hills I shuddered, for I had heard men tell of the Caldron, where no sheep ever strayed, and in whose sheer-falling waters no fish could live.

I have rarely felt a more awful eeriness than in crossing that monstrous bog. I struck far from the stream, for the Aller, which had begun as a torrent, had sunk into links of unfathomable moss-holes. The darkening was coming on, the grim hills stood out more stark and cruel, and the smell of water clung to my nostrils like the odour of salt to a half-drowned man. Forthwith I fell into the most violent ill-temper with myself and my surroundings. At last there was like to be an end of my aimless wanderings, and unless I got through the moss by nightfall, I should never see the morning. The thought nerved me to frantic endeavour. I was dog-tired and soaked to the marrow, but I plunged and struggled from tussock to tussock and through long black reaches of peat. Anything green or white I shunned, for I had lived too long in wildernesses to be ignorant that in the ugly black and brown lay my safety.

By-and-by the dusk came, and a light was kindled in the cottage, at which sign of habitation I greatly rejoiced. It gave me new heart, and when I came to a more level place I ran as well as my wearied legs would suffer me. Then for my discomfiture I fell into a great bed of peat, and came out exceeding dirty. Still the flare grew nearer, and at last, about seven o'clock, just at the thickening of darkness, I reached a stone wall and a house-end.

At the sound of my feet the door was thrown open, and a string of collies rushed out to devour me. At their tail came the master of the place, a man bent and thin, with a beard ragged and torn with all weathers, and a great scarred face roughly brown with the hill air and the reek of peat.

'Can I stay—' I began, but my words were drowned in his loud tone of welcome.

'How in the warld did ye get here, man? Come in, come in; ye'll be fair perished.'

He caught me by the arm and dragged me into the single room which formed his dwelling. Half-a-dozen hens, escaping from the hutch which was their abode, sat modestly in corners, and from a neighbouring shed came the lowing of a cow. The place was so filled with blue fine smoke that my eyes were dazed, and it was not till I sat in a chair by a glowing fire of peats that I could discern the outlines of the roof. The rafters were black and finely polished as old oak, and the floor was flagged with the grey stones of the moor. A stretch of sacking did duty for a rug, and there the tangle of dogs stretched itself to sleep. The furnishing was of the rudest, for it was brought on horseback over barren hills, and such a portage needs the stoutest of timber. But who can tell of the infinite complexity of the odour which filled the air, the pungency of peat, varied with a whiff of the snell night without and the comfortable fragrance of food?

Meat he set before me, scones and oaten-cakes, and tea brewed as strong as spirits. He had not seen loaf-bread, he told me, since the spring, when a shepherd from the Back o' the Caldron came over about some sheep, and had a loaf-end for his dinner. Then, when I was something recovered, I sat again in the fireside chair, and over pipes of the strongest black we held high converse.

'Wife!' he said, when I asked him if he dwelt alone; 'na, na, nae woman-body for me. I bide mysel', and bake my bakings, and shoo my breeks when they need it. A wife wad be a puir convanience in this pairt o' the warld. I come in at nicht, and I dae as I like, and I gang oot in the mornings, and there's naebody to care for. I can milk the coo mysel', and feed the hens, and there's little else that a man need dae.'

I asked him if he came often to the lowlands.

'Is 't like,' said he, 'when there's twenty mile o' thick heather and shairp rock atween you and a level road? I naether gang there, nor do the folk there fash me here. I havena been at the kirk for ten 'ear, no since my faither dee'd; and though the minister o' Gledsmuir, honest man, tries to win here every spring, it's no' often he gets the length. Twice in the 'ear I gang far awa' wi' sheep, when I spain the lambs in the month o' August, and draw the crocks in the back-end. I'm expectin' every day to get word to tak' off the yowes.'

'And how do you get word?' I asked.

'Weel, the post comes up the road to the foot o' the Gled. Syne some o' the fairmers up the water tak' up a letter and leave it at the foot o' the Cauldshaw Burn. A fisher, like yersel', maybe, brings it up the glen and draps it at the herd's cottage o' the Front Muneraw, whaur it lies till the herd, Simon Mruddock, tak's it wi' him on his roonds. Noo, twice every week he passes the tap o' the Aller, and I've gotten a cairn there, whaur he hides it in an auld tin box among the stanes. Twice a week I gang up that way mysel', and find onything that's lyin'. Oh, I'm no' ill off for letters; I get them in about a week, if there's no' a snawstorm.'

The man leant forward to put a fresh coal to his pipe, and I marked his eyes, begrimed with peat smoke, but keen as a hawk's, and the ragged, ill-patched homespun of his dress. I thought of the good folk in the lowlands and the cities who hugged their fancies of simple Arcadian shepherds, who, in decent cottage, surrounded by a smiling family, read God's Word of a Saturday night. In the rugged man before me I found some hint of the truth.

'And how do you spend your days?' I asked. 'Did you never think of trying a more kindly countryside?'

He looked at me long and quizzically.

'Yince,' he said, 'I served a maister, a bit flesher-body doun at Gled-foot. He was aye biddin' me dae odd jobs about the toun, and I couldna thole it, for I'm a herd, and my wark's wi' sheep. Noo I serve the Yerl o' Callowa, and there's no' a body dare say a word to me; but

I manage things according to my ain guid juidgement, wi'oot ony 'by your leave'. And whiles I've the best o' company, for yince or twice the Yerl has bided here a' nicht, when he was forewandered shooting amang thae muirs.'

But I was scarce listening, so busy was I in trying to picture an existence which meant incessant wanderings all day among the wilds, and firelit evenings, with no company but dogs. I asked him if he ever read.

'I ha'e a Bible,' he said doubtfully, 'and I whiles tak' a spell at it to see if I remember by schulin'. But I'm no keen on books o' ony kind.'

'Then what in the name of goodness do you do?' said I.

Then his tongue was unloosed, and he told me the burden of his days; how he loved all weather, fighting a storm for the fight's sake, and glorying in the conquest; how he would trap blue hares and shoot wild-fowl – for had he not the Earl's leave? – and now and then kill a deer strayed among the snow. He was full of old tales of the place, learned from a thousand old sources, of queer things that happened in these eternal deserts, and queer sights which he and others than himself had seen at dawning and sunset. Some day I will put them all down in a book, but then I will inscribe it to children and label it fantasy, for no one would believe them if told with the circumstance of truth. But, above all, he gloried in the tale of the changes of sky and earth, and the multitudinous lore of the hills. I heard of storms when the thunder echoed in the Caldron like the bleating of great sheep, and the man sat still at home in terror. He told with solemn eyes of the coming of snow, of masterful floods in the Aller, when the dead sheep came down and butted, as he said, with their foreheads against his house-wall. His voice grew high, and his figure, seen in the red glare of the peats, was like some creature of a tale.

But in time the fire sank, the dogs slumbered, our pipes went out, and he showed me my bed. It was in the garret, which you entered by a trap from the shed below. The one window had been shattered by some storm and boarded up with planks, through whose crevices I could see the driving mist and the bog lying dead under cover of night. I slept on rough blankets of homespun, and ere I lay down, in looking round the place, I came upon a book stuck fast between the rafters and the wall. It was the Bible used to brush up the shepherd's learning, and for the sake of his chances hereafter I dragged it forth and blew the dust from it.

In the morning the mist had gone, and a blue sky shone out, over which sudden gusts swept like boats on a loch. The damp earth still reeked of rain; and as I stood at the door and watched the Aller, now one line of billows, strive impetuous through the bog-land, and the hills gleam in the dawning like wet jewels, I no more wondered at the shepherd's choice. He came down from a morning's round, his voice bellowing across the uplands, and hailed me from afar. 'The hills are no vera dry,' he said, 'but they micht be passed; and if I was sure I wadna bide, he wad set me on my way.' So in a little I followed his great strides through the moss and up the hill-shoulder, till in two hours I was breathing hard on the Dreichil summit, and looking down on awful craigs, which dropped sheerly to a tarn. Here he stopped, and, looking far over the chaos of ridges, gave me my directions.

'Ye see yon muckle soo-backit hill – yon's the Yirnie Cleuch, and if ye keep alang the taps ye'll come to it in an 'oor's time. Gang doun the far shouther o't, and ye'll see a burn which flows into a loch; gang on to the loch-foot, and ye'll see a great deep hole in the hillside, what they ca' the Nick o' the Hurlstanes; gang through it, and ye'll strike the Criven Burn, which flows into the Callowa; gang doun that water till it joins the Gled, and syne ye're no' abune ten mile from whaur ye're bidin'. So guid-day to ye.'

And with these lucid words he left me and took his swinging path across the hill.

The Moor Song

This is a story that has been published in slightly different versions, under varied names and in several books. It first appeared as 'Song of the Moor' in *Macmillan's Magazine* in July 1897 and the following month in *The Living Age*. Buchan included it as 'The Moor Song' in *Grey Weather* (1899), and then under the title 'The Rime of True Thomas' in *The Moon Endureth* (1912) and the American edition of *The Watcher By The Threshold* (1918).

Subtitled 'The Tale of the Respectable Whaup and the Great Godly God', it tells the story of a shepherd, a good man called Simon Etterick, who falls into conversation with a bird, the whaup. As in 'A Journey of Little Profit' the question of a supernatural element is left to the reader and as is often the case Buchan includes the title of one of his own poems in the text — here 'The Ballad of Grey Weather'.

The Tale of the Respectable Whaup and
the Great Godly Man

THIS IS A story that I heard from the King of the Numidians, who with his tattered retinue encamps behind the peat-ricks. If you ask me where and when it happened I fear that I am scarce ready with an answer. But I will vouch my honour for its truth; and if any one seek further proof, let him go east the town and west the town and over the fields of Nomansland to the Long Muir, and if he find not the King there among the peat-ricks, and get not a courteous answer to his question, then times have changed in that part of the country, and he must continue the quest to His Majesty's castle in Spain.

Once upon a time, says the tale, there was a Great Godly Man, a shepherd to trade, who lived in a cottage among heather. If you looked east in the morning, you saw miles of moor running wide to the flames of sunrise, and if you turned your eyes west in the evening, you saw a great confusion of dim peaks with the dying eye of the sun set in a crevice. If you looked north, too, in the afternoon, when the life of the day is near its end and the world grows wise, you might have seen a country of low hills and haughlands with many waters running sweet among meadows. But if you looked south in the dusty forenoon or at hot mid-day, you saw the far-off glimmer of a white road, the roofs of the ugly little clachan of Kilmaclavers, and the rigging of the fine new kirk of Threepdaidle.

It was a Sabbath afternoon in the hot weather, and the man had been to kirk all the morning. He had heard a grand sermon from the minister (or it may have been the priest, for I am not sure of the date and the King told the story quickly) – a fine discourse with fifteen heads and three parentheses. He held all the parentheses and fourteen of the heads in his memory, but he had forgotten the fifteenth; so for the purpose of recollecting it, and also for the sake of a walk, he went forth in the afternoon into the open heather. The air was mild and cheering, and with an even step he strolled over the turf and into the deeps of the moor.

The whaups were crying everywhere, making the air hum like the twanging of a bow. *Poo-eelie, Poo-eelie*, they cried, *Kirlew, Kirlew, Whaup, Wha- -up*. Sometimes they came low, all but brushing him, till they drove settled thoughts from his head. Often had he been on the moors, but never had he seen such a stramash among the feathered clan. The wailing iteration vexed him, and he *shoo'd* the birds away with his arms. But they seemed to mock him and whistle in his very face, and at the flaff of their wings his heart grew sore. He waved his great stick; he picked up bits of loose moor-rock and flung them wildly; but the godless crew paid never a grain of heed. The morning's sermon was still in his head, and the grave words of the minister still rattled in his ear, but he could get no comfort for this intolerable piping. At last his patience failed him and he swore unchristian words. 'Deil rax the birds' thrapples,' he cried.

At this all the noise was hushed and in a twinkling the moor was empty. Only one bird was left, standing on tall legs before him with its head bowed upon its breast, and its beak touching the heather.

Then the man repented his words and stared at the thing in the moss. 'What bird are ye?' he asked thrawnly.

'I am a Respectable Whaup,' said the bird, 'and I kenna why ye have broken in on our family gathering. Once in a hundred years we foregather for decent conversation, and here we are interrupted by a muckle, sweerin' man.'

Now the shepherd was a fellow of great sagacity, yet he never thought it a queer thing that he should be having talk in the mid-moss with a bird. Truth, he had no mind on the matter.

'What for were ye making siccan a din, then?' he asked. 'D' ye no ken ye were disturbing the afternoon of the holy Sabbath?'

The bird lifted its eyes and regarded him solemnly. 'The Sabbath is a day of rest and gladness,' it said, 'and is it no reasonable that we should enjoy the like?'

The shepherd shook his head, for the presumption staggered him. 'Ye little ken what ye speak of,' he said. 'The Sabbath is for them that have the chance of salvation, and it has been decreed that Salvation is for Adam's race and no for the beasts that perish.'

The whaup gave a whistle of scorn. 'I have heard all that long ago. In my great-grandmother's time, which 'ill be a thousand years and mair sync, there came a people from the south with bright brass things on their heads and breasts and terrible swords at their thighs. And with them were some lang-gowned men who kenned the stars and would come out o' nights to talk to the deer and the corbies in their ain tongue. And one, I mind, foregathered with my great-grandmother and told her that the souls o' men flitted in the end to braw meadows where the gods bide or gaed down to the black pit which they ca' Hell. But the souls o' birds, he said, die wi' their bodies and that's the end o' them. Likewise in my mother's time, when there was a great abbey down yonder by the Threepdaidle Burn which they called the House of Kilmaclavers, the auld monks would walk out in the evening to pick herbs for their distillings, and some were wise and kenned the ways of bird and beast. They would crack often o'nights with my ain family, and tell them that Christ had saved the souls o' men, but that birds and beasts were perishable as the dew o' heaven. And now ye have a black-gowned man in Threepdaidle who threeps on the same owercome. Ye may a' ken something o' your ain kitchen-midden, but certes! ye ken little o' the warld beyond it.'

Now this angered the man, and he rebuked the bird. 'These are great mysteries,' he said, 'which are no to be mentioned in the ears of an unsanctified creature. What can a thing like you wi' a lang neb and twae legs like stilts ken about the next warld?'

'Weel, weel,' said the whaup, 'we'll let the matter be. Everything to its ain trade, and I will not dispute with ye on metapheesics. But if ye ken something about the next warld, ye ken terrible little about this.'

Now this angered the man still more, for he was a shepherd reputed to have great skill in sheep and esteemed the nicest judge of hogg and wether in all the countryside. 'What ken ye about that?' he asked. 'Ye may gang east to Yetholm and west to Kells, and no find a better herd.'

'If sheep were a',' said the bird, 'ye micht be right; but what o' the wide warld and the folk in it? Ye are Simon Etterick o' the Lowe Moss. Do ye ken aucht o' your forebears?'

'My father was a God-fearing man at the Kennel-head, and my grandfather and great-grandfather afore him. One o' our name, folk say, was shot at a dyke-back by the Black Westeraw.'

'If that's a',' said the bird, 'ye ken little. Have ye never heard o' the little man, the fourth back from yoursel', who killed the Miller o' Bewcastle at the Lammas Fair? That was in my ain time, and from my mother I have heard o' the Covenanter, who got a bullet in his wame hunkering behind the divot-dyke and praying to his Maker. There were others o' your name rode in the Hermitage forays and burned Naworth and Warkworth and Castle Gay. I have heard o' an Etterick, Sim o' the Redcleuch, who cut the throat o' Jock Johnson in his ain house by the Annan side. And my grandmother had tales o' auld Ettericks who rade wi' Douglas and the Bruce and the ancient Kings o' Scots; and she used to tell o' others in her mother's time, terrible shock-headed men, hunting the deer and rinnin' on the high moors, and bidin' in the broken stane biggings on the hill-taps.'

The shepherd stared, and he, too, saw the picture. He smelled the air of battle and lust and foray, and forgot the Sabbath.

'And you yoursel',' said the bird, 'are sair fallen off from the auld stock. Now ye sit and spell in books, and talk about what ye little understand, when your fathers were roaming the warld. But little cause have I to speak, for I too am a downcome. My bill is two inches shorter than my mother's, and my grandmother was taller on her feet. The warld is getting weaklier things to dwell in it, ever since I mind mysel'.'

'Ye have the gift o' speech, bird,' said the man, 'and I would hear mair.' You will perceive that he had no mind of the Sabbath day or the fifteenth head of the forenoon's discourse.

'What things have I to tell ye when ye dinna ken the very horn-book o' knowledge? Besides, I am no clatter-vengeance to tell stories in the middle o' the muir, where there are ears open high and low. There's others than me wi' mair experience and a better skill at the telling. Our clan was well acquaint wi' the reivers and lifters o' the muirs, and could crack fine o' wars and the taking of cattle. But the blue hawk that lives in the corrie o' the Dreichil can speak o' kelpies and the dwarfs that bide in the hill. The heron, the lang solemn fellow, kens o' the greenwood fairies and the wood elfins, and the wild geese that squatter on the tap o' the Muneraw will croak to ye of the merrymaidens and the girls o' the pool. The wren – he that hops in the grass below the birks – has the story of the 'Lost Ladies of the Land', which is ower auld and sad for any but the wisest to hear; and there is a wee bird bide in the heather – hill-lintie men call him – who sings the 'Lay of the West Wind', and the 'Glee of the Rowan Berries'. But what am I talking of? What are these things to you, if ye have not first heard the Moor-Song, which is the beginning and end o' all things?'

'I have heard no songs,' said the man, 'save the sacred psalms o' God's Kirk.'

'Bonny sangs,' said the bird. 'Once I flew by the hinder end o' the Kirk and I keekit in. A wheen auld wives wi' mutches and a wheen solemn men wi' hoasts! Be sure the Moor-Song is no like yon.'

'Can ye sing it, bird?' said the man, 'for I am keen to hear it.'

'Me sing,' cried the bird, 'me that has a voice like a craw! Na, na, I canna sing it, but maybe I can tak ye where ye may hear it. When I was young an auld bog-blitter did the same to me, and sae began my education. But are ye willing and brawly willing? – for if ye get but a sough of it ye will never mair have an ear for other music.'

'I am willing and brawly willing,' said the man.

'Then meet me at the Gled's Cleuch Head at the sun's setting,' said the bird, and it flew away.

Now it seemed to the man that in a twinkling it was sunset, and he found himself at the Gled's Cleuch Head with the bird flapping in the heather before him. The place was a long rift in the hill, made green with juniper and hazel, where it was said True Thomas came to drink the water.

'Turn ye to the west,' said the whaup, 'and let the sun fall on your face, then turn ye five times round about and say after me the Rune of the Heather and the Dew.' And before he knew, the man did as he was told, and found himself speaking strange words, while his head hummed and danced as if in a fever.

'Now lay ye down and put your ear to the earth,' said the bird, and the man did so. Instantly a cloud came over his brain, and he did not feel the ground on which he lay or the keen hill-air which blew about him. He felt himself falling deep into an abysm of space, then suddenly caught up and set among the stars of heaven. Then slowly from the stillness there welled forth music, drop by drop like the clear falling of rain, and the man shuddered, for he knew that he heard the beginning of the Moor-Song.

High rose the air, and trembled among the tallest pines and the summits of great hills. And in it were the sting of rain and the blatter of hail, the soft crush of snow and the rattle of thunder among crags. Then it quieted to the low sultry croon which told of blazing mid-day when the streams are parched and the bent crackles like dry tinder. Anon it was evening, and the melody dwelled among the high soft notes which mean the coming of dark and the green light of sunset. Then the whole changed to a great pæan which rang like an organ through the earth. There were trumpet notes in it and flute notes and the plaint of pipes. 'Come forth,' it cried; 'the sky is wide and it is a far cry to the world's end. The fire crackles fine o' nights below the firs, the smell of roasting meat and wood smoke is dear to the heart of man. Fine, too, is the sting of salt and the risp of the north-wind in the sheets. Come forth, one and all, to the great lands oversea, and the strange tongues and the fremit peoples. Learn before you die to follow the Piper's Son, and though your old bones bleach among grey rocks, what matter, if you have had your bellyful of life and come to the land of Heart's Desire?' And the tune fell low and witching, bringing tears to the eyes and joy to the heart; and the man knew (though no one told him) that this was the first part of the Moor-Song, the 'Song of the Open Road', the 'Lilt of the Adventurer', which shall be now and ever and to the end of days.

Then the melody changed to a fiercer and sadder note. He saw his forefathers, gaunt men and terrible, run stark among woody hills. He heard the talk of the bronze-clad invader, and the jar and clangour as flint met steel. Then rose the last coronach of his own people, hiding in wild glens, starving in corries, or going hopelessly to the death. He heard the cry of Border foray, the shouts of the poor Scots as they harried Cumberland, and he himself rode in the midst of them. Then the tune fell more mournful and slow, and Flodden lay before him. He saw the flower of Scots gentry around their king, gashed to the breast bone, still fronting the lines of the south, though the paleness of death sat on each forehead. 'The flowers of the Forest are gone,' cried the lilt, and through the long years he heard the cry of the lost, the desperate, fighting for kings over the water and princes in the heather. 'Who cares?' cried the air. 'Man must die, and how can he die better than in the stress of fight with his heart high and alien blood on his sword? Heigh-ho! One against twenty, a child against a host, this is the romance of life.' And the man's heart swelled, for he knew (though no one told him) that this was the 'Song of Lost Battles', which only the great can sing before they die.

But the tune was changing, and at the change the man shivered, for the air ran up to the high notes and then down to the deeps with an eldrich cry, like a hawk's scream at night, or a witch's song in the gloaming. It told of those who seek and never find, the quest that knows no fulfilment. 'There is a road,' it cries, 'which leads to the Moon and the Great Waters. No changehouse cheers it, and it has no end; but it is a fine road, a braw road – who will follow it?' And the man knew (though no one told him) that this was the 'Ballad of Grey Weather', which makes him who hears it sick all the days of his life for something which he cannot name. It is the song which the birds sing on the moor in the autumn nights, and the old crow on the tree-top hears and flaps his wing. It is the lilt which old men and women hear in the darkening of their days, and sigh for the unforgettable; and love-sick girls get catches of it and play pranks with their lovers. It is a song so old that Adam heard it in the Garden before Eve came to comfort him, so young that from it still flows the whole joy and sorrow of earth.

Then it ceased, and all of a sudden the man was rubbing his eyes on the hillside, and watching the falling dusk. 'I have heard the Moor-Song,' he said to himself, and he walked home in a daze. The whaups were crying, but none came near him, though he looked hard for the bird that had spoken with him. It may be that it was there and he did not know it, or it may be that the whole thing was only a dream; but of this I cannot say.

The next morning the man rose and went to the manse.

'I am glad to see you, Simon,' said the minister, 'for it will soon be the Communion Season, and it is your duty to go round with the tokens.'

'True,' said the man, 'but it was another thing I came to talk about,' and he told him the whole tale.

'There are but two ways of it, Simon,' said the minister. 'Either ye are the victim of witchcraft, or ye are a self-deluded man. If the former (whilk I am loth to believe), then it behoves ye to watch and pray lest ye enter into temptation. If the latter, then ye maun put a strict watch over a vagrom fancy, and ye'll be quit o' siccan whigmaleeries.'

Now Simon was not listening, but staring out of the window. 'There was another thing I had it in my mind to say,' said he. 'I have come to lift my lines, for I am thinking of leaving the place.'

'And where would ye go?' asked the minister, aghast.

'I was thinking of going to Carlisle and trying my luck as a dealer, or maybe pushing on with droves to the South.'

'But that's a cauld country where there are no faithfu' ministrations,' said the minister.

'Maybe so, but I am not caring very muckle about ministrations,' said the man, and the other looked after him in horror.

When he left the manse he went to a Wise Woman, who lived on the left side of the Kirk-yard above Threepdaidle burn-foot. She was very old, and sat by the ingle day and night, waiting upon death. To her he told the same tale.

She listened gravely, nodding with her head. 'Ach,' she said, 'I have heard a like story before. And where will you be going?'

'I am going south to Carlisle to try the dealing and droving,' said the man, 'for I have some skill of sheep.'

'And will ye bide there?' she asked.

'Maybe aye, and maybe no,' he said. 'I had half a mind to push on to the big toun or even to the abroad. A man must try his fortune.'

'That's the way of men,' said the old wife. 'I, too, have heard the Moor-Song, and many women, who now sit decently spinning in Kilmaclavers, have heard it. But a woman may hear it and lay it up in her soul and bide at hame, while a man, if he get but a glisk of it in his fool's heart, must needs up and awa' to the warld's end on some daft-like ploy. But gang your ways and fare ye weel. My cousin Francie heard it, and he went north wi' a white cockade in his bonnet and a sword at his side, singing 'Charlie's come hame'. And Tam Crichtoun o' the Bourhopehead got a sough o' it one simmer's morning, and the last we heard o' Tam he was killed among the Frenchmen fechting like a fair deil. Once I heard a tinkler play a sprig of it on the pipes, and a' the lads were wud to follow him. Gang your ways, for I am near the end o' mine.' And the old wife shook with her coughing.

So the man put up his belongings in a pack on his back and went whistling down the Great South Road.

Whether or not this tale have a moral it is not for me to say. The King (who told it me) said that it had, and quoted a scrap of Latin, for he had been at Oxford in his youth before he fell heir to his kingdom. One may hear tunes from the Moor-Song, said he, in the thick of a storm on the scarp of a rough hill, in the low June weather, or in the sunset silence of a winter's night. But let none, he added, pray to have the full music, for it will make him who hears it a footsore traveller in the ways o' the world and a masterless man till death.

A Reputation

'A Reputation' was published in *Macmillan's Magazine* in February 1898, in *The Living Age* for 2 April 1898 and then in *Grey Weather* (1899) — since when it has been out of print.

At the time this was written Buchan was also writing his novel, *The Half-Hearted*, which includes several portraits of his Oxford friends, and the story and novel have certain similarities. Arnold Layden is probably a composite of Arnold Ward, Raymond Asquith and Aubrey Herbert. Increasingly Buchan was becoming fascinated by themes such as the purpose of life and the emptiness of success, themes to be explicitly developed in subsequent short stories and novels.

I

IT WAS AT a little lonely shooting-box in the Forest of Rhynns that I first met Layden, sometime in the process of a wet August. The place belonged to his cousin Urquhart, a strange man well on in years who divided his time between recondite sport and mild antiquities. We were a small party of men held together by a shifty acquaintance of those who meet somewhere and somehow each autumn. By day we shot conscientiously over mossy hills or fished in the many turbid waters; while of an evening there would be much tobacco and sporting-talk interspersed with the sleepy, indifferent joking of wearied men. We all knew the life well from long experience, and for the sake of a certain freshness and excitement were content to put up with monotonous fare and the companionship of bleak moorlands. It was a season of brown faces and rude health, when a man's clothes smelt of peat, and he recked not of letters accumulating in the nearest post-town.

To such sombre days Layden came like a phœnix among moorfowl. I had arrived late, and my first sight of him was at dinner, where the usual listless talk was spurred almost to brilliance by his presence. He kept all the table laughing at his comical stories and quaint notes on men and things, shrewd, witty, and well-timed. But this welcome vivacity was not all, for he cunningly assumed the air of a wise man unbending, and his most random saying had the piquant hint of a great capacity. Nor was his talk without a certain body, for when by any chance one of his hearers touched upon some matter of technical knowledge, he was ready at the word for a well-informed discussion. The meal ended, as it rarely did, in a full flow of conversation, and men rose with the feeling of having returned for the moment to some measure of culture.

The others came out one by one to the lawn above the river, while he went off with his host on some private business. George Winterham sat down beside me and blew solemn wreaths of smoke toward the sky. I asked him who was the man, and it is a sign of the impression made that George gave me his name without a request for further specification.

'That's a deuced clever chap,' he said with emphasis, stroking a wearied leg.

'Who is he?' I asked.

'Don't know, – cousin of Urquhart's. Rising man, they say, and I don't wonder. I bet that fellow is at the top before he dies.'

'Is he keen on shooting?' I asked, for it was the usual question.

Not much, George thought. You could never expect a man like that to be good in the same way as fools like himself; they had better things to think about. After all, what were grouse and salmon but vanities, and the killing of them futility? said Mr. Winterham, by way of blaspheming his idols.

'I was writing to my sister, Lady Clanroyden, you know,' he went on, 'and I mentioned that a chap of the name of Layden was coming. And here she writes to me to-day and can speak about nothing but the man. She says that the Cravens have taken him up, and that he is going to marry the rich Miss Clavering, and that the Prime Minister said to somebody that he would be dashed if this chap wasn't the best they had. Where the deuce did I leave Mabel's letter?' And George went indoors upon the quest.

Shortly after Layden came out, and soon we all sat watching the dusk gather over miles of spongy moor and vague tangled birchwoods. It is hard for one who is clearly the sole representative of

light amid barbarism to escape from a certain seeming of pedantry
and a walk aloof and apart. I watched the man carefully, for he fascinated me, and if I had admired his nimble wits at dinner, the more
now did I admire his tact. By some cunning art he drove out all trace
of superiority from his air; he was the ordinary good fellow, dull,
weary like the rest, vastly relishing tobacco, and staring with vacant
eyes to the evening.

The last day of my visit to the Forest I have some occasion to
remember. It was marked by a display of weather, which I, who am
something of a connoisseur in the thing, have never seen approached
in this land or elsewhere. The morning had been hazy and damp, with
mist over the hill-tops and the air lifeless. But about mid-day a wind
came out of the south-west which sent the vapour flying, and left the
tops bald and distant. We had been shooting over the Cauldshaw
Head, and about five in the afternoon landed on a spur of the Little
Muneraw above the tarn which they call the Loch o' the Threshes.
Thence one sees a great prospect of wild country, with birchwoods like
smoke and sudden rifts which are the glens of streams. On this
afternoon the air was cool and fine, the sky a level grey, the water like
ink beneath dull-gleaming crags. But the bare details were but a
hundredth part of the scene; for over all hung an air of silence, deep,
calm, impenetrable, – the quiet distilled of the endless moors, the grey
heavens, the primeval desert. It was the incarnate mystery of Life, for
in that utter loneliness lay the tale of ages since the world's birth, the
song of being and death as uttered by wild living things since the rocks
had form. The sight had the glamour of a witch's chant; it cried aloud
for recognition, driving from the heart all other loves and fervours, and
touching the savage elemental springs of desire.

We sat in scattered places on the hillside, all gazing our fill of the
wild prospect, even the keepers, to whom it was a matter of daily
repetition. None spoke, for none had the gift of words; only in each
mind was the same dumb and unattainable longing. Then Layden
began to talk, and we listened. In another it would have been mere
impertinence, for another would have prated and fallen into easy
rhetoric; but this man had the art of speech, and his words were few
and chosen. In a second he was done, but all had heard and were
satisfied; for he had told the old tale of the tent by the running water
and the twin candle-stars in heaven, of morning and evening under the
sky and the whole lust of the gipsy life. Every man there had seen a

thousand fold more of the very thing he spoke of, had gone to the heart of savagery, pioneering in the Himalayas, shooting in the Rockies, or bearing the heat of tropical sport. And yet this slim townsman, who could not shoot straight, to whom Scots hills were a revelation of the immense, and who was in his proper element on a London pavement, – this man could read the sentiment so that every hearer's heart went out to answer.

As we went home I saw by his white face that he was overtired, and he questioned me irritably about the forwarding of letters. So there and then I prayed Heaven for the gift of speech, which makes a careless spectator the interpreter of voiceless passion.

II

Three years later I found myself in England, a bronzed barbarian fresh from wild life in north Finland, and glad of a change to the pleasant domesticity of home. It was early spring, and I drifted to my cousin's house of Heston, after the aimless fashion of the wanderer returned. Heston is a pleasant place to stay in at all times, but pleasantest in spring, for it stands on the last ridge of a Devon moor, whence rolls a wide land of wood and meadow to a faint blue line of sea. The hedgerows were already bursting into leaf, and brimming waters slipped through fresh green grasses. All things were fragrant of homeland and the peace of centuries.

At Heston I met my excellent friend Wratislaw, a crabbed, cynical, hard-working, and sore-battered man, whose excursions in high politics had not soothed his temper. His whole life was a perpetual effort to make himself understood, and as he had started with somewhat difficult theories his recognition had been slow. But it was sure; men respected him sincerely if from afar; in his own line he was pre-eminent, and gradually he was drawing to himself the work in a great office of State where difficulty was equally mated with honour.

'Well, you old madman,' he cried, 'where have you been lost all these months? We heard marvellous stories about you, and there was talk of a search-party. So you chose to kill the fatted calf here of all places. I should have gone elsewhere; it will be too much of a show this week.'

'Who are coming?' I groaned resignedly.

'Lawerdale for one,' he answered. I nodded; Lawerdale was a very great man in whom I had no manner of interest. 'Then there are Rogerson, and Lady Afflint and Charlie Erskine.'

'Is that the lot?'

'Wait a moment. Oh, by Jove, I forgot; there's Layden coming, the great Layden.'

'I once met a Layden; I wonder if it 's the same man.

'Probably, – cousin of Urquhart's.'

'But he was n't commonly called "great" then.'

'You forget, you barbarian, that you've been in the wilderness for years. Reputations have come and gone in that time. Why, Layden is a name to conjure with among most people, – Layden, the brilliant young thinker, orator, and writer, the teacher of the future!' And Wratislaw laughed in his most sardonic fashion.

'Do you know him?' I asked.

'Oh, well enough in a way. He was a year below me at Oxford, – used to talk in the Union a lot, and beat me hollow for President. He was a harebrained creature then, full of ideals and aboriginal conceit; a sort of shaggy Rousseau, who preached a new heaven and a new earth, and was worshipped by a pack of schoolboys. He did well in his way, got his First and some 'Varsity prizes, but the St. Chad's people would n't have him at any price for their fellowship. He told me it was but another sign of the gulf between the real and the ideal. I thought then that he was a frothy ass, but he has learned manners since, and tact. I suppose there is no doubt about his uncommon cleverness.'

'Do you like him?'

Wratislaw laughed. 'I don't know. You see, he and I belong to different shops, and we have n't a sentiment in common. He would call me dull; I might be tempted to call him windy. It is all a matter of taste.' And he shrugged his broad shoulders and went in to dress.

At dinner I watched the distinguished visitor with interest. That he was very much of a celebrity was obvious at once. He it was to whom the unaccountable pauses in talk were left, and something in his carefully modulated voice, his neatness, his air of entire impregnability, gave him a fascination felt even by so unemotional a man as I. He differed with Lawerdale on a political question, and his attitude of mingled deference and certainty was as engaging to witness as it must have been irritating to encounter. But the event of the meal was his treatment of Lady Afflint, a lady (it is only too well known) who is the hidden reef on which so many a brilliant talker shipwrecks. Her questions give a fatal chance for an easy and unpleasing smartness; she leads her unhappy companion into a morass of 'shop' from which there is no escape, and, worst of all, she has the shrewdness to ask those questions which can only be met by a long explanation and which leave their nervous and short-winded victim the centre of a confusing silence. I have no hesitation in calling Layden's treatment of this estimable woman a miracle of art. Her own devices were returned upon her, until we had the extraordinary experience of seeing Lady Afflint reduced to an aggrieved peace.

But the man's appearance surprised me. There was nothing of the flush of enthusiasm, the ready delight in his own powers, which are supposed to mark the popular idol. His glance seemed wandering and vacant, his face drawn and lined with worry, and his whole figure had the look of a man prematurely ageing. Rogerson, that eminent lawyer, remarked on the fact in his vigorous style. 'Layden has chosen a damned hard profession. I never cared much for the fellow, but I admit he can work. Why, add my work to that of a first-class journalist, and you have an idea of what the man gets through every day of his life. And then think of the amount he does merely for show: the magazine articles, the lecturing, the occasional political speaking. All that has got to be kept up as well as his reputation in society. It would kill me in a week, and, mark my words, he can't live long at that pitch.'

I saw him no more that night, but every paper I picked up was full of him. It was 'Mr. Layden interviewed' here, and 'Arnold Layden, an Appreciation' there, together with paragraphs innumerable, and the inscrutable allusions in his own particular journal. The thing disgusted me, and yet the remembrance of that worn-out face held me from condemning him. I am one whose interest lies very little in the minute problems of human conduct, finding enough to attract me in the breathing, living world. But here was something which demanded recognition, and in my own incapable way I drew his character.

I saw little of him during that week at Heston, for he was eternally in the train of some woman or other, when he was not shut up in the library turning out his tale of bricks. With amazing industry he contrived to pass a considerable portion of each day in serious labour, and then turned with weary eyes to the frivolity in which he was currently supposed to delight. We were the barest acquaintances, a brief nod, a chance good-morning, being the limits of our intimacy;

indeed, it was a common saying that Layden had a vast acquaintance, but scarcely a friend.

But on the Sunday I happened to be sitting with Wratislaw on an abrupt furze-clad knoll which looks over the park to meadow and sea. We had fallen to serious talking, or the random moralising which does duty for such among most of us. Wratislaw in his usual jerky fashion was commenting on the bundle of perplexities which made up his life, when to us there entered a third in the person of Layden himself. He had a languid gait, partly assumed no doubt for purposes of distinction, but partly the result of an almost incessant physical weariness. But to-day there seemed to be something more in his manner. His whole face was listless and dreary; his eyes seemed blank as a stone wall.

As I said before, I scarcely knew him, but he and Wratislaw were old acquaintances. At any rate he now ignored me wholly, and flinging himself on the ground by my companion's side, leaned forward, burying his face in his hands.

'Oh, Tommy, Tommy, old man, I am a hopeless wreck,' he groaned.

'You are overworking, my dear fellow,' said Wratislaw; 'you should hold back a little.'

Layden turned a vacant face toward the speaker. 'Do you think that is all?' he said. 'Why, work never killed a soul. I could work night and day if I were sure of my standing-ground.'

Wratislaw looked at him long and solemnly. Then he took out a pipe and lit it. 'You'd better smoke,' he said. 'I get these fits of the blues sometimes myself, and they go off as suddenly as they come. But I thought you were beyond that sort of thing.'

'Beyond it!' Layden cried. 'If I had had them years ago it might have saved me. When the Devil has designs on a man, be sure that the first thing he does is to make him contented with himself.'

I saw Wraitslaw's eyebrows go up. This was strange talk to hear from one of Layden's life.

'I would give the world to be in your place. You have chosen solid work, and you have left yourself leisure to live. And I – oh, I am a sort of ineffectual busy person running about on my little errands and missing everything.'

Wratislaw winced; he disliked all mention of himself, but he detested praise.

'It's many years since I left Oxford; I don't remember how long, and all this time I have been doing nothing. Who is it talks about being "idly busy"? And people have praised me and fooled me till I believed I was living my life decently. It is n't as if I had been slack. My God, I have worked like a nigger, and my reward is wind and smoke! Did you ever have the feeling, Tommy, as if you were without bearings and had to drift with your eyes aching for solid land?'

The other shook his head slowly, and looked like a man in profound discomfort.

'No, of course you never did, and why should you? You made up your mind at once what was worth having in the world and went straight for it. That was a man's part. But I thought a little dazzle of fame was the heavenly light. I liked to be talked about; I wanted the reputation of brilliance, so I utilised every scrap of talent I had and turned it all into show. Every little trivial thought was stored up and used on paper or in talk. I toiled terribly, if you like, but it was a foolish toil, for it left nothing for myself. And now I am bankrupt of ideas. My mind grows emptier year by year, and what little is left is spoiled by the same cursed need for ostentation. "Every man should be lonely at heart"; whoever said that said something terribly true, and the words have been driving me mad for days. All the little that I have must be dragged out to the shop-window, and God knows the barrenness of that back-parlour I call my soul.'

I saw that Wratislaw was looking very solemn, and that his pipe had gone out and had dropped on the ground.

'And what is the result of it all?' Layden went on. 'Oh, I cannot complain. It is nobody's fault but my own; but Lord, what a pretty mess it is!' and he laughed miserably. 'I cannot bear to be alone and face the naked ribs of my mind. A beautiful sight has no charms for me save to revive jaded conventional memories. I have lost all capacity for the plain, strong, simple things of life, just as I am beginning to realise their transcendent worth. I am growing wretchedly mediocre, and I shall go down month by month till I find my own degraded level. But thank God, I do not go with my eyes shut; I know myself for a fool, and for the fool there is no salvation.'

Then Wratislaw rose and stood above him. I had never seen him look so kindly at any one, and for a moment his rough, cynical face was transfigured into something like tenderness. He put his hand on the other's shoulder. 'You are wrong, old man,' he said; 'you are not a fool. But if you had not come to believe yourself one, I should have had doubts of your wisdom. As it is, you will now go on to try the real thing, and then – we shall see.'

III

The real thing, – Heaven knows it is what we are all striving after with various degrees of incompetence. I looked forward to the transformation of this jaded man with an interest not purely of curiosity. His undoubted cleverness, and the habitual melancholy of his eyes, gave him a certain romantic aloofness from common life. Moreover, Wratislaw had come to believe in him, and I trusted his judgment.

I saw no more of the man for weeks, hearing only that his health was wretched and that he had gone for a long holiday to the south. His private income had always been considerable, and his work could very well wait; but his admirers were appalled by the sudden cessation of what had been a marvellous output. I was honestly glad to think of his leisure. I pictured him once more the master of himself, gathering his wits for more worthy toil, and getting rid of the foolish restlessness which had unnerved him. Then came a chance meeting at a railway-station, where he seemed to my hasty eyes more cheerful and well looking; and then my wanderings began again, and London gossip, reputation, and chatter about letters were left a thousand miles behind.

When I returned I had almost forgotten his name; but the air of one's own land is charged with memories, and the past rises on the mind by degrees till it recovers its former world. I found Wratislaw looking older, grimmer, and more irritable, ready to throw books at me for tantalising him with glimpses of an impossible life. He walked me fiercely through Hyde Park, full of abrupt questions as of old, and ever ready with his shrewd, humorous comment. Then in my turn, I fell to asking him of people and things, of the whole complication of civilised life from which I had been shut off for years. Some stray resemblance in a passing face struck me, and I asked about Layden.

Wratislaw grunted savagely. 'In a way I am grateful to the man for showing me that I am a fool.'

'Then he has gone back to his old life?' I asked, not without anxiety.

'Listen to me,' he said gruffly. 'His health broke down, as you know, and he went abroad to recover it. He stopped work, dropped out of publicity, and I thought all was well. But the man cannot live without admiration; he must be hovering in its twopenny light like a moth round a candle. So he came back, and, well, – there was a repetition of the parable of the seven devils. Only he has changed his line. Belles-lettres, society small-talk, everything of that kind has gone overboard. He is by way of being earnest now; he talks of having found a mission in life, and he preaches a new gospel about getting down to the Truth of Things. His trash has enormous influence; when he speaks the place is crowded, and I suppose he is in hopes of becoming a Force. He has transient fits of penitence, for he is clever enough to feel now and then that he is a fool, but I was wrong to think that he could ever change. Well, well, the band-playing for the ruck, but the end of the battle for the strong! He is a mere creature of phrases, and he has got hold of the particular word which pleases his generation. Do you remember our last talk with him at Heston? Well, read that bill.'

He pointed to a large placard across the street. And there in flaming red and black type I read that on a certain day under the auspices of a certain distinguished body Mr. Arnold Layden would lecture on The Real Thing.

Comedy in the Full Moon

Originally entitled 'A Midsummer Night's Tale', 'Comedy in the Full Moon' appeared in *Chamber's Journal* for 30 December 1898 and then in *Grey Weather* (1899).

The story has resonances with several future novels. There are shades of *The Half-Hearted* (1900), *John Macnab* (1925) and *The Gap in the Curtain* (1932), and the Fairy Knowe is one of the first of the sacred spots, the *temenos*, with which Buchan remained fascinated all his life. Buchan's eye for satire and parody is often ignored by critics but here is given full rein in a story about mysterious activities under a full moon one midsummer on a Scottish moorland.

I

'I DISLIKE THAT man,' said Miss Phyllis, with energy.

'I have liked others better,' said the Earl.

There was silence for a little as they walked up the laurelled path, which wound by hazel thicket and fir-wood to the low ridges of moor.

'I call him Charles Surface,' said Miss Phyllis again, with a meditative air. 'I am no dabbler in the water-colours of character, but I think I could describe him.'

'Try,' said the Earl.

'Mr. Charles Eden,' began the girl, 'is a man of talent. He has edged his way to fortune by dint of the proper enthusiasms and a seductive manner. He is a politician of repute and a lawyer of some practice, but his enemies say that like necessity he knows no law, and even his friends shrink from insisting upon his knowledge of politics. But he believes in all honest enthusiasms, temperance, land reform, and democracy with a capital D; he is, however, violently opposed to woman suffrage.'

'Every man has his good points,' murmured the Earl.

'You are interrupting me,' said Miss Phyllis, severely. 'To continue, his wife was the daughter of a baronet of ancient family and scanty means. Her husband supplied the element which she missed in her father's household, and today she is popular and her parties famous. Their house is commonly known as the Wilderness, because there the mixed multitude which came out of Egypt mingle with the chosen people. In character he is persuasive and good-natured; but then good-nature is really a vice which is called a virtue because it only annoys a man's enemies.'

'I am learning a great deal tonight,' said the man.

'You are,' said Miss Phyllis. 'But there, I have done. What I dislike in him is that one feels that he is the sort of man that has always lived in a house and is out of place anywhere but on a pavement.'

'And you call this a sketch in water-colours?'

'No, indeed. In oils,' said the girl, and they walked through a gate on to the short bent grass and the bouldered face of a hill. Something in the place seemed to strike her, for she dropped her voice and spoke simply.

'You know I am town-bred, but I am not urban in nature. I must chatter daily, but every now and then I grow tired of myself, and I hate people like Charles Eden who remind me of my weakness.'

'Life,' said the Earl, 'may be roughly divided into – But there, it is foolish to be splitting up life by hairs on such a night.'

Now they stood on the ridge's crest in the silver-grey light of a midsummer moon. Far up the long Gled valley they looked to the towering hills whence it springs; then to the left, where the sinuous Callowa wound its way beneath green and birk-clad mountains to the larger stream. In such a flood of brightness the far-distant peaks and shoulders stood out clear as day, but full of that hint of subtle and imperishable mystery with which the moon endows the great uplands in the height of summer. The air was still, save for the falling of streams and the twitter of nesting birds.

The girl stared wide-eyed at the scene, and her breath came softly with utter admiration.

'Oh, such a land!' she cried, 'and I have never seen it before. Do you know I would give anything to explore these solitudes, and feel that I had made them mine. Will you take me with you?'

'But these things are not for you, little woman,' he said. 'You are too clever and smart and learned in the minutiae of human conduct.

You would never learn their secret. You are too complex for simple, old-world life.'

'Please don't say that,' said Miss Phyllis, with pleading eyes. 'Don't think so hardly of me. I am not all for show.' Then with fresh wonder she looked over the wide landscape.

'Do you know these places?' she asked.

'I have wandered over them for ten years and more,' said the Earl, 'and I am beginning to love them. In other ten, perhaps, I shall have gone some distance on the road to knowledge. The best things in life take time and labour to reach.'

The girl made no answer. She had found a little knoll in the opposite glen, clothed in a tangle of fern and hazels, and she eagerly asked its name.

'The folk here call it the Fairy Knowe,' he said. 'There is a queer story about it. They say that if any two people at midsummer in the full moon walk from the east and west so as to meet at the top, they will find a third there, who will tell them all the future. The old men speak of it carefully, but none believe it.'

'Oh, let us go and try,' said the girl, in glee. 'It is quite early in the evening, and they will never miss us at home.'

'But the others,' said he.

'Oh, the others,' with a gesture of amusement. 'We left Mr. Eden talking ideals to your mother, and the other men preparing for billiards. They won't mind.'

'But it's more than half a mile, and you'll be very tired.'

'No, indeed,' said the girl, 'I could walk to the top of the farthest hills tonight. I feel as light as a feather, and I do so want to know the future. It will be such a score to speak to my aunt with the prophetic accent of the things to be.'

'Then come on,' said the Earl, and the two went off through the heather.

II

If you walk into the inn-kitchen at Callowa on a winter night, you will find it all but deserted, save for a chance traveller who is storm-stayed among the uncertain hills. Then men stay in their homes, for the place is little, and the dwellers in the remoter parts have no errand to town or village. But in the long nights of summer, when the moon is up and the hills dry underfoot, there are many folk down of an evening from the glens, and you may chance on men drinking a friendly glass with half a score of miles of journey before them. It is a cheerful scene – the wide room, with the twilight struggling with the new-lit lamp, the brown faces gathered around the table, and the rise and fall of the soft southern talk.

On this night you might have chanced on a special gathering, for it was the evening of the fair-day in Gled-foot, and many shepherds from the moors were eating their suppers and making ready for the road. It was then that Jock Rorison of the Redswirehead – known to all the world as Lang Jock to distinguish him from his cousin little Jock of the Nick o' the Hurlstanes – met his most ancient friend, the tailor of Callowa. They had been at school together, together they had suffered the pains of learning; and now the one's lot was cast at the back of Creation, and the other's in a little dark room in the straggling street of Callowa. A bottle celebrated their meeting, and there and then in the half-light of the gloaming they fell into talk. They spoke of friends and kin, and the toils of life; of village gossip and market prices. Thence they drifted into vague moralisings and muttered exhortation in the odour of whisky. Soon they were amiable beyond their wont, praising each other's merit, and prophesying of good fortune. And then – alas for human nature! – there came the natural transition to argument and reviling.

'I wadna be you, Jock, for a thousand pounds,' said the tailor. 'Na, I wadna venture up that lang mirk glen o' yours for a' the wealth o' the warld.'

'Useless body,' said the shepherd, 'and what for that?'

'Bide a' nicht here,' said the tailor, 'and step on in the mornin'. Man, ye're an auld freend, and I'm wae to think that aucht ill should befa' ye.'

'Will ye no speak sense for yince, ye doited cratur?' was the ungracious answer, as the tall man rose to unhook his staff from the chimney corner. 'I'm for stertin' if I'm to win hame afore mornin'.'

'Weel,' said the tailor, with the choked voice of the maudlin, 'a' I've to say is that I wis the Lord may protect ye, for there's evil lurks i' the dens o' the way, saith the prophet.'

'Stop, John Rorison, stop,' again the tailor groaned. 'O man, bethink ye o' your end.'

'I wis ye wad bethink o' yin yoursel'.'

[127]

The tailor heeded not the rudeness . . . 'for ye ken a' the auld queer owercomes about the Gled Water. Yin Thomas the Rhymer made a word on 't. Quoth he,

> "By the Gled side
> The guid folk bide." '

'Dodsake, Robin, ye're a man o' learnin' wi' your poetry,' said the shepherd, with scorn. 'Rhymin' about auld wives' havers, sic wark for a grown man!'

A vague recollection of wrath rose to the tailor's mind. But he answered with the laborious dignity of argument, –

'I'm no sayin' that a' things are true that the body said. But I say this – that there's a heap o' queer things in the warld, mair nor you nor me nor onybody kens. Now, it's weel ken't that nane o' the folk about here like to gang to the Fairy Knowe . . .'

'It's weel ken't nae siccan thing,' said the shepherd, rudely. 'I wonder at you, a kirk member and an honest man's son, crakin' siccan blethers.'

'I'm affirmin' naething,' said the other, sententiously. 'What I say is that nae man, woman, or child in this parish, which is weel ken't for an intelligent yin, wad like to gang at the rising o' the mune up the side o' the Fairy Knowe. And it's weel ken't, tae, that when the twae daft lads frae the Rochan tried it in my faither's day and gaed up frae opposite airts, they met at the tap that which telled them a' that they ever did and a' that was ever like to befa' them, and put the fear o' death on them for ever and ever. Mind, I'm affirmin' naething; but what think ye o' that?'

'I think this o' 't – that either the folk were mair fou than the Baltic or they were weak i' the heid afore ever they set out. But I'm tired o' hearin' a sensible man bletherin', so I'm awa' to the Redswirehead.'

But the tailor was swollen with pride and romance, and filled with the audacity which comes from glasses replenished.

'Then I'll gang a bit o' the road wi' ye.'

'And what for sae?' said the shepherd, darkly suspicious. Whisky drove care to his head, and made him the most irritable of friends.

'I want the air, and its graund munelicht. Your road gangs by the Knowe, and we micht as weel mak the experiment. Mind ye, I'm affirmin' naething.'

'Will ye no haud your tongue about what ye're affirmin'?'

'But I hold that it is a wise man's pairt to try all things, and whae kens but there micht be some queer sicht on that Knowe-tap? The auld folk were nane sae ready to be inventin' havers.'

'I think the man's mad,' was the shepherd's loud soliloquy. 'You want me to gang and play daft-like pranks late at nicht among birks and stanes on a muckle knowe. Weel, let it be. It lies on my road hame, but ye'd be weel serv't if some auld Druid cam out and grippit ye.'

'Whae's blethering now,' cried the tailor, triumphantly. 'I dinna gang wi' only supersteetions. I gang to get the fresh air and admire the wonderfu' works o' God. Hech, but they're bonny.' And he waved a patronising finger to the moon.

The shepherd took him by the shoulder and marched him down the road. 'Listen,' said he, 'I maun be hame afore the morn, and if ye're comin' wi' me ye'll hae to look smerter.' So down the white path and over Gled bridge they took their way, two argumentative figures, clamouring in the silent, amber spaces of the night.

III

The farmer of the Lowe Moss was a choleric man at all times, but every now and again his temper failed him utterly. He was florid and full-blooded, and the hot weather drove him wild with discomfort. Then came the torments of a dusty market and completed the task; so it fell out that on that evening in June he drove home at a speed which bade fair to hurry him to a premature grave, and ate his supper with little thankfulness.

Then he reflected upon his manifold labours. The next day was the clipping, and the hill sheep would have to be brought down in the early morning. The shepherds would be at the folds by seven, and it would mean rising in the small hours to have the flocks in the low fields in time. Now his own shepherd was gone on an errand and would not be back till the morrow's breakfast. This meant that he, the wearied, the sorely tried, must be up with the lark and tramping the high pastures. The thought was too much for him. He could not face it. There would be no night's rest for his wearied legs, though the Lord knew how he needed it.

But as he looked through the window a thought grew upon his mind. He was tired and sore, but he might yet manage an hour or two of toil, if a sure prospect of rest lay at the end. The moon was up and bright, and he might gather the sheep to the low meadows as easily as in the morning. This would suffer him to sleep in peace to the hour of seven, which was indulgence indeed to one who habitually rose at five. He was a man of imagination and hope, who valued a prospect. Far better, he held, the present discomfort, if the certainty of ease lay before him. So he gathered his aching members, reached for his stick, whistled on his dogs, and set out.

It was a long climb up the ridges of the Lowe Burn to the stell of fir-trees which marked his boundaries. Then began the gathering of the sheep, and a great scurry of dogs, – black dots on the sleepy, moon-lit hill. With much crying of master and barking of dog the flocks were massed and turned athwart the slopes in the direction of the steading. All the while he limped grumblingly behind, thinking on bed, and leaving everything to his shaggy lieutenants. Then they crossed the Lowe Burn, skirted the bog, and came in a little to the lower meadows, while afar off over the rough crest of the Fairy Knowe twinkled the lights of the farm.

Meanwhile from another point of the hill there came another wayfarer to the same goal. The Sentimentalist was a picturesque figure on holiday, enjoying the summer in the way that still remains the best. Three weeks before he had flung the burden of work from his shoulders, and gone with his rod to the Callowa-foot, whence he fished far and near even to the utmost recesses of the hills. On this evening the soft airs and the triumphant moon had brought him out of doors. He had a dim memory of a fragrant hazelled knoll above the rocky Gled, which looked up and down three valleys. The place drew him, as it lived in his memory, and he must needs get his plaid and cross the miles of heather to the wished-for sleeping-place. There he would bide the night and see the sunrise, and haply the next morning make a raid into the near village to receive letters delayed for weeks.

He crossed the hill when the full white glory of the moon was already apparent in the valleys. The air was so still and mild that one might have slept there and then on the bare hillside and been no penny the worse. The heart of the Sentimentalist was cheered, and he scanned the prospect with a glad thankfulness. To think that three weeks ago he had been living in sultriness and dreary over-work, with a head as dazed as a spinning-top and a ruin of nerves. Now every faculty was alive and keen, he had no thought of nerves, and his old

Norfolk jacket, torn and easy, now stained with peat-water and now bleached with weather, was an index to his immediate past. In a little it would be all over, and then once more the dust and worry and heat. But meantime he was in fairyland, where there was little need for dreary prognostication.

And in truth it was a fairyland which dawned on his sight at the crest of the hill. A valley filled with hazy light, and in the middle darkly banded by the stream. All things, village, knoll, bog, and coppice, bright with a duskiness which revealed nought in detail, but only hints of form and colour. A noise of distant sheep rose from the sleeping-place, and the single, solitary note of a night-bird far over the glen. At his foot were crushed thickets of little hill-flowers, thyme and pansies and the odorous bog-myrtle. Beneath him, not half a mile distant, was a mound with two lone birches on its summit, and he knew the place of his quest. This was the far-famed Fairy Knowe, where at midsummer the little folk danced, and where, so ran the tale, lay the mystic entrance, of which True Thomas spake, to the kingdom of dreams and shadows. Twenty-five miles distant a railway ran, but here there were still simplicity and antique tales. So in a fine spirit he set himself to the tangled meadowland which intervened.

IV

Miss Phyllis looked wonderingly at the tangled, moonlit hill. 'Is this the place?' she asked.

The Earl nodded. 'Do you feel devout, madam,' said he, 'and will you make the experiment?'

Miss Phyllis looked at him gravely. 'Have I not scrambled over miles of bog, and do you think that I have risked my ankles for nothing? Besides I was always a devout believer.'

'Then this is the way of it. You wait here and walk slowly up, while I get to the other side. There is always a wonderful view at least on the top.'

'But I am rather afraid that I . . .'

'Oh, very well,' said the Earl. 'If we don't perform our part, how can we expect a hard-worked goblin to do his?'

'Then,' said Miss Phyllis, with tight lips and a sigh of melodrama, 'lead on, my lord.' And she watched his figure disappear with some misgiving.

For a little she scanned the patched shadow of birk and fern, and listened uneasily to the rustle of grasses. She heard the footsteps cease, and then rise again in the silence. Suddenly it seemed as if the place had come to life. A crackling, the noise of something in lumbering motion, came from every quarter. Then there would be a sound of scampering, and again the echo of heavy breathing. Now Miss Phyllis was not superstitious, and very little of a coward. Moreover, she was a young woman of the world, with a smattering of most things in heaven and earth, and the airs of an infinite experience. But this moonlit knoll, this wide-stretching, fantastic landscape, and the lucid glamour of the night, cast a spell on her, and for once she forgot everything. Miss Phyllis grew undeniably afraid.

She glanced timorously to the left, whence came the sounds, and then with commendable spirit began to climb the slope. If things were so queer she might reasonably carry out the letter of her injunctions, and in any case the Earl would be there to meet her. But the noise grew stranger, the sound of rustling and scrambling and breathing as if in the chase. Then to her amazement a crackle of twigs rose from her right, and as she hastily turned her head to meet the new alarum, she found herself face to face with a tall man in a plaid.

For one moment both stared in frank discomfiture. Miss Phyllis was horribly alarmed and in deepest mystery. But, she began to reflect, spirits have never yet been known to wear Norfolk jackets and knickerbockers, or take the guise of stalwart, brown-faced men. The Sentimentalist, too, after the natural surprise, recovered himself and held out his hand.

'How do you do, Miss Phyllis?' said he.

The girl gasped, and then a light of recognition came into her eyes.

'What are you doing here, Mr. Grey?' she asked.

'Surely I have the first right to the question,' the man said, smiling.

'Then, if you must know, I am looking for the customary spirit to tell the future. I thought you were the thing, and was fearfully scared.'

'But who told you that story, Miss Phyllis? I did not think you would have been so credulous. Your part was always the acute critic's.'

'Then you were wrong,' said the girl, with emphasis. 'Besides, it was Charlie Erskine's doing. He brought me here, and is faithfully keeping his compact at the other side of the hill.'

'Well, well, Callowa had always a queer way of entertaining his guests. But there, Miss Phyllis, I have not seen civilisation for weeks, and am half inclined to believe in things myself. Never again shall you taunt me with "boyish enthusiasm". Was not that your phrase?'

'I have sinned,' said the girl, 'but don't talk of it. Henceforth I belong to the sentimentalists. But you must not spoil my plans. I must get to the top and wait devoutly on the *tertium quid*. You can wait here or go round the foot and meet us at the other side. You have made me feel sceptical already.'

'I am at your service, my lady, and I hope you will get good news from the fairy-folk when . . .'

But at this juncture something held the speech and eyes of both. A figure came wildly over the brow of the hill, as if running for dear life, and took the slope in great bounds through brake and bramble and heather-tussock. Onward it came with frantic arms and ineffectual cries. Suddenly it caught sight of the two as they stood at the hill-foot, the girl in white which showed dimly beneath her cloak, and the square figure of the man. It drew itself up in a spasm, stood one moment in uncomprehending terror, and then flung itself whimpering at their feet.

V

The full history of the events of these minutes has yet to be written. But such is the rough outline of the process of disaster.

It appears that the farmer of the Lowe Moss was driving his sheep in comfort with the aid of his collies, and had just crossed the meadowland and come to the edge of the Knowe. He was not more than half a mile from home, and he was wearied utterly. There still remained the maze of tree-roots and heaps of stones known as the Broken Dykes, and here it was hard to drive beasts even in the clear moonlight. So as he looked to the far lights of his home his temper began to break, and he vehemently abused his dogs.

Just at the foot of the slope there is a nick in the dyke, and far on either side stretches the hazel tangle. If once sheep get there it is hard for the best of collies to recover them in short time. But the flock was heading right, narrow in front, marshalled by vigilant four-footed watchmen, with the leaders making straight for the narrow pass. Then suddenly something happened beyond human expectation. In front of the drove the figure of a man arose as if from the ground. It was enough for the wild hill-sheep. To right and left they scattered, flanked in their race by the worn-out dogs, and in two minutes were far and wide among the bushes.

For a moment in the extremity of his disgust the farmer's power of thought and speech forsook him. Then he looked at the cause of all the trouble. He knew the figure for that of a wandering dealer with whom he had long fought bitter warfare. Doubtless the man had come there by night to spy out the nakedness of his flock and report accordingly. In any case he had been warned off the land before, and the farmer had many old grudges against him. The memory of all overtook him at the moment and turned his brain. He rubbed his eyes. No, there could be no mistaking that yellow top-coat and that scraggy figure. So with stick upraised he ran for the intruder.

When the Earl saw the sheep fleeing wide and an irate man rushing toward him, his first impulse was to run. What possible cause could lead a man to drive sheep at night among rough meadows? But the next instant all hope of escape was at an end, for the foe was upon him. He had just time to leap aside and escape a great blow from a stick, and then he found himself in a fierce grapple with a thick-set, murderous ruffian.

Meanwhile the shepherd of the Redswirehead and the tailor of Callowa had left the high-road and tramped over the moss to the Knowe-foot. The tailor's wine-begotten bravery was somewhat lessened by the still spaces of country and the silent eye of night. His companion had no thought in the matter save to get home, and if his way lay over the crest of the Fairy Knowe it mattered little to him. But when they left the high-road it became necessary to separate, if the correct fashion of the thing were to be observed. The shepherd must slacken pace and make for the near side of the hill, while the tailor would hasten to the other, and the twain would meet at the top.

The shepherd had no objection to going slowly. He lit his pipe and marched with measured tread over the bracken-covered meadows. The tailor set out gaily for the farther side, but ere he had gone far his spirits sank. Fairy tales and old wives' fables had still a measure of credence with him, and this was the sort of errand on which he had never before embarked. He was flying straight in the face of all his most cherished traditions in company with a godless shepherd who believed in nothing but his own worthiness. He began to grow nervous and wish that he were safe in the Callowa Inn instead of scrambling on a desert hill. Yet the man had a vestige of pluck which kept him from turning back, and a fragment of the sceptical which gave him hope.

At the Broken Dyke he halted and listened. Some noise came floating over the tangle other than the fitful bleat of sheep or the twitter of birds. He listened again, and there it came, a crashing and swaying, and a confused sound as of a man muttering. Every several hair bristled on his unhappy head, till he reflected that it must be merely a bullock astray among the bushes, and with some perturbation hastened on his way. He fought through the clinging hazels, knee-deep in bracken, and stumbling ever and again over a rock of heather. The excitement of the climb for a moment drove out his terrors, and with purple face and shortened breath he gained the open. And there he was rooted still, for in the middle a desperate fight was being fought by two unearthly combatants.

He had the power left to recognise that both had the semblance of men and the dress of mortals. But never for a moment was he deceived. He knew of tales without end which told of unearthly visitants meeting at midnight on the lone hillside to settle their ghostly feuds. And even as he looked the mantle of one blew apart, and a glimpse of something strange and white appeared beneath. This was sufficient for the tailor. With a gasp he turned to the hill and climbed it like a deer, moaning to himself in his terror. Over the crest he went and down the other slope, flying wildly over little craigs, diving headlong every now and again into tussocks of bent, or struggling in a maze of birches. Then, or ever he knew, he was again among horrors. A woman with a fluttering white robe stood before him, and by her a man of strange appearance and uncanny height. He had no time to think, but his vague impression was of sheeted ghosts and awful terrors. His legs failed, his breath gave out at last, and he was floundering helplessly at Miss Phyllis' feet.

Meantime, as the young man and the girl gazed mutely at this new visitant, there entered from the left another intruder, clad in homespun, with a mighty crook in his hand and a short black pipe between his teeth. He raised his eyes slightly at the vision of the two, but heaven and earth did not contain what might disturb his composure. But at the sight of the prostate tailor he stopped short, and stared.

Slowly the thing dawned upon his brain. The sense of the ludicrous, which dwelled far down in his heart, was stirred to liveliness, and with legs apart he woke the echoes in boisterous mirth.

'God, but it's guid,' and he wiped his eyes on his sleeve. 'That man,' and again the humour of the situation shook him, 'that man thocht to frichten me wi' his ghaists and bogles, and look at him!'

The tailor raised his scared eyes to the newcomer. 'Dinna blaspheme, Jock Rorison,' he moaned with solemn unction. 'I hae seen it, the awfu' thing — twae men fechtin' a ghaistly battle, and yin o' them wi' the licht shinin' through his breistbane.'

'Hearken to him,' said the shepherd, jocularly. 'The wicked have digged a pit,' he began with dignity, and then farcically ended with 'and tumbled in 't themsel'.'

But Miss Phyllis thought fit to seek a clue to the mystery.

'Please tell me what is the meaning of all this,' she asked her companion.

'Why, the man has seen Callowa, and fled.'

'But he speaks of two and a "ghaistly combat".'

'Then Callowa with his usual luck has met the spirit of the place and fallen out with him. I think we had better go and see.'

But the tailor only shivered at the thought, till the long shepherd forcibly pulled him to his feet, and dragged his reluctant steps up the side of the hill.

The combat at the back of the knowe had gone on merrily enough till the advent of the tailor. Both were men of muscle, well-matched in height and years, and they wrestled with vigour and skill. The farmer was weary at the start, and his weariness was less fatigue than drowsiness, and as he warmed to his work he felt his strength returning. The Earl knew nothing of the game; he had not wrestled in his youth with strong out-of-door labourers, and his only resources were a vigorous frame and uncommon agility. But as the minutes passed and both breathed hard, the younger man began to feel that he was losing ground. He could scarce stand out against the strain on his arms, and his ankles ached with the weight which pressed on them.

Now it fell out that just as the tailor arrived on the scene the farmer made a mighty effort and all but swung his opponent from his feet. In the wrench that followed, the buttons on the Earl's light overcoat gave way, and to the farmer's astonished gaze an expanse of white shirtfront was displayed. For a second he relaxed his hold, while the other freed himself and leaped back to recover breath.

Slowly it dawned upon the farmer's intelligence that this was no cattle-dealer with whom he contended. Cattle-dealers do not habitually wear evening clothes when they have any work of guile on hand. And then gradually the flushed features before him awoke recognition. The next moment he could have sunk beneath the ground with confusion, for in this nightly marauder who had turned his sheep he saw no other than the figure of his master, the laird of all the countryside.

For a little the power of speech was denied him, and he stared blankly and shamefacedly while the Earl recovered his scattered wits. Then he murmured hoarsely, –

'I hope your lordship will forgi'e me. I never thocht it was yoursel', for I wad dae onything rather than lift up my hand against ye. I thocht it was an ill-daein' dealer frae east the country, whae has cheated me often, and I was vexed at his turnin' the sheep, seein' that I've had a lang day's wander.' Then he stopped, for he was a man of few words and he could go no further in apology.

Then the Earl, who had entered into the fight in a haphazard spirit, without troubling to enquire its cause, put the fitting end to the strained relations. He was convulsed with laughter, deep and over-powering. Little by little the farmer's grieved face relaxed, and he joined in the mirth, till these two made the silent place echo with unwonted sounds.

To them thus engaged entered a company of four, Miss Phyllis, the Sentimentalist, the shepherd, and the tailor. Six astonished human beings stood exchanging scrutinies under the soft moon. With the tailor the mood was still terror, with the shepherd careless amazement, and with the other two unquenchable mirth. For the one recognised the irate, and now apologetic, farmer of the Lowe Moss and the straggling sheep which told a tale to the observant; while both saw in the other of the dishevelled and ruddy combatants the once respect-able form of a friend.

Then spoke the farmer:–

'What's ta'en a' the folk? This knowe's like a kirk skailin'. And, dod, there's Jock Rorison. Is this your best road to the Redswirehead, Jock?'

But the shepherd and his friend were speechless for they had recognised their laird, and the whole matter was beyond their understanding.

'Now,' said Miss Phyllis, 'here's a merry meeting. I have seen more wonders tonight than I can quite comprehend. First, there comes Mr. Grey from nowhere in particular with a plaid on his shoulders; then a man with a scared face tumbles at our feet; then another comes to look for him; and now here you are, and you seem to have been fighting. These hills of yours are worse than any fairyland, and, do you know, they are rather exhausting.'

Meantime the Earl was solemnly mopping his brow and smiling on the assembly. 'By George,' he muttered, and then his breath failed him and he could only chuckle. He looked at the tailor, and the sight of that care-ridden face again choked him with laughter.

'I think we have all come across too many spirits tonight,' he said, 'and they have been of rather substantial flesh and bone. At least so I found it. Have you learned much about the future, Miss Phyllis?'

The girl looked shyly at her side. 'Mr. Grey has been trying to teach me,' said she.

The Earl laughed with great good-nature. 'Midsummer madness,' he said. 'The moon has touched us all.' And he glanced respectfully upward, where the White Huntress urged her course over the steeps of heaven.

The Earlier Affection

'The Earlier Affection' owes much to Buchan's three historical romances written during the 1890s – *Sir Quixote of the Moors*, *John Burnet of Barns* and most particularly his novel of the 1745 Rebellion, *A Lost Lady of Old Years*. It is taken from *Grey Weather* (1899).

———————

MY HOST ACCOMPANIED me to the foot of the fine avenue which looks from Portnacroish to the steely sea-loch. The smoke of the clachan was clear in the air, and the morn was sweet with young leaves and fresh salt breezes. For all about us were woods, till the moor dipped to the water, and then came the great shining spaces straight to the edge of Morven and the stony Ardgower Hills.

'You will understand, Mr. Townshend,' said my entertainer, 'that I do not fall in with your errand. It is meet that youth should be wild, but you had been better playing your pranks about Oxford than risking your neck on our Hieland hills, and this but two year come Whitsuntide since the late grievous troubles. It had been better to forget your mother and give your Cameron kin the go-by, than run your craig into the same tow as Ewan's by seeking him on Brae Mamore. Stewart though I be, and proud of my name, I would think twice before I set out on such a ploy. It's likely that Ewan will be blithe to see you and no less to get your guineas, but there are easier ways of helping a friend than just to go to his hidy-hole.'

But I would have none of Mr. Stewart's arguments, for my heart was hot on this fool's journey. My cousin Ewan was in the heather, with his head well-priced by his enemies and his friends dead or broken. I was little more than a boy let loose from college, and it seemed paradise itself to thus adventure my person among the wilds.

'Then if you will no take an old man's telling, here's a word for you to keep mind of on the road. There are more that have a grudge against the Cameron than King George's soldiers. Be sure there will be pickings going up Lochaber-ways, and all the Glasgow pack-men and low-country trading-bodies that have ever had their knife in Lochiel will be down on the broken house like a pack of kites. It's not impossible that ye may meet a wheen on the road, for I heard news of some going north from the Campbell country, and it bodes ill for any honest gentleman who may foregather with the black clan. Forbye, there'll be them that will come from Glenurchy-side and Breadalbin, so see you keep a quiet tongue and a watchful eye if ye happen on strangers.'

And with this last word I had shaken his hand, turned my horse to the north, and ridden out among the trees.

The sound of sea-water was ever in my ears, for the road twined in the links of coast and crooks of hill, now dipping to the tide's edge, and now rising to a great altitude amid the heather. The morn was so fresh and shining that I fell in love with myself and my errand, and when I turned a corner and saw a wall of blue hill rise gleaming to the heavens with snow-filled corries, I cried out for the fair land I had come to, and my fine adventure.

By the time I came to Duror it was mid-day, and I stopped for refreshment. There is an inn in Duror, where cheese and bread and usquebagh were to be had – fare enough for a hungry traveller. But when I was on the road again, as I turned the crook of hill by the Heugh of Ardsheal, lo! I was in the thick of a party of men.

They were five in all, dressed soberly in black and brown and grey, and riding the soberest of beasts. Mr. Stewart's word rose in my memory, and I shut my mouth and composed my face to secrecy. They would not trouble me long, this covey of merchant-folk, for they would get the ferry at Ballachulish, which was not my road to Brae Mamore.

So I gave them a civil greeting, and would have ridden by, had not Fate stepped in my way. My horse shied at a stick by the roadside, and ere I knew I was jostling and scattering them, trying to curb the accursed tricks of my beast.

After this there was nothing for it but to apologise, and what with my hurry and chagrin I was profuse enough. They looked at me with startled eyes, and one had drawn a pistol from his holster, but when they found I was no reiver they took the thing in decent part.

'It's a sma' maitter,' said one with a thick burr in his voice. 'The hert o' a man and the hoofs o' a horse are controlled by nane but our Maker, as my father aye said. Ye're no to blame, young sir.'

I fell into line with the odd man – for they rode in pairs, and in common civility. I could not push on through them. As I rode behind I had leisure to look at my company. All were elderly men, their ages lying perhaps between five and thirty and twoscore, and all rode with the air of townsmen out on a holiday. They talked gravely among themselves, now looking at the sky (which was clouding over, as is the fashion in a Highland April), and now casting inquiring glances towards my place at the back. The man with whom I rode was a little fellow, younger than the rest and more ruddy and frank of face. He was willing to talk, which he did in a very vile Scots accent which I had hard work to follow. His name he said was Macneil, but he knew nothing of the Highlands, for his abode was Paisley. He questioned me of myself with some curiosity.

'Oh, my name is Townshend,' said I, speaking the truth at random, 'and I have come up from England to see if the report of your mountains be true. It is a better way of seeing the world, say I, than to philander through Italy and France. I am a quiet man of modest means with a taste for the picturesque.'

'So, so,' said the little man. 'But I could show you corn-rigs by the Cart side which are better and bonnier than a wheen muckle stony hills. But every man to his taste, and doubtless, since ye're an Englander, ye'll no hae seen mony brae-faces?'

Then he fell to giving me biographies of each of the travellers, and as we were some way behind the others he could speak without fear. 'The lang man in the grey coat is the Deacon o' the Glesca Fleshers, a man o' great substance and good repute. He's lang had trouble wi' thae Hieland bodies, for when he bocht nowt frae them they wad seek a loan of maybe mair than the price, and he wad get caution on some o' their lands and cot-houses. 'Deed, we're a' in that line, as ye micht say'; and he raked the horizon with his hand.

'Then ye go north to recover monies?' said I, inadvertently.

He looked cunningly into my face, and, for a second, suspicion was large in his eyes. 'Ye're a gleg yin, Mr. Townds, and maybe our errand is just no that far frae what ye mean. But, speaking o' the Deacon, he has a grand-gaun business in the Trongate, and he has been elder this sax year in the Barony, and him no forty year auld. Laidly's his name, and nane mair respeckit among the merchants o' the city. Yon ither man wi' him is a Maister Graham, whae comes frae the Menteith way, a kind o' Hielander by bluid, but wi' nae Hieland tricks in his heid. He's a sober wud-merchant at the Broomielaw, and he has come up here on a job about some fir-wuds. Losh, there's a walth o' timmer in this bit,' and he scanned greedily the shady hills.

'The twae lang red-heided men are Campbells, brithers, whae deal in yairn and wabs o' a' kind in the Saltmarket. Gin ye were wantin' the guid hamespun or the fine tartan in a' the clan colours ye wad be wise to gang there. But I'm forgetting ye dinna belang to thae pairts ava'.'

By this time the heavens had darkened to a storm and the great rain-drops were already plashing on my face. We were now round the ribs of the hill they call Sgordhonuill and close to the edge of the Leven loch. It was a desolate, wild place, and yet on the very brink of the shore amid the birk-woods we came on the inn and the ferry.

I must needs go in with the others, and if the place was better than certain hostels I had lodged in on my road – notably in the accursed land of Lorne – it was far short of the South. And yet I dare not deny the comfort, for there was a peat-fire glowing on the hearth and the odour of cooking meat was rich for hungry nostrils. Forbye, the out-of-doors was now one pour of hail-water, which darkened the evening to a murky twilight.

The men sat round the glow after supper and there was no more talk of going further. The loch was a chaos of white billows, so the ferry was out of the question; and as for me, who should have been that night on Glen Leven-side, there was never a thought of stirring in my head, but I fell into a deep contentment with the warmth and a full meal, and never cast a look to the blurred window. I had not yet spoken to the others, but comfort loosened their tongues, and soon we were all on terms of gossip. They set themselves to find out every point in my career and my intentions, and I, mindful of Mr. Stewart's warning, grew as austere in manner as the Deacon himself.

'And ye say ye traivel to see the world?' said one of the Campbells. 'Man, ye've little to dae. Ye maunna be thrang at hame. If I had a son who was a drone like you, he wad never finger siller o' mine.'

'But I will shortly have a trade,' said I, 'for I shall be cutting French throats in a year, Mr. Campbell, if luck favours me.'

'Hear to him,' said the grave Campbell. 'He talks of war, bloody war, as a man wad talk of a penny-wedding. Know well, young man, that I value a sodger's trade lower than a flesher-lad's, and have no respect for a bright sword and a red coat. I am for peace, but when I speak, for battle they are strong,' said he, finishing with a line from one of his Psalms.

I sat rebuked, wishing myself well rid of this company. But I was not to be let alone, for the Deacon would play the inquisitor on the matter of my family.

'What brought ye here of a' places? There are mony pairts in the Hielands better worth seeing. Ye'll hae some freends, belike, hereaways?'

I told him, 'No,' that I had few friends above the Border; but the persistent man would not be pacified. He took upon himself, as the elder, to admonish me on the faults of youth.

'Ye are but a lad,' said he with unction, 'and I wad see no ill come to ye. But the Hielands are an unsafe bit, given up to malignants and papists and black cattle. Tak your ways back, and tell your freends to thank the Lord that they see ye again.' And then he broke into a most violent abuse of the whole place, notably the parts of Appin and Lochaber. It was, he said, the last refuge of all that was vicious and wasteful in the land.

'It is at least a place of some beauty,' I broke in with.

'Beauty,' he cried scornfully, 'd'ye see beauty in black rocks and a grummly sea? Gie me the lown fields about Lanerick, and a' the kind canty south country, and I wad let your bens and corries alane.'

And then Graham launched forth in a denunciation of the people. It was strange to hear one who bore his race writ large in his name talk of the inhabitants of these parts as liars and thieves and good-for-nothings. 'What have your Hielands done,' he cried, 'for the well-being of this land? They stir up rebellions wi' papists and the French, and harry the lands o' the god-fearing. They look down on us merchants, and turn up their hungry noses at decent men, as if cheatry were mair gentrice than honest wark. God, I wad have the lot o' them shipped to the Indies and set to earn a decent living.'

I sat still during the torrent, raging at the dull company I had fallen in with, for I was hot with youth and had little admiration for the decencies. Then the Deacon, taking a Bible from his valise, declared his intention of conducting private worship ere we retired to rest. It was a ceremony I had never dreamed of before, and in truth I cannot fancy a stranger. First the company sang a psalm with vast unction and no melody. Then the Deacon read from some prophet or other, and finally we were all on our knees while a Campbell offered up a prayer.

After that there was no thought of sitting longer, for it seemed that it was the rule of these people to make their prayers the last article in the day. They lay and snored in their comfortless beds, while I, who preferred the safety of a chair to the unknown dangers of such bedding, dozed uneasily before the peats till the grey April morning.

Dawn came in with a tempest, and when the household was stirring and we had broken our fast, a storm from the north-west was all but tearing the roof from above our heads. Without, the loch was a chasm of mist and white foam, and waves broke hoarsely over the shore-road. The landlord, who was also the ferryman, ran about, crying the impossibility of travel. No boat could live a moment in that water, and unless our honours would go round the loch-head into Mamore there was nothing for it but to kick our heels in the public.

The merchants conferred darkly among themselves, and there was much shaking of heads. Then the Deacon came up to me with a long face.

'There's nothing for't,' said he, 'but to risk the loch-head and try Wade's road to Fort William. I dinna mind if that was to be your way, Mr. Townds, but it maun be ours, for our business winna wait; so if you're so inclined, we'll be glad o' your company.'

Heaven knows I had no further desire for theirs, but I dared not evade. Once in the heart of Brae Mamore I would find means to give them the slip and find the herd's shieling I had been apprised of, where I might get shelter and news of Ewan. I accepted with as cordial a tone as I could muster, and we set out into the blinding weather.

The road runs up the loch by the clachan of Ballachulish, fords the small stream of Coe which runs down from monstrous precipices, and then, winding round the base of the hill they call Pap of Glencoe, comes fairly into Glen Levin. A more desert place I have not seen. On all sides rose scarred and ragged hills; below, the loch gleamed dully like lead; and the howling storm shook the lone fir-trees and dazed our eyes with wrack. The merchants pulled their cloak-capes over their heads and set themselves manfully to the toil, but it was clearly not to their stomach, for they said scarcely a word to themselves or me. Only Macneil kept a good temper, but his words were whistled away into the wind.

All the way along that dreary brae-face we were slipping and stumbling cruelly. The men had poor skill in guiding a horse, for though they were all well-grown fellows they had the look of those who are better used to bare-leg, rough-foot walking than to stirrup and saddle. Once I had to catch the Deacon's rein and pull him up on the path, or without doubt he would soon have been feeding the ravens at the foot of Corrynakeigh. He thanked me with a grumble, and I saw how tight-drawn were his lips and eyebrows. The mist seemed to get into my brain, and I wandered befogged and foolish in this unknown land. It was the most fantastic misery: underfoot wet rock and heather, on all sides grey dripping veils of rain, and no sound to cheer save a hawk's scream or the crying of an old blackcock from the height, while down in the glen-bottom there was the hoarse roaring of torrents.

And then all of a sudden from the darkness there sprang out a gleam of scarlet, and we had stumbled on a party of soldiers. Some twenty in all, they were marching slowly down the valley, and at the sight of us they grew at once alert. We were seized and questioned till they had assured themselves of our credentials. The merchants they let go at once, but I seemed to stick in their throat.

'What are you after, sir, wandering at such a season north of the Highland line?' the captain of them kept asking.

When I told him my tale of seeking the picturesque he would not believe it, till I lost all patience under the treatment.

'Confound it, sir,' I cried, 'is my speech like that of a renegade Scots Jacobite? I thought my English tongue sufficient surety. And if you ask for a better you have but to find some decent military head-quarters where they will tell you that Arthur Townshend is gazetted ensign in the King's own regiment and will proceed within six months to service abroad.'

When I had talked him over, the man made an apology of a sort, but he still looked dissatisfied. Then he turned roundly on us. 'Do you know young Fassiefern?' he asked.

My companions disclaimed any knowledge save by repute, and even I had the grace to lie stoutly.

'If I thought you were friends of Ewan Cameron,' said he, 'you should go no further. It's well known that he lies in hiding in these hills, and this day he is to be routed out and sent to the place he deserves. If you meet a dark man of the middle size with two-three ragged Highlanders at his back, you will know that you have foregathered with Ewan Cameron and that King George's men will not be far behind him.'

Then the Deacon unloosed the bands of his tongue and spoke a homily. 'What have I to dae,' he cried, 'with the graceless breed of the Camerons? If I saw this Ewan of Fassiefern on the bent then I wad be as hot to pursue him as any redcoat. Have I no suffered from him and his clan, and wad I no gladly see every yin o' them clapped in the Tolbooth?' And with the word he turned to a Campbell for approval and received a fierce nod of his red head.

'I must let you pass, sirs,' said the captain, 'but if you would keep out of harm's way you will go back to the Levin shore. Ewan's days of freedom are past, and he will be hemmed in by my men here and a like party from Fort William in front, and outflanked on both sides by other companies. I speak to you as honest gentlemen, and I bid you keep a good watch for the Cameron, if you would be in good grace with the King.' And without more ado he bade his men march.

Our company after this meeting was very glum for a mile or two. The Deacon's ire had been roused by the hint of suspicion, and he grumbled to himself till his anger found vent in a free cursing of the whole neighbourhood and its people. 'Deil take them,' he cried, 'and shame that I should say it, but it's a queer bit where an honest man canna gang his ways without a red-coated sodger casting een at him.' And Graham joined his plaint, till the whole gang lamented like a tinker's funeral.

It was now about mid-day, and the weather, if aught, had grown fiercer. The mist was clearing, but blasts of chill snow drove down on our ears, and the strait pass before us was grey with the fall. In front lay the sheer mountains, the tangle of loch and broken rocks where Ewan lay hid, and into the wilderness ran our bridle-path. Somewhere on the hillside were sentries, somewhere on the road before us was a troop of soldiers, and between them my poor cousin was fairly enclosed. I felt a sort of madness in my brain, as I thought of his fate. Here was I in the company of Whig traders, with no power to warn him, but going forward to see his capture.

A desperate thought struck me, and I slipped from my horse and made to rush into the bowels of the glen. Once there I might climb unseen up the pass, and get far enough in advance to warn him of his danger. My seeing him would be the wildest chance, yet I might take it. But as I left the path I caught a tree-root and felt my heels dangle in the void. That way lay sheer precipice. With a quaking heart I pulled myself up, and made my excuse of an accident as best I could to my staring companions.

Yet the whole pass was traversed without a sight of a human being. I watched every moment to see the troop of redcoats with Ewan in their grip. But no redcoats came; only fresh gusts of snow and the same dreary ribs of hill. Soon we had left the pass and were out on a windy neck of mountain where hags and lochans gloomed among the heather.

And then suddenly as if from the earth there sprang up three men. Even in the mist I saw the red Cameron tartan, and my heart leapt to my mouth. Two were great stalwart men, their clothes drenched and ragged, and the rust on their weapons. But the third was clearly the gentleman – of the middle size, slim, dressed well though also in some raggedness. At the sight the six of us stopped short and gazed dumbly at the three on the path.

I rushed forward and gripped my cousin's hand. 'Ewan,' I cried, 'I am your cousin Townshend come north to put his back to yours. Thank God you are still unharmed'; and what with weariness and anxiety I had almost wept on his neck.

At my first step my cousin had raised his pistol, but when he saw my friendliness he put it back in his belt. When he heard of my cousinship his eyes shone with kindliness, and he bade me welcome to his own sorry country. 'My dear cousin,' he said, 'you have found me in a perilous case and ill-fitted to play the host. But I bid you welcome for a most honest gentleman and kinsman to these few acres of heather that are all now left to me.'

And then before the gaping faces of my comrades I stammered out my story. 'Oh, Ewan, there's death before and behind you and on all sides. There's a troop waiting down the road and there are dragoons coming at your back. You cannot escape, and these men with me are Whigs and Glasgow traders, and no friends to the Cameron name.'

The three men straightened themselves like startled deer.

'How many passed you?' cried Ewan.

'May be a score,' said I.

He stopped for a while in deep thought.

'Then there's not above a dozen behind me. There are four of us here, true men, and five who are no. We must go back or forward, for a goat could not climb these craigs. Well-a-day, my cousin, if we had your five whiggishly-inclined gentlemen with us we might yet make a fight for it.' And he bit his lip and looked doubtfully at the company.

'We will fight nane,' said the Deacon. 'We are men o' peace, traivelling to further our lawful calling. Are we to dip our hands in bluid to please a Hieland Jaicobite?' The two Campbells groaned in acquiescence, but I thought I saw a glint of something not peaceful in Graham's eye.

'But ye are Scots folk,' said Ewan, with a soft, wheedling note in his voice. 'Ye will never see a countryman fall into the hands of redcoat English soldiers?'

'It's the law o' the land,' said a Campbell, 'and what for should we resist it to pleesure you? Besides, we are merchants and no fechtin' tinklers.'

I saw Ewan turn his head and look down the road. Far off in the stillness of the grey weather one could hear the sound of feet on the hill-gravel.

'Gentlemen,' he cried, turning to them with a last appeal, 'you see I have no way of escape. You are all proper men, and I beseech you in God's name to help a poor gentleman in his last extremity. If I could win past the gentry in front, there would be the sea-coast straight before, where even now there lies a vessel to take me to a kinder country. I cannot think that loyalty to my clan and kin should be counted an offence in the eyes of honest men. I do not know whether you are Highland or Lowland, but you are at least men, and may God do to you as you do to me this day. Who will stand with me?'

I sprang to his side, and the four of us stood looking down the road, where afar off came into sight the moving shapes of the foe.

Then he turned again to the others, crying out a word in Gaelic. I do not know what it was, but it must have gone to their hearts' core, for the little man Macneil with a sob came running toward us, and Graham took one step forward and then stopped.

I whispered their names in Ewan's ear and he smiled. Again he spoke in Gaelic, and this time Graham could forbear no more, but with an answering word in the same tongue he flung himself from his horse and came to our side. The two red-headed Campbells stared in some perplexity, their eyes bright with emotion and their hands twitching towards their belts.

Meantime the sound of men came nearer and the game grew

desperate. Again Ewan cried in Gaelic, and this time it was low entreaty, which to my ignorant ears sounded with great pathos. The men looked at the Deacon and at us, and then with scarlet faces they too dropped to the ground and stepped to our backs.

Out of the mist came a line of dark weather-browned faces and the gleam of bright coats. 'Will you not come?' Ewan cried to the Deacon.

'I will see no blood shed,' said the man, with set lips.

And then there was the sharp word of command, and ere ever I knew, the rattle of shots; and the next moment we were rushing madly down on the enemy.

I have no clear mind of what happened. I know that the first bullet passed through my coat-collar and a second grazed my boot. I heard one of the Highlanders cry out and clap his hand to his ear, and then we were at death-grips. I used my sword as I could, but I had better have had a dirk, for we were wrestling for dear life, and there was no room for fine play. I saw dimly the steel of Ewan and the Highlanders gleam in the rain; I heard Graham roaring like a bull as he caught at the throat of an opponent. And then all was mist and madness and a great horror. I fell over a little brink of rock with a man a-top of me, and there we struggled till I choked the life out of him. After that I remember nothing till I saw the air clear and the road vacant before us.

Two bodies lay on the heath, besides the one I had accounted for in the hollow. The rest of the soldiers had fled down the pass, and Ewan had his way of escape plain to see. But never have I seen such a change in men. My cousin's coat was red and torn, his shoes all but cut from his feet. A little line of blood trickled over his flushed brow, but he never heeded it, for his eyes burned with the glory of battle. So, too, with his followers, save that one had a hole in his ear and the other a broken arm, which they minded as little as midge-bites. But how shall I tell of my companions? The two Campbells sat on the ground nursing wounds, with wild red hair dishevelled and hoarse blasphemy on their lips. Every now and then one would raise his head and cry some fierce word of triumph. Graham had a gash on his cheek, but he was bending his sword-point on the ground and calling Ewan his blood-brother. The little man Macneil, who had fought like a Trojan, was whimpering with excitement, rubbing his eyes, and staring doubtfully at the heavens. But the Deacon, that man of peace – what shall I say of him? He stood some fifty yards down the pass, peering through the mist at the routed fugitives, his naked sword red in his hand, his whole apparel a ruin of blood and mire, his neatly-dressed hair flying like a beldame's. There he stood hurling the maddest oaths. 'Hell!' he cried. 'Come back and I'll learn ye, my lads. Wait on, and I'll thraw every neck and give the gleds a feed this day.'

Ewan came up and embraced me. 'Your Whigamores are the very devil, cousin, and have been the saving of me. But now we are all in the same boat, so we had better improve our time. Come, lads!' he cried, 'is it for the seashore and a kinder land?'

And all except the Deacon cried out in Gaelic the word of consent, which, being interpreted, is 'Lead, and we follow.'

The Black Fishers

'The Black Fishers' is another ironical story from *Grey Weather* (1899) about the callousness and hypocrisy of life in Gledsmuir. The references to the Procurator-fiscal reading Maupassant could well apply to Buchan's uncle Willie, Town Clerk of Peebles, who had a great interest in Maupassant and introduced his nephew to the writer. Another Buchan enthusiasm of the moment was Ibsen – he had founded an Ibsen Society in his first year at Oxford – hence the mention of Hedda Gabler.

ONCE UPON A time, as the story goes, there lived a man in Gledsmuir, called Simon Hay, who had born to him two sons. They were all very proper men, tall, black-avised, formed after the right model of stalwart folk, and by the account of the place in fear of neither God nor devil. He himself had tried many trades before he found the one which suited his talent; but in the various professions of herd, gamekeeper, drover, butcher, and carrier he had not met with the success he deserved. Some makeshift for a conscience is demanded sooner or later in all, and this Simon could not supply. So he flitted from one to the other with decent haste, till his sons came to manhood and settled the matter for themselves. Henceforth all three lived by their wits in defiance of the law, snaring game, poaching salmon, and working evil over the green earth. Hard drinkers and quick fighters, all men knew them and loved them not. But with it all they kept up a tincture of reputability, foreseeing their best interest. Ostensibly their trade was the modest one of the small crofter, and their occasional attendance at the kirk kept within bounds the verdict of an uncensorious parish.

It chanced that in spring, when the streams come down steely-blue and lipping over their brims, there came the most halcyon weather that ever man heard of. The air was mild as June, the nights soft and clear, and winter fled hotfoot in dismay. Then these three girded

themselves and went to the salmon-poaching in the long shining pools
of the Callowa in the haughlands below the Dun Craigs. The place
was far enough and yet not too far from the town, so that an active
walker could go there, have four hours' fishing, and return, all well
within the confines of the dark.

On this night their sport was good, and soon the sacks were filled
with glittering backs. Then, being drowsy from many nights out o'
bed, they bethought them of returning. It would be well to get some
hours of sleep before the morning, for they must be up betimes to
dispose of their fish. The hardship of such pursuits lies not in the toil
but the fate which hardens expediency into necessity.

At the strath which leads from the Callowa vale to Gled they
halted. By crossing the ridge of hill they would save three good miles
and find a less frequented path. The argument was irresistible;
without delay they left the highway and struck over the bent and
heather. The road was rough, but they were near its end, and a serene
glow of conscious labour began to steal over their minds.

Near the summit is a drystone dyke which girdles the breast of the
hill. It was a hard task to cross with a great load of fish, even for the
young men. The father, a man of corpulent humours and maturing
years, was nigh choked with his burden. He mounted slowly and
painfully on the loose stones, and prepared to jump. But his foothold
was insecure, and a stone slipped from its place. Then something
terrible followed. The sack swung round from his neck, and brought
him headlong to the ground. When the sons ran forward he was dead
as a herring, with a broken neck.

The two men stood staring at one another in hopeless bewilder-
ment. Here was something new in their experience, a disturbing
element in their plans. They had just the atom of affection for the
fellow-worker to make them feel the practical loss acutely. If they
went for help to the nearest town, time would be lost and the salmon
wasted; and indeed, it was not unlikely that some grave suspicion
would attach to their honourable selves.

They held a hurried debate. At first they took refuge in mutual
recriminations and well-worn regrets. They felt that some such
sentiments were due to the modicum of respectability in their reputations. But their minds were too practical to linger long in such
barren ground. It was demanded by common feeling of decency that
they should have their father's body taken home. But were there any

grounds for such feeling? None. It could not matter much to their father, who was the only one really concerned, whether he was removed early or late. On the other hand, they had trysted to meet a man seven miles down the water at five in the morning. Should he be disappointed? Money was money; it was a hard world, where one had to work for beer and skittles; death was a misfortune, but not exactly a deterrent. So picking up the old man's sack, they set out on their errand.

It chanced that the shepherd of the Lowe Moss returned late that night from a neighbour's house, and in crossing the march dyke came on the body. He was much shocked for he recognised it well as the mortal remains of one who had once been a friend. The shepherd was a dull man and had been drinking; so as the subject was beyond his special domain he dismissed its consideration till some more convenient season. He did not trouble to inquire into causes – there were better heads than his for the work – but set out with all speed for the town.

The Procurator-fiscal had been sitting up late reading in the works of M. de Maupassant, when he was aroused by a constable, who told him that a shepherd had come from the Callowa with news that a man lay dead at the back of a dyke. The Procurator-fiscal rose with much grumbling, and wrapped himself up for the night errand. Really, he reflected with Hedda Gabler, people should not do these things nowadays. But, once without, his feelings changed. The clear high space of the sky and the whistling airs of night were strange and beautiful to a town-bred man. The round hills and grey whispering river touched his poetic soul. He began to feel some pride in his vocation.

When he came to the spot he was just in the mood for high sentiment. The sight gave him a shudder. The full-blown face ashen with the grip of death jarred on his finer sensibilities. He remembered to have read of just such a thing in the works of M. Guy. He felt a spice of anger at fate and her cruel ways.

'How sad!' he said; 'this old man, still hale and fit to enjoy life, goes out into the hills to visit a friend. On returning he falls in with those accursed dykes of yours; there is a slip in the darkness, a cry, and then – he can taste of life no more. Ah, Fate, to men how bitter a task-mistress,' he quoted with a far-off classical reminiscence.

The constable said nothing. He knew Simon Hay well, and guessed shrewdly how he had come by his death, but he kept his own counsel. He did not like to disturb fine sentiment, being a philosopher in a small way.

The two fishers met their man and did their business all in the most pleasant fashion. On their way they had discussed their father's demise. It would interfere little with their profits, for of late he had grown less strong and more exacting. Also, since death must come to all, it was better that it should have taken their father unawares. Otherwise he might have seen fit to make trouble about the cottage which was his, and which he had talked of leaving elsewhere. On the whole, the night's events were good; it only remained to account for them.

It was with some considerable trepidation that they returned to the town in the soft spring dawning. As they entered, one or two people looked out and pointed to them, and nodded significantly to one another. The two men grew hotly uncomfortable. Could it be possible? No. All must have happened as they expected. Even now they would be bringing their father home. His finding would prove the manner of his death. Their only task was to give some reason for its possibility.

At the bridge-end a man came out and stood before them.

'Stop,' he cried. 'Tam and Andra Hay, prepare to hear bad news. Your auld faither was fund this morning on the back o' Callowa hill wi' a broken neck. It's a sair affliction. Try and thole it like men.'

The two grew pale and faltering. 'My auld faither,' said the chorus. 'Oh ye dinna mean it. Say it's no true. I canna believe it, and him aye sae guid to us. What'll we dae wi'oot him?'

'Bear up, my poor fellows,' and the minister laid a hand on the shoulder of one. 'The Lord gave and the Lord has taken away.' He had a talent for inappropriate quotation.

But for the two there was no comfort. With dazed eyes and drawn faces, they asked every detail, fervently, feverishly. Then with faltering voices they told of how their father had gone the night before to the Harehope shepherd's, who was his cousin, and proposed returning in the morn. They bemoaned their remissness, they bewailed his kindness; and then, attended by condoling friends, these stricken men went down the street, accepting sympathy in every public.

Summer Weather

This is the first appearance of this story in print since publication in *Grey Weather* (1899) and looks forward to another tale, 'The Green Wildebeeste'.

IN A CERTAIN year the prices of sheep at Gledsmuir sank so low that the hearts of the farmers were troubled; and one – he of Clachlands – sought at once to retrieve his fortunes and accepted an understudy. This was the son of a neighbouring laird, a certain John Anthony Dean, who by way of preparing himself for the possession of a great moorland estate thought it well to learn something of the life of the place. He was an amiable and idyllic young man, whom I once had the pleasure of knowing well. His interest was centred upon the composition of elegant verses, and all that savoured of the poetic was endeared to his soul. Therefore he had long admired the shepherd's life from afar; the word 'pastoral' conjured up a fragrant old-time world; so in a mood pleasantly sentimental he embarked upon the unknown. I need not describe his attainments as sheep-farmer or shepherd; he scarcely learned the barest rudiments; and the sage master of Clachlands trusted him only when he wrought under his own vigilant eye. Most of his friends had already labelled him a good-natured fool, and on the whole I do not feel ready to dispute the verdict. But that on one occasion he was not a fool, that once at least Mr. John Anthony Dean rose out of his little world into the air of the heroic, this tale is written to show.

It was a warm afternoon in late June, and, his dog running at heel, he went leisurely forth to the long brown ridges of moor. The whole valley lay sweltering in torrid heat; even there, on the crest of a ridge, there was little coolness. The hills shimmered blue and indeterminate through the haze, and the waters of a little loch not a mile away seemed part of the colourless benty upland. He was dressed in light flannels and reasonable shoes – vastly unlike the professional home-spuns and hob-nailed boots; but even he felt the airless drought and the flinty, dusty earth underfoot, and moderated his pace accordingly.

He was in a highly cheerful frame of mind, and tranquil enjoyment shone in his guileless face. On this afternoon certain cousins were walking over from his father's lodge to visit him at his labours. He contemplated gaily the prospect of showing them this upland Arcady, himself its high-priest and guardian. Of all times afternoon was the season when its charm was most dominant, when the mellow light lay on the far lines of mountain, and the streams were golden and russet in the pools. Then was the hour when ancient peace filled all the land, and the bleat of sheep and the calling of birds were but parts of a primeval silence. Even this dried-up noon-day moor had the charm of an elder poetry. The hot smell of earth, the glare of the sun from the rocks, were all incidents in pastoral. Even thus, he mused, must the shepherds of Theocritus have lived in that land of downs where the sun-burnt cicala hummed under the brown grass.

Some two miles from home he came to the edge of a shallow dale in whose midst a line of baked pebbles and tepid pools broke the monotonous grey. The heat was overpowering, and a vague longing for cool woods and waters stole into his mind. But the thought that this would but add to the tan of his complexion gave him comfort. He pictured the scene of his meeting with his friends; how he would confront them as the bronzed and seasoned uplander with an indescribable glamour of the poetic in his air. He was the man who lived with nature amid the endless moors, who carried always with him the romance of the inexplicable and the remote.

Such pleasing thoughts were roughly broken in on by the sight of his dog. It was a finely-bred sheep-collie, a prize-taker, and not the least costly part of his equipment. Already once in that burning summer the animal had gone into convulsions and come out of them weak and foolish. Now it lay stiffened in exactly the same way, its tongue lolling feebly, and flecks of white on its parched jaw. His sensibilities were affected, and he turned from the pitiable sight.

When he looked again it was creeping after him with tail between legs and its coat damp with sweat. Then at the crossing of a gate he missed the sound of it and looked back. There it lay again, this time more rigid than before, apparently not far from the extremities of death. His face grew grave, for he had come to like the creature and he would regret its loss.

But even as he looked the scene changed utterly. The stiffness relaxed, and before he knew the dog was on its feet and coming towards him. He rubbed his eyes with sheer amazement; for the thing looked like an incarnate devil. Its eyes glowered like coals, and its red cavern of a mouth was lined with a sickening froth. Twice its teeth met with a horrid snap as it rushed straight for him at an incredible swiftness. His mind was all but numbed, but some instinct warned him against suffering the beast to cut him off from home. The far dyke was the nearer, but he chose to make rather for the one he had already crossed. By a hairbreadth he managed to elude the rush and let the thing pass, – then with a very white face and a beating heart he ran for his life.

By a kind chance the thing had run many yards ere it saw his flight. Then it turned and with great leaps like a greyhound made after him. He heard it turn, heard every bound, with the distinctness of uttermost fear. His terror was lest it should gain on him unknown, and overpower him before he had chance to strike. Now he was almost at the dyke; he glanced round, saw the thing not five yards from him, and waited. The great scarlet jaws seemed to rise in the air before him, and with all his power he brought his thick crook down full athwart them. There was something dead and unearthly about these mad jaws; he seemed to be striking lifeless yet murderous flesh, and even as his stick crashed on the teeth his heart was sick with loathing. But he had won his end; for a second the brute fell back, and he leaped on the dyke.

It was a place built of loose moor stones, and on one larger than the rest he took his stand. He dare not trust a further chase; here he must weary the thing out, or miserably perish. Meantime it was rising again, its eyes two blazing pools of fire. Two yards forward it dragged itself, then sprang clear at his throat. He struck with all his might, but the blow missed its forehead, and, hitting the gums, sufficed only to turn it slightly aside, so that it fell on the wall two feet on his left. He lashed at it with frenzied strength, till groaning miserably it rolled off and lay panting on the turf.

The sun blazed straight on his bare head (for he had lost his cap in the chase), and sweat blinded his eyes. He felt ill, giddy, and hopelessly sick of heart. He had seen nothing of madness before in man or animal; the thing was an awful mystery, a voiceless, incredible horror. What not two hours before had been a friendly, sensible collie now lay

[157]

blinking at him with devouring eyes and jaws where foam was beginning to be dyed with blood. He calculated mechanically on each jump, and as the beast neared him his stick fell with stiff, nerveless force. To tell the truth, the man was numb with terror; his impulse was to sink to the ground; had death faced him in any form less repulsive than this assuredly he would not have striven against it.

It is a weak figure of speech to say that to him each minute seemed of an hour's length. He had no clear sense of time at all. His one sensation was an overmastering horror which directed his aim almost without his knowledge. Three times the thing leaped on him; three times he struck, and it slipped with claws grating on the stone. Then it turned and raced round a circle of heather, with its head between its forepaws like a runaway horse. The man dropped on his knees to rest, looking intently at the circling speck, now far away, now not a dozen yards distant. He vainly hoped that it would tire or leave him; vainly, for of a sudden it made for the wall and he had barely time to get to his feet before it was upon him. This time he struck it down without difficulty, for it was somewhat exhausted; but he noted with new terror that instead of leaping and falling back with open jaws, its teeth had shut with a snap as it neared him. Henceforth he must ward more closely, or the teeth might graze his flesh.

But his strength was failing, and the accursed brute seemed to grow more active and incessant. His knees ached with the attitude, and his arm still trembled with utter fear. From what he told me himself, and from the known hours of his starting and returning, he must have remained not less than two hours perched on that scorching dyke. It is probable that the heat made him somewhat light-headed and that his feet shuffled on the granite. At any rate as the thing came on him with new force he felt the whole fabric crumble beneath him, and the next second was sprawling on his back amid a ruin of stones.

He was aware of a black body hurling on the top of him as he struck feebly in the air. For a moment of agony he waited to be torn, feeling himself beyond resistance. But no savage teeth touched him, and slowly and painfully he raised his head. To his amazement he saw the dog tearing across the moorland in the direction of home.

He was conscious at once of relief, safety, a sort of weak, hysterical joy. Then his delight ceased abruptly, and he scrambled to his feet with all haste. The thing was clearly running for the farm-town, and there in the stack-yard labourers were busied with building hay-ricks,

– the result of a premature summer. In the yard women would be going to and fro, and some of the Clachlands children playing. What if the mad brute should find its way thither! There could be no issue but the most dismal tragedy.

Now Mr. John Anthony Dean was, speaking generally, a fool, but for one short afternoon he proved himself something more. For he turned and ran at his utmost speed after the fleeing dog. His legs were cramped and tottering, he was weak with fear, and his head was giddy with the sun; but he strained every muscle as if he ran for his own life and not for the life of others. His wind was poor at the best, and soon he was panting miserably, with a parched throat and aching chest; but with set teeth he kept up the chase, seeing only a black dot vanishing across the green moorland.

By some strange freak of madness the brute stopped for a second, looked round and waited. Its pursuer was all but helpless, labouring many yards behind; and had it attacked, it could have met little resistance. The man's heart leaped to his mouth, but – and to his glory I tell it – he never slackened pace. The thing suffered him to approach it, he had already conjured up the awful prospect of that final struggle, when by another freak it turned and set off once more for home.

To me it seems a miracle that under that blazing sun he ever reached the farm; but the fact remains that when the dog three minutes later dashed into an empty yard, the man followed some seconds behind it. By the grace of God the place was void; only a stray hen cackled in the summer stillness. Without swerving an inch it ran for the stable and entered the open door. With a last effort the man came up on its heels, shut the bolt, and left it secure.

He scarcely felt that his toil was ended, so painful was his bodily exhaustion. He had never been a strong man in the common sense, and now his heart seemed bursting, his temples throbbed with pain, and all the earth seemed to dance topsy-turvy. But an unknown hardiness of will seemed to drive him on to see this tragic business to an end. It was his part to shoot the dog there and then, to put himself out of anxiety and the world out of danger. So he staggered to the house, found it deserted, – one and all being busy in the stack-yard, – took down the gun from above the mantelpiece, and, slipping a cartridge in each barrel, hurried out with shambling legs.

He looked in through the stable-window, but no dog was there.

Cautiously he opened the door, and peered into the blackness of the stalls, but he could see nothing; then, lifting his eyes by chance to the other window, he saw a sash in fragments and the marks of a sudden leap. With a wild horror he realised that the dog was gone.

He rushed to the hill-road, but the place was vacant of life. Then with a desperate surmise he ran to the path which led to the highway. At first he saw nothing, so unsettled was his vision; then something grew upon his sight, – a black object moving swiftly amid the white dust.

There was but one course for him. He summoned his strength for a hopeless effort, and set off down the long dazzling roadway in mad pursuit. By this path his cousins were coming; even now the brute might be on them, and in one moment of horror he saw the lady to whom he was devoted the prey of this nameless thing of dread. At this point he lost all control of his nerves; tears of weakness and terror ran over his face; but still he ran as fast as his failing strength suffered – faster, for an overmastering fear put a false speed into his limbs and a deceptive ease in his breast. He cried aloud that the beast might turn on him, for he felt that in any case his duration was but a thing of seconds. But he cried in vain, for the thing heeded him not but vanished into the wood, as he rounded the turn of hill.

Half-way down the descent is a place shaded with thick trees, cool, green, and mossy, a hermitage from the fiercest sun. The grass is like a shorn lawn, and a little stream tinkles in a bed of grey stones. Into this cold dell the man passed from the glare without, and the shock refreshed him. This, as it chanced, was his salvation. He increased his speed, still crying hoarsely the animal's name. When he came once more into the white dust the brute was not fifty yards from him, and as he yelled more desperately, it stopped, turned, saw him, and rushed back to the attack.

He fell on his knees from extreme weakness, and waited with his gun quivering at shoulder. Now it raked the high heavens, now it was pointed to the distant hills. His hand shook like a child's, and in his blindness he crushed the stock almost against his throat. Up the highway meantime came those ravening jaws, nearer and ever nearer. Like a flash the whole picture of the future lay before him, – himself torn and dying, the wild thing leaving him and keeping its old course till it met his friends, and then – more horror and death. And all hung on two cartridges and his uncertain aim.

His nervousness made him draw the trigger when the brute was still many yards away. The shot went clear over its head to spend itself in the empty air. In desperation he nuzzled the stock below his chin, holding it tight till he was all but choked, and waited blindly. The thing loomed up before him in proportions almost gigantic; it seemed to leap to and fro, and blot out the summer heavens. He knew he was crazy; he knew, too, that life was in the balance, and that a random aim would mean a short passage to another world. Two glaring eyes shone out of the black mass, the centre, as it were, of its revolutions. With all his strength he drew the point to them and fired. Suddenly the fire seemed to go out, and the twin lights were darkened.

When the party of pretty young women in summer raiment came up the path a minute later, they saw something dark in the mid-road, and on coming nearer found that it was their cousin. But he presented a strange appearance, for in place of the elegant, bronzed young man they knew, they found a broken-down creature with a bleeding throat and a ghastly face, sitting clutching a gun and weeping hysterically beside a hideous, eyeless dog with a shattered jaw which lay dead on the ground.

Such is the tale of Mr. John Anthony Dean and his doings on that afternoon of summer. Yet it must be told – and for human nature's sake I regret it – that his sudden flash into the heroic worked no appreciable difference on his ways. He fled the hill country that very month, and during the next winter published a book of very minor poetry (dedicated to his cousin, Miss Phyllis), which contained an execrable rondeau on his adventure, with the refrain – 'From Canine Jaws', wherein the author likened the dog to Cerberus, himself to 'strong Amphitryon's son', and wound up with grateful thanksgiving to the 'Muse' for his rescue. As I said before, it is not my business to apologise for Mr. Dean; but it is my privilege to note this proof of the heroic inconsistency of man.

The Oasis in the Snow

'The Oasis in the Snow' is another story of demon possession from *Grey Weather* (1899), unpublished for almost a century. The oasis in the snow turns out to be another example of *temenos*.

THIS TALE WAS told to me by the shepherd of Callowa, when I sheltered once in his house against an April snowstorm – for he who would fish Gled in spring must fear neither wind nor weather. The shepherd was a man of great height, with the slow, swinging gait, the bent carriage, the honest eyes, and the weather-tanned face which are the marks of his class. He talked little, for life is too lonely or too serious in these uplands for idle conversation; but when once his tongue was loosened, under the influence of friendship or drink, he could speak as I have heard few men ever talk, for his mind was a storehouse of forty years' experience, the harvest of an eye shrewd and observant. This story he told me as we sat by the fire, and looked forth every now and then drearily on the weather.

They crack about snaw-storms nowadays, and ken naucht about them. Maybe there's a wee pickle driftin' and a road blockit, and there's a great cry about the terrible storm. But, lord, if they had kenned o' the storms I've kenned o' they would speak a wee thing mair serious and respectfu'. And bodies come here i' the simmer and gang daft about the bonny green hills, as they ca' them, and think life here sae quate and peacefu', as if the folk here had nocht to dae but daunder roond their hills and follow their wark as trig and easy as if they were i' the holms o' Clyde and no i' the muirs o' Gled. But they dinna ken, and weel for them, how cauld and hungry and cruel are the hills, how easy a man gangs to his death i' thae braw glens, how the wind stings i' the morn and the frost bites at nicht, o' the bogs and sklidders and dreich hillsides, where there's life neither for man nor beast.

[162]

Weel, about this story, it was yince in a Februar' mony year syne that it a' happened, when I was younger and lichter on my feet and mair gleg i' the seein'.

Ye mind Doctor Crichton – he's deid thae ten 'ear, but he was a braw doctor in his time. He could cure when anither was helpless, and the man didna leeve whae wad ride further on less errand.

Now the doctor was terrible keen on fishin' and shootin' and a' manner o' sport. I've heard him say that there were three things he likit weel abune ithers. Yin was the back o' a guid horse, anither a guid water and a clear wast wind, and the third a snawy day and a shot at the white hares. He had been crakin' on me for mony a day to gang wi' him, but I was thrang that 'ear wi' cairtin' up hay for the sheep frae lower doon the glens and couldna dae't. But this day I had trystit to gang wi' him, for there had been a hard frost a' the week, and the hares on the hills wad be in graund fettle. Ye ken the way o' the thing. Yae man keeps yae side o' the hill and the ither the ither, and the beasts gang atween them, back and forrit. Whiles ye'll see them pop round the back o' a dyke and aff again afore ye can get a shot. It's no easy wark, for the skins o' the craturs are ill to tell frae the snawy grund, and a man taks to hae a gleg ee afore he can pick them oot, and a quick hand ere he can shoot. But the doctor was rale skilfu' at it and verra proud, so we set aff brisk-like wi' our guns.

It was snawin' lichtly when we startit, and ere we had gone far it begood to snaw mair. And the air was terrible keen, and cut like a scythe-blade. We were weel wrappit up and walkit a' our pith, but our fingers were soon like to come off, and it was nane sae easy to handle the gun. We tried the Wildshaw Hichts first, and got nane there, though we beat up and doon, and were near smoored wi' snaw i' the gullies. I didna half like the look o' things, for it wasna canny that there should be nae hares, and, forbye, the air was gettin' like a rusty saw to the face. But the doctor wad hear naething o' turnin' back, for he had plenty o' speerit, had the man, and said if we didna get hares on yae hill we wad get them on the ither.

At that time ye'll mind that I had twae dowgs, baith guid but verra contrar' in natur'. There was yin ca'ed Tweed, a fine, canty sort o' beast, very freendly to the bairns, and gien to followin' me to kirk and things o' that sort. But he was nae guid for the shootin', for he was mortal feared at the sound o' a gun, and wad rin hame as he were shot. The ither I ca'ed Voltaire, because he was terrible against releegion.

On Sabbath day about kirk-time he gaed aff to the hills, and never lookit near the hoose till I cam back. But he was a guid sheep dowg and, forbye, he was broken till the gun, and verra near as guid 's a retriever. He wadna miss a day's shootin' for the warld, and mony a day he's gane wi'oot his meat ower the heid o't. Weel, on this day he had startit wi' us and said nae words about it; but noo he began to fa' ahint, and I saw fine he didna like the business. I kenned the dowg never did onything wi'oot a guid reason, and that he was no easy to fricht, so I began to feel uneasy. I stopped for a meenute to try him, and pretended I was gaun to turn hame. He cam rinnin' up and barkit about my legs as pleased as ye like, and when I turned again he looked awfu' dowie.

I pointed this oot to the doctor, but he paid nae attention. 'Tut, tut,' says he, 'if ye're gaun to heed a dowg's havers, we micht gie a' thing up at yince.'

'It's nae havers,' I said, hot-like, for I didna like to hear my dowg misca'ed. 'There's mair sense in that beast than what's in a heap o' men's heids.'

'Weel, weel,' he says, 'sae let it be. But I'm gaun on, and ye can come or no, just as ye like.'

'Doctor,' says I again, 'ye dinna ken the risk ye're rinnin'. I'm a better juidge o' the wather than you, and I tell ye that I'm feared at this day. Ye see that the air is as cauld 's steel, and yet there's mist a' in front o' ye and ahint. Ye ken the auld owercome, "Rouk is snaw's wraith," and if we dinna see a fearsome snaw afore this day's dune, I'll own my time's been wastit.'

But naething wad move him, and I had to follow him for fair shame. Sune after, too, we startit some hares, and though we didna get ony, it set the excitement o' the sport on us. I sune got as keen as himsel', and sae we trampit on, gettin' farther intil the hills wi' every step, and thinkin' naething about the snaw.

We tried the Gledscleuch and got naething, and syne we gaed on to the Allercleuch, and no anither beast did we see. Then we struck straucht for the Cauldhope Loch, which lies weel hoddit in hills miles frae ony man. But there we cam nae better speed, for a' we saw was the frozen loch and the dowie threshes and snaw, snaw everywhere, lyin' and fa'in'. The day had grown waur, and still that dour man wadna turn back. 'Come on,' says he, 'the drift's clearin', and in a wee we'll be on clear grund'; and he steppit oot as he were on the laigh road. The air wasna half as cauld, but thick just like a nicht in hairst; and though there wasna muckle snaw fa'in' yet, it felt as though there were miles o' 't abune in the cluds and pressin' doun to the yirth. Forbye, it was terrible sair walkin', for though the snaw on the grund wasna deep, it was thick and cloggin'. So on we gaed, the yin o' us in high fettle, the ither no verra carin', till we cam to the herd's shielin' o' the Lanely Bield, whilk lies in the very centre o' the hills, whaur I had never been afore.

We chappit at the door and they took us in. The herd was a dacent man, yin Simon Trumbull, and I had seen him aften at kirk and market. So he bade us welcome, and telled us to get our claes dried, for we wadna gang anither step that nicht. Syne his wife made us tea, and it helpit us michtily, for we had drank a' our whisky lang syne. They had a great fire roarin' up the lum, and I was sweired, I can tell ye, to gang oot o' the warm place again into the ill wather.

But I must needs be aff if I was to be hame that nicht, and keep my wife from gaun oot o' her mind. So I gets up and buttons to my coat.

'Losh, man,' says the herd, 'ye're never thinkin' o' leavin'. It'll be the awfu'est nicht that ever man heard tell o'. I've herdit thae hills this mony 'ear, and I never saw sic tokens o' death i' the air. I've my sheep fauldit lang syne, and my hoose weel stockit, or I wadna bide here wi' an easy hert.'

'A' the mair need that I should gang,' says I, 'me that has naething dune. Ye ken fine my wife. She wad die wi' fricht, if I didna come hame.'

Simon went to the door and opened it. It blew back on the wa', and a solid mass o' snaw fell on the floor. 'See that,' he says. 'If ye dinna believe me, believe your ain een. Ye need never think o' seein' Callowa the nicht.'

'See it or no,' said I, 'I'll hae to try 't. Ye'd better bide, doctor; there's nae cause for you to come wi' me.'

'I'll gang wi' you,' he said. 'I brocht ye intil this, and I'll see ye oot o't.' And I never liked the man sae weel as at the word.

When the twae o' us walkit frae that hoose it was like walkin' intil a drift o' snaw. The air was sae thick that we couldna richt see the separate flakes. It was just a great solid mass sinkin' ever doun, and as heavy as a thousand ton o' leid. The breath went frae me at the verra outset. Something clappit on my chest, and I had nocht to dae but warstle on wi' nae mair fushion than a kittlin'. I had a grip o' the doctor's hand, and muckle we needit it, for we wad sune hae been separate and never mair heard o'. My dowg Voltaire, whae was gien for ordinar' to rinnin' wide and playin' himsel', kept close rubbin' against my heels. We were miles frae hame, and unless the thing cleared there was sma' chance o' us winnin' there. Yae guid thing, there was little wind, but just a saft, even fa'; so it wasna so bad as though it had been a fierce driftin'. I had a general kind o' glimmer o' the road, though I had never been in thae hills afore. If we held doun by the Lanely Bield Burn we wad come to the tap o' the Stark Water, whilk cam into Gled no a mile abune Callowa. So on we warstled, prayin' and greetin' like bairns, wi' scarce a thocht o' what we were daein'.

'Whaur are we?' says the doctor in a wee, and his voice sounded as though he had a naipkin roond his mouth.

'I think we should be somewhere near the Stark heid,' said I. 'We're gaun doun, and there's nae burn hereaways but it.'

'But I aye thocht the Stark Glen was a' sklidders at the heid,' said he; 'and this is as saft a slope as a hoose riggin'.'

'I canna help that,' says I. 'It maun e'en be it, or we've clean missed the airt.'

So on we gaed again, and the snaw aye got deeper. It wasna awfu' saft, so we didna sink far as we walkit, but it was terrible wearin'. I sune was sae tired that I could scarce drag mysel'; forbye being frichtit oot o' my senses. But the doctor was still stoot and hopefu', and I just followed him.

Suddenly, ere ever we kenned, the slope ceased, and we were walkin' on flat grund. I could scarce believe my een, but there it was at my feet, as laigh as a kitchen floor. But the queer thing was that while a' around was deep snaw, this place was a' but bare, and here and there rigs o' green land stuck oot.

'What in the warld's this?' says I, as I steppit oot boldly, and I turned to my companion. When I saw him I was fair astonished. For his face was white as the snaw, and he was tremblin' to his fingers.

'Ye're no feared, are ye?' I asked. 'D' ye no ken guid land when ye see 't?"

His teeth were chattering in his heid. 'You hae na sense to be feared. The Almichty help us, but I believe we're daein' what nae man ever did afore.'

I never saw sae queer a place. The great wecht o' snaw was still fa'in' on us, but it seemed to disappear when it cam to the grund. And our feet when we steppit aye sank a wee bit, but no in snaw. The feel i' the air wasna cauld, but if onything 't was het and damp. The sweat began to rin doon aff my broo, and I could hear the man ahint me pantin' like a broken-winded horse. I lookit roond me for the dowg, but nae dowg was to be seen; for at the first step we took on the queer land he had ta'en himsel' aff. I didna like the look o't, for it wad hae ta'en muckle to drive the beast frae my side.

Every now and then we cam on a wee hillock whaur the snaw lay deeper, but the spaces atween were black and saft, and crunkled aneath the feet. Ye ken i' the spring about the burn-heids how the water rins oot o' the grund, and a' the colour o' the place is a sodden grey. Weel, 't was the same here. There was a seepin', dreepin' feel i' the grund whilk made it awesome to the eye. Had I been i' my clear senses, I wad hae been rale puzzled about the maitter, but I was donnered wi' the drifts and the weariness, and thocht only o' gettin' by 't. But sune a kind o' terror o' the thing took me. Every time my feet touched the grund, as I walkit, a groo gae'd through my body. I grat wi' the fair hate o' the place, and when I lookit at my neebor it didna mak me better. For there he was gaun along shakin' like a tree-tap, and as white 's a clout. It made it waur that the snaw was sae thick i' the air that we couldna see a foot in front. It was like walkin' blindfold roond the tap o' a linn.

Then a' of a sudden the bare grund stopped, and we were flounderin' among deep drifts up to the middle. And yet it was a relief, and my hert was strengthened. By this time I had clean lost coont o' the road, but we keepit aye to the laigh land, whiles dippin' intil a glen and whiles warstlin' up a brae face. I had learned frae mony days in hill mists to keep frae gaun roond about. We focht our way like fair deevils, for the terror o' the place ahint had grippit us like a vice. We ne'er spak a word, but wrocht till our herts were like to burst and our een felt fou o' bluid. It got caulder and caulder, and thicker and ever thicker. Hope had lang syne gane frae us, and fricht had ta'en its place. It was just a maitter o' keepin' up till we fell down, and then . . .

It wasna lang ere they fund us, for find us they did, by God's grace and the help o' the dowg. For the beast went hame and made sic a steer that my wife roused the nearest neebor and got folk startit oot to seek us. And wad ye believe it, the dowg took them to the verra bit. They fund the doctor last, and he lay in his bed for a month and mair wi' the effects. But for mysel', I was nane the waur. When they took me hame, I was put to bed, and sleepit on for twenty hoor, as if I had been streikit oot. They waukened me every six hoor, and put a spoonfu' o' brandy doon my throat, and when a' was feenished, I rase as weel as ever.

It was about fower months after that I had to gang ower to Annandale wi' sheep, and cam back by the hills. It was a road I had never been afore, and I think it was the wildest that ever man trod. I mind it was a warm, bricht day, verra het and wearisome for the walkin'. Bye and bye I cam to a place I seemed to ken, though I had never been there to my mind, and I thocht hoo I could hae seen it afore. Then I mindit that it was abune the heid o' the Stark, and though the snaw had been in my een when I last saw it, I minded the lie o' the land and the saft slope. I turned verra keen to ken what the place was whaur me and the doctor had had sic a fricht. So I went oot o' my way, and climbed yae hill and gaed doun anither, till I cam to a wee rig, and lookit doun on the verra bit.

I just lookit yince, and then turned awa' wi' my hert i' my mooth.

For there below was a great green bog, oozing and blinking in the sun.

Gideon Scott

This unpublished story was found amongst Buchan's papers in the National Library of Scotland by Kate Love and has hitherto only appeared in *The John Buchan Journal*.

Gideon Scott is landlord of the Crook Inn, a Border inn that Buchan often frequented and which figures in several stories.

IF ANYONE SHOULD travel up the pleasant valley of Tweed from Peebles, some distance up on the right hand bank of the river he would see a green spur on the side of a dark heath-clad hill. And if he were inclined to examine it further, he would find on the summit the ruins of what was once a castle. Across the river, among the trees, he would see a grey ivy-covered wall. These few stones are all that remain of two famous castles, the abode of a still more remarkable family. The Tweedies of Tinnis and Drumelzier were one of the oldest families in Scotland. They derived their name and origin from the genius, or water spirit of Tweed. For centuries they lorded over the whole district of Upper Tweeddale. But in more civilized times, like many other noble families, they got into debt, and in the beginning of the seventeenth century we find the last of the clan in a debtors' prison in Edinburgh. The estates passed into other hands, and the place where once they were now knows them no more.

I

One of these spring days in which winter had completely got the predominance of summer was merging into darkness and the light of day was gradually leaving the kitchen of the Crook Inn to make way for the more cheerful light of the fire. The Crook Inn, as all travellers between Edinburgh and Dumfries know, is situated on the top of the high bank of the Tweed, a few miles below its junction with the Talla.

It was the haunt of all the drovers who came from the south to the Scottish fairs, and every other day the mail coach stopped to change horses. Now and then a shepherd or a farmer dropped in or a belated traveller in that stormy region. On this particular night several shepherds from the hills, a sprinkling of drovers and two men, who by their dress appeared to be travelling chapmen, thronged around the ample fireplace in the inn kitchen. The great black oak rafters were plentifully adorned with smoked hams, shoulders of beef and white hares, as beseemed the season of the year. One of the shepherds got up and opened the door. A great blast blew in with a few raindrops.

'What kind o' nicht is it, shepherd?' said one of the packmen.

'Nae nicht for me to get back to the Hopehead in,' was the surly answer. The great black clouds were coming thick over the sky, while on the horizon a grey vapour was slowly arising. The hills looked near and black. The roar of the Tweed, swollen high by recent rains, came up above the noise of the wind. The shepherd slammed the door, let down the bar which closed it, and returned once more to his seat at the fire.

'There's nae lack o' wet weather in the air,' said he. 'There'll be nae crossing Tweed the nicht, and less the morn. It's a guid thing Biggar fair is past, and I have my stock sell't.'

'It will be a bad look out for us,' said one of the drovers, 'we'll never see Dumfries this week.'

'It's a providence for me,' said the landlord of the inn, Gideon Scott by name, a big burly man of about forty, with a shrewd, quiet face, 'it's a clear godsend that I havena' to go to Edinburgh this month. Ye ken I have to go in every month in the way of business. But who should be going in this week but Jamie Hislop my wife's brother, so he got my commission, and, being a man of his word, I can lippen to him. It's an awful time this to travel in. Just in this week last year the coach fell over the Blyth Bridge and killed two passengers. And the driver of the mail told me that there is a tale of terrible robberies in the Lothians, and even hinted that the Dumfries coach hersel wasna over safe. Lord preserve Jamie Hislop and my commission.'

By this time the candles had been brought in and set down on the high oak dressser. At this period the shepherd of Kingledores rose to go, and a tall dark man, who stood by the fireplace and was evidently a shepherd, rose to follow him. The latter man was by far the most striking-looking in the company. He was dressed in rough home-spuns, marked here and there with spots of tar and tufts of wool from his recent operations with sheep at Biggar fair. His face was tanned brown with the weather but there was a certain nobility, not so often found among shepherds, in his clear cut features and proud bearing. He must have been considerably over six feet high, and his brawny legs, broad shoulders, and muscular arms showed that he possessed great bodily strength. As he rose to go he picked up his stout horn-handled stick and whistled on his dog which was lying below the table.

'Yeddie, Yeddie,' cried the host in astonishment, 'guidsakes, man, you're no going to try to get to Talla the nicht. No mortal man could get halfway.'

'Psa, what's a blast o' rain to me, Gidden, it's no' the first time I been out in it.'

'Sit down, ye loon,' said the host angrily, 'I'll let no man go away frae my hoose the nicht. It wisna' half sic an ill nicht last Martinmas when Tam Laidlaw, the herd of Stanhope, was drowned trying to cross the ford down there. Ye ken the bridge was washed away wi' the last flood and ye'll never ford the river when it is like this.'

'It maun be done,' said Yeddie, as without another word he wrapped his plaid around his shoulders and went out into the night.

'An obstinate mule if ever there was one,' said the landlord. 'Aweel, he'll wish he had taen my advice when he finds himself in the Black Linn.' Supper, which two centuries ago was taken at a much earlier hour than in our times, was now set on the table. The company took their seats before viands which were admirably adapted to satisfy hungry men – a salmon from the Tweed, a piece of black-faced mutton from the hills, and a large bowl of porridge, which stood at one end of the table and from which platefuls were ladled out to each man. When the supper was finished, a large china bowl, a number of glasses and a silver ladle were brought in and the landlord proceeded to brew a bowl of toddy. It was served round to the guests and, as their glasses were replenished pretty frequently, their spirits became somewhat exuberant. One of the packmen entered upon a lengthy tale, stopping every now and then to laugh loudly at some joke, which the company invariably failed to appreciate. As a diversion a drover sang a bacchanalian song very popular in that part of the country, and the rest took up the chorus, which emphatically declared that they had hitherto trusted to Providence and would still continue to do it. Then a draught board was produced and one of the shepherds and the sober packman played a game. The other drovers produced a dirty pack of cards and began to play for money. The rest of the shepherds, who cared for none of these things, sat down round the fire with the host and discussed the prices of sheep and the prospects of the weather. Gideon had been somewhat gloomy all the evening. He had failed to enter heartily into the mirth at the supper table, and had talked to his guests with the air of a man performing a disagreeable duty. Now he broke in upon the conversation with an abrupt question:

'What in the world made Yeddie tak' the road for Talla the nicht?'

'I'm sure I dinna ken, Gidden,' said one of the shepherds who hailed from Moffat Water, 'he's a queer body, is Yeddie, but when once he's set his heart on onything, I'd like to see the man that wad stop him.'

'There's ower mony o' his kind in the country the noo, and we could weel be rid o' half o' them. Restless, peppery chiels, wha canna bide to hear a word against them. I saw a better man hang't in the Grassmarket afore I left Edinburgh.'

'I am no caring what he is, but I wish he hadna' tried the Tweed the nicht.'

There was silence for a while, broken only by the crackling of the wood in the fire and the howling of the storm outside. Then came a gust of wind stronger than the rest and with a crash the door was blown open. Up jumped Gideon to shut the door, while the candles were almost blown out by the violence of the blast.

'Guidsakes, come and look at the water!' roared the astonished landlord.

One or two shepherds came, the rest being either too drunk or too busy to attend. They looked out from the door porch and a wonderful sight met their eyes. The Tweed had burst the barriers of its banks and was bearing down the valley a wilderness of swirling yellow water. The roar was like that of the North Sea in the winter storms. Trunks of trees and broken fragments of wooden bridges floated on the surface. Far down the glen a line of white foam marked where the river plunged over the Black Linn. The air was almost free from rain, but the murky blackness in the southern sky told of a terrible rainfall further up the stream. Broad Law on the other side of the river was almost wholly enveloped in mist, the which stood out in peculiar contrast to the blackness of the moorlands beneath. They looked on for a few minutes in silence, then Gideon went into the kitchen again.

He took down his bonnet from a peg, wrapped a plaid round his shoulders and took a large ash stick which stood in the corner. He then put a flask of brandy in his pocket and rejoined his comrades at the door.

'I'm going doon to the ford to see if I can see onything o' Yeddie. Will ony o' ye come with me?'

Two shepherds, Wat Fletcher from Drumelzier and Robert Senton of Fruid, went out with him. Down the rough hillside they went for a few paces and then turned down the valley for about half a mile, gradually approaching nearer the river till they came to where a small cart track led down to the water's edge. Here was the ford, though on this night, ford there was none. A small rowan tree marked where the road began on the other side. Between them and this tree lay many yards of brown, unpassable water.

'If Yeddie tried the ford, he was drowned,' said Gideon in a mournful tone. For a considerable time they waited there scanning the stream and shouting the name of the lost shepherd. Then they began sadly to go away when a dog's barking came on their ear. They listened and waited. Again it was heard further down the river.

'I could swear onywhere that that was Maisie's bark,' said Fletcher.

'If that's Yeddie's dog, Yeddie's no' far off,' said Rob Senton. Quickly, with Gideon in front, they rushed down the bank of the Tweed, guided by the barking of the dog. They were now close upon that terrible fall, known all over the district as the Black Linn. The waters of the Tweed rush into a narrow channel, with high precipitous rocks on both sides. Then the river dashes over a linn some thirty feet high, into a deep black pool, from which the fall gets its name. The pool is thickly fringed with hazel and rowan trees, many bending far over the water. On the banks they found a small collie, black and tan in colour, rushing up and down the grass, barking wildly. When it saw the three men, it immediately made for them and, crouching at their feet, whined and moaned in the most piteous manner. Then it sprang up again and rushed along the bank, every now and then looking back to see that it was followed. At last it reached a gap in the trees above where the river made a turn. An old oak, knotted and gnarled with very age ran out into the water, bending its boughs close to the stream. Here the collie stopped and with one long-drawn howl attempted to crawl along a bough of the oak. Gideon caught it by the tail and swung it back, for he had caught a glimpse of something at the end of the branch which moved him to rapid action. The current had washed down a large wooden plank, probably from some ruined bridge, against an arm of the oak. Wedged in between the tree and the plank, with his legs in the water, was the unconscious form of Yeddie. Knowing that there was not a moment to lose, since at any moment the stream might wash away the plank, Gideon flung off his plaid, and prepared to crawl along the bough. Slowly and painfully he made his way, with the wood creaking at every movement. Sometimes he lost his footing and clutched the branch to save himself. Sometimes a larger wave than usual washed over his legs. At last he was within reach, and was able to grip the shepherd's coat. But now a new difficulty faced him. He could not re-cross the branch with such a burden in his arms. There was no alternative but to leap into the flood and carry Yeddie with him. The tide was running hard, but he saw that it would carry him close to the bank which a strong man might catch. With a cry to the men to run for the turning he clutched Yeddie more tightly and slipped off the branch. The water surged over his head and he felt as if he would never rise again. But up he came and struck out boldly. The weight of his burden was a sad hindrance to him; without it he felt that he might have saved himself. Once more he sunk and once more he rose. The bank loomed black before, and he saw that now was his chance or never. With one great effort he clutched a tree root which projected, and felt himself being washed in towards the side: then two pairs of strong hands gripped him and he and his burden were lifted into safety.

Gideon was soon restored to himself by a mouthful of brandy, and then he turned to the man he had rescued. To bring him back to consciousness was a much more difficult task. He had abandoned the idea of crossing at the ford and attempted the river below the linn, where the breadth is not so great but that a strong man might leap over it. The attempt had failed and he had been carried down by the current. His head had been badly cut by a sharp rock and after being borne along for about a hundred yards he had been caught by the tree. Here, weak with fatigue and the loss of blood, he had been exposed for more than three hours with the water dashing over him.

At first, the treatment of Gideon and his men had no effect. But, after a time, through vigorous rubbing and repeated doses of brandy, their patient showed signs of consciousness. Then he opened his eyes and recovered so far as to be able to speak and thank his preservers. Weak and faint he was conveyed to the inn by the strong arms of the three men and there put to bed. But Yeddie was blessed with an iron constitution, and, though the night's adventures might have killed most men, they had little or no effect on him. In a week his cut was almost healed and he was able to proceed to his house at Talla.

II

The springtime had passed into the summer and the time of the long, hot days had come, when Gideon Scott made preparations for his journey to Edinburgh. This was always a great event to the household at the moorland inn. The night before the appointed day few of the inmates got any sleep, for the coach passed at three o'clock in the morning. On this occasion Gideon's journey was more important than usual, for he had to receive a sum of money which was owing him from a cattle dealer in Edinburgh, and had also resolved to buy an additional horse, on which he might make his journey home. Accordingly, early on Tuesday morning, when the fleecy mist had not yet lifted from the hilltops, and the sun was beginning to make himself seen over the hills of Kingledores, Gideon stood on the doorstep of the Crook Inn, accoutred for his journey. He had not waited long, when the lumbering, crazy old coach came round the turn of the hill, and drew up at the inn door. Gideon hoisted himself into it along with what little luggage he had, and soon was carried out of sight of his home. With what transpired till he reached Edinburgh we have little to do. Suffice it to say that he had an uneventful journey, unattended by any of the usual accidents which befell the unhappy coach; that he transacted his business in Edinburgh, bought his horse, and set out on his return journey. His purchase, which was a fine brown mare, had been warranted by Jock Scott, his cousin from whom he had bought it, to be able to outrun any animal in the Lothians. Gideon took his road through the village of Liberton and thence out into the pleasant valley of the Esk. Ere nightfall he arrived at Leadburn, where he put up for the night. Next morning he remembered an old friend of his who lived at Bordlands, whom he resolved to visit. Accordingly, he pushed on, and about midday arrived at Bordlands. His friend was of a sociable character, and prevailed upon him to stay longer than his better judgment required. Thus it came about that it was nearly six o'clock when he left Bordlands with the intention of reaching Broughton that night.

All went well until he passed through the little village of Kirkurd, and reached the wild moorland, which extends without a human dwelling to the village of Broughton, twelve miles away. Gideon rode on for a considerable distance until he became aware of three men riding at right angles to the highway. Whether it was the influence of the farmer of Bordlands' ale or not, I do not know, but Gideon instantly conceived the idea that these men intended to block the road. They might be highwaymen or they might not but he had heard of daring attacks lately and he had a large sum of money in his pocket, so he clapped spurs to his horse and rode at full speed along the highway. Now the three horsemen did a still more suspicious thing; they directed their horses for a point in the road where it made a sharp turn. Gideon felt that if he did not get to this place first he was a lost man, for he dare not trust himself to the bogs on the side of the road. He knew that his mare could hold her own on the highway, so he strained every nerve to get the lead. She responded gallantly to his calls, everything seemed to dance before Gideon's eyes; he saw only the white spot which marked where the bend was, and the black forms of his pursuers. Now to his joy he saw that he was gaining ground; the three horsemen saw this also and endeavoured with might and main to recover it. At last the turn was reached and with one great bound the mare swept round it with the three men about twelve yards behind her. Then began a race grim and long. The horses of the highwaymen though inferior in quality to Gideon's mare were very much fresher. The road from this point leads in an almost straight line down the valley of a small stream to the village of Broughton. It was now about nine o'clock and the dusk was creeping up the sky. Gideon felt faint and giddy; the landscape swam before his eyes, he dared not look behind him but he knew his pursuers were near. He wondered that no shot had been fired, but he concluded that they had no firearms. Now he could see the lights of Broughton twinkling through the gathering gloom six miles ahead. New courage grew up within him. He stood up in his stirrups and coaxed and patted his mare. She made one gallant effort more and gained other ten yards. Then she fell back again to her old pace. But now the highwaymen made a fresh effort also and Gideon felt with a sickening sense of terror that they were gaining on him. On and on they swept, gaining at every step. Now he could feel their horses' breath on the back of his neck. One more gallant effort the mare made, and increased the distance between them by a few yards. But it was her last; her breath came up in great pants; the gallop was changed to a canter, the canter to a trot, and the trot to a walk. Then, with a rush, the three horsemen dashed past the terror-stricken Gideon and caught his mare's bridle. The unhappy man gave himself up for lost, and thought woefully of the fate of his money, when an extraordinary thing happened. As soon as the leader cast his eyes on Gideon's face,

'Stand back,' he roared in a voice of thunder, 'and let him past.'

The highwaymen wheeled their horses round and galloped away, leaving the astonished Gideon to proceed on his way in safety. But by the dim light that remained, he had recognised in the leader of the three the saturnine features of Yeddie.

III

Gideon, one afternoon in the month of October, might be seen mounting his mare in the courtyard of the Cross Keys Inn at Peebles. He had come down from the hills for the autumn fair; for Gideon was a versatile man in his way, and in addition to his occupation of inn-keeper, he was a small sheep farmer. The day was one of those fine clear autumn days, with just a touch of frost in the air. As he rode along through the pleasant woods of Neidpath, his heart was glad within him, and he felt at peace with all men, that is with the exception of Robin the drover who had cheated him out of thirty pounds, at the last fair, at Biggar. Gideon was one of these men who remember an injury for about two months, and then forget it entirely. At first he had thought he would have liked to kill Robin, now he simply wished to make him pay back. On this special afternoon the air was the air of spring, and had it not been for the withered leaves one might have thought it March. Gideon crossed the bridge over the Lyne Water, then but newly erected, and remembered how he had to swim his horse over the stream the last time he came this road. Then he rode along through the rich meadows which make the valley of the Tweed at this point like a nobleman's estate. One would hardly have thought it the same river here gliding slowly through among high reeds and between banks as smooth as a lawn, as that which half a dozen miles further up tumbles and rushes among desolate brown

moors, and rocky hills. About five o'clock in the afternoon he
bethought himself that he was thirsty, and being near the little village
of Stobo, he resolved to pay a visit to the inn and taste its ale. He
alighted from his horse at the inn door and marched in and called
loudly for the master, Sandilands. The master appeared, a tall stout
man, renowned in his younger days for his feats at hammer throwing.

'Well, Gidden, how have ye come't on at Peebles?'

'Very weel, very weel, Jamie, considering the folk that were there,'
said Gideon.

'Are ye bidin' here a' nicht? Come awa' in, come awa' in,' said the
host.

'No, no man, I just want a glass o' ale; I've to be at the Crook the
nicht.'

'Ye should hae been sooner on the road then, Gidden.'

Gideon looked out at the gathering dusk and reflected that the
landlord's observation was true.

'What in the world's that noise, Jamie? I thocht ye kept a quieter
hoose.'

'It's a party o' dragoons frae Embro', Gidden. I wish folk like them
came oftener. It would be a blessing for this inn. Lord save us, but
they've drunk an awfu' quantity o' yale the day.'

'What do ye think they're here for, lad? I've heard o' naething
lately.'

'Oh, they winna tell that. But there's something brewing up the
muirs, that we'll hear tell o' afore long.' The ale had meantime been
brought, and Gideon quenched his thirst.

'Well, guid day, Jamie. I maun off, if I've to get to the Crook the
nicht.'

He mounted his horse and rode slowly down the village street. He
crossed the bridge of Tweed and turned up the river. No sooner had he
got out of sight of the village than he changed his slow walk into a
gallop. The mention of soldiers had brought the name of Yeddie
before his mind. Since his adventure on the Edinburgh road, he had
heard little about Yeddie. He kept the events of that night a profound
secret, but on making enquiries in a way which would excite no
suspicion he found that Yeddie was but little at home. Moreover he
had heard of great robberies in the Lothians and Clydesdale, and from
the descriptions which he got of the chief actors in them he had but
little doubt that Yeddie was one. Now when he heard of the dragoons'

expedition into so remote a part of the country, he instinctively guessed that they had traced him nearer home. With that thought a resolution was formed in his mind. He would get the start of them and warn their victims. How to do it he did not know but he had an idea that if he once got up into the moors he would meet Yeddie. There was only one road up the river and at this time of the year, in a wild part of the country the dragoons would likely keep to it. There is no analysing the motives of some men. What could induce a sober respectable man like Gideon to strain every nerve and even risk his own life to shield a notorious highwayman, is a mystery. But in the most prosaic of men there is always some strain of the romantic. Here in this sober inn-keeper, the Border strain derived from his reiving ancestors, the tendency to defend any breaker of the law at the risk of his own neck, comes out.

The night was now getting darker, and he was some four miles up the water from Stobo. Still he had not met a soul, not even a shepherd or a ploughman, everything was as quiet as a Sabbath morning.

In a little while he saw a great dark mass looming before him, which he knew was the spur of the hill on which Tinnis castle stands, formerly the home of the Tweedies. Here the road for the Crook left the main path, so here Gideon came to a standstill. Perhaps the soldiers had no thought of Yeddie. Perhaps they meant to go to Broughton or Biggar; or perhaps their expectations were wrong, and the object of their pursuit was not there. At any rate he would go home, he couldn't do anything more. Just then far down the valley he heard the sound of horses' feet; 'these were the soldiers,' thought he, he would wait for them and watch them pass before he went home. Up the brown hillside along the rocky pathway he directed his horse's steps, till he came to a small plateau from which he could command a full view of the valley. Here he dismounted from his mare and let her graze while he himself sat down on a boulder close by. From the road they could not have been distinguished from boulders, although on account of the moonlight they could see up and down the valley almost to Stobo. The night grew chilly, and Gideon began to feel cold perched up on that hillside. He remembered that he had left his plaid at Stobo, and he called himself a fool for his madcap haste.

From his watch-tower he saw the soldiers moving like snails along the road. 'Ah,' thought Gideon, 'they are near somebody, they are going cautiously.' Now they were not half a mile distant but still they kept at the same slow pace. Sometimes when the mind of a man is most intent upon anything, some trivial thing or other comes in and distracts his attention. Gideon happened to look up at the sky and there he saw a flock of birds flying, which he knew by their flight to be wild geese. Then he fell to wondering why so few wild geese had come to the moors this year. He remembered the sport he had had in his younger days, stalking these same birds in the marshy ground beside the Tweed at three o'clock on a frosty winter morning. He remembered the peculiar cry with which they rose; but at this point his ornithological memories were rudely interrupted by a gunshot from the valley. Up he sprang and looked down; he saw a confused mass of men standing in different attitudes on the road; another man fleeing on foot towards Stobo, and another man on horseback galloping up in the opposite direction. Gideon's attention was divided between watching this man and soothing his horse, now terrified by the number of shots. He saw several men ride in pursuit of him; then the fugitive's riding began to get peculiar; he swayed backwards in his saddle, and finally dropped off at the point where the mountain path left the main road while his horse galloped on. 'He kens the path,' said Gideon to himself, 'he'll be up here in five minutes.' He watched the pursuers ride after the riderless horse and then looked down among the brackens through which the footway ran. For some minutes he saw and heard nothing except the cries of troopers, and the sound of their horses' feet. Then he heard the brackens in front of him rustle and Yeddie's head and shoulders emerged from among them. The look of fear which crossed his face when he saw a man, was immediately changed to one of joy as he recognised Gideon.

The latter bent over and grasped his arms and pulled him up beside him. The thin stream of blood which trickled down from below Yeddie's left shoulder, together with his slow and painful breathing, showed that he was badly wounded.

'O, Gidden,' he gasped, 'we saw ye pass and let ye go on. But, fules that we were, we took the dragoons for drovers, and – I doubt they've done for me.'

'Na, na, Yeddie, I'll get ye off yet. But ye see the end your ill doings hae brocht ye to. Man, man, could ye no hae bidden at hame, instead of ridin' and reivin' ower a' the country?'

A groan from the wounded man was the only answer.

'I'll no preach to ye my puir lad; ye're punished enuch.'

By this time the soldiers had discovered the ruse and were retracing their steps. Gideon felt that there was no time to be lost. Carefully he placed Yeddie on his mare's back, and mounted behind him, putting one arm around his body to support him. Then he rode slowly up the path till he reached the brow of the hill overhanging Drumelzier Burn. Up that glen and over the back of Glenheurie Rig lay Talla. If once he got there he knew that no trooper could reach them. But the way was long and dangerous and the burden was heavy for his mare. Now a shout arose from below, which told that his pursuers had discovered the track. This renewed his resolution. He rode quickly down the broken pathway into the glen. Thus began the ride which is famous in Upper Tweeddale. The country people still speak of Gideon Scott's Ride as something uncanny. The mare also, which carried two men ten miles over a rough country, still enjoys a reputation in the stories of the district.

Gideon knew that if the mare could but keep up, he would never be overtaken, for the dragoons must needs ride very slow, since they had no knowledge of the windings of the road. Moreover, he felt that if he could not get to Talla, and dress Yeddie's wound, Yeddie would die. On the crest of the hill ere he started he had wrapped a portion of his plaid over the wound, but the blood kept coming through the cloth and dropping on his hand. No sound came from the wounded man except an occasional groan when the motion of the mare hurt him.

It was about nine o'clock at night when he started on his ride; ere they reached Talla the light was beginning to appear over the grey hills of Holmes Water. Many times the mare had stumbled, twice she had sunk in a bog and was extricated by Gideon with great difficulty. Her knees and legs were bleeding from contact with sharp rocks, her wind was almost gone and her eyes shone like blood in her head. Gideon also was sore spent between the labour of supporting his burden and assisting the horse. As for Yeddie, he had fallen into a sort of stupor; he lay resting on Gideon's arm, with a face as pale as death in strange contrast to his blood-drenched plaid. The troopers had long since fallen off. Weary, jaded and well nigh dead, the horse and its two riders stopped at the door of the small shepherd's hut at Talla. Gideon, though scarce able to stand from fatigue, managed to undo the door and carry Yeddie in. He placed him on the bed and tottered out to see to his horse. But the mare had looked after herself. She had dragged herself to the stream's edge and was now lying drinking great draughts of water and resting her weary limbs. Then he went back and sat down in a chair by Yeddie's bed. A great sleep came over him and completely overpowered him. For five hours he slept and then he was wakened by the mare, who had come in to the hut in search of food. He arose and found some oats for her. Then he rummaged about and got some cold mutton for himself. Then and not till then he remembered Yeddie. He found a flask of brandy on a shelf, and succeeded in forcing some of it between his lips. In time Gideon succeeded in getting him out of the death-like stupor into which he had fallen. He went down to the stream for water, and dressed his wound, which had now stopped bleeding, as well as he could. Yeddie lay perfectly still watching Gideon's operations.

'I doubt I'm done for, Gidden,' said he.

'Na, na, I saved your life afore and I think I'll get ye roond this time.'

'I've a bullet in my breast, Gidden; there's nae hope for me, lad. I'm done for this time.' Then he burst out, 'O, I'll never dae't noo, I'll never dae't noo. I dinna care a whistle for death, if I just had finished it.'

'Whisht, man, whisht,' said Gideon, but he saw with a sinking heart the signs on Yeddie's face which told too clearly of death.

Then Yeddie spoke, 'Gideon, ye've been a guid friend to me, and I have just one mair thing to ask ye. I am going to tell ye something which you'll promise me never to tell to anyone.' (Gideon noticed that Yeddie had dropped the Tweeddale dialect and spoke, as he thought, more like a gentleman than a shepherd.) He promised what he required.

'Ye've heard,' said the dying man, 'of the Tweedies of Drumelzier, who used to be great folks in this countryside?'

'Ay, ay,' said Gideon. 'They were awfu' folk, they keepit a' Tweedside under their feet.'

'Well, my name is Adam Tweedie, and I am the last of the line. My grandfather had to sell the estates, and my father was a lawyer in Edinburgh. I was brought up to succeed him, but I had little love for the work. I had heard of the doings of my ancestors, and I resolved to do my best to get back the family possessions. When my father died I kept on his business, for my first idea was to make a fortune as a lawyer. But when I saw that I was not fitted to do anything of the kind, I gave up the idea and looked out for something else. Then I fell in with some wild fellows of my own age who first put the idea into my head of taking to the road. The upshot was that I sold the business and came up to Talla, where I had still this sheep farm belonging to me. I stayed in this cottage and with three other companions whose names I cannot tell, I became a –, call it highwayman, it was no better. Jamie Morrison, the lawyer in Edinburgh, was my banker; he thought I made the money from my farms. If I had lived another year, I would have accomplished my work; but it will never be done now.'

Yeddie's voice now became faint and his breathing more difficult. 'I can trust you to tell no one, Gideon. I would'na' like folk to know that the last of the clan came so low, though it was the trade of my forebears. Ye might do me the last favour of carrying news of my death to the laird of Mossfennan; he'll tell the others.' His voice failed him and he was silent.

Gideon sat in silence by his bed till the short day faded into night and then Yeddie died. Gideon arose and went down the valley to Mossfennan. Along with the laird he returned next morning and buried the dead man and then rode home alone with a heavy heart.

No-Man's Land

During his last year at Oxford Buchan began his life-long association with the Edinburgh-based *Blackwood's Magazine*. *Blackwood's* would publish some forty stories and articles, as well as serialise such novels as *The Thirty-Nine Steps* (1915) and *Sick-Heart River* (1940). 'No-Man's Land' was the first of his *Blackwood's* stories, appearing in the January 1899 issue; when submitting it in November 1898 Buchan described it as the 'story of a primitive survival among Scottish moorland. It is a piece of rather wild fancy'. It is the first story in his short-story collection *The Watcher By The Threshold* (1902) and at over 20,000 words is the longest of Buchan's short stories.

The story has certain similarities to Conan Doyle's *The Lost World* and Buchan's novel *The Dancing Floor* (1926). It is a good example of how Buchan's imagination invested a familiar countryside with mysterious properties and he demonstrates the same ambivalence as in 'A Journey of Little Profit' as to whether the strange events are real or a figment of the imagination.

I
The Shieling of Farawa

IT WAS WITH a light heart and a pleasing consciousness of holiday that I set out from the inn at Allermuir to tramp my fifteen miles into the unknown. I walked slowly, for I carried my equipment on my back – my basket, fly-books and rods, my plaid of Grant tartan (for I boast myself a distant kinsman of that house), and my great staff, which had tried ere then the front of the steeper Alps. A small valise with books and some changes of linen clothing had been sent on ahead in the shepherd's own hands. It was yet early

April, and before me lay four weeks of freedom — twenty-eight blessed days in which to take fish and smoke the pipe of idleness. The Lent term had pulled me down, a week of modest enjoyment thereafter in town had finished the work; and I drank in the sharp moorish air like a thirsty man who has been forwandered among deserts.

I am a man of varied tastes and a score of interests. As an undergraduate I had been filled with the old mania for the complete life. I distinguished myself in the Schools, rowed in my college eight, and reached the distinction of practising for three weeks in the Trials. I had dabbled in a score of learned activities, and when the time came that I won the inevitable St. Chad's fellowship on my chaotic acquirements, and I found myself compelled to select if I would pursue a scholar's life, I had some toil in finding my vocation. In the end I resolved that the ancient life of the North, of the Celts and the Northmen and the unknown Pictish tribes, held for me the chief fascination. I had acquired a smattering of Gaelic, having been brought up as a boy in Lochaber, and now I set myself to increase my store of languages. I mastered Erse and Icelandic, and my first book — a monograph on the probable Celtic elements in the Eddic songs — brought me the praise of scholars and the deputy-professor's chair of Northern Antiquities. So much for Oxford. My vacations had been spent mainly in the North — in Ireland, Scotland, and the Isles, in Scandinavia and Iceland, once even in the far limits of Finland. I was a keen sportsman of a sort, an old-experienced fisher, a fair shot with gun and rifle, and in my hill-craft I might well stand comparison with most men. April has ever seemed to me the finest season of the year even in our cold northern altitudes, and the memory of many bright Aprils had brought me up from the South on the night before to Allerfoot, whence a dogcart had taken me up Glen Aller to the inn at Allermuir; and now the same desire had set me on the heather with my face to the cold brown hills.

You are to picture a sort of plateau, benty and rock-strewn, running ridge-wise above a chain of little peaty lochs and a vast tract of inexorable bog. In a mile the ridge ceased in a shoulder of hill, and over this lay the head of another glen, with the same doleful accompaniment of sunless lochs, mosses, and a shining and resolute water. East and west and north, in every direction save the south, rose walls of gashed and serrated hills. It was a grey day with blinks of sun, and when a ray chanced to fall on one of the great dark faces, lines of light and colour sprang into being which told of mica and granite. I was in high spirits, as on the eve of holiday; I had breakfasted excellently on eggs and salmon-steaks; I had no cares to speak of, and my prospects were not uninviting. But in spite of myself the landscape began to take me in thrall and crush me. The silent vanished peoples of the hills seemed to be stirring; dark primeval faces seemed to stare at me from behind boulders and jags of rock. The place was so still, so free from the cheerful clamour of nesting birds, that it seemed a *temenos* sacred to some old-world god. At my feet the lochs lapped ceaselessly; but the waters were so dark that one could not see bottom a foot from the edge. On my right the links of green told of snake-like mires waiting to crush the unwary wanderer. It seemed to me for the moment a land of death, where the tongues of the dead cried aloud for recognition.

My whole morning's walk was full of such fancies. I lit a pipe to cheer me, but the things would not be got rid of. I thought of the Gaels who had held those fastnesses; I thought of the Britons before them, who yielded to their advent. They were all strong peoples in their day, and now they had gone the way of the earth. They had left their mark on the levels of the glens and on the more habitable uplands, both in names and in actual forts, and graves where men might still dig curios. But the hills – that black stony amphitheatre before me – it seemed strange that the hills bore no traces of them. And then with some uneasiness I reflected on that older and stranger race who were said to have held the hill-tops. The Picts, the Picti – what in the name of goodness were they? They had troubled me in all my studies, a sort of blank wall to put an end to speculation. We knew nothing of them save certain strange names which men called Pictish, the names of those hills in front of me – the Muneraw, the Yirnie, the Calmarton. They were the *corpus vile* for learned experiment; but Heaven alone knew what dark abyss of savagery once yawned in the midst of this desert.

And then I remembered the crazy theories of a pupil of mine at St. Chad's, the son of a small landowner on the Aller, a young gentleman who had spent his substance too freely at Oxford, and was now dreeing his weird in the Backwoods. He had been no scholar; but a certain imagination marked all his doings, and of a Sunday night he would come and talk to me of the North. The Picts were his special subject, and his ideas were mad. 'Listen to me,' he would say, when I had mixed him toddy and given him one of my cigars; 'I believe there are traces – ay, and more than traces – of an old culture lurking in those hills and waiting to be discovered. We never hear of the Picts being driven from the hills. The Britons drove them from the lowlands, the Gaels from Ireland did the same for the Britons; but the hills were left unmolested. We hear of no one going near them except outlaws and tinklers. And in that very place you have the strangest mythology. Take the story of the Brownie. What is that but the story of a little swart man of uncommon strength and cleverness, who does good and ill indiscriminately, and then disappears? There are many scholars, as you yourself confess, who think that the origin of the Brownie was in some mad belief in the old race of the Picts, which still survived somewhere in the hills. And do we not hear of the Brownie in authentic records right down to the year 1756? After that, when people grew more incredulous, it is natural that the belief should have begun to die out; but I do not see why stray traces should not have survived till late.'

'Do you not see what that means?' I had said in mock gravity. 'Those same hills are, if anything, less known now than they were a hundred years ago. Why should not your Picts or Brownies be living to this day?'

'Why not, indeed?' he had rejoined, in all seriousness.

I laughed, and he went to his rooms and returned with a large leather-bound book. It was lettered, in the rococo style of a young man's taste, 'Glimpses of the Unknown', and some of the said glimpses he proceeded to impart to me. It was not pleasant reading; indeed, I had rarely heard anything so well fitted to shatter sensitive nerves. The early part consisted of folk-tales and folk-sayings, some of them wholly obscure, some of them with a glint of meaning, but all of them with some hint of a mystery in the hills. I heard the Brownie story in countless versions. Now the thing was a friendly little man, who wore grey breeches and lived on brose; now he was a twisted being, the sight of which made the ewes miscarry in the lambing-time. But the second part was the stranger, for it was made up of actual tales, most of them with date and place appended. It was a most Bedlamite catalogue of horrors, which, if true, made the wholesome moors a place instinct with tragedy. Some told of children carried away from villages, even from towns, on the verge of the uplands. In almost every case they were girls, and the strange fact was their utter disappearance. Two little girls would be coming home from school, would be seen last by a neighbour just where the road crossed a patch of heath or entered a wood and then – no human eye ever saw them again. Children's cries had startled outlying shepherds in the night, and when they had rushed to the door they could hear nothing but the night wind. The instances of such disappearances were not very common – perhaps once in twenty years – but they were confined to this one tract of country, and came in a sort of fixed progression from the middle of the last century, when the record began. But this was only one side of the history. The latter part was all devoted to a chronicle of crimes which had gone unpunished, seeing that no hand had ever been traced. The list was fuller in last century;[1] in the earlier years of the present it had dwindled; then came a revival about the 'Fifties; and now again in our own time it had sunk low. At the little cottage of Auchterbrean, on the roadside in Glen Aller, a labourer's wife had been found pierced to the heart. It was thought to be a case of a woman's jealousy, and her neighbour was accused, convicted, and hanged. The woman, to be sure, denied the charge with her last breath; but circumstantial evidence seemed sufficiently strong against her. Yet some people in the glen believed her guiltless. In particular, the carrier who had found the dead woman declared that the way in which her neighbour received the news was a sufficient proof of innocence; and the doctor who was first summoned professed himself unable to tell with what instrument the wound had been given. But this was all before the days of expert evidence, so the woman had been hanged without scruple. Then there had been another story of peculiar horror, telling of the death of an old man at some little lonely shieling called Carrickfey. But at this point I had risen in protest, and made to drive the young idiot from my room.

'It was my grandfather who collected most of them,' he said. 'He

---

[1] The narrative of Mr. Graves was written in the year 1898.

had theories,[1] but people called him mad, so he was wise enough to hold his tongue. My father declares the whole thing mania; but I rescued the book, had it bound, and added to the collection. It is a queer hobby; but, as I say, I have theories, and there are more things in heaven and earth—'

But at this he heard a friend's voice in the Quad., and dived out, leaving the banal quotation unfinished.

Strange though it may seem, this madness kept coming back to me as I crossed the last few miles of moor. I was now on a rough tableland, the watershed between two lochs, and beyond and above me rose the stony backs of the hills. The burns fell down in a chaos of granite boulders, and huge slabs of grey stone lay flat and tumbled in the heather. The full waters looked prosperously for my fishing, and I began to forget all fancies in anticipation of sport.

Then suddenly in a hollow of land I came on a ruined cottage. It had been a very small place, but the walls were still half-erect, and the little moorland garden was outlined on the turf. A lonely apple-tree, twisted and gnarled with winds, stood in the midst.

From higher up on the hill I heard a loud roar, and I knew my excellent friend the shepherd of Farawa, who had come thus far to meet me. He greeted me with the boisterous embarrassment which was his way of prefacing hospitality. A grave reserved man at other times, on such occasions he thought it proper to relapse into hilarity. I fell into step with him, and we set off for his dwelling. But first I had the curiosity to look back to the tumble-down cottage and ask him its name.

A queer look came into his eyes. 'They ca' the place Carrickfey,' he

---

[1] In the light of subsequent events I have jotted down the materials to which I refer. The last authentic record of the Brownie is in the narrative of the shepherd of Clachlands, taken down towards the close of last century by the Reverend Mr. Gillespie, minister of Allerkirk, and included by him in his 'Songs and Legends of Glen Aller'. The authorities on the strange carrying-away of children are to be found in a series of articles in a local paper, the *Allerfoot Advertiser*, September and October 1878, and a curious book published anonymously at Edinburgh in 1848, entitled *The Weathergaw*. The records of the unexplained murders in the same neighbourhood are all contained in Mr. Fordoun's 'Theory of Expert Evidence', and an attack on the book in the *Law Review* for June 1881. The Carrickfey case has a pamphlet to itself – now extremely rare – a copy of which was recently obtained in a bookseller's shop in Dumfries by a well-known antiquary, and presented to the library of the Supreme Court in Edinburgh.

said. 'Naebody has daured to bide there this twenty year sin' – but I see ye ken the story.' And, as if glad to leave the subject, he hastened to discourse on fishing.

II
Tells of an Evening's Talk

The shepherd was a masterful man; tall, save for the stoop which belongs to all moorland folk, and active as a wild goat. He was not a new importation, nor did he belong to the place; for his people had lived in the remote Borders, and he had come as a boy to this shieling of Farawa. He was unmarried, but an elderly sister lived with him and cooked his meals. He was reputed to be extraordinarily skilful in his trade; I know for a fact that he was in his way a keen sportsman; and his few neighbours gave him credit for a sincere piety. Doubtless this last report was due in part to his silence, for after his first greeting he was wont to relapse into a singular taciturnity. As we strode across the heather he gave me a short outline of his year's lambing. 'Five pairs o' twins yestreen, twae this morn; that makes thirty-five yowes that hae lambed since the Sabbath. I'll dae weel if God's willin'.' Then, as I looked towards the hill-tops whence the thin mist of morn was trailing, he followed my gaze. 'See,' he said with uplifted crook – 'see that sicht. Is that no what is written of in the Bible when it says, "The mountains do smoke."' And with this piece of exegesis he finished his talk, and in a little we were at the cottage.

It was a small enough dwelling in truth, and yet large for a moorland house, for it had a garret below the thatch, which was given up to my sole enjoyment. Below was the wide kitchen with box-beds, and next to it the inevitable second room, also with its cupboard sleeping-places. The interior was very clean, and yet I remember to have been struck with the faint musty smell which is inseparable from moorland dwellings. The kitchen pleased me best, for there the great rafters were black with peat-reek, and the uncovered stone floor, on which the fire gleamed dully, gave an air of primeval simplicity. But the walls spoiled all, for tawdry things of to-day had penetrated even there. Some grocers' almanacs – years old – hung in places of honour, and an extraordinary lithograph of the Royal Family in its youth. And this, mind you, between crooks and fishing-rods and old guns, and horns of sheep and deer.

The life for the first day or two was regular and placid. I was up early, breakfasted on porridge (a dish which I detest), and then off to the lochs and streams. At first my sport prospered mightily. With a drake-wing I killed a salmon of seventeen pounds, and the next day had a fine basket of trout from a hill-burn. Then for no earthly reason the weather changed. A bitter wind came out of the north-east, bringing showers of snow and stinging hail, and lashing the waters into storm. It was now farewell to fly-fishing. For a day or two I tried trolling with the minnow on the lochs, but it was poor sport, for I had no boat, and the edges were soft and mossy. Then in disgust I gave up the attempt, went back to the cottage, lit my biggest pipe, and sat down with a book to await the turn of the weather.

The shepherd was out from morning till night at his work, and when he came in at last, dog-tired, his face would be set and hard, and his eyes heavy with sleep. The strangeness of the man grew upon me. He had a shrewd brain beneath his thatch of hair, for I had tried him once or twice, and found him abundantly intelligent. He had some smattering of an education, like all Scottish peasants, and, as I have said, he was deeply religious. I set him down as a fine type of his class, sober, serious, keenly critical, free from the bondage of superstition. But I rarely saw him, and our talk was chiefly in monosyllables – short interjected accounts of the number of lambs dead or alive on the hill. Then he would produce a pencil and note-book, and be immersed in some calculation; and finally he would be revealed sleeping heavily in his chair, till his sister wakened him, and he stumbled off to bed.

So much for the ordinary course of life; but one day – the second I think of the bad weather – the extraordinary happened. The storm had passed in the afternoon into a resolute and blinding snow, and the shepherd, finding it hopeless on the hill, came home about three o'clock. I could make out from his way of entering that he was in a great temper. He kicked his feet savagely against the door-post. Then he swore at his dogs, a thing I had never heard him do before. 'Hell!' he cried, 'can ye no keep out o' my road, ye britts?' Then he came sullenly into the kitchen, thawed his numbed hands at the fire, and sat down to his meal.

I made some aimless remark about the weather.

'Death to man and beast,' he grunted. 'I hae got the sheep doun frae the hill, but the lambs will never thole this. We maun pray that it will no last.'

[191]

His sister came in with some dish. 'Margit,' he cried, 'three lambs away this morning, and three deid wi' the hole in the throat.'

The woman's face visibly paled. 'Guid help us, Adam; that hasna happened this three year.'

'It has happened noo,' he said, surlily. 'But, by God! if it happens again I'll gang mysel' to the Scarts o' the Muneraw.'

'O Adam!' the woman cried shrilly, 'haud your tongue. Ye kenna wha hears ye.' And with a frightened glance at me she left the room.

I asked no questions, but waited till the shepherd's anger should cool. But the cloud did not pass so lightly. When he had finished his dinner he pulled his chair to the fire and sat staring moodily. He made some sort of apology to me for his conduct. 'I'm sore troubled, sir; but I'm vexed ye should see me like this. Maybe things will be better the morn.' And then, lighting his short black pipe, he resigned himself to his meditations.

But he could not keep quiet. Some nervous unrest seemed to have possessed the man. He got up with a start and went to the window, where the snow was drifting unsteadily past. As he stared out into the storm I heard him mutter to himself, 'Three away, God help me, and three wi' the hole in the throat.'

Then he turned round to me abruptly. I was jotting down notes for an article I contemplated in the *Revue Celtique*, so my thoughts were far away from the present. The man recalled me by demanding fiercely, 'Do ye believe in God?'

I gave him some sort of answer in the affirmative.

'Then do ye believe in the Devil?' he asked.

The reply must have been less satisfactory, for he came forward and flung himself violently into the chair before me.

'What do ye ken about it?' he cried. 'You that bides in a southern toun, what can ye ken o' the God that works in thae hills and the Devil – ay, the manifold devils – that He suffers to bide here? I tell ye, man, that if ye had seen what I have seen ye wad be on your knees at this moment praying to God to pardon your unbelief. There are devils at the back o' every stane and hidin' in every cleuch, and it's by the grace o' God alone that a man is alive upon the earth.' His voice had risen high and shrill, and then suddenly he cast a frightened glance towards the window and was silent.

I began to think that the man's wits were unhinged, and the thought did not give me satisfaction. I had no relish for the prospect of being left alone in this moorland dwelling with the cheerful company of a maniac. But his next movements reassured me. He was clearly only dead-tired, for he fell sound asleep in his chair, and by the time his sister brought tea and wakened him, he seemed to have got the better of his excitement.

When the window was shuttered and the lamp lit, I set myself again to the completion of my notes. The shepherd had got out his Bible, and was solemnly reading with one great finger travelling down the lines. He was smoking, and whenever some text came home to him with power he would make pretence to underline it with the end of the stem. Soon I had finished the work I desired, and, my mind being full of my pet hobby, I fell into an inquisitive mood, and began to question the solemn man opposite on the antiquities of the place.

He stared stupidly at me when I asked him concerning monuments or ancient weapons.

'I kenna,' said he. 'There's a heap o' queer things in the hills.'

'This place should be a centre for such relics. You know that the name of the hill behind the house, as far as I can make it out, means the 'Place of the Little Men'. It is a good Gaelic word, though there is some doubt about its exact interpretation. But clearly the Gaelic peoples did not speak of themselves when they gave the name; they must have referred to some older and stranger population.'

The shepherd looked at me dully, as not understanding.

'It is partly this fact – besides the fishing, of course – which interests me in this countryside,' said I, gaily.

Again he cast the same queer frightened glance towards the window. 'If ye'll tak the advice of an aulder man,' he said, slowly, 'ye'll let well alane and no meddle wi' uncanny things.'

I laughed pleasantly, for at last I had found out my hard-headed host in a piece of childishness. 'Why, I thought that you of all men would be free from superstition.'

'What do ye call supersteetion?' he asked.

'A belief in old wives' tales,' said I, 'a trust in the crude supernatural and the patently impossible.'

He looked at me beneath his shaggy brows. 'How do ye ken what is impossible? Mind ye, sir, ye're no in the toun just now, but in the thick of the wild hills.'

'But, hang it all, man,' I cried, 'you don't mean to say that you believe in that sort of thing? I am prepared for many things up here, but not for the Brownie, – though, to be sure, if one could meet him in the flesh, it would be rather pleasant than otherwise, for he was a companionable sort of fellow.'

'When a thing pits the fear o' death on a man he aye speaks well of it.'

It was true – the Eumenides and the Good Folk over again; and I awoke with interest to the fact that the conversation was getting into strange channels.

The shepherd moved uneasily in his chair. 'I am a man that fears God, and has nae time for daft stories; but I havena traivelled the hills for twenty years wi' my een shut. If I say that I could tell ye stories o' faces seen in the mist, and queer things that have knocked against me in the snaw, wad ye believe me? I wager ye wadna. Ye wad say I had been drunk, and yet I am a God-fearing temperate man.'

He rose and went to a cupboard, unlocked it, and brought out something in his hand, which he held out to me. I took it with some curiosity, and found that it was a flint arrow-head.

Clearly a flint arrow-head, and yet like none that I had ever seen in any collection. For one thing it was larger, and the barb less clumsily thick. More, the chipping was new, or comparatively so; this thing had not stood the wear of fifteen hundred years among the stones of the hillside. Now there are, I regret to say, institutions which manufacture primitive relics; but it is not hard for a practised eye to see the difference. The chipping has either a regularity and a balance which is unknown in the real thing, or the rudeness has been overdone, and the result is an implement incapable of harming a mortal creature. But this was the real thing if it ever existed; and yet – I was prepared to swear on my reputation that it was not half a century old.

'Where did you get this? I asked with some nervousness.

'I hae a story about that,' said the shepherd. 'Outside the door there ye can see a muckle flat stane aside the buchts. One simmer nicht I was sitting there smoking till the dark, and I wager there was naething on the stane then. But that same nicht I awoke wi' a queer thocht, as if there were folk moving around the house – folk that didna mak' muckle noise. I mind o' lookin' out o' the windy, and I could hae sworn I saw something black movin' amang the heather and intil the buchts. Now I had maybe threescore o' lambs there that nicht, for I had to tak' them many miles off in the early morning. Weel, when I gets up about four o'clock and gangs out, as I am passing the muckle stane I finds this bit errow. "That's come here in the nicht," says I, and I wunnered a wee and put it in my pouch. But when I came to my faulds what did I see? Five o' my best hoggs were away, and three mair were lying deid wi' a hole in their throat.'

'Who in the world—?' I began.

'Dinna ask,' said he. 'If I aince sterted to speir about thae maitters. I wadna keep my reason.'

'Then that was what happened on the hill this morning?'

'Even sae, and it has happened mair than aince sin' that time. It's the most uncanny slaughter, for sheep-stealing I can understand, but no this pricking o' the puir beasts' wizands. I kenna how they dae't either, for it's no wi' a knife or ony common tool.'

'Have you never tried to follow the thieves?'

'Have I no?' he asked, grimly. 'If it had been common sheep-stealers I wad hae had them by the heels, though I had followed them a hundred miles. But this is no common. I've tracked them, and it's ill they are to track; but I never got beyond ae place, and that was the Scarts o' the Muneraw that ye've heard me speak o'.'

'But who in Heaven's name are the people? Tinklers or poachers or what?'

'Ay,' said he, drily. 'Even so. Tinklers and poachers whae wark wi' stane errows and kill sheep by a hole in their throat. Lord, I kenna what they are, unless the Muckle Deil himsel'.'

The conversation had passed beyond my comprehension. In this prosaic hard-headed man I had come on the dead-rock of superstition and blind fear.

'That is only the story of the Brownie over again, and he is an exploded myth,' I said, laughing.

'Are ye the man that exploded it?' said the shepherd, rudely. 'I trow no, neither you nor ony ither. My bonny man, if ye lived a twalmonth in thae hills, ye wad sing safter about exploded myths, as ye call them.'

'I tell you what I would do,' said I. 'If I lost sheep as you lose them, I would go up the Scarts of the Muneraw and never rest till I had settled the question once and for all.' I spoke hotly, for I was vexed by the man's childish fear.

'I daresay ye wad,' he said, slowly. 'But then I am no you, and maybe I ken mair o' what is in the Scarts o' the Muneraw. Maybe I ken that whilk, if ye kenned it, wad send ye back to the South Country wi' your hert in your mouth. But, as I say, I am no sae brave as you, for I saw something in the first year o' my herding here which put the terror o' God on me, and makes me a fearfu' man to this day. Ye ken the story o' the gudeman o' Carrickfey?'

I nodded.

'Weel, I was the man that fand him. I had seen the deid afore and I've seen them since. But never have I seen aucht like the look in that man's een. What he saw at his death I may see the morn, so I walk before the Lord in fear.'

Then he rose and stretched himself. 'It's bedding-time, for I maun be up at three,' and with a short good night he left the room.

III

The Scarts of the Muneraw

The next morning was fine, for the snow had been intermittent, and had soon melted except in the high corries. True, it was deceptive weather, for the wind had gone to the rainy south-west, and the masses of cloud on that horizon boded ill for the afternoon. But some days' inaction had made me keen for a chance of sport, so I rose with the shepherd and set out for the day.

He asked me where I proposed to begin.

I told him the tarn called the Loch o' the Threshes, which lies over the back of the Muneraw on another watershed. It is on the ground of the Rhynns Forest, and I had fished it of old from the Forest House. I knew the merits of the trout, and I knew its virtues in a south-west wind, so I had resolved to go thus far afield.

The shepherd heard the name in silence. 'Your best road will be ower that rig, and syne on to the weater o' Caulds. Keep abune the moss till ye come to the place they ca' the Nick o' the Threshes. That will take ye to the very lochside, but it's a lang road and a sair.'

The morning was breaking over the bleak hills. Little clouds drifted athwart the corries, and wisps of haze fluttered from the peaks. A great rosy flush lay over one side of the glen, which caught the edge of the sluggish bog-pools and turned them to fire. Never before had I seen the mountain-land so clear, for far back into the east and west I saw mountain-tops set as close as flowers in a border, black crags seamed with silver lines which I knew for mighty waterfalls, and below at my feet the lower slopes fresh with the dewy green of spring. A name stuck in my memory from the last night's talk.

'Where are the Scarts of the Muneraw?' I asked.

The shepherd pointed to the great hill which bears the name, and which lies, a huge mass, above the watershed.

'D'ye see yon corrie at the east that runs straucht up the side? It looks a bit scart, but it's sae deep that it's aye derk at the bottom o't. Weel, at the tap o' the rig it meets anither corrie that runs doun the ither side, and that one they ca' the Scarts. There is a sort o' burn in it that flows intil the Dule and sae intil the Aller, and, indeed, if ye were gaun there it wad be from Aller Glen that your best road wad lie. But it's an ill bit, and ye'll be sair guidit if ye try't.'

There he left me and went across the glen, while I struck upwards over the ridge. At the top I halted and looked down on the wide glen of the Caulds, which there is little better than a bog, but lower down grows into a green pastoral valley. The great Muneraw still dominated the landscape, and the black scaur on its side seemed blacker than before. The place fascinated me, for in that fresh morning air the shepherd's fears seemed monstrous. 'Some day,' said I to myself, 'I will go and explore the whole of that mighty hill.' Then I descended and struggled over the moss, found the Nick, and in two hours' time was on the loch's edge.

I have little in the way of good to report of the fishing. For perhaps one hour the trout took well; after that they sulked steadily for the day. The promise, too, of fine weather had been deceptive. By mid-day the rain was falling in that soft soaking fashion which gives no hope of clearing. The mist was down to the edge of the water, and I cast my flies into a blind sea of white. It was hopeless work, and yet from a sort of ill-temper I stuck to it long after my better judgment had warned me of its folly. At last, about three in the afternoon, I struck my camp, and prepared myself for a long and toilsome retreat.

And long and toilsome it was beyond anything I had ever encountered. Had I had a vestige of sense I would have followed the burn from the loch down to the Forest House. The place was shut up, but the keeper would gladly have given me shelter for the night. But foolish pride was too strong in me. I had found my road in mist before, and could do it again.

Before I got to the top of the hill I had repented my decision; when I got there I repented it more. For below me was a dizzy chaos of grey; there was no landmark visible; and before me I knew was the bog through which the Caulds Water twined. I had crossed it with some trouble in the morning, but then I had light to pick my steps. Now I could only stumble on, and in five minutes I might be in a bog-hole, and in five more in a better world.

But there was no help to be got from hesitation, so with a rueful courage I set off. The place was if possible worse than I had feared. Wading up to the knees with nothing before you but a blank wall of mist and the cheerful consciousness that your next step may be your last — such was my state for one weary mile. The stream itself was high, and rose to my armpits, and once and again I only saved myself by a violent leap backwards from a pitiless green slough. But at last it was past, and I was once more on the solid ground of the hillside.

Now, in the thick weather I had crossed the glen much lower down than in the morning, and the result was that the hill on which I stood was one of the giants which, with the Muneraw for centre, guard the watershed. Had I taken the proper way, the Nick o' the Threshes would have led me to the Caulds, and then once over the bog a little ridge was all that stood between me and the glen of Farawa. But instead I had come a wild cross-country road, and was now, though I did not know it, nearly as far from my destination as at the start.

Well for me that I did not know, for I was wet and dispirited, and had I not fancied myself all but home, I should scarcely have had the energy to make this last ascent. But soon I found it was not the little ridge I had expected. I looked at my watch and saw that it was five o'clock. When, after the weariest climb, I lay on a piece of level ground which seemed the top, I was not surprised to find that it was now seven. The darkening must be at hand, and sure enough the mist seemed to be deepening into a greyish black. I began to grow desperate. Here was I on the summit of some infernal mountain, without any certainty where my road lay. I was lost with a vengeance, and at the thought I began to be acutely afraid.

I took what seemed to me the way I had come, and began to descend steeply. Then something made me halt, and the next instant I was lying on my face trying painfully to retrace my steps. For I had found myself slipping, and before I could stop, my feet were dangling over a precipice with Heaven alone knows how many yards of sheer mist between me and the bottom. Then I tried keeping the ridge, and took that to the right, which I thought would bring me nearer home. It was no good trying to think out a direction, for in the fog my brain was running round, and I seemed to stand on a pin-point of space where the laws of the compass had ceased to hold.

It was the roughest sort of walking, now stepping warily over acres of loose stones, now crawling down the face of some battered rock, and now wading in the long dripping heather. The soft rain had begun to fall again, which completed my discomfort. I was now seriously tired, and, like all men who in their day have bent too much over books, I began to feel it in my back. My spine ached, and my breath came in short broken pants. It was a pitiable state of affairs for an honest man who had never encountered much grave discomfort. To ease myself I was compelled to leave my basket behind me, trusting to return and find it, if I should ever reach safety and discover on what pathless hill I had been strayed. My rod I used as a staff, but it was of little use, for my fingers were getting too numb to hold it.

Suddenly from the blankness I heard a sound as of human speech. At first I thought it mere craziness – the cry of a weasel or a hill-bird distorted by my ears. But again it came, thick and faint, as through acres of mist, and yet clearly the sound of 'articulate-speaking men'. In a moment I lost my despair and cried out in answer. This was some forwandered traveller like myself, and between us we could surely find some road to safety. So I yelled back at the pitch of my voice and waited intently.

But the sound ceased, and there was utter silence again. Still I waited, and then from some place much nearer came the same soft mumbling speech. I could make nothing of it. Heard in that drear place it made the nerves tense and the heart timorous. It was the strangest jumble of vowels and consonants I had ever met.

A dozen solutions flashed through my brain. It was some maniac talking Jabberwock to himself. It was some belated traveller whose wits had given out in fear. Perhaps it was only some shepherd who was amusing himself thus, and whiling the way with nonsense. Once again I cried out and waited.

Then suddenly in the hollow trough of mist before me, where things could still be half discerned, there appeared a figure. It was little and squat and dark; naked, apparently, but so rough with hair that it wore the appearance of a skin-covered being. It crossed my line of vision, not staying for a moment, but in its face and eyes there seemed to lurk an elder world of mystery and barbarism, a troll-like life which was too horrible for words.

The shepherd's fear came back on me like a thunderclap. For one awful instant my legs failed me, and I had almost fallen. The next I had turned and ran shrieking up the hill.

If he who may read this narrative has never felt the force of an overmastering terror, then let him thank his Maker and pray that he never may. I am no weak child, but a strong grown man, accredited in general with sound sense and little suspected of hysterics. And yet I went up that brae-face with my heart fluttering like a bird and my throat aching with fear. I screamed in short dry gasps; involuntarily, for my mind was beyond any purpose. I felt that beast-like clutch at my throat; those red eyes seemed to be staring at me from the mist; I heard ever behind and before and on all sides the patter of those inhuman feet.

Before I knew I was down, slipping over a rock and falling some dozen feet into a soft marshy hollow. I was conscious of lying still for a second and whimpering like a child. But as I lay there I awoke to the silence of the place. There was no sound of pursuit; perhaps they had lost my track and given up. My courage began to return, and from this it was an easy step to hope. Perhaps after all it had been merely an illusion, for folk do not see clearly in the mist, and I was already done with weariness.

But even as I lay in the green moss and began to hope, the faces of my pursuers grew up through the mist. I stumbled madly to my feet; but I was hemmed in, the rock behind and my enemies before. With a cry I rushed forward, and struck wildly with my rod at the first dark body. It was as if I had struck an animal, and the next second the thing was wrenched from my grasp. But still they came no nearer. I stood trembling there in the centre of those malignant devils, my brain a mere weathercock, and my heart crushed shapeless with horror. At last the end came, for with the vigour of madness I flung myself on the nearest, and we rolled on the ground. Then the monstrous things seemed to close over me, and with a choking cry I passed into unconsciousness.

IV

The Darkness that is Under the Earth

There is an unconsciousness that is not wholly dead, where a man feels numbly and the body lives without the brain. I was beyond speech or thought, and yet I felt the upward or downward motion as the way lay in hill or glen, and I most assuredly knew when the open air was changed for the close underground. I could feel dimly that lights were flared in my face, and that I was laid in some bed on the earth. Then with the stopping of movement the real sleep of weakness seized me, and for long I knew nothing of this mad world.

Morning came over the moors with birdsong and the glory of fine weather. The streams were still rolling in spate, but the hill-pastures were alight with dawn, and the little seams of snow were glistening like white fire. A ray from the sunrise cleft its path somehow into the abyss, and danced on the wall above my couch. It caught my eye as I wakened, and for long I lay crazily wondering what it meant. My head was splitting with pain, and in my heart was the same fluttering nameless fear. I did not wake to full consciousness; not till the twinkle of sun from the clean bright out-of-doors caught my senses did I realise that I lay in a great dark place with a glow of dull firelight in the middle.

In time things rose and moved around me, a few ragged shapes of men, without clothing, shambling with their huge feet and looking towards me with curved beast-like glances. I tried to marshal my thoughts, and slowly, bit by bit, I built up the present. There was no question to my mind of dreaming; the past hours had scored reality upon my brain. Yet I cannot say that fear was my chief feeling. The first crazy terror had subsided, and now I felt mainly a sickened disgust with just a tinge of curiosity. I found that my knife, watch, flask, and money had gone, but they had left me a map of the countryside. It seemed strange to look at the calico, with the name of a London printer stamped on the back, and lines of railway and highroad running through every shire. Decent and comfortable civilisation! And here was I a prisoner in this den of nameless folk, and in the midst of a life which history knew not.

Courage is a virtue which grows with reflection and the absence of the immediate peril. I thought myself into some sort of resolution, and lo! when the Folk approached me and bound my feet I was back at once in the most miserable terror. They tied me, all but my hands, with some strong cord, and carried me to the centre, where the fire was glowing. Their soft touch was the acutest torture to my nerves, but I stifled my cries lest some one should lay his hand on my mouth. Had that happened, I am convinced my reason would have failed me.

So there I lay in the shine of the fire, with the circle of unknown things around me. There seemed but three or four, but I took no note of number. They talked huskily among themselves in a tongue which sounded all gutturals. Slowly my fear became less an emotion than a habit, and I had room for the smallest shade of curiosity. I strained my ear to catch a word, but it was a mere chaos of sound. The thing ran and thundered in my brain as I stared dumbly into the vacant air. Then I thought that unless I spoke I should certainly go crazy, for my head was beginning to swim at the strange cooing noise.

I spoke a word or two in my best Gaelic, and they closed round me inquiringly. Then I was sorry I had spoken, for my words had brought them nearer, and I shrank at the thought. But as the faint echoes of my speech hummed in the rock-chamber, I was struck by a curious kinship of sound. Mine was sharper, more distinct, and staccato; theirs was blurred, formless, but still with a certain root-resemblance.

Then from the back there came an older being, who seemed to have heard my words. He was like some foul grey badger, his red eyes sightless, and his hands trembling on a stump of bog-oak. The others made way for him with such deference as they were capable of, and the thing squatted down by me and spoke.

To my amazement his words were familiar. It was some manner of speech akin to the Gaelic, but broadened, lengthened, coarsened. I remembered an old book-tongue, commonly supposed to be an impure dialect once used in Brittany, which I had met in the course of my researches. The words recalled it, and as far as I could remember the thing, I asked him who he was and where the place might be.

He answered me in the same speech – still more broadened, lengthened, coarsened. I lay back with sheer amazement. I had found the key to this unearthly life.

For a little an insatiable curiosity, the ardour of the scholar, prevailed. I forgot the horror of the place, and thought only of the fact that here before me was the greatest find that scholarship had ever made. I was precipitated into the heart of the past. Here must be the fountainhead of all legends, the chrysalis of all beliefs. I actually grew light-hearted. This strange folk around me were now no more shapeless things of terror, but objects of research and experiment. I almost came to think them not unfriendly.

For an hour I enjoyed the highest of earthly pleasures. In that strange conversation I heard – in fragments and suggestions – the history of the craziest survival the world has ever seen. I heard of the struggles with invaders, preserved as it were in a sort of shapeless poetry. There were bitter words against the Gaelic oppressor, bitterer words against the Saxon stranger, and for a moment ancient hatreds flared into life. Then there came the tale of the hill-refuge, the morbid hideous existence preserved for centuries amid a changing world. I heard fragments of old religions, primeval names of god and goddess, half-understood by the Folk, but to me the key to a hundred puzzles. Tales which survive to us in broken disjointed riddles were intact here in living form. I lay on my elbow and questioned feverishly. At any moment they might become morose and refuse to speak. Clearly it was my duty to make the most of a brief good fortune.

And then the tale they told me grew more hideous. I heard of the circumstances of the life itself and their daily shifts for existence. It was a murderous chronicle – a history of lust and rapine and unmentionable deeds in the darkness. One thing they had early recognised – that the race could not be maintained within itself; so that ghoulish carrying away of little girls from the lowlands began, which I had heard of but never credited. Shut up in those dismal holes, the girls soon died, and when the new race had grown up the plunder had been repeated. Then there were bestial murders in lonely cottages, done for God knows what purpose. Sometimes the occupant had seen more than was safe, sometimes the deed was the mere exuberance of a lust of slaying. As they gabbled their tales my heart's blood froze, and I lay back in the agonies of fear. If they had used the others thus, what way of escape was open for myself? I had been brought to this place, and not murdered on the spot. Clearly there was torture before death in store for me, and I confess I quailed at the thought.

But none molested me. The elders continued to jabber out their stories, while I lay tense and deaf. Then to my amazement food was brought and placed beside me – almost with respect. Clearly my murder was not a thing of the immediate future. The meal was some form of mutton – perhaps the shepherd's lost ewes – and a little smoking was all the cooking it had got. I strove to eat, but the tasteless morsels choked me. Then they set drink before me in a curious cup, which I seized on eagerly, for my mouth was dry with thirst. The vessel was of gold, rudely formed, but of the pure metal, and a coarse design in circles ran round the middle. This surprised me enough, but a greater wonder awaited me. The liquor was not water, as I had guessed, but a sort of sweet ale, a miracle of flavour. The taste was curious, but somehow familiar; it was like no wine I had ever drunk, and yet I had known that flavour all my life. I sniffed at the brim, and there rose a faint fragrance of thyme and heather honey and the sweet things of the moorland. I almost dropped it in my surprise; for here in this rude place I had stumbled upon that lost delicacy of the North, the heather ale.

For a second I was entranced with my discovery, and then the wonder of the cup claimed my attention. Was it a mere relic of pillage, or had this folk some hidden mine of the precious metal? Gold had once been common in these hills. There were the traces of mines on Cairnsmore; shepherds had found it in the gravel of the Gled Water; and the name of a house at the head of the Clachlands meant the 'Home of Gold'.

Once more I began my questions, and they answered them willingly. There and then I heard that secret for which many had died in old time, the secret of the heather ale. They told of the gold in the hills, of corries where the sand gleamed and abysses where the rocks were veined. All this they told me, freely, without a scruple. And then, like a clap, came the awful thought that this, too, spelled death. These were secrets which this race aforetime had guarded with their lives; they told them generously to me because there was no fear of betrayal. I should go no more out from this place.

The thought put me into a new sweat of terror – not at death, mind you, but at the unknown horrors which might precede the final suffering. I lay silent, and after binding my hands they began to leave me and go off to other parts of the cave. I dozed in the horrible half-swoon of fear, conscious only of my shaking limbs, and the great dull glow of the fire in the centre. Then I became calmer. After all, they had treated me with tolerable kindness: I had spoken their language, which few of their victims could have done for many a century; it might be that I had found favour in their eyes. For a little I comforted myself with this delusion, till I caught sight of a wooden box in a corner. It was of modern make, one such as grocers use to pack provisions in. It had some address nailed on it, and an aimless curiosity compelled me to creep thither and read it. A torn and weather-stained scrap of paper, with the nails at the corner rusty with age; but something of the address might still be made out. Amid the stains my feverish eyes read, 'To Mr M — , Carrickfey, by Allerfoot Station.'

The ruined cottage in the hollow of the waste with the single gnarled apple-tree was before me in a twinkling. I remembered the shepherd's shrinking from the place and the name, and his wild eyes when he told me of the thing that had happened there. I seemed to see the old man in his moorland cottage, thinking no evil; the sudden entry of the nameless things; and then the eyes glazed in unspeakable terror. I felt my lips dry and burning. Above me was the vault of rock; in the distance I saw the fire-glow and the shadows of shapes moving around it. My fright was too great for inaction, so I crept from the couch, and silently, stealthily, with tottering steps and bursting heart, I began to reconnoitre.

But I was still bound, my arms tightly, my legs more loosely, but yet firm enough to hinder flight. I could not get my hands at my leg-straps, still less could I undo the manacles. I rolled on the floor, seeking some sharp edge of rock, but all had been worn smooth by the use of centuries. Then suddenly an idea came upon me like an inspiration. The sounds from the fire seemed to have ceased, and I could hear them repeated from another and more distant part of the cave. The Folk had left their orgy round the blaze, and at the end of the long tunnel I saw its glow fall unimpeded upon the floor. Once there, I might burn off my fetters and be free to turn my thoughts to escape.

I crawled a little way with much labour. Then suddenly I came abreast an opening in the wall, through which a path went. It was a long straight rock-cutting, and at the end I saw a gleam of pale light. It must be the open air; the way of escape was prepared for me; and with a prayer I made what speed I could towards the fire.

I rolled on the verge, but the fuel was peat, and the warm ashes would not burn the cords. In desperation I went farther, and my clothes began to singe, while my face ached beyond endurance. But yet I got no nearer my object. The strips of hide warped and cracked, but did not burn. Then in a last effort I thrust my wrists bodily into the glow and held them there. In an instant I drew them out with a groan of pain, scarred and sore, but to my joy with the band snapped in one place. Weak as I was, it was now easy to free myself, and then came the untying of my legs. My hands trembled, my eyes were dazed with hurry, and I was longer over the job than need have been. But at length I had loosed my cramped knees and stood on my feet, a free man once more.

I kicked off my boots, and fled noiselessly down the passage to the tunnel mouth. Apparently it was close on evening, for the white light had faded to a pale yellow. But it was daylight, and that was all I sought, and I ran for it as eagerly as ever runner ran to a goal. I came out on a rock-shelf, beneath which a moraine of boulders fell away in a chasm to a dark loch. It was all but night, but I could see the gnarled and fortressed rocks rise in ramparts above, and below the unknown screes and cliffs which make the side of the Muneraw a place only for foxes and the fowls of the air.

The first taste of liberty is an intoxication, and assuredly I was mad when I leaped down among the boulders. Happily at the top of the gully the stones were large and stable, else the noise would certainly have discovered me. Down I went, slipping, praying, my charred wrists aching, and my stockinged feet wet with blood. Soon I was in the jaws of the cleft, and a pale star rose before me. I have always been timid in the face of great rocks, and now, had not an awful terror been dogging my footsteps, no power on earth could have driven me to that descent. Soon I left the boulders behind, and came to long spouts of little stones, which moved with me till the hillside seemed sinking under my feet. Sometimes I was face downwards, once and again I must have fallen for yards. Had there been a cliff at the foot, I should have gone over it without resistance; but by the providence of God the spout ended in a long curve into the heather of the bog.

When I found my feet once more on soft boggy earth, my strength was renewed within me. A great hope of escape sprang up in my heart. For a second I looked back. There was a great line of shingle with the cliffs beyond, and above all the unknown blackness of the cleft. There lay my terror, and I set off running across the bog for dear life. My mind was clear enough to know my road. If I held round the loch in front I should come to a burn which fed the Farawa stream, on whose banks stood the shepherd's cottage. The loch could not be far; once at the Farawa I would have the light of the shieling clear before me.

Suddenly I heard behind me, as if coming from the hillside, the patter of feet. It was the sound which white hares make in the winter-time on a noiseless frosty day as they patter over the snow. I have heard the same soft noise from a herd of deer when they changed their pastures. Strange that so kindly a sound should put the very fear of death in my heart. I ran madly, blindly, yet thinking shrewdly. The loch was before me. Somewhere I had read or heard, I do not know where, that the brutish aboriginal races of the North could not swim. I myself swam powerfully; could I but cross the loch I should save two miles of a desperate country.

There was no time to lose, for the patter was coming nearer, and I was almost at the loch's edge. I tore off my coat and rushed in. The bottom was mossy, and I had to struggle far before I found any depth. Something plashed in the water before me, and then something else a little behind. The thought that I was a mark for unknown missiles made me crazy with fright, and I struck fiercely out for the other shore. A gleam of moonlight was on the water at the burn's exit, and thither I guided myself. I found the thing difficult enough in itself, for my hands ached, and I was numb from my bonds. But my fancy raised a thousand phantoms to vex me. Swimming in that black bog water, pursued by those nameless things, I seemed to be in a world of horror far removed from the kindly world of men. My strength seemed inexhaustible from my terror. Monsters at the bottom of the water seemed to bite at my feet, and the pain of my wrists made me believe that the loch was boiling hot, and that I was in some hellish place of torment.

I came out on a spit of gravel above the burn mouth, and set off down the ravine of the burn. It was a strait place, strewn with rocks; but now and then the hill turf came in stretches, and eased my wounded feet. Soon the fall became more abrupt, and I was slipping down a hillside, with the water on my left making great cascades in the granite. And then I was out in the wider vale where the Farawa water flowed among links of moss.

Far in front, a speck in the blue darkness, shone the light of the cottage. I panted forward, my breath coming in gasps and my back shot with fiery pains. Happily the land was easier for the feet as long as I kept on the skirts of the bog. My ears were sharp as a wild beast's with fear, as I listened for the noise of pursuit. Nothing came but the rustle of the gentlest hill-wind and the chatter of the falling streams.

Then suddenly the light began to waver and move athwart the window. I knew what it meant. In a minute or two the household at the cottage would retire to rest, and the lamp would be put out. True, I might find the place in the dark, for there was a moon of sorts and the road was not desperate. But somehow in that hour the lamplight gave a promise of safety which I clung to despairingly.

And then the last straw was added to my misery. Behind me came the pad of feet, the pat-patter, soft, eerie, incredibly swift. I choked with fear, and flung myself forward in a last effort. I give my word it was sheer mechanical shrinking that drove me on. God knows I would have lain down to die in the heather, had the things behind me been a common terror of life.

I ran as man never ran before, leaping hags, scrambling through green well-heads, straining towards the fast-dying light. A quarter of a mile and the patter sounded nearer. Soon I was not two hundred yards off, and the noise seemed almost at my elbow. The light went out, and the black mass of the cottage loomed in the dark.

Then, before I knew, I was at the door, battering it wearily and yelling for help. I heard steps within and a hand on the bolt. Then something shot past me with lightning force and buried itself in the wood. The dreadful hands were almost at my throat, when the door was opened and I stumbled in, hearing with a gulp of joy the key turn and the bar fall behind me.

V

The Troubles of a Conscience

My body and senses slept, for I was utterly tired, but my brain all the night was on fire with horrid fancies. Again I was in that accursed cave; I was torturing my hands in the fire; I was slipping barefoot among jagged boulders; and then with bursting heart I was toiling the last mile with the cottage light – now grown to a great fire in the heavens – blazing before me.

It was broad daylight when I awoke, and I thanked God for the comfortable rays of the sun. I had been laid in a box-bed off the inner room, and my first sight was the shepherd sitting with folded arms in a chair regarding me solemnly. I rose and began to dress, feeling my legs and arms still tremble with weariness. The shepherd's sister bound up my scarred wrists and put an ointment on my burns; and, limping like an old man, I went into the kitchen.

I could eat little breakfast, for my throat seemed dry and narrow; but they gave me some brandy-and-milk, which put strength into my body. All the time the brother and sister sat in silence, regarding me with covert glances.

'Ye have been delivered from the jaws o' the Pit,' said the man at length. 'See that,' and he held out to me a thin shaft of flint. 'I fand that in the door this morning.'

I took it, let it drop, and stared vacantly at the window. My nerves had been too much tried to be roused by any new terror. Out of doors it was fair weather, flying gleams of April sunlight and the soft colours of spring. I felt dazed, isolated, cut off from my easy past and pleasing future, a companion of horrors and the sport of nameless things. Then suddenly my eye fell on my books heaped on a table, and the old distant civilisation seemed for the moment inexpressibly dear.

'I must go – at once. And you must come too. You cannot stay here. I tell you it is death. If you knew what I know you would be crying out with fear. How far is it to Allermuir? Eight, fifteen miles; and then ten down Glen Aller to Allerfoot, and then the railway. We must go together while it is daylight, and perhaps we may be untouched. But quick, there is not a moment to lose.' And I was on my shaky feet, and bustling among my possessions.

'I'll gang wi' ye to the station,' said the shepherd, 'for ye're clearly no fit to look after yourself. My sister will bide and keep the house. If naething has touched us this ten year, naething will touch us the day.'

'But you cannot stay. You are mad,' I began; but he cut me short with the words, 'I trust in God.'

'In any case let your sister come with us. I dare not think of a woman alone in this place.'

'I'll bide,' said she. 'I'm no feared as lang as I'm indoors and there's steeks on the windies.'

So I packed my few belongings as best I could, tumbled my books into a haversack, and, gripping the shepherd's arm nervously, crossed the threshold. The glen was full of sunlight. There lay the long shining links of the Farawa burn, the rough hills tumbled beyond, and far over all the scarred and distant forehead of the Muneraw. I had always looked on moorland country as the freshest on earth – clean, whole-some, and homely. But now the fresh uplands seemed like a horrible pit. When I looked to the hills my breath choked in my throat, and the feel of soft heather below my feet set my heart trembling.

It was a slow journey to the inn at Allermuir. For one thing, no power on earth would draw me within sight of the shieling of Carrickfey, so we had to cross a shoulder of hill and make our way down a difficult glen, and then over a treacherous moss. The lochs were now gleaming like fretted silver; but to me, in my dreadful knowledge, they seemed more eerie than on that grey day when I came. At last my eyes were cheered by the sight of a meadow and a fence; then we were on a little byroad; and soon the fir-woods and corn-lands of Allercleuch were plain before us.

The shepherd came no farther, but with brief good-bye turned his solemn face hillwards. I hired a trap and a man to drive, and down the ten miles of Glen Aller I struggled to keep my thoughts from the past. I thought of the kindly South Country, of Oxford, of anything comfortable and civilised. My driver pointed out the objects of interest as in duty bound, but his words fell on unheeding ears. At last he said something which roused me indeed to interest – the interest of the man who hears the word he fears most in the world. On the left side of the river there suddenly sprang into view a long gloomy cleft in the hills, with a vista of dark mountains behind, down which a stream of considerable size poured its waters.

'That is the Water o' Dule,' said the man in a reverent voice. 'A graund water to fish, but dangerous to life, for it's a' linns. Awa' at the heid they say there's a terrible wild place called the Scarts o' Muneraw, – that's a shouther o' the muckle hill itsel' that ye see, – but I've never been there, and I never kent ony man that had either.'

At the station, which is a mile from the village of Allerfoot, I found I had some hours to wait on my train for the south. I dared not trust myself for one moment alone, so I hung about the goods-shed, talked vacantly to the porters, and when one went to the village for tea I accompanied him, and to his wonder entertained him at the inn. When I returned I found on the platform a stray bagman who was that evening going to London. If there is one class of men in the world which I heartily detest it is this; but such was my state that I hailed him as a brother, and besought his company. I paid the difference for a first-class fare, and had him in the carriage with me. He must have thought me an amiable maniac, for I talked in fits and starts, and when he fell asleep I would wake him up and beseech him to speak to me. At wayside stations I would pull down the blinds in case of recognition, for to my unquiet mind the world seemed full of spies sent by that terrible Folk of the Hills. When the train crossed a stretch of moor I would lie down on the seat in case of shafts fired from the heather. And then at last with utter weariness I fell asleep, and woke screaming about midnight to find myself well down in the cheerful English midlands, and red blast-furnaces blinking by the railway-side.

In the morning I breakfasted in my rooms at St. Chad's with a dawning sense of safety. I was in a different and calmer world. The lawn-like quadrangles, the great trees, the cawing of rooks, and the homely twitter of sparrows – all seemed decent and settled and pleasing. Indoors the oak-panelled walls, the shelves of books, the pictures, the faint fragrance of tobacco, were very different from the gimcrack adornments and the accursed smell of peat and heather in that deplorable cottage. It was still vacation-time, so most of my friends were down; but I spent the day hunting out the few cheerful pedants to whom term and vacation were the same. It delighted me to hear again their precise talk, to hear them make a boast of their work, and narrate the childish little accidents of their life. I yearned for the childish once more; I craved for women's drawing-rooms, and women's chatter, and everything which makes life an elegant game. God knows I had had enough of the other thing for a lifetime!

That night I shut myself in my rooms, barred my windows, drew my curtains, and made a great destruction. All books or pictures which recalled to me the moorlands were ruthlessly doomed. Novels, poems, treatises I flung into an old box, for sale to the second-hand bookseller. Some prints and water-colour sketches I tore to pieces with my own hands. I ransacked my fishing-book, and condemned all tackle for moorland waters to the flames. I wrote a letter to my solicitors, bidding them go no further in the purchase of a place in Lorn I had long been thinking of. Then, and not till then, did I feel the bondage of the past a little loosed from my shoulders. I made myself a night-cap of rum-punch instead of my usual whisky-toddy, that all associations with that dismal land might be forgotten, and to complete the renunciation I returned to cigars and flung my pipe into a drawer.

But when I woke in the morning I found that it is hard to get rid of memories. My feet were still sore and wounded, and when I felt my arms cramped and reflected on the causes, there was that black memory always near to vex me.

In a little term began, and my duties – as deputy-professor of Northern Antiquities – were once more clamorous. I can well believe that my hearers found my lectures strange, for instead of dealing with my favourite subjects and matters, which I might modestly say I had made my own, I confined myself to recondite and distant themes, treating even these cursorily and dully. For the truth is, my heart was no more in my subject. I hated – or I thought I hated – all things Northern with the virulence of utter fear. My reading was confined to science of the most recent kind, to abstruse philosophy, and to foreign classics. Anything which savoured of romance or mystery was abhorrent; I pined for sharp outlines and the tangibility of a high civilisation.

All the term I threw myself into the most frivolous life of the place. My Harrow schooldays seemed to have come back to me. I had once been a fair cricketer, so I played again for my college, and made decent scores. I coached an indifferent crew on the river. I fell into the slang of the place, which I had hitherto detested. My former friends looked on me askance, as if some freakish changeling had possessed me. Formerly I had been ready for pedantic discussion, I had been absorbed in my work, men had spoken of me as a rising scholar. Now I fled the very mention of things I had once delighted in. The Professor of Northern Antiquities, a scholar of European reputation, meeting me once in the Parks, embarked on an account of certain novel rings recently found in Scotland, and to his horror found that, when he had got well under weigh, I had slipped off unnoticed. I heard afterwards that the good old man was found by a friend walking disconsolately with bowed head in the middle of the High Street. Being rescued from among the horses' feet, he could only murmur, 'I am thinking of Graves, poor man! And a year ago he was as sane as I am!'

But a man may not long deceive himself. I kept up the illusion valiantly for the term; but I felt instinctively that the fresh schoolboy life, which seemed to me the extreme opposite to the ghoulish North, and as such the most desirable of things, was eternally cut off from me. No cunning affectation could ever dispel my real nature or efface the memory of a week. I realised miserably that sooner or later I must fight it out with my conscience. I began to call myself a coward. The chief thoughts of my mind began to centre themselves more and more round that unknown life waiting to be explored among the wilds.

One day I met a friend – an official in the British Museum – who was full of some new theory about primitive habitations. To me it seemed inconceivably absurd; but he was strong in his confidence, and without flaw in his evidence. The man irritated me, and I burned to prove him wrong, but I could think of no argument which was final against his. Then it flashed upon me that my own experience held the disproof; and without more words I left him, hot, angry with myself, and tantalised by the unattainable.

I might relate my *bona-fide* experience, but would men believe me? I must bring proofs, I must complete my researches, so as to make them incapable of disbelief. And there in those deserts was waiting the key. There lay the greatest discovery of the century – nay, of the millennium. There, too, lay the road to wealth such as I had never dreamed of. Could I succeed, I should be famous for ever. I would revolutionise history and anthropology; I would systematise folklore; I would show the world of men the pit whence they were digged and the rock whence they were hewn.

And then began a game of battledore between myself and my conscience.

'You are a coward,' said my conscience.

'I am sufficiently brave,' I would answer. 'I have seen things and yet lived. The terror is more than mortal, and I cannot face it.'

'You are a coward,' said my conscience.

'I am not bound to go there again. It would be purely for my own aggrandisement if I went, and not for any matter of duty.'

'Nevertheless you are a coward,' said my conscience.

'In any case the matter can wait.'

'You are a coward.'

Then came one awful midsummer night, when I lay sleepless and fought the thing out with myself. I knew that the strife was hopeless, that I should have no peace in this world again unless I made the attempt. The dawn was breaking when I came to the final resolution; and when I rose and looked at my face in a mirror, lo! it was white and lined and drawn like a man of sixty.

VI

Summer on the Moors

The next morning I packed a bag with some changes of clothing and a collection of notebooks, and went up to town. The first thing I did was to pay a visit to my solicitors. 'I am about to travel,' said I, 'and I wish to have all things settled in case any accident should happen to me.' So I arranged for the disposal of my property in case of death, and added a codicil which puzzled the lawyers. If I did not return within six months, communications were to be entered into with the shepherd at the shieling of Farawa – post-town Allerfoot. If he could produce any papers, they were to be put into the hands of certain friends, published, and the cost charged to my estate. From my solicitors I went to a gunmaker's in Regent Street and bought an ordinary six-chambered revolver, feeling much as a man must feel who proposed to cross the Atlantic in a skiff and purchased a small life-belt as a precaution.

I took the night express to the North, and, for a marvel, I slept. When I awoke about four we were on the verge of Westmoreland, and stony hills blocked the horizon. At first I hailed the mountain-land gladly; sleep for the moment had caused forgetfulness of my terrors. But soon a turn of the line brought me in full view of a heathery moor, running far to a confusion of distant peaks. I remembered my mission and my fate, and if ever condemned criminal felt a more bitter regret I pity his case. Why should I alone among the millions of this happy isle be singled out at the repository of a ghastly secret, and be cursed by a conscience which would not let it rest?

I came to Allerfoot early in the forenoon, and got a trap to drive me up the valley. It was a lowering grey day, hot and yet sunless. A sort of heat-haze cloaked the hills, and every now and then a smurr of rain would meet us on the road, and in a minute be over. I felt wretchedly dispirited; and when at last the white-washed kirk of Allermuir came into sight and the broken-backed bridge of Aller, man's eyes seemed to have looked on no drearier scene since time began.

I ate what meal I could get, for, fears or no, I was voraciously hungry. Then I asked the landlord to find me some man who would show me the road to Farawa. I demanded company, not for protection – for what could two men do against such brutish strength? – but to keep my mind from its own thoughts.

The man looked at me anxiously.

'Are ye acquaint wi' the folks, then?' he asked.

I said I was, that I had often stayed in the cottage.

'Ye ken that they've a name for being queer. The man never comes here forbye once or twice a-year, and he has few dealings wi' other herds. He's got an ill name, too, for losing sheep. I dinna like the country ava. Up by yon Muneraw – no that I've ever been there, but I've seen it afar off – is enough to put a man daft for the rest o' his days. What's taking ye thereaways? It's no the time for the fishing?'

I told him that I was a botanist going to explore certain hill-crevices for rare ferns. He shook his head, and then after some delay found me an ostler who would accompany me to the cottage.

The man was a shock-headed, long-limbed fellow, with fierce red hair and a humorous eye. He talked sociably about his life, answered my hasty questions with deftness, and beguiled me for the moment out of myself. I passed the melancholy lochs, and came in sight of the great stony hills without the trepidation I had expected. Here at my side was one who found some humour even in those uplands. But one thing I noted which brought back the old uneasiness. He took the road which led us farthest from Carrickfey, and when to try him I proposed the other, he vetoed it with emphasis.

After this his good spirits departed, and he grew distrustful.

'What mak's ye a freend o' the herd at Farawa?' he demanded a dozen times.

Finally, I asked him if he knew the man, and had seen him lately.

'I dinna ken him, and I hadna seen him for years till a fortnicht syne, when a' Allermuir saw him. He cam doun one afternoon to the public-hoose, and begood to drink. He had aye been kenned for a terrible godly kind o' a man, so ye may believe folk wondered at this. But when he had stuck to the drink for twae days, and filled himsel' blind-fou half-a-dozen o' times, he took a fit o' repentance, and raved and blethered about siccan a life as he led in the muirs. There was some said he was speakin' serious, but maist thocht it was juist daftness.'

'And what did he speak about?' I asked sharply.

'I canna verra weel tell ye. It was about some kind o' bogle that lived in the Muneraw – that's the shouthers o't ye see yonder – and it seems that the bogle killed his sheep and frichted himsel'. He was aye bletherin', too, about something or somebody ca'd Grave; but oh! the man wasna wise.' And my companion shook a contemptuous head.

And then below us in the valley we saw the shieling, with a thin shaft of smoke rising into the rainy grey weather. The man left me, sturdily refusing any fee. 'I wantit my legs stretched as weel as you. A walk in the hills is neither here nor there to a stoot man. When will ye be back, sir?'

The question was well-timed. 'To-morrow fortnight,' I said, 'and I want somebody from Allermuir to come out here in the morning and carry some baggage. Will you see to that?'

He said 'Ay,' and went off, while I scrambled down the hill to the cottage. Nervousness possessed me, and though it was broad daylight and the whole place lay plain before me, I ran pell-mell, and did not stop till I reached the door.

The place was utterly empty. Unmade beds, unwashed dishes, a hearth strewn with the ashes of peat, and dust thick on everything, proclaimed the absence of inmates. I began to be horribly frightened. Had the shepherd and his sister, also, disappeared? Was I left alone in this bleak place, with a dozen lonely miles between me and human dwellings? I could not return alone; better this horrible place than the unknown perils of the out-of-doors. Hastily I barricaded the door, and to the best of my power shuttered the windows; and then with dreary forebodings I sat down to wait on fortune.

In a little I heard a long swinging step outside and the sound of dogs. Joyfully I opened the latch, and there was the shepherd's grim face waiting stolidly on what might appear.

At the sight of me he stepped back. 'What in the Lord's name are ye daein' here?' he asked. 'Didna ye get enough afore?'

'Come in,' I said, sharply. 'I want to talk.'

In he came with those blessed dogs, – what a comfort it was to look on their great honest faces! He sat down on the untidy bed and waited.

'I came because I could not stay away. I saw too much to give me any peace elsewhere. I must go back, even though I risk my life for it. The cause of scholarship demands it as well as the cause of humanity.'

'Is that a' the news ye hae?' he said. 'Weel, I've mair to tell ye. Three weeks syne my sister Margit was lost, and I've never seen her mair.'

My jaw fell, and I could only stare at him.

'I cam hame from the hill at nightfa' and she was gone. I lookit for her up hill and doun, but I couldna find her. Syne I think I went daft. I went to the Scarts and huntit them up and doun, but no sign could I see. The Folk can bide quiet enough when they want. Syne I went to Allermuir and drank mysel' blind, – me, that's a God-fearing man and a saved soul; but the Lord help me, I didna ken what I was at. That's my news, and day and night I wander thae hills, seekin' for what I canna find.'

'But, man, are you mad?' I cried. 'Surely there are neighbours to help you. There is a law in the land, and you had only to find the nearest police-office and compel them to assist you.'

'What guid can man dae?' he asked. 'An army o' sodgers couldna find that hidy-hole. Forby, when I went into Allermuir wi' my story the folk thocht me daft. It was that set me drinking, for – the Lord forgive me! – I wasna my ain maister. I threepit till I was hairse, but the bodies just lauch'd.' And he lay back on the bed like a man mortally tired.

Grim though the tidings were, I can only say that my chief feeling was of comfort. Pity for the new tragedy had swallowed up my fear. I had now a purpose, and a purpose, too, not of curiosity but of mercy.

'I go to-morrow morning to the Muneraw. But first I want to give you something to do.' And I drew roughly a chart of the place on the back of a letter. 'Go into Allermuir to-morrow, and give this paper to the landlord at the inn. The letter will tell him what to do. He is to raise at once all the men he can get, and come to the place on the chart marked with a cross. Tell him life depends on his hurry.'

The shepherd nodded. 'D'ye ken the Folk are watching for you? They let me pass without trouble, for they've nae use for me, but I see fine they're seeking you. Ye'll no gang half a mile the morn afore they grip ye.'

'So much the better,' I said. 'That will take me quicker to the place I want to be at.'

'And I'm to gang to Allermuir the morn,' he repeated, with the air of a child conning a lesson. 'But what if they'll no believe me?'

'They'll believe the letter.'

'Maybe,' he said, and relapsed into a doze.

I set myself to put that house in order, to rouse the fire, and prepare some food. It was dismal work; and meantime outside the night darkened, and a great wind rose, which howled round the walls and lashed the rain on the windows.

VII

In Tuas Manus, Domine!

I had not gone twenty yards from the cottage door ere I knew I was watched. I had left the shepherd still dozing, in the half-conscious state of a dazed and broken man. All night the wind had wakened me at intervals, and now in the half-light of morn the weather seemed more vicious than ever. The wind cut my ears, the whole firmament was full of the rendings and thunders of the storm. Rain fell in blinding sheets, the heath was a marsh, and it was the most I could do to struggle against the hurricane which stopped my breath. And all the while I knew I was not alone in the desert.

All men know – in imagination or in experience – the sensation of being spied on. The nerves tingle, the skin grows hot and prickly, and there is a queer sinking of the heart. Intensify this common feeling a hundredfold, and you get a tenth part of what I suffered. I am telling a plain tale, and record bare physical facts. My lips stood out from my teeth as I heard, or felt, a rustle in the heather, a scraping among stones. Some subtle magnetic link seemed established between my body and the mysterious world around. I became sick – acutely sick – with the ceaseless apprehension.

My fright became so complete that when I turned a corner of rock, or stepped in deep heather, I seemed to feel a body rub against mine. This continued all the way up the Farawa water, and then up its feeder to the little lonely loch. It kept me from looking forward; but it likewise kept me in such a sweat of fright that I was ready to faint. Then the notion came upon me to test this fancy of mine. If I was tracked thus closely, clearly the trackers would bar my way if I turned back. So I wheeled round and walked a dozen paces down the glen.

Nothing stopped me. I was about to turn again, when something made me take six more paces. At the fourth something rustled in the heather, and my neck was gripped as in a vice. I had already made up my mind on what I would do. I would be perfectly still, I would conquer my fear, and let them do as they pleased with me so long as they took me to their dwelling. But at the touch of the hands my resolutions fled. I struggled and screamed. Then something was clapped on my mouth, speech and strength went from me, and once more I was back in the maudlin childhood of terror.

In the cave it was always a dusky twilight. I seemed to be lying in the same place, with the same dull glare of firelight far off, and the same close stupefying smell. One of the creatures was standing silently at my side, and I asked him some trivial question. He turned and shambled down the passage, leaving me alone.

Then he returned with another, and they talked their guttural talk to me. I scarcely listened till I remembered that in a sense I was here of my own accord, and on a definite mission. The purport of their speech seemed to be that, now I had returned, I must beware of a second flight. Once I had been spared; a second time I should be killed without mercy.

I assented gladly. The Folk, then, had some use for me. I felt my errand prospering.

Then the old creature which I had seen before crept out of some corner and squatted beside me. He put a claw on my shoulder, a horrible, corrugated, skeleton thing, hairy to the finger-tips and nailless. He grinned, too, with toothless gums, and his hideous old voice was like a file on sandstone.

I asked questions, but he would only grin and jabber, looking now and then furtively over his shoulder towards the fire.

I coaxed and humoured him, till he launched into a narrative of which I could make nothing. It seemed a mere string of names, with certain words repeated at fixed intervals. Then it flashed on me that this might be a religious incantation. I had discovered remnants of a ritual and a mythology among them. It was possible that these were sacred days, and that I had stumbled upon some rude celebration.

I caught a word or two and repeated them. He looked at me curiously. Then I asked him some leading question, and he replied with clearness. My guess was right. The midsummer week was the holy season of the year, when sacrifices were offered to the gods.

The notion of sacrifices disquieted me, and I would fain have asked further. But the creature would speak no more. He hobbled off, and left me alone in the rock-chamber to listen to a strange sound which hung ceaselessly about me. It must be the storm without, like a park of artillery rattling among the crags. A storm of storms surely, for the place echoed and hummed, and to my unquiet eye the very rock of the roof seemed to shake!

Apparently my existence was forgotten, for I lay long before any one returned. Then it was merely one who brought food, the same strange meal as before, and left hastily. When I had eaten I rose and stretched myself. My hands and knees still quivered nervously; but I was strong and perfectly well in body. The empty, desolate, tomb-like place was eerie enough to scare any one; but its emptiness was comfort when I thought of its inmates. Then I wandered down the passage towards the fire which was burning in loneliness. Where had the Folk gone? I puzzled over their disappearance.

Suddenly sounds began to break on my ear, coming from some inner chamber at the end of that in which the fire burned. I could scarcely see for the smoke; but I began to make my way towards the noise, feeling along the sides of rock. Then a second gleam of light seemed to rise before me, and I came to an aperture in the wall which gave entrance to another room.

This in turn was full of smoke and glow – a murky orange glow, as if from some strange flame of roots. There were the squat moving figures, running in wild antics round the fire. I crouched in the entrance, terrified and yet curious, till I saw something beyond the blaze which held me dumb. Apart from the others and tied to some stake in the wall was a woman's figure, and the face was the face of the shepherd's sister.

My first impulse was flight. I must get away and think, – plan, achieve some desperate way of escape. I sped back to the silent chamber as if the gang were at my heels. It was still empty, and I stood helplessly in the centre, looking at the impassable walls of rock as a wearied beast may look at the walls of its cage. I bethought me of the way I had escaped before and rushed thither, only to find it blocked by a huge contrivance of stone. Yards and yards of solid rock were between me and the upper air, and yet through it all came the crash and whistle of the storm. If I were at my wits' end in this inner darkness, there was also high commotion among the powers of the air in that upper world.

As I stood I heard the soft steps of my tormentors. They seemed to think I was meditating escape, for they flung themselves on me and bore me to the ground. I did not struggle, and when they saw me quiet, they squatted round and began to speak. They told me of the holy season and its sacrifices. At first I could not follow them; then when I caught familiar words I found some clue, and they became intelligible. They spoke of a woman, and I asked, 'What woman?' With all frankness they told me of the custom which prevailed – how every twentieth summer a woman was sacrificed to some devilish god, and by the hand of one of the stranger race. I said nothing, but my whitening face must have told them a tale, though I strove hard to keep my composure. I asked if they had found the victims. 'She is in this place,' they said: 'and as for the man, thou art he.' And with this they left me.

I had still some hours; so much I gathered from their talk, for the sacrifice was at sunset. Escape was cut off for ever. I have always been something of a fatalist, and at the prospect of the irrevocable end my cheerfulness returned. I had my pistol, for they had taken nothing from me. I took out the little weapon and fingered it lovingly. Hope of the lost, refuge of the vanquished, ease to the coward, – blessed be he who first conceived it!

The time dragged on, the minutes grew to hours, and still I was left solitary. Only the mad violence of the storm broke the quiet. It had increased in fury, for the stones at the mouth of the exit by which I had formerly escaped seemed to rock with some external pressure, and cutting shafts of wind slipped past and cleft the heat of the passage. What a sight the ravine outside must be, I thought, set in the forehead of a great hill, and swept clean by every breeze! Then came a crashing, and the long hollow echo of a fall. The rocks are splitting, said I; the road down the corrie will be impassable now and for evermore.

I began to grow weak with the nervousness of the waiting, and by-and-by I lay down and fell into a sort of doze. When I next knew consciousness I was being roused by two of the Folk, and bidden get ready. I stumbled to my feet, felt for the pistol in the hollow of my sleeve, and prepared to follow.

When we came out into the wider chamber the noise of the storm was deafening. The roof rang like a shield which has been struck. I noticed, perturbed as I was, that my guards cast anxious eyes around them, alarmed, like myself, at the murderous din. Nor was the world quieter when we entered the last chamber, where the fire burned and the remnant of the Folk waited. Wind had found an entrance from somewhere or other, and the flames blew here and there, and the smoke gyrated in odd circles. At the back, and apart from the rest, I saw the dazed eyes and the white old drawn face of the woman.

They led me up beside her to a place where there was a rude flat stone, hollowed in the centre, and on it a rusty iron knife, which seemed once to have formed part of a scythe-blade. Then I saw the ceremonial which was marked out for me. It was the very rite which I had dimly figured as current among a rude people, and even in that moment of horror I had something of the scholar's satisfaction.

The oldest of the Folk, who seemed to be a sort of priest, came to my side and mumbled a form of words. His fetid breath sickened me; his dull eyes, glassy like a brute's with age, brought my knees together. He put the knife in my hands, dragged the terror-stricken woman forward to the altar, and bade me begin.

JOHN BUCHAN

I began by sawing her bonds through. When she felt herself free she would have fled back, but stopped when I bade her. At that moment there came a noise of rending and crashing as if the hills were falling, and for one second the eyes of the Folk were averted from the frustrated sacrifice.

Only for a moment. The next they saw what I had done, and with one impulse rushed towards me. Then began the last scene in the play. I sent a bullet through the right eye of the first thing that came on. The second shot went wide; but the third shattered the hand of an elderly ruffian with a club. Never for an instant did they stop, and now they were clutching at me. I pushed the woman behind, and fired three rapid shots in blind panic, and then, clutching the scythe, I struck right and left like a madman.

Suddenly I saw the foreground sink before my eyes. The roof sloped down, and with a sickening hiss a mountain of rock and earth seemed to precipitate itself on the foremost of my assailants. One, nipped in the middle by a rock, caught my eye by his hideous writhings. Two only remained in what was now a little suffocating chamber, with embers from the fire still smoking on the floor.

The woman caught me by the hand and drew me with her, while the two seemed mute with fear. 'There's a road at the back,' she screamed. 'I ken it. I fand it out.' And she pulled me up a narrow hole in the rock.

How long we climbed I do not know. We were both fighting for air, with the tightness of throat and chest, and the craziness of limb which mean suffocation. I cannot tell when we first came to the surface, but I remember the woman, who seemed to have the strength of extreme terror, pulling me from the edge of a crevasse and laying me on a flat rock. It seemed to be the depth of winter, with sheer-falling rain and a wind that shook the hills.

Then I was once more myself and could look about me. From my feet yawned a sheer abyss, where once had been a hill-shoulder. Some great mass of rock on the brow of the mountain had been loosened by the storm, and in its fall had caught the lips of the ravine and blocked the upper outlet from the nest of dwellings. For a moment I feared that all had been destroyed.

My feeling – Heaven help me! – was not thankfulness for God's mercy and my escape, but a bitter mad regret. I rushed frantically to

[222]

the edge, and when I saw only the blackness of darkness I wept weak tears. All the time the storm was tearing at my body, and I had to grip hard by hand and foot to keep my place.

Suddenly on the brink of the ravine I saw a third figure. We two were not the only fugitives. One of the Folk had escaped.

I ran to it, and to my surprise the thing as soon as it saw me rushed to meet me. At first I thought it was with some instinct of self-preservation, but when I saw its eyes I knew the purpose of fight. Clearly one or other should go no more from the place.

We were some ten yards from the brink when I grappled with it. Dimly I heard the woman scream with fright, and saw her scramble across the hillside. Then we were tugging in a death-throe, the hideous smell of the thing in my face, its red eyes burning into mine, and its hoarse voice muttering. Its strength seemed incredible; but I, too, am no weakling. We tugged and strained, its nails biting into my flesh, while I choked its throat unsparingly. Every second I dreaded lest we should plunge together over the ledge, for it was thither my adversary tried to draw me. I caught my heel in a nick of rock, and pulled madly against it.

And then, while I was beginning to glory with the pride of conquest, my hope was dashed in pieces. The thing seemed to break from my arms, and, as if in despair, cast itself headlong into the impenetrable darkness. I stumbled blindly after it, saved myself on the brink, and fell back, sick and ill, into a merciful swoon.

VIII
Note in conclusion by the editor

At this point the narrative of my unfortunate friend, Mr. Graves of St. Chad's, breaks off abruptly. He wrote it shortly before his death, and was prevented from completing it by the attack of heart failure which carried him off. In accordance with the instructions in his will, I have prepared it for publication, and now in much fear and hesitation give it to the world. First, however, I must supplement it by such facts as fall within my knowledge.

The shepherd seems to have gone to Allermuir and by the help of the letter convinced the inhabitants. A body of men was collected under the landlord, and during the afternoon set out for the hills. But unfortunately the great midsummer storm — the most terrible of recent climatic disturbances – had filled the mosses and streams, and they found themselves unable to proceed by any direct road. Ultimately late in the evening they arrived at the cottage of Farawa, only to find there a raving woman, the shepherd's sister, who seemed crazy with brain-fever. She told some rambling story about her escape, but her narrative said nothing of Mr. Graves. So they treated her with what skill they possessed, and sheltered for the night in and around the cottage. Next morning the storm had abated a little, and the woman had recovered something of her wits. From her they learned that Mr. Graves was lying in a ravine on the side of the Muneraw in imminent danger of his life. A body set out to find him; but so immense was the landslip, and so dangerous the whole mountain, that it was nearly evening when they recovered him from the ledge of rock. He was alive, but unconscious, and on bringing him back to the cottage it was clear that he was, indeed, very ill. There he lay for three months, while the best skill that could be got was procured for him. By dint of an uncommon toughness of constitution he survived; but it was an old and feeble man who returned to Oxford in the early winter.

The shepherd and his sister immediately left the countryside, and were never more heard of, unless they are the pair of unfortunates who are at present in a Scottish pauper asylum, incapable of remembering even their names. The people who last spoke with them declared that their minds seemed weakened by a great shock, and that it was hopeless to try to get any connected or rational statement.

The career of my poor friend from that hour was little short of a tragedy. He awoke from his illness to find the world incredulous; even the country-folk of Allermuir set down the story to the shepherd's craziness and my friend's credulity. In Oxford his argument was received with polite scorn. An account of his experiences which he drew up for *The Times* was refused by the editor; and an article on 'Primitive Peoples of the North', embodying what he believed to be the result of his discoveries, was unanimously rejected by every responsible journal in Europe. At first he bore the treatment bravely. Reflection convinced him that the colony had not been destroyed. Proofs were still awaiting his hand, and with courage and caution he might yet triumph over his enemies. But unfortunately, though the ardour of the scholar burned more fiercely than ever and all fear seemed to have been purged from his soul, the last adventure had grievously sapped his bodily strength. In the spring following his accident he made an effort to reach the spot – alone, for no one could be persuaded to follow him in what was regarded as a childish madness. He slept at the now deserted cottage of Farawa, but in the morning found himself unable to continue, and with difficulty struggled back to the shepherd's cottage at Allercleuch, where he was confined to bed for a fortnight. Then it became necessary for him to seek health abroad, and it was not till the following autumn that he attempted the journey again. He fell sick a second time at the inn of Allermuir, and during his convalescence had himself carried to a knoll in the inn garden, whence a glimpse can be obtained of the shoulder of the Muneraw. There he would sit for hours with his eyes fixed on the horizon, and at times he would be found weeping with weakness and vexation. The last attempt was made but two months before his last illness. On this occasion he got no farther than Carlisle, where he was taken ill with what proved to be a premonition of death. After that he shut his lips tightly, as though recognising the futility of his hopes. Whether he had been soured by the treatment he received, or whether his brain had already been weakened, he had become a morose silent man, and for the two years before his death had few friends and no society. From the obituary notice in *The Times* I take the following paragraph, which shows in what light the world had come to look upon him: –

'At the outset of his career he was regarded as a rising scholar in one department of archæology, and his Taffert lectures were a real contribution to an obscure subject. But in after-life he was led into fantastic speculations; and when he found himself unable to convince his colleagues, he gradually retired into himself, and lived practically a hermit's life till his death. His career, thus broken short, is a sad instance of the fascination which the recondite and the quack can exercise even over men of approved ability.'

And now his own narrative is published, and the world can judge as it pleases about the amazing romance. The view which will doubtless find general acceptance is that the whole is a figment of the brain, begotten of some harmless moorland adventure and the company of such religious maniacs as the shepherd and his sister. But some who knew the former sobriety and calmness of my friend's mind may be disposed timorously and with deep hesitation to another verdict. They may accept the narrative, and believe that somewhere in those moorlands he met with a horrible primitive survival, passed through the strangest adventure, and had his fingers on an epoch-making discovery. In this case they will be inclined to sympathise with the loneliness and misunderstanding of his latter days. It is not for me to decide the question. Though a fellow-historian, the Picts are outside my period, and I dare not advance an opinion on a matter with which I am not fully familiar. But I would point out that the means of settling the question are still extant, and I would call upon some young archæologist, with a reputation to make, to seize upon the chance of the century. Most of the expresses for the North stop at Allerfoot; a ten-miles' drive will bring him to Allermuir; and then with a fifteen-miles' walk he is at Farawa and on the threshold of discovery. Let him follow the burn and cross the ridge and ascend the Scarts of the Muneraw, and, if he return at all, it may be with a more charitable judgment of my unfortunate friend.

The Far Islands

'The Far Islands' is another story from *Blackwood's* (1899).

In a letter to Gilbert Murray's wife, Mary, in February 1900 Buchan called it 'a sort of fairy tale for old people'. The story is a return to the Celtic theme of the journey to the Islands of the Blest but also looks forward to Adam Melfort's dream about Eilean Ban in Buchan's own novel *A Prince of the Captivity* (1933).

Indeed the story has important links with several Buchan novels. The Radens will later figure in *John Macnab* (1925), while the theme 'Can a particular form of hallucination run in a family for generations' has certain resonances with Buchan's exploration of how noble virtues can be passed between generations in his novel *The Path of the King* (1921). It is also possible to discern certain identifiable characters. Colin Raden is a composite of Oxford contemporaries, such as Auberon Herbert, and Buchan himself, while Medway, 'the foremost scholar of his acquaintance', is probably Buchan's friend from Oxford, Cuthbert Medd.

Lady Alice, Lady Louise,
Between the wash of the tumbling seas—

I

WHEN BRAN THE Blessed, as the story goes, followed the white bird on the Last Questing, knowing that return was not for him, he gave gifts to his followers. To Heliodorus he gave the gift of winning speech, and straightaway the man went south to the Italian seas, and, becoming a scholar, left many descendants who sat in the high places of the Church. To Raymond he gave his steel battle-axe, and bade him go out to the warrior's path and hew his way to a throne;

which the man forthwith accomplished, and became an ancestor in the fourth degree of the first king of Scots. But to Colin, the youngest and the dearest, he gave no gift, whispering only a word in his ear and laying a finger on his eyelids. Yet Colin was satisfied, and he alone of the three, after their master's going, remained on that coast of rock and heather.

In the third generation from Colin, as our elders counted years, came one Colin the Red, who built his keep on the cliffs of Acharra and was a mighty sea-rover in his day. Five times he sailed to the rich parts of France, and a good score of times he carried his flag of three stars against the easterly Vikings. A mere name in story, but a sounding piece of nomenclature well garnished with tales. A master-mind by all accounts, but cursed with a habit of fantasy; for, hearing in his old age of a land to the westward, he forthwith sailed into the sunset, but three days later was washed up, a twisted body, on one of the outer isles.

So far it is but legend, but with his grandson, Colin the Red, we fall into the safer hands of the chroniclers. To him God gave the unnumbered sorrows of story-telling, for he was a bard, cursed with a bard's fervours, and none the less a mighty warrior among his own folk. He it was who wrote the lament called 'The White Waters of Usna,' and the exquisite chain of romances, 'Glede-red Gold and Grey Silver.' His tales were told by many fires, down to our grandfathers' time, and you will find them still pounded at by the folk-lorists. But his airs – they are eternal. On harp and pipe they have lived through the centuries; twisted and tortured, they survive in many song-books; and I declare that the other day I heard the most beautiful of them all murdered by a band at a German watering-place. This Colin led the wanderer's life, for he disappeared at middle-age, no one knew whither, and his return was long looked for by his people. Some thought that he became a Christian monk, the holy man living in the sea-girt isle of Cuna, who was found dead in extreme old age, kneeling on the beach, with his arms, contrary to the fashion of the Church, stretched to the westward.

As history narrowed into bonds and forms the descendants of Colin took Raden for their surname, and settled more firmly on their lands in the long peninsula of crag and inlets which runs west to the Atlantic. Under Donald of the Isles they harried the Kings of Scots, or, on their own authority, made war on Macleans and Macranalds, till their flag of the three stars, their badge of the grey-goose feather, and their on-cry of 'Cuna' were feared from Lochalsh to Cantire. Later they made a truce with the King, and entered into the royal councils. For years they warded the western coast, and as king's lieutenants smoked out the inferior pirates of Eigg and Toronsay. A Raden was made a Lord of Sleat, another was given lands in the low country and the name Baron of Strathyre, but their honours were transitory and short as their lives. Rarely one of the house saw middle-age. A bold, handsome, and stirring race, it was their fate to be cut off in the rude warfare of the times, or, if peace had them in its clutches, to man vessel and set off once more on those mad western voyages which were the weird of the family. Three of the name were found drowned on the far shore of Cuna; more than one sailed straight out of the ken of mortals. One rode with the Good Lord James on the pilgrimage of the Heart of Bruce, and died by his leader's side in the Saracen battle. Long afterwards a Raden led the western men against the Cheshire archers at Flodden, and was slain himself in the steel circle around the king.

But the years brought peace and a greater wealth, and soon the cold stone tower was left solitary on the headland, and the new house of Kinlochuna rose by the green links of the stream. The family changed its faith, and an Episcopal chaplain took the place of the old mass-priest in the tutoring of the sons. Radens were in the '15 and the '45. They rose with Bute to power, and they long disputed the pride of Dundas in the northern capital. They intermarried with great English houses till the sons of the family were Scots only in name, living much abroad or in London, many of them English landowners by virtue of a mother's blood. Soon the race was of the common over-civilised type, graceful, well-mannered, with abundant good looks, but only once in a generation reverting to the rugged northern strength. Eton and Oxford had in turn displaced the family chaplain, and the house by the windy headland grew emptier and emptier save when grouse and deer brought home its fickle masters.

II

A childish illness brought Colin to Kinlochuna when he had reached the mature age of five, and delicate health kept him there for the greater part of the next six years. During the winter he lived in London, but from the late northern spring, through all the long bright summers, he lived in the great tenantless place without company – for he was an only child. A French nurse had the charge of his doings, and when he had passed through the formality of lessons there were the long pinewoods at his disposal, the rough moor, the wonderful black holes with the rich black mud in them, and best of all the bay of Acharra, below the headland, with Cuna lying in the waves a mile to the west. At such times his father was busy elsewhere; his mother was dead; the family had few near relatives; so he passed a solitary childhood in the company of seagulls and the birds of the moor.

His time for the beach was the afternoon. On the left as you go down through the woods from the house there runs out the great headland of Acharra, red and grey with mosses, and with a nimbus always of screaming sea-fowl. To the right runs a low beach of sand, passing into rough limestone boulders and then into the heather of the wood. This in turn is bounded by a reef of low rocks falling by gentle breaks to the water's edge. It is crowned with a tangle of heath and fern, bright at most seasons with flowers, and dwarf pine-trees straggle on its crest till one sees the meaning of its Gaelic name, 'The Ragged Cock's-Comb'. This place was Colin's playground in fine weather. When it blew rain or snow from the north he dwelt indoors among dogs and books, puzzling his way through great volumes from his father's shelves. But when the mild west-wind weather fell on the sea, then he would lie on the hot sand – Amèlie the nurse reading a novel on the nearest rock – and kick his small heels as he followed his fancy. He built great sand castles to the shape of Acharra old tower, and peopled them with preposterous knights and ladies; he drew great moats and rivers for the tide to fill; he fought battles innumerable with crackling seaweed, till Amèlie, with her sharp cry of 'Colin, Colin,' would carry him houseward for tea.

Two fancies remained in his mind through those boyish years. One was about the mysterious shining sea before him. In certain weathers it seemed to him a solid pathway. Cuna, the little ragged isle, ceased to block the horizon, and his own white road ran away down into the west, till suddenly it stopped and he saw no farther. He knew he ought to see more, but always at one place, just when his thoughts were pacing the white road most gallantly, there came a baffling mist to his sight, and he found himself looking at a commonplace sea with Cuna lying very real and palpable in the offing. It was a vexatious limitation, for all his dreams were about this pathway. One day in

June, when the waters slept in a deep heat, he came down the sands barefoot, and lo! there was his pathway. For one moment things seemed clear, the mist had not gathered on the road, and with a cry he ran down to the tide's edge and waded in. The touch of water dispelled the illusion, and almost in tears he saw the cruel back of Cuna blotting out his own magic way.

The other fancy was about the low ridge of rocks which bounded the bay on the right. His walks had never extended beyond it, either on the sands or inland, for that way lay a steep hillside and a perilous bog. But often on the sands he had come to its foot and wondered what country lay beyond. He made many efforts to explore it, difficult efforts, for the vigilant Amèlie had first to be avoided. Once he was almost at the top when some sea-weed to which he clung gave way, and he rolled back again to the soft warm sand. By-and-by he found that he knew what was beyond. A clear picture had built itself up in his brain of a mile of reefs, with sand in bars between them, and beyond all a sea-wood of alders slipping from the hill's skirts to the water's edge. This was not what he wanted in his explorations, so he stopped, till one day it struck him that the westward view might reveal something beyond the hog-backed Cuna. One day, pioneering alone, he scaled the steepest heights of the sea-weed and pulled his chin over the crest of the ridge. There, sure enough, was his picture – a mile of reefs and the tattered sea-wood. He turned eagerly seawards. Cuna still lay humped on the waters, but beyond it he seemed to see his shining pathway running far to a speck which might be an island. Crazy with pleasure he stared at the vision, till slowly it melted into the waves, and Cuna the inexorable once more blocked the skyline. He climbed down, his heart in a doubt between despondency and hope.

It was the last day of such fancies, for on the morrow he had to face the new world of school.

At Cecil's Colin found a new life and a thousand new interests. His early delicacy had been driven away by the sea-winds of Acharra, and he was rapidly growing up a tall, strong child, straight of limb like all his house, but sinewy and alert beyond his years. He learned new games with astonishing facility, became a fast bowler with a genius for twists, and a Rugby three-quarters full of pluck and cunning. He soon attained to the modified popularity of a private school, and, being essentially clean, strong, and healthy, found himself a mark for his juniors' worship and a favourite with masters. The homage did not spoil him, for no boy was ever less self-possessed. On the cricket-ground and the football-field he was a leader, but in private he had the nervous, sensitive manners of the would-be recluse. No one ever accused him of 'side' – his polite, halting address was the same to junior and senior; and the result was that wild affection which simplicity in the great is wont to inspire. He spoke with a pure accent, in which lurked no northern trace; in a little he had forgotten all about his birthplace and his origin. His name had at first acquired for him the sobriquet of 'Scottie', but the title was soon dropped from its manifest inaptness.

In his second year at Cecil's he caught a prevalent fever, and for days lay very near the brink of death. At his worst he was wildly delirious, crying ceaselessly for Acharra and the beach at Kinlochuna. But as he grew convalescent the absorption remained, and for the moment he seemed to have forgotten his southern life. He found himself playing on the sands, always with the boundary ridge before him, and the hump of Cuna rising in the sea. When dragged back to his environment by the inquiries of Bellew, his special friend, who came to sit with him, he was so abstracted and forgetful that the good Bellew was seriously grieved. 'The chap's a bit cracked, you know,' he announced in hall. 'Didn't know me. Asked me what "footer" meant when I told him about the Bayswick match, and talked about nothing but a lot of heathen Scotch names.'

One dream haunted Colin throughout the days of his recovery. He was tormented with a furious thirst, poorly assuaged at long intervals by watered milk. So when he crossed the borders of dreamland his first search was always for a well. He tried the brushwood inland from the beach, but it was dry as stone. Then he climbed with difficulty the boundary ridge, and found little pools of salt water, while far on the other side gleamed the dark black bog-holes. Here was not what he sought, and he was in deep despair, till suddenly over the sea he caught a glimpse of his old path running beyond Cuna to a bank of mist. He rushed down to the tide's edge, and to his amazement found solid ground. Now was the chance for which he had long looked, and he ran happily westwards, till of a sudden the solid earth seemed to sink with him, and he was in the waters struggling. But two curious things he noted. One was that the far bank of mist seemed to open for a pin-point of time, and he had a gleam of land. He saw nothing distinctly, only a line which was not mist and was not water. The second was that the water was fresh, and as he was drinking from this curious new fresh sea he awoke. The dream was repeated three times before he left the sick-room. Always he wakened at the same place, always he quenched his thirst in the fresh sea, but never again did the mist open for him and show him the strange country.

From Cecil's he went to the famous school which was the tradition in his family. The Head spoke to his house-master of his coming. 'We are to have another Raden here,' he said, 'and I am glad of it, if the young one turns out to be anything like the others. There's a good deal of dry-rot among the boys just now. They are all too old for their years and too wise in the wrong way. They haven't anything like the enthusiasm in games they had twenty years ago when I first came here. I hope this young Raden will stir them up.' The house-master agreed, and when he first caught sight of Colin's slim, well-knit figure, looked into the handsome kindly eyes, and heard his curiously diffi-dent speech, his doubts vanished. 'We have got the right stuff now,' he told himself, and the senior for whom the new boy fagged made the same comment.

From the anomalous insignificance of fagdom Colin climbed up the School, leaving everywhere a record of honest good-nature. He was allowed to forget his cricket and football, but in return he was initi-ated into the mysteries of the river. Water had always been his delight, so he went through the dreary preliminaries of being coached in a tub-pair till he learned to swing steadily and get his arms quickly forward. Then came the stages of scratch fours and scratch eights, till after a long apprenticeship he was promoted to the dignity of a thwart in the Eight itself. In his last year he was Captain of Boats, a position which joins the responsibility of a Cabinet Minister to the rapturous popular applause of a successful warrior. Nor was he the least distinguished of a great band. With Colin at seven the School won the Ladies' after the closest race on record.

The Head's prophecy fell true, for Colin was a born leader. For all his good-humour and diffidence of speech, he had a trick of shutting his teeth which all respected. As captain he was the idol of the school, and he ruled it well and justly. For the rest, he was a curious boy with none of the ordinary young enthusiasms, reserved for all his kindliness. At house 'shouters' his was not the voice which led the stirring strains of 'Stroke out all you know,' though his position demanded it. He cared little about work, and the School-house scholar, who fancied him from his manner a devotee of things intellectual, found in Colin but an affected interest. He read a certain amount of modern poetry with considerable boredom; fiction he never opened. The truth was that he had a romance in his own brain which, willy nilly, would play itself out, and which left him small relish for the pale second-hand inanities of art. Often, when with others he would lie in the deep meadows by the river on some hot summer's day, his fancies would take a curious colour. He adored the soft English landscape, the lush grasses, the slow streams, the ancient secular trees. But as he looked into the hazy green distance a colder air would blow on his cheek, a pungent smell of salt and pines would be for a moment in his nostrils, and he would be gazing at a line of waves on a beach, a ridge of low rocks, and a shining sea-path running out to – ah, that he could not tell! The envious Cuna would suddenly block all the vistas. He had constantly the vision before his eyes, and he strove to strain into the distance before Cuna should intervene. Once or twice he seemed almost to achieve it. He found that by keeping on the top of the low rock-ridge he could cheat Cuna by a second or two, and get a glimpse of a misty something out in the west. The vision took odd times for recurring, – once or twice in lecture, once on the cricket-ground, many times in the fields of a Sunday, and once while he paddled down to the start in a Trials race. It gave him a keen pleasure: it was his private domain, where at any moment he might make some enchanting discovery.

As this time he began to spend his vacations at Kinlochuna. His father, an elderly ex-diplomat, had permanently taken up his abode there, and was rapidly settling into the easy life of the Scots laird. Colin returned to his native place without enthusiasm. His childhood there had been full of lonely hours, and he had come to like the warm south country. He found the house full of people, for his father entertained hugely, and the talk was of sport and sport alone. As a rule, your very great athlete is bored by Scots shooting. Long hours of tramping and crouching among heather cramp without fully exercising the body; and unless he has the love of the thing ingrained in him, the odds are that he will wish himself home. The father, in his new-found admiration for his lot, was content to face all weathers; the son found it an effort to keep pace with such vigour. He thought upon the sunlit fields and reedy watercourses with regret, and saw little in the hills but a rough waste scarred with rock and sour with mosses.

He read widely throughout these days, for his father had a taste for modern letters, and new books lay littered about the rooms. He read queer Celtic tales which he thought 'sickening rot', and mild Celtic poetry which he failed to understand. Among the guests was a noted manufacturer of fiction, whom the elder Raden had met somewhere and bidden to Kinlochuna. He had heard the tale of Colin's ancestors and the sea headland of Acharra, and one day he asked the boy to show him the place, as he wished to make a story of it. Colin assented unwillingly, for he had been slow to visit this place of memories, and he did not care to make his first experiment in such company. But the gentleman would not be gainsaid, so the two scrambled through the sea-wood and climbed the low ridge which looked over the bay. The weather was mist and drizzle; Cuna had wholly hidden herself, and the bluff Acharra loomed hazy and far. Colin was oddly disappointed: this reality was a poor place compared with his fancies. His companion stroked his peaked beard, talked nonsense about Colin the Red and rhetoric about 'the spirit of the misty grey weather having entered into the old tale'. 'Think,' he cried; 'to those old warriors beyond that bank of mist was the whole desire of life, the Golden City, the Far Islands, whatever you care to call it.' Colin shivered, as if his holy places had been profaned, set down the man in his mind most unjustly as an 'awful little cad', and hurried him back to the house.

Oxford received the boy with open arms, for his reputation had long preceded him. To the majority of men he was the one freshman of his year, and gossip was busy with his prospects. Nor was gossip disappointed. In his first year he rowed seven in the Eight. The next year he was captain of his college boats, and a year later the O.U.B.C. made him its president. For three years he rowed in the winning Eight, and old coaches agreed that in him the perfect seven had been found. It was he who in the famous race of 18– caught up in the last three hundred yards the quickened stroke which gave Oxford victory. As he grew to his full strength he became a splendid figure of a man – tall, supple, deep-chested for all his elegance. His quick dark eyes and his kindly hesitating manners made people think his face extraordinarily handsome, when really it was in no way above the common. But his whole figure, as he stood in his shorts and sweater on the raft at Putney, was so full of youth and strength that people involuntarily smiled when they saw him — a smile of pleasure in so proper a piece of manhood.

Colin enjoyed life hugely at Oxford, for to one so frank and well equipped the place gave of its best. He was the most distinguished personage of his day there, but, save to school friends and the men he met officially on the river, he was little known. His diffidence and his very real exclusiveness kept him from being the centre of a host of friends. His own countrymen in the place were utterly nonplussed by him. They claimed him eagerly as a fellow, but he had none of the ordinary characteristics of the race. There were Scots of every description around him — pale-faced Scots who worked incessantly, metaphysical Scots who talked in the Union, robustious Scots who played football. They were all men of hearty manners and many enthusiasms, — who quoted Burns and dined to the immortal bard's honour every 25th of January; who told interminable Scotch stories, and fell into fervours over national sports, dishes, drinks, and religions. To the poor Colin it was all inexplicable. At the remote house of Kinlochuna he had never heard of a Free Kirk or a haggis. He had never read a line of Burns, Scott bored him exceedingly, and in all honesty he thought Scots games inferior to southern sports. He had no great love for the bleak country, he cared nothing for the traditions of his house, so he was promptly set down by his compatriots as 'denationalised and degenerate'.

He was idle, too, during these years as far as his 'schools' were concerned, but he was always very intent upon his own private business. Whenever he sat down to read, when he sprawled on the grass at river picnics, in chapel, in lecture — in short, at any moment when his body was at rest and his mind at leisure — his fancies were off on the same old path. Things had changed, however, in that country. The boyish device of a hard road running over the waters had gone, and now it was invariably a boat which he saw beached on the shingle. It differed in shape. At first it was an ugly salmon-coble, such as the fishermen used for the nets at Kinlochuna. Then it passed, by rapid transitions, through a canvas skiff which it took good watermanship to sit, a whiff, an ordinary dinghey, till at last it settled itself into a long rough boat, pointed at both ends, with oar-holes in the sides instead of row-locks. It was the devil's own business to launch it, and launch it anew he was compelled to for every journey; for though he left it bound in a little rock hollow below the ridge after landing, yet when he returned, lo! there was the clumsy thing high and dry upon the beach.

The odd point about the new venture was that Cuna had ceased to trouble him. As soon as he had pulled his first stroke the island disappeared, and nothing lay before him but the sea-fog. Yet, try as he might, he could come little nearer. The shores behind him might sink and lessen, but the impenetrable mist was still miles to the westward. Sometimes he rowed so far that the shore was a thin line upon the horizon, but when he turned the boat it seemed to ground in a second on the beach. The long laboured journey out and the instantaneous return, puzzled him at first, but soon he became used to them. His one grief was the mist, which seemed to grow denser as he neared it. The sudden glimpse of land which he had got from the ridge of rock in the old boyish days was now denied him, and with the denial came a keener exultation in the quest. Somewhere in the west, he knew, must be land, and in this land a well of sweet water – for so he had interpreted his feverish dream. Sometimes, when the wind blew against him, he caught scents from it – generally the scent of pines, as on the little ridge on the shore behind him.

One day on his college barge, while he was waiting for a picnic party to start, he seemed to get nearer than before. Out on that western sea, as he saw it, it was fresh, blowing weather, with a clear hot sky above. It was hard work rowing, for the wind was against him, and the sun scorched his forehead. The air seemed full of scents – and sounds, too, sounds of far-away surf and wind in trees. He rested for a moment on his oars and turned his head. His heart beat quickly, for there was a rift in the mist, and far through a line of sand ringed with snow-white foam.

Somebody shook him roughly, – 'Come on, Colin, old man. They're all waiting for you. Do you know you've been half asleep?'

Colin rose and followed silently, with drowsy eyes. His mind was curiously excited. He had looked inside the veil of mist. Now he knew what was the land he sought.

He made the voyage often, now that the spell was broken. It was short work to launch the boat, and, whereas it had been a long pull formerly, now it needed only a few strokes to bring him to the Rim of the Mist. There was no chance of getting farther, and he scarcely tried. He was content to rest there, in a world of curious scents and sounds, till the mist drew down and he was driven back to shore.

The change in his environment troubled him little. For a man who has been an idol at the University to fall suddenly into the comparative insignificance of Town is often a bitter experience; but Colin, whose thoughts were not ambitious, scarcely noticed it. He found that he was less his own master than before, but he humbled himself to his new duties without complaint. Many of his old friends were about him; he had plenty of acquaintances; and, being 'sufficient unto himself', he was unaccustomed to ennui. Invitations showered upon him thick and fast. Match-making mothers, knowing his birth and his father's income, and reflecting that he was the only child of his house, desired him as a son-in-law. He was bidden welcome everywhere, and the young girls, for whose sake he was thus courted, found in him an attractive mystery. The tall good-looking athlete, with the kind eyes and the preposterously nervous manner, wakened their maidenly sympathies. As they danced with him or sat next to him at dinner, they talked fervently of Oxford, of the north, of the army, of his friends. 'Stupid, but nice, my dear,' was Lady Afflint's comment; and Miss Clara Etheridge, the beauty of the year, declared to her friends that he was a 'dear boy, but so awkward'. He was always forgetful, and ever apologetic; and when he forgot the Shandwicks' theatre-party, the Herapaths' dance, and at least a dozen minor matters, he began to acquire the reputation of a cynic and a recluse.

'You're a queer chap, Col,' Lieutenant Bellew said in expostulation.

Colin shrugged his shoulders; he was used to the description.

'Do you know that Clara Etheridge was trying all she knew to please you this afternoon, and you looked as if you weren't listening? Most men would have given their ears to be in your place.'

'I'm awfully sorry, but I thought I was very polite to her.'

'And why weren't you at the Marshams' show?'

'Oh, I went to polo with Collinson and another man. And, I say, old chap, I'm not coming to the Logans to-morrow. I've got a fence on with Adair at the school.'

Little Bellew, who was a tremendous mirror of fashion and chevalier in general, looked up curiously at his tall friend.

'Why don't you like the women, Col, when they're so fond of you?'

'They aren't,' said Colin hotly, 'and I don't dislike 'em. But, Lord! they bore me. I might be doing twenty things when I talk nonsense to one of 'em for an hour. I come back as stupid as an owl, and besides there's heaps of things better sport.'

The truth was that, while among men he was a leader and at his ease, among women his psychic balance was so oddly upset that he grew nervous and returned unhappy. The boat on the beach, ready in general to appear at the slightest call, would delay long after such experiences, and its place would be taken by some woman's face for which he cared not a straw. For the boat, on the other hand, he cared a very great deal. In all his frank wholesome existence there was this enchanting background, this pleasure-garden which he cherished more than anything in life. He had come of late to look at it with somewhat different eyes. The eager desire to search behind the mist was ever with him, but now he had also some curiosity about the details of the picture. As he pulled out to the Rim of the Mist sounds seemed to shape themselves on his lips, which by-and-by grew into actual words in his memory. He wrote them down in scraps, and after some sorting they seemed to him a kind of Latin. He remembered a college friend of his, one Medway, now reading for the Bar, who had been the foremost scholar of his acquaintance; so with the scrap of paper in his pocket he climbed one evening to Medway's rooms in the Temple.

The man read the words curiously, and puzzled for a bit. 'What's made you take to Latin comps so late in life, Colin? It's baddish, you know, even for you. I thought they'd have licked more into you at Eton.'

Colin grinned with amusement. 'I'll tell you about it later,' he said. 'Can you make out what it means?'

'It seems to be a kind of dog-Latin or monkish Latin or something of the sort,' said Medway. 'It reads like this: *"Soles occidere solent"* (that's cribbed from Catullus, and besides it's the regular monkish pun) ... *qua* ... then *blandula* something. Then there's a lot of Choctaw, and then *illæ insulæ dilectæ in quas festinant somnia animulæ gaudia*. That's pretty fair rot. Hullo, by George! here's something better – *Insula pomorum insula vitæ*. That's Geoffrey of Monmouth.'

He made a dive to a bookcase and pulled out a battered little calf-bound duodecimo. 'Here's all about your Isle of Apple-trees. Listen. "Situate far out in the Western ocean, beyond the Utmost Islands, beyond even the little Isle of Sheep where the cairns of dead men are, lies the Island of Apple-trees where the heroes and princes of the nations live their second life."' He closed the book and put it back.

'It's the old ancient story, the Greek Hesperides, the British Avilion, and this Apple-tree Island is the northern equivalent.'

Colin sat entranced, his memory busy with a problem. Could he distinguish the scents of apple-trees among the perfumes of the Rim of the Mist. For the moment he thought he could. He was roused by Medway's voice asking the story of the writing.

'Oh, it's just some nonsense that was running in my head, so I wrote it down to see what it was.'

'But you must have been reading. A new exercise for you, Colin!'

'No, I wasn't reading. Look here. You know the sort of pictures you make for yourself of places you like.'

'Rather! Mine is a Yorkshire moor with a little red shooting-box in the heart of it.'

'Well, mine is different. Mine is a sort of beach with a sea and a lot of islands somewhere far out. It is a jolly place, fresh, you know, and blowing, and smells good. 'Pon my word, now I think of it, there's always been a scent of apples.'

'Sort of cider-press? Well, I must be off. You'd better come round to the club and see the telegrams about the war. *You* should be keen about it.'

One evening, a week later, Medway met a friend called Tillotson at the club, and, being lonely, they dined together. Tillotson was a man of some note in science, a dabbler in psychology, an amateur historian, a ripe genealogist. They talked of politics and the war, of a new book, of Mrs. Runnymede, and finally of their hobbies.

'I am writing an article,' said Tillotson. 'Craikes asked me to do it for the *Monthly*. It's on a nice point in psychics. I call it "The Transmission of Fallacies", but I do not mean the logical kind. The question is, Can a particular form of hallucination run in a family for generations? The proof must, of course, come from my genealogical studies. I maintain it can. I instance the Douglas-Ernotts, not one of whom can see straight with the left eye. That is one side. In another class of examples I take the Drapiers, who hate salt water and never go on board ship if they can help it. Then you remember the Durwards? Old Lady Balcrynie used to tell me that no one of the lot could ever stand the sight of a green frock. There's a chance for the romancer. The Manorwaters have the same madness, only their colour is red.'

A vague remembrance haunted Medway's brain.

'I know a man who might give you points from his own case. Did you ever meet a chap Raden – Colin Raden?'

Tillotson nodded. 'Long chap – in the Guards? 'Varsity oar, and used to be a crack bowler? No, I don't know him. I know him well by sight, and I should like to meet him tremendously – as a genealogist, of course.'

'Why?' asked Medway.

'Why? Because the man's family is unique. You never hear much about them nowadays, but away up in that north-west corner of Scotland they have ruled since the days of Noah. Why, man, they were aristocrats when our Howards and Nevilles were greengrocers. I wish you would get this Raden to meet me some night.'

'I am afraid there's no chance of it just at present,' said Medway, taking up an evening paper. 'I see that his regiment has gone to the front. But remind me when he comes back, and I'll be delighted.'

III

And now there began for Colin a curious divided life, – without, a constant shifting of scene, days of heat and bustle and toil, – within, a slow, tantalising, yet exquisite adventure. The Rim of the Mist was now no more the goal of his journeys, but the starting-point. Lying there, amid cool, fragrant sea-winds, his fanciful ear was subtly alert for the sounds of the dim land before him. Sleeping and waking the quest haunted him. As he flung himself on his bed the kerosene-filled air would change to an ocean freshness, the old boat would rock beneath him, and with clear eye and a boyish hope he would be waiting and watching. And then suddenly he would be back on shore, Cuna and the Acharra headland shining grey in the morning light, and with gritty mouth and sand-filled eyes he would awaken to the heat of the desert camp.

He was kept busy, for his good-humour and energy made him a willing slave, and he was ready enough for volunteer work when others were weak with heat and despair. A thirty-mile ride left him untired; more, he followed the campaign with a sharp intelligence and found a new enthusiasm for his profession. Discomforts there might be, but the days were happy; and then – the cool land, the bright land, which was his for the thinking of it.

Soon they gave him reconnoitring work to do, and his wits were put to the trial. He came well out of the thing, and earned golden praise from the silent colonel in command. He enjoyed it as he had enjoyed a hard race on the river or a good cricket match, and when his worried companions marvelled at his zeal he stammered and grew uncomfortable.

'How the deuce do you keep it up, Colin?' the major asked him. 'I'm an old hand at the job, and yet I've got a temper like devilled bones. You seem as chirpy as if you were going out to fish a chalkstream on a June morning.'

'Well, the fact is—' and Colin pulled himself up short, knowing that he could never explain. He felt miserably that he had an unfair advantage of the others. Poor Bellew, who groaned and swore in the heat at his side, knew nothing of the Rim of the Mist. It was really rough luck on the poor beggars, and who but himself was the fortunate man?

As the days passed a curious thing happened. He found fragments of the Other world straying into his common life. The barriers of the two domains were falling, and more than once he caught himself looking at a steel-blue sea when his eyes should have found a mustard-coloured desert. One day, on a reconnoitring expedition, they stopped for a little on a hillock above a jungle of scrub, and, being hot and tired, scanned listlessly the endless yellow distances.

'I suppose yon hill is about ten miles off,' said Bellew with dry lips.

Colin looked vaguely. 'I should say five.'

'And what's that below it – the black patch? Stones or scrub?'

Colin was in a day-dream. 'Why do you call it black? It's blue, quite blue.'

'Rot,' said the other. 'It's grey-black.'

'No, it's water with the sun shining on it. It's blue, but just at the edges it's very near sea-green.'

Bellew rose excitedly. 'Hullo, Col, you're seeing the mirage! And you the fittest of the lot of us! You've got the sun in your head, old man!'

'Mirage!' Colin cried in contempt. He was awake now, but the thought of confusing his own bright western sea with a mirage gave him a curious pain. For a moment he felt the gulf of separation between his two worlds, but only for a moment. As the party remounted he gave his fancies the rein, and ere he reached camp he had felt the oars in his hand and sniffed the apple-tree blossom from the distant beaches.

The major came to him after supper.

'Bellew told me you were a bit odd to-day, Colin,' he said. 'I expect your eyes are getting baddish. Better get your sand-spectacles out.'

Colin laughed. 'Thanks. It's awfully good of you to bother, but I think Bellew took me up wrong. I never was fitter in my life.'

By-and-by the turn came for pride to be humbled. A low desert fever took him, and though he went through the day as usual, it was with dreary lassitude; and at night, with hot hands clasped above his damp hair, he found sleep a hard goddess to conquer.

It was the normal condition of the others, so he had small cause to complain, but it worked havoc with his fancies. He had never been ill since his childish days, and this little fever meant much to one whose nature was poised on a needle-point. He found himself confronted with a hard bare world, with the gilt rubbed from its corners. The Rim of the Mist seemed a place of vague horrors; when he reached it his soul was consumed with terror; he struggled impotently to advance; behind him Cuna and the Acharra coast seemed a place of evil dreams. Again, as in his old fever, he was tormented with a devouring thirst, but the sea beside him was not fresh, but brackish as a rock-pool. He yearned for the apple-tree beaches in front; there, he knew, were cold springs of water; the fresh smell of it was blown towards him in his nightmare.

But as the days passed and the misery for all grew more intense, an odd hope began to rise in his mind. It could not last, coolness and health were waiting near, and his reason for the hope came from the odd events at the Rim of the Mist. The haze was clearing from the foreground, the surf-lined coast seemed nearer, and though all was obscure save the milk-white sand and the foam, yet here was earnest enough for him. Once more he became cheerful; weak and light-headed he rode out again; and the major, who was recovering from sun-stroke, found envy take the place of pity in his soul.

The hope was near fulfilment. One evening when the heat was changing into the cooler twilight, Colin and Bellew were sent with a small picked body to scour the foot-hills above the river in case of a flank attack during the night-march. It was work they had done regularly for weeks, and it is possible that precautions were relaxed. At any rate, as they turned a corner of hill, in a sandy pass where barren rocks looked down on more barren thorn thickets, a couple of rifle-shots rang out from the scarp, and above them appeared a line of dark faces and white steel. A mere handful, taken at a disadvantage, they could not hope to disperse numbers, so Colin gave the word to wheel about and return. Again shots rang out, and little Bellew had only time to catch at his friend's arm to save him from falling from the saddle.

The word of command had scarcely left Colin's mouth when a sharp pain went through his chest, and his breath seemed to catch and stop. He felt as in a condensed moment of time the heat, the desert smell, the dust in his eyes and throat, while he leaned helplessly forward on his horse's mane. Then the world vanished for him. . . . The boat was rocking under him, the oars in his hand. He pulled and it moved, straight, arrow-like towards the forbidden shore. As if under a great wind the mist furled up and fled. Scents of pines, of apple-trees, of great fields of thyme and heather, hung about him; the sound of wind in a forest, of cool waters falling in showers, of old moorland music, came thin and faint with an exquisite clearness. A second and the boat was among the surf, its gunwale ringed with white foam, as it leaped to the still waters beyond. Clear and deep and still the water lay, and then the white beaches shelved downward, and the boat grated on the sand. He turned, every limb alert with a strange new life, crying out words which had shaped themselves on his lips and which an echo seemed to catch and answer. There was the green forest before him, the hills of peace, the cold white waters. With a passionate joy he leaped on the beach, his arms outstretched to this new earth, this light of the world, this old desire of the heart – youth, rapture, immortality.

Bellew brought the body back to camp, himself half-dead with fatigue and whimpering like a child. He almost fell from his horse, and when others took his burden from him and laid it reverently in his tent, he stood beside it, rubbing sand and sweat from his poor purblind eyes, his teeth chattering with fever. He was given something to drink, but he swallowed barely a mouthful.

'It was some d-d-damned sharpshooter,' he said. 'Right through the breast, and he never spoke to me again. My poor old Col! He was the best chap God ever created, and I do-don't care a dash what becomes of me now. I was at school with him, you know, you men.'

'Was he killed outright?' asked the major hoarsely.

'N-no. He lived for about five minutes. But I think the sun had got into his head or he was mad with pain, for he d-d-didn't know where he was. He kept crying out about the smell of pine-trees and heather and a lot of pure nonsense about water.'

'*Et dulces reminiscitur Argos*,' somebody quoted mournfully, as they went out to the desert evening.

Glossary

A
a' – all
aboon/abune – above/over
aboot – about
ae – one
ahint – behind
aiblins – perhaps
ain – own
aince – once
aiten – oaten
alang – along
amang – among
ane – one
anither – another
atween – between
aucht – anything
auchteen – eighteen
auld – old
auldfarrant – old-fashioned
awa – away

B
bade – bid
bannocks – pancakes
bairn – child
bairnliest – babiest
baith – both
bauchled – distorted
bauks – untilled land
bauld – bold
bawbee – halfpenny
bawl – shout
bawsened – white-faced
begood – begun

belchin' – preaching
ben – through
beuk – book
bicker – drinking cup
bickerin' – arguing
biddins – orders
bield – shelter
birk – birch
blae – blue
blate – shy
blaw – blow
bleeze – blaze
bluid – blood
brae – hill
braid – broad
braw – fine
braxy – diseased
breeks – trousers
broo – brow
bucht – sheep pen
buid – bid
buits – boots
bund – bond/bound
burnie – brook
buskit – dressed
busses – bushes
bye – beside/near
byliff – bailiff

C
ca' – call
ca'ed – called
canna – cannot
canty – lively

GLOSSARY

carle – old man
cauld – cold
chappin – knocking
chaumer – chamber
cheild – boy
chuckies – chickens
claes – clothes
clamjamfried – worthless
clart/y – dirt/y
claught – clutched
clinkit – struck
cockit – heaped
coorts – courts
coup – upset
couthy – kindly
crackin' – chatting
craw – crow/boast
creashy – greasy
crood – crowd
croun – crown
crously – briskly
cuif – fool
cuisten – cast
cundies – conduits

D

dacent – decent
dae – do
dander – stroll
daunder – saunter
daured – dared
dawf – remove
delve – dig
denty – dainty
ding – knock
dochter – daughter
Dod – George
doo – dove/pigeon
doots – doubts
doucely – quiet
doun – down
dowie – sad

drée – endure
dreich/est – dull/est
drooned – drowned
dwaibly – feeble

E

een – eyes
eneuch – enough
errin' – errant
ettle – attempt

F

faes – foes
farles – oatcakes
fauld – fold
faun – fallen
fauts – faults
ferlie – strange
feucht – fight
fleechin' – flattering
fleein' – flying
floo'rs – flowers
flytit – scolded
frae – from
freend – friend
frem't – foreign
fricht – fright
fan – when
furthy – frank

G

gaed – went
gait – stride
gangs – goes
garred – made
gaucy – plump
ghaist – ghost
gie/n – give/n
glaikit – stupid
glaury – muddy
gleg – horsefly
gleg's – bright

[247]

gloomin' – frowning
glower – glare
glumchin – looking sad
goud – gold
gowans – daisies
gowk – fool
greetin' – crying
grue – ice
grumlin' – grumbling
grund – ground
guddlin' – tickling trout
guid – good

H
hae – have
hain/in's -enclose/ures
hairst – harvest
hale – whole
halms – stalks/shaws
hame – home
happit – wrapped
haughlands – highlands
heid – head
heinchin – chicken
hert – heart
heuchs – exclamations
hirsel – collection
hoddit – held
hoodie craws – black-head crows
howkin' – digging
hunkerin' – squatting

I
ilka – every
ither – other

J
jee – stir
jimped – leaped
jouked – ducked

K
kent – known
kenned – knew
kep – cap
kets – carrion
kittle – tickle
kinle – light
kye – cattle

L
lauchin' – laughing
lee – lie
lickit – defeated
licht – light
loon – boy
Losh – Lord
loup – leap
louse – free
lowe – flame

M
mair – more
mairrit – married
maist – most
makkers – poets
maud – plaid
maukit – infested
maun – must
massy – massive
meuse – honour
micht – might
midden – dung heap
misdoot – misdoubt
mools – moles
mou – mouth
muckle – much/great

N
nae – no
nane – none
neebors – neighbours
niffer – barter/haggle

nieves – fists
nocht – nothing
nou – now

O

'oo – wool
ower – over
orra – odd

P

paiks – strikes/pokes
pairt – part
parritch – porridge
piked – gathered
plock – third of a penny
ploom – plum
ploos – ploughs
plowtered – waded
poke – grope
pooches – pockets/pouches
poopits – pulpits
poether – powder
puir – poor
puirtith – poverty

Q

quate – quiet

R

rade – afraid
rape – rope
raws – rows
rax – stretch
reddin' – clearing
reid – read
richt – right
roopy – hoarsely
rauk – fag
roup – auction
rows – rolls

S

sae – so
sair – sore
saunts – saints
scabbit – scabbed
scaith – scathe
scaud – scald
schauchled – shackled
schauchlin' – shaking
sel – self
shairn/y – cows dung/daubed in
shouther – shoulder
shilpit – pale
siccan – such
siller – silver
sin – since
skeely – skilled
skelped – smacked
skreich – break of day
snoddit – tidied
snoukin' – to smell as a dog
snoutit – snouted
spainin' – weaning
spak – spoke
speir – ask
speldered – split
splore – explore
staig – stag
staucherin' – staggering
stausome – disgusting
steeked – latched
stell – prop
stench – strong
stert/it – start/ed
stievest – stiffest
stirk – cow
stramash – uproar
straucht – straight
sudna – should not
swirds – swords

JOHN BUCHAN

T

tackets – tacks
taen – taken
tak – take
tautit – matted
tawmont – two months
tentier – careful
teuch – tough
thack – thatch
thegither – together
thocht – thought
thole – bear
thrall – worry
thrang – stubborn
thrapple – throat
threep/it – whistle/d
thristles – thistles
tine – lose
tippeny – two pence
toddy – whisky
toom – empty
toun – town
traivelled – travelled
trig/s – trim/tidy
tups – rams
twae – two

U

unco – extraordinarily
unction – auction

W

wae/fu' – woe/ful
walie – feeble
wame – belly/womb
wanchancy – unlucky
warstled – wrestled
wauf – wave
wauks – wakens
wean – child
wecht – weight
weird – fate
whae – who
whaup – curlew
whaur – where
whase – whose
whilk – which
wight – creature
wrocht – worked

Y

yaird – yard
yammerin' – whining
ye – you
yestreen – yesterday
yett – gate
yill – ale
yin – one
yon – that/yonder
yowe – cattle